Wicked Pleasure

Nina Bangs

BERKLEY SENSATION, NEW YORK

For Curt Groff

THE BERKLEY PUBLISHING GROUP
Published by the Penguin Group
Penguin Group (USA) Inc.
375 Hudson Street, New York, New York 10014, USA
Penguin Group (Canada), 90 Eglinton Avenue East, Suite 700, Toronto, Ontario M4P 2Y3, Canada
(a division of Pearson Penguin Canada Inc.)
Penguin Books Ltd., 80 Strand, London WC2R 0RL, England
Penguin Group Ireland, 25 St. Stephen's Green, Dublin 2, Ireland (a division of Penguin Books Ltd.)
Penguin Group (Australia), 250 Camberwell Road, Camberwell, Victoria 3124, Australia
(a division of Pearson Australia Group Pty. Ltd.)
Penguin Books India Pvt. Ltd., 11 Community Centre, Panchsheel Park, New Delhi—110 017, India
Penguin Group (NZ), Cnr. Airborne and Rosedale Roads, Albany, Auckland 1310, New Zealand
(a division of Pearson New Zealand Ltd.)
Penguin Books (South Africa) (Pty.) Ltd., 24 Sturdee Avenue, Rosebank, Johannesburg 2196, South Africa

Penguin Books Ltd., Registered Offices: 80 Strand, London WC2R 0RL, England

This book is an original publication of The Berkley Publishing Group.

This is a work of fiction. Names, characters, places, and incidents either are the product of the author's imagination or are used fictitiously, and any resemblance to actual persons, living or dead, business establishments, events, or locales is entirely coincidental. The publisher does not have any control over and does not assume any responsibility for author or third-party websites or their content.

Copyright © 2006 by Nina Bangs.
Cover design by Bruce Emmett.
Cover art by Lesley Worrell.

First edition: June 2006

Library of Congress Cataloging-in-Publication Data

Bangs, Nina.
    Wicked pleasure / Nina Bangs.— 1st ed.
        p. cm.
    ISBN 0-425-20371-9
  1. Vampires—Fiction. 2. Brothers—Fiction. 3. Amusement parks—Fiction. I. Title.

PS3602.A636W54 2006
813'.6—dc22   2006003159

PRINTED IN THE UNITED STATES OF AMERICA

10 9 8 7 6 5 4 3 2 1

I

Throbthrobthrob. "You can vibrate all night, Fo, but I don't feeeeel you." Kim ignored the frantic pulsing going on in her jacket pocket and concentrated on the Castle of Dark Dreams.

The castle was definitely male. Sensory ripples of overpowering sexuality, danger, and frightening secrets glided over her exposed skin. She smiled. Perfect for a castle, but everything she *didn't* want in a man.

Kim still couldn't believe she'd gotten the job. Her family would go ballistic if they found out she'd broken her promise, but a little sneakiness and lots of creative lying should guarantee they'd never find out. They thought she'd come here to hunt demons. She was really here to live her dream.

Kim pulled the collar of her jacket over her ears. Galveston might not be freezing in March, but a drizzly night could still be miserable and chilly.

"Take me out, Kimmie. I'm your partner, your electronic identifier of all things demonic."

Kim glanced at her pocket. Fo could express any emotion that suited her annoying little self, and right now she was into an irritating mix of wheedling and whiny.

"Uh-uh. Isn't going to happen. Your success rate in fingering demons is in single digits, Fo. Remember the White House? The president? Can we say humiliating? Our nation's commander in chief *wasn't* amused. Don't think we'll be getting an invite to the Oval Office anytime soon."

Kim continued to admire the castle's exterior. She had the gut feeling that the Castle of Dark Dreams only came alive when night shadows enveloped it. Words like *threatening* and *brooding* came to mind. Even though spotlights bathed it in a brilliant glow, she'd bet its heart still lived in darkness.

Threatening, brooding. Suddenly she felt uneasy. Nothing physical. Just a faint tap on the door of her consciousness, a warning that anger and desperation waited outside. More disturbing was the darkly erotic flow of something she sensed hiding behind these emotions. An uninvited visitor.

Erotic flow? Okay, so she hadn't been with a man for a while, but this didn't feel like a playful, gotta-have-some-great-lovin' moment. This wasn't ordinary need. It was a compulsion. Not something she'd feel or *want* to feel. Angry and desperate? Nooo. Sure Dad ticked her off by assuming she'd want to spend the rest of her life in the family business, but that didn't come anywhere near desperate.

Kim took a deep breath. She was probably way too deep into the castle's mood. A few in her family were still intuitive to a certain degree, not enough to recognize demons as their ancestors did, but enough to *sense* things. And yeah, she had a vivid imagination. Still, she'd never experienced this kind of feeling before. For once, she was relieved when Fo spoke.

"Fine, so I made one little mistake. The president forgave you. Besides, all of those cameras and mikes confused my sensors. But this time I'm right. I detect all kinds of supernatural activity here. You need me." Fo sounded positive about that.

Right. Like she needed a big fat wart on her nose. Kim had passed up the more technologically advanced versions of the Vaughn family's demon detectors exactly because they, well, detected demons. She hated the family business, so she'd chosen Fo, short for First One, specifically because Fo couldn't find a demon even if the devil drop-kicked her into hell. This was a good thing. The fewer demons detected, the less demon destroying Kim had to do. And Kim was all about avoiding her destiny.

A brief pause for conscience-appeasing justifications. Unlike the rest of her family, she hadn't swallowed whole the belief that every entity identified by her ancestors as evil was a demon. Back when her family used their enhanced sensitivity to root out demonic beings, the Vaughns hadn't always come down on the side of goodness and light.

She'd found proof in the family's record books that the accused "demon" was sometimes a very human enemy destroyed under the guise of ridding mankind of evil. Besides, in ancient times all entities painted with the name "demon" weren't considered wicked or minions of Satan. Her family chose to ignore that fact.

"Kimmie, I sense demons dead ahead. Umm, if you take me out right now I can be ready to destroy the soul-sucking slime buckets with no muss and no fuss. Then you can just kick their ashes into the grass."

"Not now, Fo." Lately, a disturbing trend in the demon-hunting business had further alienated her from her family and relatives. Family heads had decided that the current crop of detectors was behind the curve, that some demons had found a way to circumvent their sensors. The more dedicated hunters hated the safety feature that made it impossible to destroy anything the detectors didn't identify as demonic. Fail-safe devices were a pain in the butt.

"The demons are really close, Kimmie. I bet they're close enough for you to smell their disgusting sulfur breath. What are you going to do?"

"Give them a breath mint." And so, a few of the far-flung members of the demon-hunting Vaughn family had decided to destroy "evil entities" in the old way, by lopping off their heads with a sword, even if the detectors didn't agree.

Now this is where things got sticky. If the demon was manifesting in its true form, no problem. But if the demon had possessed a human, then lopping off a head sort of did permanent damage to the innocent vessel. Some of the Vaughns, though, had no patience with drawn-out exorcisms. What the hey, it was worth some collateral damage to rid the world of evil entities. It was all good to the fanatical few.

"You'll be sorry you didn't take me out, Kimmie. While they're kicking your sorry behind all over the courtyard, I'll be stuck in your pocket."

"Uh-huh. Then you'll be able to lay an I-told-you-so on me as I eat dirt." Kim wasn't a destroyer. She was a builder. If she came across something truly evil, and she had proof that it was a malevolent spirit, she'd destroy it. But she wouldn't make demon destroying the driving force in her life. There were enough obsessed hunters in her family to more than make up for her lack of enthusiasm. Besides, she intended to have a husband and children someday. She refused to put them in danger from a bunch of ticked-off malevolent spirits.

"Just take me out for a minute so I can see everything. How would you like it if someone stuck *you* in their pocket and forgot about you?" Fo knew how to play the guilt card.

The only flaw in Fo's reasoning was that she *never* let Kim forget about her. Surrendering to the inevitable, Kim reached into her pocket, pulled Fo out, and flipped her open. To anyone who didn't know better, Fo looked like a camera phone. Only Kim knew that Fo's true function in life was to be a little pain in the butt.

Fo's small screen lit up, and her huge purple eyes outlined in neon pink blinked open. Fo was *not* into subtle.

"You know, the whole goal in demon hunting is to sneak up on the demons. We're talking low-key here. Cell phones don't have eyes." Kim had allowed Fo to have eyes and choose her own eye color. Fine, so she'd said okay to the eyes because she felt conflicted about her demon detector.

The rest of Kim's family treated their detectors as necessary pieces of technology like their computers. No angst over the true nature of *their* demon-hunting tools. But Kim had to constantly hum loudly over an inner voice that tried to whisper "AI" in her ear.

Everyone in her family had cracked up the one time she'd mentioned the words "artificial intelligence" in relation to Fo. They'd agreed between guffaws that, yeah, Fo was AI all right—Absolutely Ineffectual. Offended for Fo—who of course had no feelings to hurt, who was just the creation of an inept programmer—Kim had never again voiced any doubts about the detector to her family.

"Forget it, Kimmie. I like my eyes." Fo paused almost as though she was actually . . . thinking.

Kim rushed to assure herself that Fo wasn't thinking. Any pause was due to the detector's flawed innards.

"Look at it from my point of view. I don't have a body. I don't have one single physical thing that can express my personality, my *individuality*. Just my eyes. So purple and pink is who I am."

Fo was wrong. Her voice was *always* expressing something. Fo should've put a mouth on her screen instead of eyes. Better yet, Kim would feel a lot more comfortable if Fo looked like all of the other demon detectors—no human features, just a screen filled with technical info pertinent to the evil entity in question.

"Be quiet now so I can concentrate on the castle, get a feel for it, absorb its essence." Okay, so all Kim really wanted to do was wallow in the joy of her first job as an architect.

When Holgarth—not Holgarth Jones or Bob Holgarth, just Holgarth—had written to express the owner's desire that she be the one to make a few changes to the castle, she'd been thrilled but cautious. When something seemed too good to be true, it often was. So she'd done some investigating and found the offer was legit. Holgarth explained that the owner, whose name he never men-

tioned, was looking for new and enthusiastic as opposed to experienced and jaded. Well, Kim was certainly new and could out-
enthuse *anyone*. This was a breathtaking opportunity to start her
career with a bang.

She turned the screen toward the castle so Fo could see it, too.

As theme park attractions went, this one was awesome. Live the
Fantasy Theme Park advertised that it was a place where adults
could role-play their fantasies, childhood or otherwise. From the pirate ship to the Wild West street scene, it invited customers to
throw away their inhibitions and play.

But the Castle of Dark Dreams was something more. It looked as
authentic as everything else in the park—a keep with four square
towers, a curtain wall, moat, and drawbridge—but the white walls
that imitated the lime-washed color of ancient castles didn't fool
her. This was no Magic Kingdom castle. Its master planner had captured a spirit of danger and mystery in every sharp angle and blunt
line. Wonderful. Of course, whatever she did would have to maintain that ominous aura.

"Ooooh! Scary." Fo was happy again. "I'll have to do a scan of my
systems to make sure I'm ready to off dozens of demons. I like it here."

Oh, jeez. "Look, Fo, you can't keep seeing demons behind every
bush. I mean, I can't believe you shouted *demon* at that woman in
the shop we just left. Sparkle Stardust isn't a demon. She's just a
nice lady who owns a candy store. Sure, her name's a little strange,
but hey, lots of people have unusual names. That doesn't make
them demons."

She held up her hand to forestall Fo's interruption. "I know, I
know. So my fifth grade teacher, Mr. Ozzlehoot, *was* a demon. But
he was an exception. And Mom took care of him at the first parent-
teacher conference. I don't sense mobs of demons hanging around
this castle. Loads of atmosphere but no demons." Maybe a little too
much atmosphere. Kim walked across the drawbridge, through the
open gates, and into the courtyard. She paused to look back at the
gates. "The castle needs a gatehouse."

This time when the emotions hit her, they were strong enough to make her gasp—fury, hopelessness, and sexual hunger that wasn't about pleasure. What the hell . . . ? They weren't *her* emotions. And they couldn't be someone else's because she was the quintessential ordinary person, other than her job, of course. Ordinary people didn't get slammed with unexplained emotions. Kim gloried in her ordinariness. She had no psychic abilities. Thank God. She pushed the emotions aside to be taken out later and examined from every angle and then reasoned away.

Fo laughed, a light trill of amusement. "You couldn't sense a demon even if it tattooed the words *Malevolent Spirit* across its forehead." Pause. "You know, that would be a lot to get on a forehead, but if it had a really wide forehead—"

"Drifting off topic, Fo." Kim's reminder was automatic. Fo jumped from subject to subject like the frenetic zigzagging of a water beetle.

Fo blinked. "Oh, yeah. Anyway, over the centuries, your whole family has lost its ability to sense demons. That's why you need a demon detector. And Sparkle *is* a demon, a very old and evil one."

Kim didn't bother arguing with Fo. It wouldn't do any good. Besides, Fo was right about one thing. Kim couldn't sense demons, didn't *want* to sense demons. During her short career as a demon destroyer, she'd used Fo to zap a measly five of the evil entities. And that was only because they'd been really dumb. Even she couldn't miss a demon when it attacked her in its true disgustingly gross form. Ugh.

Besides, before they'd attacked her, four of them had given her indisputable proof of their demon status. They'd mooned her. Together. And there on all of their repulsive bare butts, she'd seen the imprint of a small bat.

For the last six hundred years or so, demons had taken to imprinting an animal shape somewhere on their bodies, usually on a spot normally covered by clothing. They picked an animal with ambiguous symbolism, one that throughout history had both good and evil connotations, as a representation of their ability to confuse humans. The bat was a sign of good fortune in the East, but it represented demons and spirits in medieval Europe. The animal thing was a stupid affectation because it was just one more way for destroyers to identify them. But then, demons weren't the brightest sparks in the fire.

"You know, your heart isn't in this business, Kimmie. Why don't you quit? You can build big beautiful houses, and I can be your interior design consultant." Fo blinked her large purple eyes. "I'm great with color."

"Can't do it." Kim shuddered at the concept of Fo as interior designer. "I made a deal with Dad. I stay in the family business until I marry. Then I'm gone." She continued walking toward the massive doors leading into the great hall. Holgarth had overnighted the castle's blueprints to her, and she'd seen photos on the Web, so she felt she knew every inch of it now. But studying blueprints and looking at photos hadn't prepared her for the total impact of the place. It was WOW on a gigantic scale.

"Humph! At the rate you're going, you won't find Mr. Right or even Mr. Sort-of-Okay until you're a card-carrying AARP member. Not that AARP isn't a great organization. It gives its members—"

"Floating off course again." Kim fixed her attention on the grotesque gargoyles protecting the castle's doors. Very effective details. But would they really keep evil from entering the castle? Her ancestors thought so.

Only a short distance now and she'd be inside and hopefully safe from random attacks by weird emotions.

"I knew that. Now what was I talking about . . . ? Oh, I remember. The search for Mr. Right." Fo narrowed her eyes to indicate her displeasure with Kim's ongoing, and for the most part futile, hunt for the perfect guy. "What exactly do you *want* in a man?" Fo's tone suggested that at the advanced age of twenty-seven, Kim should settle for anything human and male that had the right sexual organs and would marry her. "Just tell me, Kimmie, and I'll help you find him."

Kim glanced up at the keep where light streamed from the many arrow slits. "Cool place. Tour the castle, buy stuff in the shops, eat in the restaurant, take part in a fantasy, and then sleep in your cozy chamber for the night. Great view of the Gulf of Mexico, too. Bet this place makes tons of money."

"I want to talk about Mr. Right." Fo was in sulky mode.

Kim sighed. "I want an *ordinary* man so I can have *ordinary* kids and live an *ordinary* life." Qualifications for her perfect mate? He'd never seen a ghost or wanted to see one, never glimpsed a UFO or wondered about alien abductions, and laughed at even the suggestion that vampires, werewolves, or demons existed. And he'd have to have a job that could never, *ever* intersect with the paranormal world.

Chances of her finding and actually settling down with Mr. Ordinary? None. Because he'd be gone as soon as he met her family.

"Sounds sort of boring. But then what do I know about exciting?" Fo's tone said that if she had a body to go along with her eyes, she'd aim a lot higher than ordinary.

"Forget men. I have to think about the castle. Holgarth wanted me here right away, so I didn't get a chance to pull together any ideas at home." She didn't want to talk about her love life. It gave her a headache. Call her picky, but she couldn't seem to find a man who lit her lamp *and* fulfilled her perfectly reasonable qualifications. Was she expecting too much? She firmly shut the door in her mind labeled Hunky Normal Husband and concentrated on something more accessible, like getting a quick look at the great hall.

Since Dad had assured Kim that no way was Fo a sentient being, and because Kim had always believed Dad knew everything, it followed that she should put Fo back in her pocket. Kim kept her out. Fo liked to see things.

As she drew nearer to the doors closed against the damp and chill, Kim noticed a corner protected from the spotlight's glare. Within the shadows lurked a darker shape, massive with no identifiable form. And for the moment it took her to catch her breath, fear rippled through her. Strange emotions, dark shadows—this place was messing with her mind.

Kim glanced around. Castle and surrounding area lit by bright spotlights, people still walking around even in the drizzle. Fear? What was that about? Hello? She was a demon destroyer. Black blobs skulking in the shadows didn't scare someone who hunted demons. She wasn't even afraid of a big butt-ugly minion of the Supreme Scumbag. Okay, maybe she was a little afraid. Very little.

Throwing whatever stood in the shadows a casual and totally fearless smile—she was still practicing her totally fearless smile in front of her mirror—Kim reached for the door.

"Do you really want to go inside? You're not dressed to kill." The voice was light, female, and amused.

Startled, Kim almost dropped Fo.

The scary blob separated, revealing the shapes of two people, a man and woman. The woman stepped out of the shadows. Short blond hair, a pixie face, and large, dark eyes. She looked perky. Kim winced at the description. Ms. Perky's long black sleeveless dress was slit up the side, plunged low in front, and was set off by the sparkle of diamonds at throat and ears. Silver sandals with four-inch heels helped with the height thing, but Kim figured that she'd barely break five feet two in her bare feet. Wasn't she freezing to death out here without a coat?

"Dressed to kill?" Kim glanced down. "Well, no, I guess not. Can't I go in wearing jeans?" Why didn't the man step out of the shadows?

The woman's laughter was friendly, her smile contagious. Kim smiled back. Sheesh, how embarrassing. Lucky her family wasn't here. Kim could see the black-bordered blurb in the family newsletter: Kimberly Vaughn, formerly known as a tiger in the demon-destroying world, has been disowned by her family for the crime of being afraid of her own and other people's shadows. The Council of Demon Destroyers has reduced her to the rank of scared rabbit.

Fine, so even on her most ferocious day, Kim would never de-scribe herself as a "tiger of the demon-destroying world." That title would go to her sister, Lynsay.

"No one will stop you." The woman inventoried Kim's outfit. "But you're still not dressed to *kill*."

"Kill?" Kim didn't get it.

The shadow man hadn't moved, didn't seem to even breathe. *He* certainly wasn't filled with friendly perkiness. In fact, something about his complete stillness made her shiver. She pulled her jacket more tightly around her.

"Only vampires pass through these doors on a Saturday night." The woman's smile widened. "The Castle of Dark Dreams holds a Vampire Ball every Saturday night. Everyone does the basic black clothes and fake fangs thing. Oh, and I'm Liz. I've been staying here for a few weeks. Really neat place." Liz's expectant pause meant Kim would have to reciprocate with name and trivial info.

"Kim Vaughn, and I'm an architect." She got an adrenaline rush just saying that out loud. "The owner hired me to plan a few addi-tions to the castle. So we'll probably run into each other again."

"I'll only be here for two more days, but I'll look for you." She slid her tongue across her lower lip. Liz sounded really eager, and her smile was really friendly, but Kim decided that something about Liz and Shadow Man was really creeping her out. Probably just a by-product of the last few minutes' weirdness and her scared-rabbit syndrome.

Fo's paranoia must be catching. "Guess I'll go in and take a peek at the great hall." Kim reached for the door again.

"Psst, Kimmie."

Damn, Kim had forgotten she was still holding Fo.

"Uh, she's a demon."

Kim glared at Fo.

"I'm whispering. She can't hear me." Fo looked aggrieved that Kim didn't appreciate her attempt to be discreet.

Kim cast Liz a cautious glance. Yep, Liz had heard Fo. "It's just my cell phone. My brother did some creative programming. He has a warped sense of humor." She hoped her smile said amused embarrassment.

Kim never found out what Liz thought of her brother's warped sense of humor because at that moment the man stepped from the shadows.

Oh. My. God. Kim felt frozen in place, not able to close her mouth or blink as she got her first look at him. At the same moment, the emotions struck again with enough force to almost bring her to her knees.

"Umm, Kimmie? Did you hear me? I said she's a D-E-M-O—"

Kim flipped Fo shut and crammed her back into her pocket, all without taking her gaze from the man. She couldn't reason away what she'd just felt. Even as she stared at him, she could feel her ordinariness trickling away, and she hated him for that. Because the emotions were coming from him. She knew it, felt it on a primitive level.

He narrowed his gaze on her, *through* her, to the confused person inside. She tried to rub away a slight pressure between her eyes. Great. A sinus headache would complete the night.

"So your cell phone thinks Liz is a demon?" His voice was a husky murmur that would be right at home on a foggy London street at midnight, quietly menacing with a promise that danger could be deliciously tempting.

Kim forced herself to blink before her eyeballs dried out. "It thinks *everyone's* a demon." True. "My brother programmed it to accuse people of being demons as a joke." Not true.

"The laws of probability would suggest that it might be right sometimes." His soft laughter shivered along all of her nerve endings. "If demons existed."

He leaned closer to her, but she couldn't move, couldn't *breathe.* Thankfully, the scary emotions had disappeared. She didn't question why.

But holy cow, would you look at him! Six feet plus of broad-shouldered, hard-muscled body. Fine, so she couldn't testify to any bare-body specifics because he was wearing a black tux and what looked like a black silk shirt. But only a hard-muscled body would do justice to that *face*.

Kim drew in a deep breath before she turned as purple as Fo's eyes. "Sure. *If* demons existed. They don't, so the message is a big ha-ha."

Right now demons weren't on her personal radar screen. Where did great looking cross the line into spectacular? This guy not only had leaped across the spectacular line but was closing in fast on unbelievable. *No one* looked this good. If he were a building, he'd be the Chrysler Building in New York City, one of her personal choices for most magnificent building in the world.

Liz moved up to put a proprietary hand on his arm. "We need to get going, Brynn."

The man, Brynn, deliberately glanced at his watch. "Not yet." He didn't look at Liz, and his words were shards of chipped ice. Didn't sound too lover-like to Kim. In fact, he moved away from Liz's grasp and closer to Kim.

While Brynn was eyeing the time, Kim was ogling him. Hey, scenery this good came along once in a millennium. She couldn't tell much about his hair other than it was at least shoulder-length, because he'd pulled it away from his face and secured it with a leather tie. In the uncertain mixture of light and shadow she wasn't sure about its color. Maybe rain-darkened blond.

He shifted his attention back to Kim. "You don't believe in demons, but let's say they existed, in theory of course. And just for the hell of it, let's say your cell phone could really identify them. Would your cell phone also be able to destroy them?"

There was a dark eagerness to his question that would've normally registered on her really-weird scale, but she was still too wrapped up in the glory of his face.

"Yeah, I guess so." His *face*. If you just listed each feature—firm jaw, full lower lip, wide-spaced eyes—you might dismiss him as merely another example of yummy maleness in a world loaded with delish guys.

This man had all the intangibles, though. Every woman who ever looked at him would recognize his sensual, dangerous, and primal call. Kim didn't know many women who wouldn't answer. He was simply perfect. And since Kim never trusted perfect in an imperfect world, she was instantly suspicious.

Uh-huh. Time for a teeny tiny bit of self-honesty here. If Mr. Sinfully Sexy crooked his perfect finger, she'd probably leap on him, knock him down right here in front of the castle, rip his clothes from his body, and have her wicked way with him. Kim took a deep, calming breath. Yeah, she'd still be suspicious, but who said she couldn't have a good time while she waited for him to do something dastardly, hmm?

"Come on, Brynn. I'm cold, and it'll be time in"—Liz leaned over to glance at his watch—"five minutes."

She sounded whiny, and the malicious enjoyment Kim got from the thought surprised her. And what exactly would happen in five minutes?

"You may as well go back inside, Liz, because I want to talk to Kim for a few minutes about her cell phone. In fact, I guess I've officially been with *Kim* for the last four minutes. So all bets are off. Enjoy the rest of your night." More shocking than Brynn's terse dismissal of Liz, was Liz's response.

"You'll pay for this next time." She didn't look perky anymore, just royally pissed off. "I'm starved." Liz speared him with her gaze, and Kim couldn't remember ever seeing such open sexual hunger on any woman's face. She cast Kim a speculative glance before turning and striding away from the castle, anger in every click of her heels.

Away from the castle? Didn't they have food inside? Maybe she didn't want food. Kim figured Liz had a pretty healthy appetite for Brynn's body. *Say something.* "Uh, this is probably none of my business, but I think I missed something."

He lifted his face to the light breeze that had suddenly kicked up and closed his eyes. "Liz and I play a game each night. She lost this time." He opened his eyes and then stepped closer.

For the first time she got a good look at his eyes in the full light . . . and forgot to breathe. The big bang theory became real for Kim in that moment, because looking into Brynn's eyes opened up a whole new personal universe for her.

She was surprised he couldn't hear the kaboom kaboom of her heartbeat. Kim controlled the need to flatten her hand over the organ in question so it wouldn't leap from her chest. Chasing your heart down the street would be so not cool.

There were a thousand stories in his eyes, and they were all sexual. Color? Old whiskey held up to candlelight so that the rich gold shone through—potent, ageless, and . . . *Warm* should be the next word on her list. It wasn't. Every emotion she'd felt just a few minutes ago shone in those eyes. Cold. So cold. She exhaled sharply and shivered.

Forcing her gaze away from those eyes, she tried to concentrate on what he was saying.

"You saved me from a night of mindless sex." He didn't smile when he said it.

Mindless sex? The men she'd known would salivate like Pavlov's pooch at the mention of mindless sex. She didn't understand him, and she certainly didn't understand his emotions that had sort of wandered off course and found her. "Gotcha. Well, I guess I'll take a peek into the great hall. Are you coming in, too?"

"No." His gaze drifted beyond her into the night. "I think I'll walk for a while. There's a certain pleasure in aloneness. Don't you feel it? The quiet. The *peace*." His voice was smoke, sex, and warm, secret places.

She would've believed his voice if she hadn't looked into his eyes first. Warm wasn't part of his agenda. Kim finally managed to move. She stepped back. Standing too close to those waves of pheromones couldn't be good for her sensual well-being. "You're right. I wouldn't mind being alone more." She couldn't help it if she sounded a little wistful. She was supposed to keep Fo with her all the time, and the detector didn't have an Off button. So essentially Kim was never alone.

She had a feeling that *his* "alone" meant something else. Could a man ever get too much female adoration? The thought was revolutionary. But Kim could almost imagine what would happen inside the castle if all the women knew he was outside by himself. There'd be a bloody catfight, dozens of women scratching and clawing at each other. The winner would eventually drag her battered body out here to claim her prize. Kim frowned. Something touched her that felt uncomfortably close to envy.

"Would you mind if I took a quick look at your cell phone before you go inside?" He'd shifted closer again, invading her space, bringing with him the scent of wicked joys and dark fantasies.

"Oh, sure." She reached for her real cell phone in her other pocket and prayed he hadn't seen which pocket held Fo.

"I don't think so." He covered her hand with his larger one, and she swore she felt the heat from his touch all the way to her backbone. "I think *this* is your talkative little phone." He dipped his fingers into her other pocket and pulled out Fo.

Damn. Kim snatched Fo from his fingers, flipped the detector open so he could see, and hoped for a miracle. One in which the screen remained blank and Fo remained silent.

It wasn't her night for miracles. Fo's huge purple eyes blinked open, and she stared at Brynn. Only the slight widening of Fo's eyes gave warning, but Kim knew what was coming and was helpless to stop it. Now Kim knew how the Wicked Witch of the East had felt just before Dorothy's house flattened her.

"Woohoo! DemondemonDEMON!" Fo's small case pulsed with excitement. "Big beeeautiful DEMON. Can we keep him for a while before we destroy him? Huh, can we?"

Kim closed her eyes and wished for an out-of-body experience. Preferably one that would take her at least a mile from this man. "I'm already visualizing the duct tape over your mouth, Fo." Kim's hissed threat didn't seem to slow down Fo's happy vibrating.

All right, she'd have to open her eyes sometime. He'd either be surprised or amused. Those were the usual responses to one of Fo's outbursts. Except for the president's secret service. It took a lot to surprise or amuse them. Fo had barely escaped with her nano-parts intact.

Drawing in a deep breath of courage, Kim opened her eyes. Then blinked. He was fascinated. Really fascinated. He carefully removed Fo from her nerveless fingers.

"It's a joke. It's only a cell phone. My brother programmed her, umm, it, to say that. It didn't mean what it said. I mean, she's, uh, it's not real, so it didn't know . . ." *Shut up.* Kim closed her mouth and waited for his response to that bit of hysteria.

He narrowed his eyes as he studied Fo. Fo studied him right back. "What happens if I press this button?" He indicated the red Destroy button.

"Not much. A little noise, a little light. Pretty harmless." *Unless you're a demon.* "The whole thing's a gag. I've been trying to tell you that."

She reached for Fo and then watched in horror as his finger hovered over the red button. The demon-destroying beam would get him right in the face. It wouldn't kill a human, but it would blind him for about a half hour. She didn't need to start her new job with him clutching his face and accusing her of trying to kill him.

Kim ripped Fo from his fingers. "It was great meeting you, but it's chilly standing out here." She clicked Fo shut and put the detector back into her pocket.

She refused to meet his gaze, but Kim sensed his amusement . . . and something more, something darker.

"When you're ready to go in, just press that button, and someone will greet you." He pointed to a button beside the doors. "Welcome to the Castle of Dark Dreams, Kim." Then he turned and strode away.

Bemused, she watched him until he disappeared in the darkness, and then she reached for the doorbell.

"Would you like a brochure, dearie?" The voice behind her said, senior citizen with a capital S.

Kim gave a startled squeak and leaped away from the door. Okay, so with everything that had happened tonight she had a right to be jumpy. She turned to meet the sharp gaze of a walking stereotype.

The woman looked old. Very old. Her white hair was short with waves that marched across her head in perfect order. Small wire-framed glasses perched on the end of her nose. A round face, faded blue eyes, a small mouth, and many many wrinkles completed the picture of everybody's grandmother.

Trouble was, Kim's grandmother didn't look like this. Grandma was slim, trim, and stylish, with great hair. She'd threatened to give all her money to cat charities unless her family promised to make sure when they laid her out that no gray roots showed and that she had fresh highlights. Grandma wasn't going to knock on the pearly gates looking like a night hag.

Kim glanced down at the brochure the woman held out to her. The grandma image continued. White cardigan, baggy, flowered dress that showed the tops of knee-highs when the wind caught the edges of her skirt, and black, chunky shoes.

Kim took the brochure because she didn't want to insult the woman. "Thanks."

The woman smiled at Kim. It was a prim smile. "I'm Miss Abby. Taught first grade for thirty-five years here in Galveston. Kids'll either kill you or make you stronger. I got stronger. When I retired, I started my own business. Ye Olde Victorian Wedding Chapel. I'll marry you in style."

What to say? "Umm, I don't think—"

"That's the trouble today, youngsters don't think. Keep the brochure. You never know when you might meet the perfect young man and want to hitch up with him in a hurry. In my day, young ladies didn't just up and marry someone fast unless they were in a family way. But times change." Her expression said not for the better.

Family way? Who said things like that nowadays? "I guarantee I won't be needing a wedding chapel." Not unless Mr. Ordinary popped out of the castle wall.

The woman waved at her. "Keep the brochure. Pass it on if you can't use it." She walked past Kim. "I have to leave a pile of them in the lobby. Get a lot of business from the castle."

Strange. Miss Abby's walk was a lot more chipper than the rest of her. But a faint squeaking distracted Kim from Miss Abby's walk. Birds? Not at night. "Do you hear a squeaking noise?"

Miss Abby glanced back at Kim. "That's my girdle, dearie. Every lady should wear one." Her gaze said no girdle, no lady. She didn't give the button a second glance as she pulled the door open and disappeared inside.

Kim was on Miss Abby's slut list, but somehow she couldn't drum up the energy to care. She'd take a look at the great hall and then spend the rest of her night trying to reason away Brynn's very scary emotions that had scraped off on her.

Finally, she noticed the whispering coming from her pocket.

"She's a demon, Kimmie. I've been trying to tell you, but you weren't paying attention." Pregnant pause. "Someday a demon is going to get you, and you'll be dead, dead, dead. And I'll make sure they put 'I told you so. Love, Fo' on your tombstone."

Kim sighed. *What a sweetheart.* She pushed the button.

2

Kim stared at the closed doors. Well, that was a freaky little scene. Not her weirdest, though.

Her weirdest had been when a demon wearing a chicken costume had attacked her. The restaurant manager who'd hired him really got bent out of shape when Fo turned Mr. Chicken into a pile of ash. Kim had to sweep Mr. Chicken off the walk and then wear the stupid costume for the rest of the night to calm the manager down.

But this was close. Very close. At least the strange emotions hadn't returned. Maybe they'd just been an anomaly, a moment in time and space that would never happen again. She could hope.

The creak of heavy doors opening refocused her on the here and now. Flickering lights along with the sounds of music and voices washed over her. And a man, no, a wizard, stood in the doorway. Gold-trimmed blue robe, tall, conical hat decorated with gold suns, moons, and stars—yeah, definitely a wizard.

The thin, gray-haired man peered at her from narrowed gray

eyes. His pursed lips announced his disapproval of her appearance at his door. He tugged at his long, pointy beard.

"Holgarth, at your service, madam." His expression said he'd eat dirt before *ever* being at anyone's service. "Your clothing is distressingly inappropriate for tonight's ball. Please pay for your ticket and then come with me." He waved imperiously toward a ticket counter.

This man was Holgarth? "I don't want—"

"You don't want to be seen in those disreputable garments?" He looked down his long nose at her and then dismissed her jeans, T-shirt, boots, and jacket with a contemptuous sniff. "And rightly so. One always wonders why people don't consider their apparel more carefully." He arched one haughty brow to indicate how puzzled he was by such thoughtless behavior on the part of the unwashed masses.

"No, you don't understand. I'm—"

"Appallingly late. I know." He glanced around at the sea of fake vamps filling the great hall. "Come, come. I have other duties to perform besides greeting and finding presentable gowns for all the local Cinderellas." Ignoring her attempt to introduce herself, he tried to propel her toward the counter where he obviously expected her to meekly pay for a ticket.

Kim didn't do meekness well. "Whoa, your Wizardy Worship. We need to get a few things straight. First off, I didn't come here for your Vampire Ball. I'm Kimberly Vaughn, and you wrote to offer me the job of making a few improvements to ye olde castle."

He stared at her with eyes that looked a little too ancient, a little too crafty. Not a comfy feeling. "Ah, yes. Ms. Vaughn. The owner insisted that you were the only one who could capture the true vision of the castle." He pressed his lips into thin lines of displeasure. "I was not consulted on the choice." Once again, he did the looking-up-and-down thing. "I dread to ask what your vision might be." He held up a hand. "No, don't tell me. Let it all be a marvelous surprise." His expression said he expected a disastrous surprise.

Kim couldn't help it, she grinned. He was so obnoxious he was funny. "Oh, but I have tons of great ideas. The first thing I'll do is knock down one side of the great hall and create a wall of glass. Bring the castle into the twenty-first century. Hey, and how about a gatehouse with a murder hole so you can shoot fiery arrows down on customers? How does that work for you?"

He actually blanched. But before he could express his opinion, Fo expressed hers.

"He's too old for you, Kimmie. I can tell by his voice. Why're you wasting your time on an old fart when you could be searching for a young *ordinary* guy? Take me out so I can look at him." Fo vibrated to emphasize her demand.

Kim clamped her hand over her pocket. Damn.

Holgarth paused to stare at her pocket. "Your pocket spoke, Ms. Vaughn. The 'old fart' will wait while you answer it." His bored expression said that pockets spoke to people on a regular basis.

Fine, so she had a situation here, but nothing she hadn't faced before. She'd take Fo out, act like she was answering a call, and then roll right into the familiar it's-just-a-novelty explanation. *Uh-huh, and that worked so well with Brynn.* She took Fo from her pocket and flipped her open.

But before she had a chance to put the detector to her ear and carry on a pretend conversation, Holgarth plucked Fo from her hand. He narrowed his gimlet gaze on Fo, and Fo blinked her big purple eyes at him.

"I think he's a demon, too, Kimmie. A mean one. But he's not hot like the one we met outside. So can I destroy him now?" Fo didn't seem to realize she was in the hands of the enemy, so to speak.

"How fascinating. A tiny homicidal being." Holgarth seemed intrigued, which was a step up from obnoxious. "Perhaps I'll take her apart to see how she works."

Fo's eyes widened in alarm. "Get me away from him, Kimmie. And then press my Destroy button. Do it nownownow!" Fo's alarm was escalating into all-out panic.

Luckily for Galveston, Fo's creator hadn't programmed her with the ability to destroy demons on her own. Kim still had to press the button. "Give Fo back to me before I yank off your pointy hat and beat you over your pointy head with it." *Way to go, Vaughn.* She wondered if Holgarth had the power to fire her. "Besides, you don't need to take her—er, it—apart. It's just a cell phone with some clever programming. My brother likes to mess with electronics."

Holgarth's gaze seemed to strip away all her bravado and expose the lie festering beneath. "You don't tell untruths very well, Ms. Vaughn. Not even to yourself. We both know what Fo is."

What *did* he know? Okay, a moment of self-truth. Kim didn't believe her family. Fo wasn't merely a piece of useful equipment like all their other demon detectors. The scientist they'd commissioned to create the perfect demon-detector-slash-destroyer had made Fo first. Then he had the nerve to drop dead. Dad was really ticked at first because he had to find someone else to build all the other detectors. Later, Dad said they'd caught a lucky break because Fo was a useless piece of junk.

And what did *Kim* believe? Fo had a personality. Her technology was flawed, so she made decisions based on her emotions. Kim still had trouble taking that last step and demanding that her family accept what Fo truly was, but *she* knew. Heaven help all of them, she knew. "Give Fo back to me *now.*"

Surprisingly, Holgarth handed Fo over, and for the first time Kim thought she saw a slight lift of his lips that was almost, but not quite, a smile. "Perhaps I misjudged you. Your stay could prove to be quite entertaining."

That didn't sound good. "Look, I don't want to do any dancing or anything. I just want to take a quick look around the great hall and then get some sleep. I drove down from Dallas, and it's been a long day." *Too long if I'm picking up on the emotions of godlike strangers.*

She'd already checked in and had her bags taken to her room, but she'd wanted to get the full impact of the castle by walking around to the front where, for a few moments, she could forget that the other side of the castle was a hotel entrance.

Holgarth nodded. "When you decide to retire, you can go through that door." He pointed toward a door tucked away in one of the great hall's corners. "It leads to the hotel lobby and elevators. Of course, if you feel energetic, you can always take the scenic route to your room. The four spiral stone staircases lead all the way to the top of the towers. Authentic but exhausting."

Kim nodded. "One question. What's your job description here?" Maybe she should've asked that question when she first received his letter.

"I do many things, Ms. Vaughn."

Something in his tone sent an unexplained ripple of unease through her. "Fine, so name a few."

"I'm the owner's attorney, but I also take care of various . . . things here. The owner pays me well to devote myself exclusively to the well-being of the castle." He seemed ready to walk away from her, but then paused. "Fo mentioned a demon you'd met outside, one that was 'hot' as opposed to an old fart."

"You can forget the demon part. Fo thinks if it breathes, it's a demon." Kim ignored Fo, who'd narrowed her eyes to angry purple slits. "I met two people, Brynn and Liz. I guess they're both staying in the hotel." The warm slide of pleasure when she mentioned Brynn's name surprised her, because the emotion was hers, all hers.

For some reason, her comment seemed to bother Holgarth. "They were together?"

Kim nodded. "Before you run off to harass more late-comers—and heaven knows how the castle keeps any business when you greet customers with such joyous enthusiasm—I have two more questions. What's the owner's name, and is the owner a man or a woman?" Stupid of her not to have asked these questions sooner.

Holgarth's expression turned sly. "The owner prefers to remain anonymous." He shrugged. "Man or woman? One can never be quite sure, can one? Oh, and we keep customers because my bubbling personality grows on them." He turned toward the door to welcome another unfortunate late arrival.

"Like mold." Her muttered comment drew no response from Holgarth. Left alone, Kim looked down at a subdued Fo. "See what happens when you open your mouth without thinking?" Yes, *mouth*, not speaker or sound box. Kim didn't give Fo a chance to reply before closing her and returning the detector to her pocket.

She wandered through the crowd of dancers. A group of musicians played in one corner of the hall while a long banquet table in front of the large, blazing fireplace was set up as a buffet. A bar was kept busy in another corner. Kim tried to wrap her imagination around an image of hordes of drunken vampires hitting the streets after the ball.

She ignored the small candlelit tables around the periphery of the room while she tried to picture the great hall the way it normally looked—wall sconces with lights that imitated the flickering flames of many candles, authentic-looking tapestries, armor, and weapons of war, high vaulted ceilings with exposed beams. Yes, she could work with all of this.

"Spectacular, isn't it?" The deep male voice dragged her attention back to the ball.

She smiled automatically as she turned to the man who'd stopped beside her. "Yes, it's really . . ." Kim had to make trips to Galveston more often. The Gulf breezes seemed to blow in more than the normal smattering of hot guys. "Beautiful."

Tall, broad-shouldered, with long black hair just tousled enough to tempt a woman's fingers, and brilliant blue eyes that hinted at secrets, he was a major wow. Okay, maybe not as major a wow as Brynn, but still totally gorgeous.

"I heard you talking to Holgarth. We've been expecting you. I'm Eric McNair. My brothers and I run the place, so I wanted to officially welcome you to the Castle of Dark Dreams." He smiled and held out his hand. "I know how Holgarth greets newcomers, so I figured I'd better rush over to do some damage control."

Kim clasped his hand and duly noted that actual physical contact with Eric didn't trigger her body's awesome-impact alarm. Brynn sure had. Interesting. And how had he heard her conversation with Holgarth? She hadn't seen him anywhere nearby, and she'd definitely have noticed a man like Eric.

"I caught a mention of my brother Brynn in your conversation. You said you met him outside, and Liz was with him." Eric's gaze might be on Kim, but behind those blue eyes his thoughts were elsewhere.

Brynn and Eric were brothers? Kim studied Eric more closely. No resemblance other than a sensuality rating that was off the scale. And why were Holgarth and Eric both so concerned that Brynn and Liz were together? *Concern* was the right word. She sensed worry in both men's questions. She mentally shrugged away her curiosity. It wasn't any of her business.

"Well, when Liz first spoke to me they were together, but then for some reason Liz left. Don't ask me why; I don't know." But she'd like to. Fine, so she couldn't dismiss her curiosity about Brynn with just a mental shrug. That worried her. She didn't believe in mixing business with pleasure, and she sensed that Brynn would bring pleasure on a mythic scale.

Eric nodded, but there was still a line of worry between his eyes. "I'll leave you alone so you can look around. Make sure you ask the staff for anything you need. I probably won't see you again until tomorrow night, but maybe we can all get together then and toss around ideas." Eric turned away and strode to the bar where he joined a tall, muscular man with shaggy dark hair who looked like he'd be more at home wearing a kilt and wielding a sword than dressed in a tux and holding a drink.

Eric and the other man spoke intently. The other man glanced her way once, so she assumed Eric was passing on the info she'd given him. Then both men left. Hmm. Strange, but she was too tired to think about the undercurrents she felt. Yawning, she headed for the door to the hotel lobby. She'd try to sort out all her first impressions tomorrow when her head was clearer.

She grinned at Fo's tentative vibration. Surprise, surprise, Holgarth had scared Fo into blessed silence. Kim would listen while Fo told her Eric was a demon *after* she'd had a good night's sleep.

*   *   *

Brynn stood on the curtain wall's walkway looking out over the battlements at the Gulf of Mexico. He didn't have Eric's enhanced senses, so he couldn't see too much of the Gulf through the fog that was moving in. But that was okay, because the fog also blanked out most of the traffic on Seawall Boulevard, the street that separated the castle from the Gulf. On a night like this—damp, chilly, and with the fog rolling in—he could almost believe he was the only person alive. And that suited him just fine.

But he wasn't allowed to enjoy his fantasy long. Eric and Conall joined him, one on each side, and all three stared in silence at the fog.

"Hey, relax, I'm not going to jump. Leaping from high places puts a major hurting on me without achieving the desired goal. And if the impact messes up a few body parts, they heal as good as new faster than I can say ouch. Been there, done that, don't want to go there again." He could write the definitive book on creative attempts to end demonic existence, but since none of them worked, he didn't think publishers would put out the big bucks.

Eric and Conall chose to ignore his comment.

"I guess you're here because someone told you I was with Liz." He figured that *someone* was about five seven with a mop of curly red hair, huge green eyes, and named Kim. Amazing he remembered even that much about her. There'd been so many women over the centuries, women he'd tried to wipe from his memory as soon as he left them. He'd gotten good at forgetting women.

But he'd have to be careful around Kim. When he'd probed her mind to find an explanation for her reaction to him, he'd found the echo of his own emotions. From the amazed look on her face, she didn't understand how it had happened. He'd have to guard his feelings when she was close so it didn't happen again. His emotions were ugly and not to be shared with anyone.

Eric turned his deadly vampire stare on Brynn, the one meant to scare him into submission. "I'm going to stop Liz."

"No." Greatest word in any language. *No* wasn't a word he got to say often, so he savored moments like this.

"Stubborn son of a bitch." Conall's contribution to the discussion.

"You're letting pride get in the way of common sense." Eric's input.

"Right on both counts." Brynn kept his gaze fixed on the Gulf, almost obscured now by the thick fog. Nice metaphor for his life before coming to the Castle of Dark Dreams. Surround your soul with white nothingness where no emotions could find you, and you learned to survive. Oops. Forgot. He didn't have a soul. "Now that we've got that straight, you can leave."

"Uh-uh. Don't think so." Eric turned his back to the Gulf and stared down instead at the castle's courtyard where two fanged fakes were weaving unsteadily toward the drawbridge. "Don't know why the owner insisted on a real moat. Someone's going to fall in one night and then sue our asses."

Conall turned to follow Eric's gaze. "I liked Holgarth's idea about stocking the moat with gators. Can't sue from inside a gator's belly." Conall sounded like he'd gleefully chuck Brynn into the moat as gator food.

Brynn exhaled slowly. Conall was pissed. Previous experience had taught him a rant wouldn't be far behind.

"Dammit, look at me, Brynn." Conall got into his face and smacked him on the shoulder, forcing Brynn to meet his gaze.

Eric and Conall were the only two beings he'd take that from. Anyone else would find himself on a one-way flight to the courtyard below. Brynn forced himself to relax. Good thing that Conall was a friend. Even demons and vampires didn't go around flinging six foot five inch tall immortal warriors from castle walls.

"We're pretending to be three ordinary brothers running a theme park attraction, but we're not brothers and we're not ordinary. Don't forget for one minute that you have a vampire and a cursed warrior with a bad attitude watching your back." Conall speared Brynn with a hard stare and then stepped back.

Eric continued to watch the two who would be vampires below as they crawled into a cab. "I think you're wrong not to accept our help, but I guess I understand. When Taurin was out to get me, I wanted to take him down by myself. It was an ego thing."

Brynn allowed himself a smile that was more grimace than anything else. "Don't know how much pride there is in doing battle with a woman who barely reaches my shoulders."

Eric shook his head. "Not a woman. Liz is a vampire. She's only a few hundred years old, but she's powerful and used to getting her own way. And she wants you. A locked door will keep a human out of your room, but a lock won't stop Liz. It'll just tick her off."

"So how'd you get rid of her tonight?" Conall seemed to have accepted that Brynn wouldn't allow him to kick Liz's evil little behind out of Galveston.

Brynn's smile was more real this time. "Our shiny new architect saved me. I'd gone outside thinking maybe the cold and damp would eventually drive Liz back inside, but no luck. Then the architect showed up. I think Liz was sizing her up for a midnight snack, and while they were talking I attached myself to the architect. Just in time, too. I only had a few minutes left." Only a few minutes before he would've had to offer Liz his body. Again.

"Don't worry, though. Liz will only be here for two more days. I have five hundred years of coping skills behind me, so I should be able to avoid her for that long. And if I don't?" He shrugged. "What's one more night of sex?" Just another piece of his humanity torn off and chewed up. Of course, he'd never been human, not even for one day of his existence.

Eric frowned. Ever since he'd married Donna, he'd gone all serious about this only-one-life-mate crap. "There has to be a way to find out who or what did this to you." He lifted his lips to expose his fangs, hinting at what would happen if the entity refused to release Brynn. "Tell me again what you remember about that day."

"He's told us the story a dozen times, Eric." Even Conall seemed to understand the futility of searching for clues where none existed.

Brynn shrugged. "Nothing to tell. I woke up at an inn with no memory of who I was or how I'd gotten there. I rolled out of bed, looked at myself in what passed for a mirror, and knew *what* I was and what I was expected to do. No one at the inn recognized me, but there was a horse waiting for me in the stable, and I had gold to buy what I wanted." He frowned. "Wait. I do remember something I never told you before. There was a cat in the room with me. Big black-and-white tomcat. I didn't know how it got into the room and didn't care. I had other things to worry about."

Eric nodded. "Someday you'll remember something important, and then we'll nail the bastard that did this to you."

Brynn grinned. Eric and Conall were fierce in their friendships, and that's what made the Castle of Dark Dreams a place he intended to call home for a long time. "Get over it. I'm a demon. No rhyme or reason, no miracle cure." He glanced at his watch. "If I'm lucky, Liz will spend the rest of the night hunting dinner."

"Just to make sure you get some uninterrupted sleep, I'll put a shield across your door and window. Liz isn't powerful enough to get through it." Eric's mouth was set in a determined line.

Brynn said nothing as he followed Eric and Conall back into the castle. Eric would try to protect him no matter how much he argued, so he let it go.

And as he lay in his bed a short time later, he thought about Kim and her strange . . . Cell phone? Demon destroyer? Gag toy?

By rights he should be more intrigued by the possibility of a machine that could destroy demons than by the castle's resident architect. But amazingly, the memory of full lips with a tempting shine that dared him to slide his tongue across them, and green eyes that shone with all the emotions *he* kept carefully hidden, wouldn't let him concentrate.

Scary. After five hundred years, women only stirred him sexually when he was under the compulsion. Kim Vaughn was a whole new ball game.

3

"Ack! Wake up, Kimmie. Kitty demon alert." Fo's screeches poked holes in the warm, comfy lethargy of Kim's sleep, letting the new day in. "Push my Destroy button. Now!"

Kim scrunched her eyes more tightly shut and tried to recapture the fast-fading dream of a perfect male face attached to a perfect male body. Obviously a Brynn-induced fantasy. The whole magnificent package was in the act of performing erotic acts on her willing body. She clenched her teeth. Fo was cheating her out of an awesome orgasm.

"Get your butt out of bed and help me nuke the demon. It's our job, our purpose in life. The demon's sitting on your chest, and it's getting ready to suck your soul out through your mouth. WAKE UP!" Fo was working herself into a frenzy.

Fo's paranoia had taken a sharp right turn from the moment they hit Galveston. Kim would have to do something about her. She got a sudden mental image of Fo's small case resting in the middle of a psychiatrist's couch. She could hear it all now. "So tell me, Ms. Fo, do you harbor deeply repressed memories of Ms. Vaughn attacking you with a can opener, hmm? And how do you feel about that?"

Kim smiled but didn't open her eyes.

"Wake up, Kimmie! You have to teach me how to push the button by myself, because we'll never off any demons if you can't get your lazy behind out of bed." Fo sounded ticked off. "Fine, just let it sit on your chest all day and suck out your soul, your brain, your heart, your—"

Kim frowned as she tried to ignore Fo's litany of vital organs she was about to lose to the "kitty demon." She must've caught something, because her chest did have that heavy, hard-to-take-a-breath feel. Great, all she needed on top of Fo's caterwauling was a chest cold.

"You'll be sorry you didn't get up when I tell Lynsay about how you let a demon escape." Fo had progressed to vindictiveness.

Lynsay and Fo, what a scary duo. Kim's sister would cheerfully zap every person Fo said was a demon—Lynsay was totally into her job—leaving a trail of outraged citizens in her wake. Can we say many, many lawsuits?

"*Are you awake yet? Oh, and if you can't make mini-mouth be quiet, I'll be glad to bury it in someone's backyard. Did I ask if you're awake yet?*"

Not Fo's voice. The voice was impatient, female, and . . . in her head.

In her head? Kim opened her eyes to meet the unblinking blue eyes of a Siamese cat. It sat in regal splendor on her chest, its tail curled around its slender, elegant body.

"*Good. You're up. I was going to meow to wake you, but the noisy ninny on your night table would've drowned me out. Please make it stop that god-awful shrieking.*" The cat slid its gaze to Fo.

Kim stared up at the cat and tried to force words past the boulder in her throat.

"Yo, Kimmie, are you okay? Did it suck out your—"

"*Shut. Up.*" The cat studied Fo through slitted eyes. "*Do it. Oth-*

erwise I might be forced to abandon my civilized veneer and loose the beast within. The maid would be vacuuming up bits of you for weeks."

Fo fell silent.

The cat calmly returned her attention to Kim. "*See, you just need to be firm with it.*"

Kim concentrated on talking. She could do this. She hunted demons, but she'd never awakened to find one sitting on her chest. *Was* the cat a demon? Had Fo cried wolf once too often, and Kim hadn't believed her?

"What are you?" Three words. Hey, this talking wasn't so hard.

"*Not* what, *Kim. Who.*" The cat began to wash its face. "*I'm Asima, messenger of Bast, the Egyptian cat goddess. Oh, and to clear up the usual stereotypical misconceptions, Bast is not just a happy, fluffy sex goddess. She's an Eye of Ra, and her wrath is legendary.*" Asima sent Fo a meaningful glare. "*I'm not free to tell you what my true mission is here, but while I'm waiting to fulfill it, I amuse myself by taking an interest in a few select humans.*"

Lucky me. "So you're not a demon?" Stupid question. Lying was a national sport to demons. She'd bet they even had a Lying World Series.

Asima looked down her long, haughty nose at Kim. "*Bite your tongue. Demons are the Neanderthals of the nonhuman entity world. Great bumbling boobies. No sense of taste or culture. I love the opera, ballet, and Shakespearean plays. Demons love mud wrestling and Cheeze Doodles.*"

"Why'd you choose me, and would you please get off my chest?" Kim ignored Fo's small noises of outrage.

Asima stood, stretched leisurely, and then leaped gracefully onto the night table, landing beside Fo. Kim always left Fo open at night on the off chance a demon might feel the need to sneak into her room. She sighed. Okay, really so that Fo could see something besides the inside of her case. Now Fo stared up at Asima with wide purple eyes that filled her whole screen. Probably visualizing the maid vacuuming.

"*I knew the moment I saw you that you were a woman of culture and good taste—although you really need some help with your wardrobe, and your undies beg for an upgrade from slutty to elegant, but we'll deal with that at another time. Anyway, since you're our new architect, I decided to run a few ideas past you.*"

"You poked around in my closet and drawers?" Messenger of Bast or not, enough was enough. "And how'd you get into my room? I locked the door last night."

Asima did the equivalent of a cat shrug. "*I unlocked it and walked in. When you have goddess connections, you can do things like that. Now can we talk about perhaps adding a small theater to the castle? Nothing fancy, just an intimate area where we could hold the occasional cultural event—Swan Lake, or maybe The Taming of the Shrew.*"

"No."

Asima blinked. "*No?*"

Obviously those with goddess connections weren't used to the word *no*. "I'm not talking about anything until I've had my coffee, eaten breakfast, and taken a shower, in that order. Then I'll put on my tacky undies and something totally uncool from my closet. Finally I'll take a long walk to see if I can get my head on straight." Kim pointed to the door. "You may leave now." She didn't know how much longer she could hold it all together. First feeling someone else's emotions and now listening to a cat in her head. And in between the two, she'd met a few people who seemed just a tiny bit off.

Asima twitched her tail, plainly irritated. "*Well, I suppose I should give you some time to settle in.*" She glanced down at Fo. "*And please do something with those eyes. Purple makes me shudder. Silver or gold would project a more stylish image. Perception is everything, my tiny demon destroyer.*"

Fo narrowed her eyes slightly. "My name is Fo, and I like my eyes."

Asima yawned. "*Whatever.*" She leaped from the night table, padded to the door, stared at it, and when it swung open, she left with her tail waving serenely in the air.

Kim closed her eyes for the moment of blessed silence she knew would be all too short.

"Kimmie?" Fo sounded hesitant. "I heard her in my head."

In my head. More and more Fo was attributing human characteristics to herself. Kim didn't have the heart to correct her.

"Yeah. Me, too." Kim rubbed the middle of her forehead where a headache was trying to form. Then she opened her eyes. "Let's not talk about Asima now." She called room service for breakfast and a whole pot of coffee. Then she crawled out of bed to begin the rest of this really terrific day.

Kim wasn't looking forward to the moment when Fo found out she wasn't going with Kim today.

Brynn reached the top step and paused. He'd purposely taken the stairs instead of the elevator so he'd have more time to think over the pros and cons of what he was about to do—knock on Kim Vaughn's door.

It would be a *good* thing to get a closer look at that cell phone. If it was a fake, fine. If it was the real deal, he'd have to decide what to do about that.

It would be a *bad* thing to purposely initiate contact with the enemy. And women *were* his enemies, to be treated with suspicion and avoided whenever possible.

Each floor of the towers only had two rooms, so he didn't have to search far to find Kim's. He strode to her door and smiled grimly as he noted that she was in the Wicked Pleasure room. A fitting description of what he brought to the sexual table. Brynn hesitated before knocking. He could still walk away.

The sound of angry screaming from inside the room caught him by surprise.

"You can't leave me here, Kimmie. It's against the rules. I'll tell your dad. I'll tell Lynsay. I'll tell—"

The screams belonged to Kim's cell phone. He couldn't hear Kim's response.

"I can't help it if everyone in this castle is a demon. I'm supposed to tell you when I find one. You can't leave me here all day. Who am I supposed to talk to, the plants?"

Again he couldn't hear how Kim countered that argument.

"It's dangerous out there. If a demon knows you don't have me with you, it'll kill you. Then you'll be sorry." The phone seemed to get a lot of satisfaction from that thought.

Kim evidently had an answer for that argument, too.

"Pleasepleaseplease take me with you, Kimmie. I won't say one word. Even if I sense demons closing in on all sides, I'll just vibrate. Very hard. Maybe I'll just whisper the word 'demon.' Very softly."

Kim finally raised her voice. "No. Ever since we hit Galveston, you've accused everyone we met of being a demon. What're the chances, huh? You're embarrassing me, Fo."

"But they *were* demons." Fo's voice slid easily from emotion to emotion. She was now trying on her petulant little girl voice for size. It seemed that even female machines were adept at manipulation.

Brynn was fascinated—by Fo and by Kim. He couldn't remember the last time a woman had dredged up any interest in him at all, let alone fascination. It wouldn't last, but he'd ride the wave until it died on the beach.

"The little ladies are having quite a dustup in there, aren't they?" The voice spun Brynn around.

The man was tall with brown hair, brown eyes, and a wide smile. Brynn smiled back even as he touched the man's mind. Force of habit. His smile faded.

The man's smile turned mocking. "Yeah, I'm a demon. I could've told you that and saved you the trouble of rooting around in my mind." He held up his hand to keep Brynn from interrupting. "I'm a eudemon, one of the good guys." His expression turned thoughtful. "Maybe good guys is going too far. Eudemons don't give a crap about humans. We just want to be left alone to do our own thing."

His expression cleared. "Don't sense any cacodemons around. Those are the ones the Vaughn woman and her demon detector are hunting." Bitterness crept into his voice. "Not that any of the Vaughns ever stop long enough to realize there's a difference. Their motto is, 'Kill them all.' Oh, and I'm Wade Thomas."

"Brynn McNair. My brothers and I help run the castle. The Vaughn family? Sounds like you know them." *And why don't you sense I'm a demon like you?* "Bad luck that you have a room right across from a Vaughn."

Wade laughed. "I don't believe in coincidences, but I'll investigate that later. No problem, though. That's one crazy demon detector. Someone must've dropped it once too often, because it thinks everyone's a demon. Ms. Demon Hunter won't have a clue who is and who isn't one. It's all good."

"How'd you find out so much about your neighbor?" Talk about bad luck. A demon hunter right across from a demon. A hotel's reservation nightmare. It had to be a coincidence.

"I did some snooping. It pays to know who's nearby." Thoughts of the Vaughn family seemed to drain his good humor. "The freakin' Vaughn family has been a pain in the butt for centuries. There're hundreds of them. They get their kicks from destroying, and some of them aren't too selective about what they kill."

"But the detectors only destroy demons, right?" Brynn wasn't afraid for himself. He'd learned centuries ago that fear didn't make anything better. Besides, there were things worse than fear. But he had to make sure both humans and nonhumans in the castle were safe.

Wade shrugged. "Some of the old-timers don't trust the detectors and go with their gut feelings. They carry their swords with them to lop off heads. Must think we're damned vampires."

Brynn followed the logic path. "But if the demon's possessing a human body, they'll destroy the host, too."

"Doesn't matter to them." His smile returned. "I don't think the little lady in there is one of the fanatics. But watch out for the loose cannons in that family."

"Yeah, I'll do that." Brynn tried to gather his scattered thoughts. The Vaughn family sounded like scary people. "So what brings you to the Castle of Dark Dreams?"

"What am I doing here? I'm staying in a cool castle with a Gulf view while I get ready for my next fishing tournament. Bay fishing. Trailered my boat in from Louisiana. Love to fish. Do any fishing yourself?" Wade looked eager for some male bonding.

"A little. But it's more of an excuse to be alone. No one's going to walk out to talk to you in the middle of a lake." A demon who entered fishing tournaments. A first as far as Brynn knew.

"Any excuse is a good excuse to go fishing." He slapped Brynn on the shoulder. "I'm on my way down to breakfast. I'll be here for a week, so if you feel the need to get away and don't mind country music, give a shout." He started toward the elevator but stopped and turned around. "I can't make you, man. You're not human, but damned if I can figure out where you belong." He shrugged. "Guess that's none of my business." Then he stepped into the elevator, and the doors closed.

I don't belong anywhere. No, that wasn't true anymore. For the first time in five hundred years he had some real friends, so he belonged right here in the castle. And no woman like Liz or the hundreds of others who'd taken what they'd wanted from his body would drive him away.

He'd confront Kim with what he knew about Fo and her. This was his home, and no one would make him cower or hide in it. Brynn knocked on her door.

Silence fell inside the room, and then Kim pulled open the door. He slid his gaze the length of her body, taking in the boots, brown pants, and cream-colored top. She was studying him with the unblinking, wide-eyed stare he'd seen on women's faces down through the centuries. They loved the shiny wrapping paper, but they'd hate the ugly gift that passed for his heart locked inside the box. Lucky for them, they never got that far.

"I'm walking over to the candy store. Thought you might want to go with me. I could answer any questions you have, and you might even be able to answer a few of mine." He smiled at her. Brynn didn't use his smile too often, because women liked to see him smile. That was reason enough to wear a perpetual scowl. But he wanted something from Kim, so he smiled.

"Candy store?" She blinked. "Oh, sure. Sounds like fun. Let me get my jacket, and I'll be right with you."

She turned away. Probably thought he'd wait outside the door. He didn't. Brynn followed her into the room and stopped beside the bureau where Fo lay open, her purple eyes narrowed with temper. "Not taking Fo?"

Kim spun around with her leather jacket in her hand. "Why are you in my room? And are you talking about my phone?"

Time to play hardball. "Let's cut the it's-a-cell-phone story. I was standing outside your door. Fo isn't a quiet little being." He ignored her question about why he was in her room.

He had to give her credit. Once she realized she wouldn't be able to lie her way out of this one, she didn't go all sullen on him.

Instead, she flung her jacket over a chair and sat down. "What do you want to know, and how will what I tell you impact this job?"

Brynn almost smiled. She'd sure gotten over her wide-eyed reaction to him fast. Her gaze was now direct and cold. He didn't smile. "I know Fo is some kind of combination demon detector and destroyer. And I know demon destroying is a family business. What you tell me here stays here. The owner won't find out." Okay, so he was lying. But considering what he was, lying was almost a positive character trait. He wouldn't tell the owner because he didn't know who the damned owner was, but he'd tell Eric and Conall. He wouldn't have to tell Holgarth, because Holgarth probably already knew.

A small smile played at the corners of her sexy mouth. He slipped into her mind. She didn't think he'd believe her story, thereby saving her butt. Her small, perfectly rounded, and made-to-be-kneaded butt.

Made-to-be-kneaded butt? Where had that come from? When he wasn't under the compulsion, Brynn could objectively admire a woman's body, but the admiration was emotionless and analytical. The sway of Kim's behind stirred the beginnings of definite sensual interest. Something that *never* happened, that he didn't *allow* to happen.

Brynn could feel a line of worry forming between his eyes. It would be great if the crease became permanent. He needed some character lines in his face. But he knew from past experience that his face would remain unlined, forever freakin' perfect.

"You're right. The Vaughn family has hunted demons for centuries. My true love is architecture, but I have an obligation to destroy any evil entities I happen to stumble across." She shrugged. "Over the years, the family has lost its sensitivity to demons, so it had to turn to technology. Fo was the first combination detector and destroyer created. She's not like the other detectors, she's . . ." For the first time, Kim seemed unsure what to say.

Brynn finished for her. "She's a bust at finding demons, but she's developed emotions and the ability to think for herself." Artificial intelligence. Although Kim would probably argue the intelligence part.

Kim looked suspicious. "You got all that from standing outside my door?"

"Fo's volume control was turned way up." He glanced down at Fo who was staring up at him with those huge purple eyes.

"You don't believe my story, right?" Kim looked hopeful. "It's just too far out there to be real, right?"

"I believe in what I see and hear." *And in a lot of things that are so far out there they would blow you away, sweetheart.* "From the little I heard you say, Fo thinks anything that walks and talks is a demon."

Fo's eyes narrowed slightly. Amazing. A machine that showed an emotional response to a perceived insult.

"That's about it." Kim looked worried.

A quick peek into her thoughts revealed her concern that not only had she found the one person who'd swallow her story, but that he might have the ear of the owner, who wouldn't be quite so accepting of his architect moonlighting as a demon destroyer. She didn't believe Brynn wouldn't tell anyone. Smart lady.

What to do? He should try to get rid of them, because Kim might eventually believe Fo when she said he was a demon. Funny, because just a few years ago he would've pressed Fo's red button himself. Now? He had friends and an interesting job. And as hard as it was for him to believe, he was enjoying Kim and Fo.

"Do you mind if I ask Fo a few questions?" Who better to ask about her take on demon detecting?

"I guess it's okay." Kim looked confused. Probably no one had ever asked to talk to Fo.

Fo, on the other hand, looked ecstatic. He'd bet no one except Kim had ever treated her as a sentient being.

"Scan your systems, Fo, and tell me how your creator programmed you to recognize demons." It was a shot in the dark, but if his idea was right, it would explain why she was seeing demons everywhere.

Fo blinked at him. It amazed him that she could express puzzlement with only her eyes. "The one who made me believed as the Greeks believed. Daimons are minor deities, not necessarily good or evil. So he chose to program me to recognize all nonhuman entities, just to be safe."

Beside him, Kim gasped. "That's it? It was that simple all along? Fo, you identify any being that isn't human?"

"Yes. Isn't that what I'm supposed to do?" Fo sounded hesitant. "Did the one who created me make a mistake?"

"No, no." Kim raked her fingers through all that thick red hair. "I can't believe this. The family had Fo checked out at least three times, but no one came up with anything. Why didn't I know this?"

"They didn't believe Fo was a sentient being, so they never talked to her. They never asked her the right questions." To take his mind from her hair and his sudden desire to bury his fingers in the silken mass, he glanced at his watch. If he timed things perfectly, he could walk with her to the candy store and back in less than an hour. "Fo, if Kim agrees to take you with her, will you promise to keep quiet?" *Tell me I'm not feeling sorry for a demon destroyer.*

"Not one word. I promise." Fo's eyes gleamed with excitement. "I won't even point out to Kimmie again that you're a demon."

"Thanks. I think." Kim had remained silent for a little too long. Whatever she was thinking might not be good. "Let's get moving. There's a bag of candy calling my name."

Kim nodded absently as she slipped into her jacket and put Fo in her pocket. She said nothing until they'd almost reached Sweet Indulgence. When she did speak, he realized he was right to think that a quiet woman was a dangerous woman.

"All right, I guess I have things figured out." She cast him a suspicious sidelong glance. "Everyone Fo has identified as a demon since last night is nonhuman but not necessarily a demon in the strictest sense of how demon is defined in today's culture."

Brynn grimaced. A lot of words to lead up to the punch line. "Sounds logical."

"Sooo, that means you're not human." She sounded calm, but her eyes looked more intensely green in her suddenly pale face. "And if I didn't have this sudden overwhelming need to eat candy, we'd stop right now so you could explain things to me."

Thanks to whatever gods cared enough to protect stupid demons, they'd reached the candy store just in time. Brynn grabbed for the door with the same heartfelt relief as a marathoner flinging his body across the finish line.

Saved by Sparkle Stardust.

4

"It's getting really tough to maintain my sensitive and caring persona when you are so ticking me off, cuddle bunny." Sparkle Stardust perched with legs crossed on the stool behind the counter of her candy store, Sweet Indulgence.

Holding her cell phone to her ear, she used her free hand to scroll down the page on her laptop to a particularly yummy ring on her fave site, expensivethings.com. Could a woman ever have too many diamonds? Sparkle didn't think so. The latest issue of *Cosmo* waited beside the laptop. A dreary Sunday morning in March meant slow candy sales. Sparkle would fill in the blanks with lots of impulse buying.

"Uh-huh. I totally understand. You're a cosmic troublemaker, and you're hard at work doing what you do best—causing trouble. So of course you can't drop everything and rush to my side." She narrowed her eyes as she flipped the *Cosmo* open. The more Mede pissed her off, the more money it made her want to spend. Maybe a new car. Hmm. A shiny Jaguar would help rekindle her warm and fuzzy Sunday spirit. "I can tell from the drunken revelry I hear in the background that you've been putting in long, hard hours on the job."

Blah, blah, blah. Mede needed to renew his subscription to *Lame Excuses* because she'd heard all the old ones. Sighing, she traced the neckline of her black silk top. It didn't show nearly enough of what was important to a man. And Sparkle was always tuned into what turned men on. So much sexual knowledge, so few to share it with.

"Look, sugar fluff, here's the deal. Don't give me all that crap about you being a big bad cosmic troublemaker who's lived thousands of years, ruined more lives than you can remember, and can't find the time in your busy schedule to fix one of those lives. I want you here by the end of the week to take care of Brynn." Sometimes she just had to verbally slap Mede upside his gorgeous head.

Sparkle only half listened to Mede's dumb-assed reasons why he couldn't help Brynn, because she'd riveted her attention on the man and woman approaching her store. She allowed herself a brief surge of triumph. Kim and Brynn were together.

Sparkle hadn't gotten too personal with Kim last night, just an exchange of names and Kim's reason for visiting Galveston—all of which she'd already known. But this time she'd begin working on the most important strand of the intricate sexual web she intended to weave around Brynn.

While they paused just inside the door to discuss something, Sparkle turned away to deliver her ultimatum to Mede. "You might be Ganymede the Great to all the sorry losers at the bottom of the cosmic troublemaker barrel, but I don't look up to anyone, Mede." Damn straight. She was as powerful as he was in her chosen sphere of influence—sex. For more than a thousand years she'd spread sexual chaos throughout the universe by luring unsuspecting couples into playing her favorite game—Sex with the Wrong Stranger. She got off on watching all their roiling emotions churn up lots of erotic action.

She lowered her voice to the husky temptation she knew Mede couldn't resist. "You're the hottest being I've ever spent quality sexual time with. Do this for me, and I'll be so grateful that . . ."

Sparkle paused to enjoy Mede's heavy breathing. "Well, I just won't be able to control myself from dragging you off to one of the Castle of Dark Dreams' towers so I can try out all the new sensual ways I've learned to bring a man to screaming completion." She sighed her regret. "But I guess if you don't have time—"

Sparkle took the phone from her ear and stared at it. Wow, was she good or what? Mede had shouted, "I'm coming," and hung up on her. She paused to consider which meaning of "coming" he'd intended and then shrugged off the thought. It didn't matter. They were both positive.

With a practiced smile that invited confidences, Sparkle turned back to her victims . . . er customers, who'd finally reached the counter. Kim looked a little dazed. Nothing new there. Every woman's eyes glazed over when they were around Brynn.

He'd left his hair loose this morning. A little past shoulder length, it would slide through a woman's fingers and live in her memory every time silk lay smooth against her breasts, renewing the visual of old gold and warm honey—erotic and incredibly masculine.

But a woman stopped thinking about his hair once they looked into his eyes—dark possibilities backlit by the heated glow of promised passion. Brynn was such a hottie that . . . No, Mede was still her guy. Unless he didn't help with her latest plan, of course.

"Right on schedule, Brynn." Sparkle turned a playful glance Kim's way. She did playful well. "Every Sunday morning, Brynn comes in to buy a week's supply of Wicked Red Blow Pops. I think that's endearingly symbolic."

Kim just stared at her. Sparkle hoped Kim wasn't one of those women who didn't get sexual innuendoes. Jeez, how much more in your face could she get? Wicked, blow, hello? Sparkle couldn't communicate with someone who didn't understand that it was all about sex. Okay, so maybe that wasn't quite true. She communicated with Deimos. Sort of.

"Welcome back, Kim. No one stays away from my candy long. Wicked morning out there." *Wicked.* One of her favorite words.

"No kidding. It's starting to rain." Kim smiled at Sparkle. "Brynn invited me to tag along with him, but I didn't think I wanted any candy. As soon as I got close to your store, though, this amazing need just grabbed me by the throat. I've never felt anything like it."

That's because you've never been the target of one of Sparkle Stardust's designer compulsions, sister. Sparkle widened her eyes in the culturally accepted expression of surprise. "Hmm. Strange. But hey, I'm glad you both got here in time. This is the ultimate danger." She waved her hand over the candy counter to emphasize the total menace of her store. "Unlimited supply of candy plus boredom equals an infinity of hours at the local gym. You saved me from uncontrolled gorging followed closely by exercise hell."

Sparkle watched as Brynn wandered away to collect his week's supply of blow pops from the jar she kept at the end of the counter.

"Yeah, I'm trying not to inhale. Just breathing chocolate fumes expands my waist like a helium balloon." Kim edged away from the section of the long glass case filled with chocolates. "Give me a small bag of lemon drops."

Sparkle blinked. "Lemon drops?" Uh-oh. Any woman who chose lemon drops over chocolate wouldn't last long in the sensual playground that was the Castle of Dark Dreams. "Where's your cell phone, the one that decided I was the Candy Demon?" She might have to take care of that little item if it became a pest. "Oops, never mind. Your pocket is vibrating. You must have the phone set on pulse. What brand is it? I don't think I've ever seen a pulse that . . . enthusiastic."

Kim shrugged. "It's not supposed to do that." She raised her voice. "In fact, if I can't get it fixed, I might have to buy a new one." The pulsing stopped.

She slid her gaze to Sparkle's hair. Sparkle sensed a convenient change of subject coming. "We have the same shade of red hair, but that's where the similarity ends. Your hair's incredible. How do you keep it from frizzing up on a day like this?"

Sparkle tried to keep her smile open and human-friendly as she slipped from her stool to get Kim's candy, but she was afraid a little slyness was creeping into it. "Magic and good hair products." Heavy on the magic. "Last night you said the park's owner hired you to tweak the castle. Any ideas?"

"A few." Kim frowned as she paid for the candy. "I still don't know why the owner chose *me*, but the project sounded too intriguing to turn down."

The owner chose you because you're perfect, simply perfect, for the masterful manipulation she's planning. Sparkle smiled as she handed Kim the bag. "The people in the castle are pretty intriguing, too." More intriguing than Kim could probably handle, but her good buddy, Sparkle, would be there to guide her in the wrong direction.

Behind Kim, Brynn caught Sparkle's attention and pointed to his watch. She sighed. Sparkle and the three faux McNair brothers understood each other. Okay, so Brynn and the others could never *truly* understand all that she was. Only Mede had plumbed her true depths. She allowed herself a small, secret smile. His plumbing skills were excellent.

But Brynn's whole I-can't-spend-more-than-an-hour-with-a-woman thing was a gigantic pain in the butt. And speaking of butts, Mede had better get his sexy tush here fast before Brynn's compulsion interfered with Sparkle's plans.

On the positive side, though, Brynn had shown up with Kim when he never purposely initiated contact with a woman. And he'd stayed strangely quiet. That meant he was thinking, hopefully about Kim.

"Intriguing? Sure." Kim looked uncertain. "Umm, I saw a Siamese cat in the castle. Do you know who it belongs to?"

Cat? Sparkle slid into Kim's mind. Not good news. The snooty, scheming witch was back. Asima had kept a low profile since interfering with Sparkle's plans for Eric. Sparkle wouldn't let that sneaky Bast gofer mess with her business again.

"That's Asima. Keep her out of your room. She'll claw your clothes and pee on your bed. If you feel the need for a pet, I'll get you one. In fact, I have the perfect pet in mind." Oh, yesss, the

Court of Cosmic Justice was in session. Mede would hate what she had in mind, but when had she ever let that stop her?

Kim looked alarmed as she started backing toward the door. "Hey, thanks, but I don't need a pet. Definitely not in the castle. And I travel a lot, so I'd have to park it with someone. That wouldn't be fair to the animal."

Brynn cast Sparkle a warning glance as he paid for his blow pops. With his back to Kim, he spoke quietly. "Be careful. Her cell phone—"

Kim opened the door, letting in the chill and damp. She glanced back at Sparkle. "Oh, your pet idea almost made me forget what I wanted to say. Next time I drop in for candy, you can tell me what kind of nonhuman entity you are." She stepped outside to wait for Brynn.

Brynn shrugged. "We're all busted. I talked to Fo, Kim's fake cell phone. Kim thought Fo was just a defective demon detector, but Fo told us she was programmed to identify anyone who isn't human. She can't differentiate between us, so that's why she calls everyone a demon." After dropping that little bombshell, he turned and followed Kim out the door.

Well, thank you very much, Mr. Demon of Sensual Desire, for helping Kim out all of us. Sometimes Sparkle didn't know why she bothered with men. Fine, so that was a lie. She knew exactly why she bothered with them. A hot bod with sex on his mind was at the tippy top of her personal evolutionary scale.

She smoothed her fingers over her black leather skirt and then checked her fuchsia nails. Good. No chips. If there was anything that could put her in a worse mood than a man doing something stupid, it was chipped nails. She listened to the sound of footsteps coming from her storage room. Deimos was lucky her nails were perfect.

"I unpacked all the new candy, so what should I do next?" His sulky voice preceded Deimos. "Hey, can I go out to do some action hero stuff? Maybe someone is drowning in the surf or something." His eyes brightened. "Or maybe he isn't drowning. Maybe he's being attacked by a great white."

Sparkle narrowed her eyes to annoyed slits as she glared at her Vin Diesel knockoff. "It's March. It's chilly. It's raining. I don't think anyone's frolicking in the surf today."

The next time she agreed to mentor a cosmic troublemaker newbie, she'd lay a five-page questionnaire on him. And every question would have the word sex in it.

Look at him. Six feet plus of massive muscle and he was still . . . "Are you still a virgin?"

"Yeah." Red crept up his neck. "Look, I'm too busy learning to be an action hero to bother with that stuff."

Okay, now she was royally ticked. "*That stuff* is what I'm all about. And since I'm mentoring you, you need to be about *that stuff*, too."

"I've only been in existence five years. I need more time to—"

She was losing it. If he wasn't careful, she'd break the heels of her favorite Jimmy Choo stilettos over his hard head, and then she'd really be pissed.

"You look like Vin Diesel and you're . . . *still* . . . *a* . . . *virgin*. You're a damned minion of the Queen Of All Things Sexual, and you've . . . *never* . . . *had* . . . *sex*. Does anyone else think that's strange, hmm?" Sparkle hadn't a clue why steam wasn't coming out of her ears. "Go somewhere and have sex, sex, sex, sex, sex!" Watching the red creep farther and farther over his shaved head every time she said the word "sex" gave her a little satisfaction.

Oh, hell. What was the use? She'd made him watch videos, read books, and even go to a lecture given by a former madam who knew her stuff. Results? Nothing.

"So what should I do now?" He was edging toward the front door.

"I don't know. Go separate the M&M's into piles according to color. I don't give a damn."

She knew he sensed freedom as he eased the door open, and she purposely waited for the moment when he thought he'd escaped.

"Whoa, big guy. A little later I want you to drop by Kim's room and check on the plants." She smiled, her good humor restored by his disgusted groan. "And while you're there you can explain to Kim how she can keep the plants healthy."

His grumbles were cut off as he slammed the door behind him. She studied the door, her thoughts on Deimos. He wasn't cut out for the job of spreading sexual chaos. He'd never follow in her footsteps. But she kind of liked him. The way she'd like a big, clumsy puppy. Not something she'd ever admit to anyone, least of all Deimos. She couldn't send him away in disgrace. Sparkle shrugged. She'd worry about what to do with Deimos later.

Suddenly the front door was flung open as if punched by a giant fist. Wind whistled, lightning flashed, and a clap of thunder shook the store.

Sparkle ran around to the front of the counter just as a large black cat stalked through the open door. It leaped onto the counter and stared at her from brilliant amber eyes.

She felt the warm glow of joy that only one being in the universe could make her feel. "Mede."

The cat's eyes gleamed with evil laughter. "Your big bad lover boy is in the house, babe. Where's the fridge?"

"I'm going to my room, suck on lemon drops until I'm permanently puckered, and then I want us to meet for dinner so you can explain to me what you are and what's going on around here." Kim sounded quietly desperate. "I'd say come to my room right now, but I need a few hours to scream, pound my head against the wall, and come to terms with Fo's new status as detector of all things weird."

Brynn used Kim's own logic against her. "Have you considered that no matter how Fo was programmed she still might be flawed? Maybe she's just taking wild guesses. What're the chances that almost everyone you've met here isn't human?" *Damned good.*

Brynn glanced at his watch as he waited for the elevator with Kim. He'd made it with twenty minutes to spare. He'd go to his room, take care of some paperwork, do the things he had to do around the castle, and then catch some more sleep so he'd be ready for tonight's fantasies. At least he didn't have to worry about Liz until sunset.

"I guess it's possible." She looked uncertain. "Except for the cat. Asima talked in my head. Not a normal feline trait." Kim didn't sound uncertain about the cat.

Asima. Brynn didn't try to explain the cat because there was no logical explanation. But he'd have a lot to say when he got a chance to track down that pain-in-the-butt interfering messenger of Bast. It was dry cat food for her royal nuisance.

"Are you telling me you're totally human?" Her voice said she was hoping for a yes.

"Totally." He fixed his gaze on the lighted numbers tracking the descending elevator while Kim tugged Fo from her jacket pocket.

Come on. Hurry. Kim could be a bigger danger than Liz. Brynn understood the Lizes of the world—their greed, their hunger.

He used his body to give them sexual pleasures they'd never have with their human mates. That was his small revenge on them. Once he reclaimed his body after a few hours, he used his mind to take away the reality of what they'd experienced. They remembered it as a dream.

Whatever entity had created him had at least given him that much protection. Without it, some of the powerful women who'd commanded his body would've imprisoned him like a genie in a bottle, something to be taken out and used at their own pleasure. But unlike a genie, he couldn't hide in a bottle between wishes.

He frowned as he watched Kim take Fo from her pocket and flip her open. Kim and Liz. Two different problems. Liz was a vampire with a mind powerful enough to block his suggestions that sex with him was only a dream. So once she realized he was a sex machine that she could turn on anytime she wanted just by staying with him for more than an hour, she'd taken full advantage.

He could easily walk away from the castle forever during the day-light hours, lose himself in a distant city where she couldn't find him. But the castle was his home now—Eric, Conall, and Holgarth his friends. Besides, she'd only be here for one more day. If she ever returned, he'd deal with her.

So that left Kim. Kim with the tiny sentient being that could destroy him when he no longer wished to be destroyed. Brynn didn't miss the irony there. Kim whose wide eyes showed every one of her emotions, and whose full, lush lips stirred his sexual interest when no woman had done so for centuries, except while he was under the compulsion.

She was the real danger, because the rock-hard ground made up of his centuries-long contempt and loathing for all things female supported the wall he'd carefully erected around his emotions. Sprinkle that ground with a little sexual awareness, and the ground might soften, allowing the wall to tumble down on top of him— baring his feelings, making him vulnerable. The wall was all he had left of his self-respect.

Thoughts of walls and awareness scattered as the elevator door opened. Kim waited for several people to get out before stepping in and hitting the button for the top floor. As Brynn followed her in and prepared to press the button for his floor, he could see Fo's big purple eyes watching him. But just before he pressed the button, someone charged into the elevator behind him. He turned to see Wade, the demon fisherman, squeezing past him, a coffee container in one hand and a glazed doughnut in the other.

But before Brynn could turn back to press the button for his floor, Wade bumped into Kim, knocking Fo from her hand. As Wade tried to right himself without spilling his coffee or dropping his doughnut, he stomped on Fo.

The elevator door swished shut, and at Kim's horrified cry, Brynn forgot about pushing buttons. He shoved Wade away from Fo, but even as the demon lifted his foot from the detector, he managed to kick her into the corner. Kim dove for the floor to rescue Fo.

"Oh, jeez, I'm sorry, ma'am." Wade was still juggling his coffee and doughnut. "Lost my balance. Look, I'll get you another cell phone." He glanced at Brynn. "The only place I'm not clumsy is on my boat. Wasn't meant for life on land."

Brynn narrowed his gaze on Wade even as he bent down to help Kim. He reached for Wade with his mind. *"What the hell were you thinking? You said Fo wasn't any danger to you."* Fo didn't look too good. Her back cover had come off. It was still in one piece, but it had a crack in it. There were a lot of little bits of her lying around the case.

"Thought about that and decided it never hurts to be too careful." Wade looked big, clumsy, and apologetic.

But Brynn knew the demon wasn't clumsy, and he was a long way from apologetic. *"Real smart move, Wade. She'll just get another detector, and the new one might actually be able to point out the real deal. Did you think about that?"* He picked up the few pieces of Fo that Kim had missed and placed them in her shaking hands.

"Doesn't matter to me. It'll probably take her a week or so to get a new one. By that time the fishing tournament will be over, and I'll be gone." Wade edged away from where Kim still crouched and moved to the front of the elevator, ready to step off as soon as the doors slid open. *"Once I leave, I don't give a damn if she wipes out a whole army of demons. Eudemons are pretty laid back that way. Just leave us alone to do our thing. And my thing is fishing."* The door opened, but he paused before heading toward his room. "Want to apologize again, ma'am. I'll be over to get some info from you. You'll have the best phone I can find." And then he strode away.

Kim looked up at Brynn as she held the pitifully small pile of Fo's remains. Tears glistened in her eyes. "She . . ."

Brynn slipped into Kim's mind to hear the words she couldn't speak aloud. Sorrow. Kim mourned the loss of a being she hadn't even known she cared for. Hopelessness. Fo was lost to her. Kim hadn't a clue how to fix her, and the detector's creator was dead. Kim doubted anyone in her family could or would even want to put Fo back together again.

Brynn glanced at his watch. Fifteen minutes. He couldn't believe what he was considering. But the sadness he'd touched in Kim's mind plus the thought of those ridiculous purple eyes closed forever, bothered him. So he was feeling compassion, was that a crime? Yeah, for a demon. He was pretty sure the Big Bad who created him wouldn't be happy. Brynn exhaled sharply. He'd worry about the Big Dickhead Bad later.

"Give Fo to me. Let's see what I can do." Silently, Kim handed Fo's pieces to him and then fished in her jacket pocket for her key.

Once inside, she threw her jacket on the bed and then joined him in the small sitting area. He'd set Fo on the coffee table, taken off his own jacket, and now sat on the couch studying the pieces. Kim sat beside him on the couch. "What're you going to do?"

I'm going to use my mind to interface with whatever power still remains in Fo and see if it can tell me how to fix her. All in fifteen minutes before I'm compelled to do my sex demon routine. "I know a little about electronics. Don't think I can do much more damage." From the looks of Fo, he'd have more luck with Humpty Dumpty.

"Who would've thought I was so attached? I mean, Fo drove me crazy most of the time." She shook her head and then bit her bottom lip.

Probably trying to control her emotions, but the damp sheen of her full bottom lip brought a low growl from the sexual beast within him. A beast that never roused itself except when compelled. He forced himself to concentrate on Fo.

"Yeah, friends do that sometimes. Now be quiet so I can concentrate." He thought his suggestion that Fo was her friend shocked Kim into silence. Good.

Brynn had a powerful mind, made more powerful over the centuries, but he'd never tried interfacing with a sentient machine. He poured his mind into Fo and searched among the ruins for anything that remained of her. *"I don't know how to fix you, Fo, unless you tell me how."*

At first he saw only blackness, and then a screen opened within the darkness. It faded in and out, but he could see some sort of schematics. Hopefully Fo's. Too bad he didn't have a clue what to do with it. While he was pondering where to start studying the maze of parts and letters, a cursor appeared. It blinked beside a small, distinctly shaped piece.

Brynn studied the piece and where it was. Then he looked down at Fo. It took him a few minutes to find the piece spread among the others on the table, but when he did, he put it back into Fo according to what he'd seen.

Once that piece was in place, he glanced at his watch. Uh-oh. This was going to take longer than fifteen minutes. He pulled a few dollars from his wallet. "Would you do me a favor and get me some coffee? Black. Helps me concentrate." Once Kim was out of the room, he was safe until she returned. And then the countdown for the next hour would begin. He didn't think it would take longer than that to get Fo's innards back in place.

Kim waved off his money. "Hey, you're trying to fix Fo. I'll be back."

She left, and he went back to painstakingly accessing Fo's memory to find where each piece belonged. Somewhere along the way Kim returned because a Styrofoam container of coffee appeared on the table close to where he was working, and he felt Kim ease down beside him. But he was too focused on what he was doing to stop long enough to even look at his watch.

He'd just completed all the things he'd seen in the instructions, replaced the back of Fo's case, and was considering going down to his room for some tape to make sure the crack didn't get worse, when he felt it. The warm flow of desire he hated, couldn't control. The lengthening and thickening of his cock—automatic, attached to no emotion, only ravenous physical hunger. Unstoppable.

Brynn didn't need to look at his watch. He was too late to stop what was about to happen. He closed his eyes for a moment of deep regret. His budding friendship with Kim was over. She'd either accept his body and what it could offer her, or she'd turn from him in disgust. Either way, he lost.

He carefully closed Fo, pushed her away from him, and then stood. The compulsion washed over him.

5

Kim was reaching for Fo when Brynn got up and strode away from the couch. Was Fo okay now? Kim was almost afraid to look. Would she see huge purple eyes or a blank screen?

And then she forgot about Fo. Suddenly, everything in the room seemed to shift. Not physically. The couch was still in place, but it was as if the room swirled with energy, an energy that warmed the air around her and changed the reality of what had been just a few seconds ago. Did that make any sense? Uh, no.

What the . . . ? Kim looked up and automatically sought Brynn. But Brynn had evidently left the building, because the man standing in the middle of the room was *not* Brynn. Oh, he had Brynn's size and shape, his features, but his *essence* had become something else, something totally . . . No, that didn't make sense. She blinked, and then blinked again. Nothing changed. She drew in a deep breath, trying to balance her disbelief with what was standing right in front of her. He'd become a totally sexual creature right in front of her it-ain't-happening eyes.

His hair. The lamplight, the pale daylight streaming through the arrow slits, all faded, leaving only the glory of Brynn's hair framing his face. Not blond. It was hot summer sunlight, the kind that made her sweat as she tried to pull her clinging clothes away from her damp body. The kind that made her want to run naked in it, letting the air flow over her and the warmth sink into every inch of exposed skin. The kind that tempted her to lie in the cool grass, open her legs, and let the heat touch her *there*. Kim's body clenched around the imagined sensation.

Heavy-lidded, he watched her from eyes that shone knowing and wicked, that promised he could slide his fingers across her bared body, touch her with his mouth in ways that would make her cry out with need. She allowed her senses a silent scream at the awesome possibilities.

She couldn't hold his gaze, so she lowered her attention to his mouth. Deliberately, he gripped his bottom lip between his teeth and then released it. He smiled, a slow erotic suggestion, daring her to accept his sensual invitation, to cover his mouth with hers, to smooth her tongue over the soft sheen of that lip.

Kim tried to turn away from his in-your-face seduction. She couldn't. What did that say about her? And where had this whole scene come from? No sexy buildup, no conversational foreplay, just wham. It didn't make sense.

"Uh, well, thanks for putting Fo back together again. Um, I guess I'll see you later." From the deepening glow in his spectacular eyes, Kim guessed that she'd be seeing a lot more of him now than later. God, what to say? This was out of her realm of experience. Hey, demon destroying was easy compared to this.

"Let yourself go, Kim. Live the moment." He pulled his white T-shirt over his head in one smooth motion, exposing a wide expanse of muscular chest. "My hands, my mouth, my *body*, can bring you physical pleasure you've never dreamed you could experience."

"Sure. Lots of pleasure. Got it." *This is wrong. He's a sleaze. Next he'll probably hand you his business card listing his hourly rates. Throw him out.* Kim's brain was issuing orders with machine gun rapidity, but her body wasn't paying much attention. It was otherwise engaged. Her eyes had dropped to where his fingers were unbuttoning his jeans and sliding them, along with his briefs, down powerful thighs and legs. Somewhere along the way he'd rid himself of his shoes. Her mouth was hanging open, and commands to her jaw were being ignored. The rest of her body? All remaining body parts thought he was totally ripped and wanted to get on with the physical pleasure thing.

Ignoring her wide-eyed and slack-jawed response, he strode to her bed and lay down. With his hands clasped behind his head, he studied her. "Come to me. Enjoy my body. Use me in any way you wish. There's nothing I won't do to please you."

Nothing? Absolutely nothing? She'd always wanted to . . . Kim mentally slapped herself upside her head. *Stay focused.*

In a moment of lucidity, she noted that his voice had changed. It had deepened to a husky murmur, a sexual temptation to join him on her bed and explore his muscular expanse of smooth flesh and hard body. His speech pattern seemed from an older time, but it only made him more sensual.

Kim swallowed with an audible gulp. She was torn between making a cowardly dash for the door and flinging herself onto the bed for a shot at living *la vida loca*. This was beyond bizarre. But while she was contemplating the weirdness of the whole thing, she slid her gaze over his broad chest and wondered what he would taste like if she touched one tempting male nipple with her tongue.

Resisting arousal—or not—she watched his body sheen with a thin layer of sweat. And as her gaze moved lower, his erection swelled, demanding her attention. She fought the good fight— weak and pitifully ineffective though it was—against the mental picture forming. A visual of his sex buried deep inside her burst triumphantly onto the scene. Against her brain's express orders, she edged closer to the bed.

Did he know what she was thinking? Kim hoped not. She had to get out of here. His overwhelming sexuality was messing with her mind. Yeah, she was going to run from her own room. But if she opened her mouth to order him out, they'd both know she didn't mean it.

And then he spread his legs, a primitive and erotic call to everything female in her. But that's not what tore a startled gasp from her.

High on his inner thigh was the tattoo of a cat's head. Even while she reeled from the shock, Kim dispassionately noted the details—a black cat with strange amber eyes. Even though it was only a tattoo, she could swear the eyes watched her with a wicked gleam. She shook her head to get rid of the impression. Then she backed away from him.

A cat. One of the preferred symbolic animals for a demon. Cats had at one time or other in past ages been worshipped as gods and condemned as familiars.

Brynn was a demon. For once, Fo had called it right. A demon. That explained the erotic spell he seemed to be casting over her. She understood her instant horror but not her soul-deep disappointment. She took a step toward Fo.

He watched her move away from him, his gaze still dark with sexual hunger. If he could read her mind—and demons had no difficulty worming their way into human thoughts—he must know she realized what he was. The knowledge didn't seem to effect his single-minded drive for the almighty orgasm.

"Do you want my body, Kim?" His eyes said he already knew the answer to that.

"You're a demon. I'm a demon hunter. So what're we going to do about that, hmm?" There. She'd said it. The Vaughn family book of demon-hunting rules stated that a destroyer should never let the demon know she'd made him. But Brynn had saved Fo, so Kim sort of owed him. Kim clung to that bit of logic and pushed away her conscience's command to zap him.

Now he'd leap from her bed and flee, thereby saving his beautiful butt from . . . From what? Could she coldly walk over to Fo, pick her up, and push the red button? Duty to her family said she had to, but her emotional reaction to the visual of Brynn reduced to nothing more than a pile of hot ash made her queasy. In the short time she'd known him, she'd grown to like him. Good grief, she'd watched him buy a bag of blow pops. How could she hate a demon that got pleasure from sucking on a blow pop? She couldn't. She was such a wuss. *Bad, bad demon hunter.*

"Do you want my body, Kim?" There was an urgency to his question that hadn't been there before.

"No." *Well, maybe a little.* "No, definitely not." Self-denial. It was one of her special talents. She moved closer to Fo, still fighting the battle between duty and emotion.

Kim wasn't prepared for what happened the moment she told him she didn't want his body. Gone was the sensual animal luring her to perform unspeakable sexual acts on his magnificent body. A primal part of her mind mourned lost opportunities.

With a few lithe movements that showcased the flow of supple skin over hard muscle, he rose from the bed and reached Fo before Kim could make a grab for her. He picked Fo up and flipped her open.

Kim didn't know what worried her more, being in the same room with a very bare demon or waiting to see if Fo was back. She exhaled a breath she hadn't known she was holding as Fo's big purple eyes appeared on the screen. Other than looking a little confused, they were vintage Fo.

"Give Fo to me." She spoke quietly with the same fake calmness she'd use if she were locked in a cage with a hungry tiger.

"I don't think so. Not just yet." Brynn smiled at her, but the smile didn't reach his eyes. "Hand my clothes to me. Naked demons roaming the castle are bad for business." He glanced down at Fo. "Feeling okay?"

"I think so. But I don't have any memory of the events during my near-death experience. Who did this to me?" Fo still looked unfocused.

Near-death experience? Fo's continuing referral to herself in human terms couldn't be good for her long-term emotional health.

But Kim hadn't a clue how to handle the problem. "Wade, the man across the hall from us, accidentally knocked you out of my hands and then stepped on you."

"I do remember something." Fo blinked up at Brynn. "You saved me." Fo's gaze was clear now, and Kim swore she saw hero worship shining in those purple eyes.

Uh-oh. "Fo, Brynn is a demon. So that isn't a good place for you to be." What did she expect Fo to do?

Fo's eyes didn't lose any of their shine, but they did roll to the bottom of her screen. "Woohoo! A hot hunky demon, all bare and gorgeous. Tip me down a little so I can see everything. It's important for me to view and record images of demons in all their forms. I've never seen a naked one before."

Damn. Kim didn't know who she was more aggravated with, Fo or herself. Angrily, she kicked his clothes toward Brynn. She should've reacted faster, made a dash for Fo the second she saw the cat.

Her shoulders slumped. Time for some self-honesty. It didn't matter. She still wouldn't have destroyed Brynn. Kim wasn't like some of the more dedicated members of her family who zapped first and asked questions later. She'd need indisputable proof of Brynn's demonic nature, like seeing him in his true, disgusting form, or witnessing him mooning her right before he tried to rip out her throat.

Okay, okay, so she'd have to see him doing something really evil that proved he deserved to be destroyed. Getting naked and then offering his body wasn't threatening enough, except to her sexual self. In fact, her sexual self was pretty ticked off that she'd passed up a chance at some sizzling heat between the sheets.

Brynn continued to watch Fo. "What do you think, Fo? Should Kim use you to destroy me?" He didn't sound too worried.

Kim narrowed her gaze. He should be very worried, unless . . . "Are you in my mind?"

He raised his gaze from Fo long enough to smile at Kim. "You bet. And I'm insulted. Offering you my body was supposed to be very threatening. Guess I'm a demonic failure. Won't be moving up the demon corporate ladder anytime soon." His smile remained fixed in place as he set Fo gently on the table.

But his eyes . . . For just a moment, Kim thought she saw something close to despair in his gaze. She blinked. Demons didn't feel despair. At least according to the Vaughn family records of demonic behavior. But then she remembered the emotions rolling off him last night. Maybe the Vaughn family records were wrong.

Maybe he wasn't a demon. He'd claimed he was human before. Was this just his idea of black humor? Her surge of hope surprised her. Sure, she didn't want him to be a demon. That was her normal response when facing a possible malevolent spirit. But usually her emotions were all about *her*. How would *she* feel, what would *she* do? This time? It was all about Brynn. Faced with destruction, how would he feel?

While she'd been thinking, he'd been dressing. Once dressed, he grabbed his jacket and headed for the door. "Oh, and I'd stay away from Wade, Fo. I can't guarantee that I could put you together again."

Kim couldn't believe it. He was leaving. Just turning his back so she could pick up Fo and test exactly how demonic he was. A real demon wouldn't take that chance. She had to know one way or another.

"Whoa. You don't leave this room without telling me what you are." Oh, please. She wasn't going to race across the room and tackle him. Was she? The image of his bare, buff body teased her memory. Not a totally bad idea.

Stop it. Get a grip. There, she was focused again.

He paused with his hand on the doorknob. "I'm a demon of sensual desire, Kim. I thought you'd have figured that out by now."

Breathe, breathe, breathe. "An incubus?"

His harsh laughter mocked her. "Not hardly. An incubus has choices. I don't. And I don't sneak up on women while they're sleeping. I lay everything out while they're wide awake. Maybe that makes me a little more honest." He started to turn the knob.

What had happened to his demon's mantra—deny, deny, deny? Somehow he couldn't work up the energy to think that through. She'd either let him walk or pick up Fo to end his existence. Right now, Brynn didn't much care which. Her choice.

"Come back and talk to me, Brynn." She sounded calm, but he felt her fear and uncertainty as an acid trickle along the edges of what passed for his heart.

Strange. He didn't usually feel any emotions after the compulsion other than his own frustration and despair. And he never cared enough about the women who did or didn't claim his body to tap into their emotions.

She didn't know it, but she was giving him that oh-so-rare gift, a choice. And he'd lied about not caring what decision she made. He always felt self-disgust after the compulsion ended, but he no longer hated himself enough to invite destruction.

Brynn had pretty much figured that Kim wouldn't use Fo to end his existence after he'd put Fo's tiny bits and pieces back together again. He'd based his belief on the gut feeling that she was one of the few Vaughn family members without a shriveled raisin for a conscience.

He weighed his possible responses—keep walking and let her think he was pond scum who got off on offering sex to every woman he met, or go back and explain that he had no options.

Turning back was the coward's path. Since he had no defenses against the compulsion, he'd compensated by taking pride in his strengths. Throughout his existence he'd never begged for sympathy. He did what he did and then walked away. The women who turned him down could think what they damned well pleased. And the ones who used him? They didn't remember it as a real event, so they didn't matter. Only since coming to the Castle of Dark Dreams had he lowered his defenses enough to allow a few friends to know about the compulsion. But never an outsider. No, he definitely had to walk away from Kim.

He turned back. And that surprised him enough to keep him

quiet until he'd dropped onto the couch. Kim sat in the chair across from him. He smiled. "Keeping the table between us?"

She pulled Fo to her side of the table. "Keeping Fo between us." Kim didn't return his smile. "Let's talk about your job description. When did you first realize your calling?" She pushed a strand of hair from her face.

Now that he'd decided to tell her his story, he'd make it short and get his dumb butt out of here. Because opening up to a Vaughn couldn't have a good ending. Kim might not hunt him down, but all she had to do was tell one of her relatives, and he'd have to run, kill, or go down. Not the kind of choices he had in mind.

"I woke up in an inn five hundred years ago knowing I was a demon and that I was the proud owner of a compulsion. If I stay with a woman for more than an hour, I have to offer her my body. If she accepts, I'm hers until she can't do it anymore." He shrugged. "Usually a few hours, maybe a night. Once it's over, I have the power to make her think it was all a dream. If the woman turns me down, I'm home free until the next time."

Kim frowned, a line forming between her eyes. He fixed his gaze on that line.

"And if you try to resist the compulsion?"

"Pain. Lots and lots of pain."

"How about if you go off by yourself for a while?"

"After a few days away from women, more pain."

The crease between her eyes deepened. "Can't you resist the pain?"

"Ever been kicked in the balls?" He knew his smile was just a baring of his teeth. "No, guess not. It's a man thing. You'll just have to use your imagination. Not much chance of resisting it for more than say . . . three minutes."

"How did you survive for five centuries?" The horror in her voice shocked him into meeting her gaze. The few women who'd discovered the truth about him had one of two reactions—disgust or fascination. None of them gave a damn about his take on the whole sexual compulsion scenario.

Her eyes were soft with sympathy.

Not the response he'd expected. Not the one he wanted. "Don't waste any pity on me. It didn't take me long to develop a few coping skills." Very few.

"Like what?" She leaned forward, her gaze intent on him.

Didn't she know that her clear green eyes hid nothing, not her interest or her feelings? Suddenly uneasy, he looked away. He focused his attention on the two plants that sat on a small stand beneath one of the arrow slits. He didn't know their names, but they had to be disappointed. They expected more from him. Too bad he wouldn't be here when Kim found out about them.

But she'd asked him a question. He raised his gaze to meet hers. "I was a little more subtle than usual with you." And if he could figure out why, he'd feel a lot more in control.

"Subtle?" She didn't try to hide the disbelief in her voice. "Yeah, I guess if you think a ten-point quake is just a 'subtle' tremblor. Me? I thought there was a whole lotta shakin' going on."

Brynn took a quick glance at his watch. Better keep track of the minutes this time. "Here's how it usually plays out." He purposely met her gaze, letting the heat and hunger shine through. All fake. Then why didn't it feel fake? His cock thought it felt damned real.

He watched her swallow and let his gaze slide down to the smooth curve of her neck. Eric would appreciate a world-class neck like hers.

But he wasn't the only one with sliding-gaze syndrome. Hers was slipping and skipping down his torso, but it came to a skidding stop when it reached his arousal.

He'd use his erection as part of his demonstration. Purposely, he spread his legs, stretching the material of his jeans taut across the bulge of his cock. "When I make the mistake of losing track of the time, the compulsion hits me. It's instant arousal. Getting naked and offering my body is part of the compulsion. I don't have any choice. But I *can* decide how I'll offer myself."

Kim looked wary now. "And I assume the *how* is meant to be a major turnoff?"

He didn't need to do this. *Sure you do.* Because for the first time in hundreds of years, he had a hard-on that wasn't compulsion generated. He couldn't want one particular woman when he belonged to any female who put in her hour and said yes to his offer. It would hurt too much. And he was into avoiding pain wherever he found it. So yeah, he had to do this. Gross her out before he started liking her for her mind.

Rising, he walked around the coffee table to stand behind her chair. He could feel tension along with excitement thrumming through her. Her scent was of warm, sunlit beaches and dark, tropical nights. And when the hell had he started noticing what women smelled like? It must be the whole opposites attract thing, because if he had a scent it was of rocky cliffs and blinding ice storms. Not compatible.

"Normally, I'd just say . . ." He couldn't help it. He bent down, ran his tongue over the sensitive skin behind her ear, and laughed softly as she stiffened. "Want to fuck, babe?"

Brynn waited expectantly for her to cringe away from him. She didn't. Instead, she turned her head to study him with cool green eyes. "Does it work? Do they turn you down?"

He shrugged. "Not often enough."

"I have an answer to your question, Brynn." Fo's eyes somehow managed to express deep thought.

"Question?" Brynn had forgotten what he'd asked.

"You wanted to know if Kimmie should use me to destroy you." Fo paused as if contemplating the ethical enormity of her decision. "It wouldn't be right for her to make me destroy a being who'd saved me from death. I might not survive the trauma. Kimmie would have to put me in a mental health facility at enormous expense."

"Thanks, Fo." Interesting. Fo thought of herself in human terms—dead as opposed to inoperative.

Kim's cell phone rang, stopping any possible rebuttal to Fo's reasoning. Kim got up and walked to her bed. She pulled the phone from her jacket pocket, then looked at him expectantly. She thought he'd leave. No chance.

Annoyed, she turned her back to him, as though that would stop him from hearing. "Hey, Lynsay. What's happening?"

Pause.

"What? You're kidding. You can't."

Pause.

"Absolutely not. Don't even think about it. I . . ." Kim blinked and pulled the phone away from her ear to look at it. "She hung up on me."

"Who's Lynsay?" He could reach into her mind, but clattering around inside Fo's consciousness had tired him out.

"My sister."

He waited.

"Good-bye, Brynn." Her expression said he was dismissed.

With a slashing smile aimed at both Fo and her, he nodded and left, closing the door softly behind him. Kim collapsed onto the bed. Her very first morning at the Castle of Dark Dreams, and she felt like she needed to spend some quality time with her head buried under the covers.

But she didn't have time to hide in a dark place contemplating her navel. She had to call Lynsay back and stop her from coming to the castle. And Lynsay was bringing Uncle Dirk. *Who* was Uncle Dirk? Probably one of the far-flung Vaughn family members she'd never met. Lynsay said he'd contacted Mom and Dad with info about possible demon activity here.

Kim had to convince Lynsay she could handle things on her own. But since Kim had never even gotten within sniffing distance of the Demon Hunter of the Year award, Lynsay—who'd won it three times—might be a hard sell.

Kim rubbed the back of her neck to dispel some of her tension. No way did she want her family here messing up her first job as an architect. *Is that your only reason?*

Fine, so she didn't want Lynsay to discover that Brynn was a demon. She owed him for Fo. Besides, he had enough problems without having to hide from rabid demon hunters. Lynsay and Uncle Dirk wouldn't spend even a second wondering if Brynn was truly demonic. They'd destroy him. It must be nice to have no doubts about the rightness of your cause, no twinges of conscience.

Any other reasons you don't want them to destroy Brynn?

Nope. None at all.

Liar.

The bottom line? She wouldn't help her family out demons in the Castle of Dark Dreams. Later on she'd think of a nice, satisfying rationalization—one without the name *Brynn* in it—that didn't sound like a betrayal of all her family stood for.

Exhaling deeply, Kim reached for her phone. But a knock on the door stopped her in mid-reach. What now? So far, she hadn't met one single normal human in this blasted place. No, wait. The guy who'd stomped on Fo seemed pretty normal.

Sighing, she climbed off her bed and walked to the door. Steeling herself for whatever might be on the other side, she pulled the door open.

Ohmigod! A man. A very *big* man. Kim tipped her head back and looked way, *way* up. She gulped. He was huge, all bulky muscle and dangerous scowl. His shaved head gleamed in the dim light, and his sleeveless T-shirt exposed some scary tattoos on his massive arms. When she finally dropped her gaze because she was getting a crick in her neck, she noticed he clutched a plant food container in one giant fist. She would've tried to slam the door in his face, but he'd probably just rip it off its hinges and eat it.

"Hi, Ms. Vaughn. I, um, hate to bother you, but I have to take care of the plants." He shuffled his very large feet and looked uneasy.

See, now that blew her Jack-and-the-Beanstalk fantasy. Someone like him should never look uneasy. He should stride through life flattening small buildings and shaking the earth as he walked.

"The plants?" She glanced around and spotted them on the stand beneath what passed for a window.

"Yeah, I have a couple of jobs like taking care of the plants in the castle and spelling Sparkle when she wants a few hours away from her store." He edged around Kim—as well as someone who was that big could edge—and walked over to the plants. "Hey, don't get the idea that these jobs are forever. They're just something to do until I get started in the action hero business." He cast her a shy glance. "If you ever need an action hero, let me know. I gotta have lots of practice."

"Sure. I'll keep you in mind." How could someone that big sound so going-on-sixteen?

Kim trailed behind him as she tried to imagine little kids running screaming from the candy store while jelly beans fell unnoticed from their bags. He was one scary-looking dude.

"Do you have to take care of the plants *now*?" Kim shifted her gaze from him long enough to study the plants. Ordinary, bushy plants. Didn't look like they needed emergency care.

"These two plants are Sweetie Pie and Jessica. I can't tell them apart, but I bet the owner could. Holgarth says the owner is really into plants. We have to keep them happy." He refused to meet her gaze. "And I had to come now because the owner wants me to tell you about them. Oh, and I'm Deimos."

Happy? "Deimos, they're plants. Plants don't do happy." Kim could see Fo's big purple eyes fixed on Deimos. Please, no. She'd had enough weirdness since last night to last her for the next twenty years.

"Kimmie, I think Deimos is a nonhuman entity. Since Brynn pointed out the flaw in my programming, I now understand that I can't definitely say he's a demon." Fo blinked her eyes. "Yo, Deimos, are you a demon? Kimmie, you should always keep me with you."

Deimos widened his amber eyes as he shifted his attention to Fo. "What's that?"

Kim looked more closely at his eyes. A strange color. Where had she seen eyes . . . Sparkle Stardust. Sparkle's eyes were the same color as Deimos's. Maybe they were related. Hmm, come to think of it, they were the same color as the eyes of the cat on Brynn's body. No, didn't want to go there. Or maybe she should say she wanted to go there too much. She would *not* think about Brynn's inner thigh now.

"You don't have to ask Kimmie. I can answer for myself. I'm—"

"Fo is a high-tech toy that I'm thinking about leaving with Wade, my neighbor across the hall." Kim hoped Fo got the message.

She did.

Silence stretched between Kim and Deimos for a moment. "So are you a demon?" Under the circumstances, she figured the direct approach would be best.

Deimos shook his head as he continued to avoid her gaze. She sensed an unspoken *but* there somewhere. He bent over the plants and began pouring some of the plant food around their roots. Suddenly, he paused. "Jeez, I can't believe it. Look, they both have flower buds." He sounded endearingly excited about the buds.

Deimos glanced up at her, and once again she got the impression of someone young and innocent trapped in that massive body. "Wow, you'll have to take really good care of them. They've never had flowers before." He frowned. "I guess I'll have to tell you what the owner wants you to know."

"That might be a good idea." Kim felt her frustration with him fading away in the face of his happiness over the flower buds.

He straightened and locked his gaze on a point about a foot above her head. "The owner has spent lots of time studying plants. He . . . Well, I don't know for sure if the owner's a he. Holgarth says the owner might be a he, she, or possibly it. Anyway, the owner says that plants can pick up on human emotions. They stay really healthy and happy in a room where people . . ."

Kim watched in bemused silence as red crept up Deimos's neck, flooded his face, and then swept across his shaven head. He was experiencing a full-head blush. He'd have to get a handle on that if he wanted to be an action hero. She didn't think action heroes spent much time blushing.

He coughed and blushed some more. "They stay healthy in a room where people . . ." He made a meaningless gesture with his hand she supposed was meant to symbolize what he couldn't quite put into words. "Where people, you know, do it. I mean, the plants don't watch, but they get off on all the energy." He finished in a rush.

"Do it?" She raised one brow. "You mean have sex?"

The word *sex* spoken out loud deepened his blush to neon red. "Yeah." He backed toward the door.

Kim spent a few moments of silence contemplating the plants. What could she possibly add to that? "From all those buds, I'd say these girls must've been in a room with a sex tag team. Only sex twenty-four/seven would've made them this happy." Wait, why did the owner want her to know this? "Maybe you should move the plants to another room before they lose all their buds, because there won't be any doing-it in my room. You can tell the owner that."

"But the owner says—" He'd paused in the process of backing out the door.

Kim didn't waste any more time arguing. She picked up a plant in each hand, marched over to Deimos, and shoved the plants into his arms. "*You* keep the plants. *You* keep them happy."

She gave him an irritated push, and he stumbled into the hall, still gripping Sweetie Pie and Jessica. She started to slam the door in his face.

"But I'm a virgin."

Kim finished slamming the door and then leaned her back against it. She closed her eyes.

"Oh, boy."

6

"Get this straight; I'm nobody's pet. I don't do wimpy meows. I don't do lap cuddling. And I never purr—except when I'm digging into a great meal." Ganymede crouched on Sparkle's candy counter. With ears pinned, amber eyes narrowed to angry slits, and black tail whipping back and forth, he was one steamed kitty.

Sparkle allowed herself a deliciously secret smile. Did he know how sexy he was when he got all angry and aggressive? Mede was always a challenge. He never said yes without a fight. She loved that about him.

"You need to calm down and relax. Here, have a caramel." She reached into her display case.

"You've got a mean streak, evil woman. That's what keeps me coming back. Notice the cat form? If I chomp down on a caramel, it'll glue my jaws shut for an hour."

Sparkle leaned forward to slide her fingertips over the smooth fur of his back. He arched into the caress. Mmm. Mede's hair when he was in human form felt the same way, all soft and sensual. "Exactly, sugar fluff. You need to do some quality listening."

"Hmmph." He sat down on the counter and then wrapped his tail around him. "Give it your best shot, but I'm not going to change my mind. I only came for the sex."

She perched herself on the high stool behind her counter, crossed her legs—she was glad she'd chosen to wear her barely-there leather skirt today—and studied her nails so Mede wouldn't see the laughter in her eyes. He always said he came for the sex, but he always stayed for so much more.

"This is your lucky day, Mede." Rats. The nail color on her ring finger was chipped. When had that happened? Now that she knew it was chipped, she wouldn't be able to concentrate on anything else.

"We can get it on *before* you nag me? Hey, changing forms is tough for me, but it'll only take about twenty minutes if I start right now." For the first time, his eyes gleamed with excitement.

"What?" Could she call Deimos back so he could watch the store while she zipped home to get her bottle of Torrid Tiger? "No. Absolutely not. We don't get to play until you fix Brynn's life. But the good news is that if you take away his compulsion, I bet you earn a barrel of brownie points with the Big Boss." Was she imagining it, or was the chipped spot getting bigger?

Mede's expression returned to narrow-eyed bad temper. "What's the big deal with Brynn? I gave him every man's fantasy. He gets to have great sex every day of his life if he wants it, with no consequences or responsibilities. Besides that, he's immortal. So the great sex just goes on and on. Doesn't get much better than that."

Mede was such a cosmic troublemaker. He didn't understand humans. Never had. "If he *wants* it. That's the problem. Brynn doesn't have a choice. He thinks he's a sex slave."

Mede blinked. "And your point is? Look, I can't help it if he's a negative kind of guy. I gave him lemonade, and he turned it into lemons." His expression said he knew there was a flaw in his analogy, but he wasn't quite sure what it was.

Sparkle did a few mental eye rolls. "The point is you shouldn't have given him anything having to do with lemons in the first place. Humans don't think like us. We rose from the primordial ooze knowing we were meant to be bad. Our whole existence is spent causing trouble, living in the moment, and working on instant gratification. We never have identity crises."

She frowned at the chipped nail color. It was like if she took her attention off it for too long it would spread to her other nails, a chipped-nail-color pandemic. "I'm still working on the instant gratification part, because sometimes it's damned hard to convince two people who're completely wrong for each other that everything's good. Anyway, humans eventually want to fall in love, settle down, and have a family. I know, sounds boring, but that's humanity for you." She glanced at Mede. "You might want to get off the counter. Personally, I find your kitty form cute and endearing, but customers would get all bent out of shape if they found cat hair on their fudge."

"Primordial ooze? What's that about?" Amusement flickered in his eyes. "And no, I'm not getting off the counter. I like it here. So I still don't get it. Why isn't Brynn happy? He could get married and just ask his wife to have sex with him every hour. No problem."

Sparkle fixed her attention on her absolutely fave Manolo Blahnik sandals and tried not to think about her ruined nail. Could she help it if she obsessed over her sensual appearance? Did that make her shallow? Sparkle didn't think so.

"I gave Brynn his compulsion a long time ago, back when I never did *anything* to make humans happy. He was lucky because I'd just released a plague of locusts on some unsuspecting boobies and was feeling pumped. You know, all kind and charitable. Only feel that way once in say a thousand years. So I made sure he wouldn't feel guilty about using women by letting him think he was a demon. See, everybody knows demons are slimeballs, so Brynn could ease his conscience by telling himself he was just doing what came naturally." He shook his head at the folly of trying to make humans feel good.

Mede got a faraway look in his eyes. "I was a real badass back then—destroying planets, creating black holes, messing with the time-space continuum." He exhaled deeply. "Those were the bad old days, before the Big Boss brought his hammer down." His eyes shone with the memory of past glory. "I was the baddest of the bad for thousands of years. I was the most powerful cosmic trouble-maker in the universe." The glow slowly faded. "Now I can't do one damned thing to hurt anyone without the Big Boss getting on my case."

"I feel your pain, love button." And she did, as much as she was able to empathize with another being. "That's why you have to do this for me. The Big Boss will think you've gone good and not pay so much attention to you. That way you can slip in a few wicked deeds without him noticing."

Mede washed his face with one black paw as he thought over Sparkle's logic. "Yeah, maybe you're right. But I don't know if I can reverse the compulsion. I don't usually build in fail-safes for this kind of thing."

"You've got to try . . . for me." Okay, so that wasn't the smartest thing to say. She should've appealed to his troublemaker nature in-stead of making it personal. Sometimes Mede muddled her thinking.

The silence dragged on a little too long, and Sparkle knew her big bad cat was doing it on purpose. "Well?"

"I'll give it a shot, but I'm not doing the telepathy crap this time. Anything I have to say, I'll say it out loud." His belligerent stare dared her to defy him.

Sparkle nodded. She knew when to give in. Mede needed to feel he'd won a point to make up for him agreeing to help her. Males were so transparent. "Just make sure you don't talk to Kim. She'll lose it, and you'll be out of there. I have it all worked out. I prom-ised Kim a pet, so I'll take you over in the carrier and—"

"Whoa, stop, cut it freakin' off right there. What part of I . . . am . . . not . . . a . . . pet didn't you understand?" He stood and in one graceful motion leaped to the floor. "I'll just mosey over to the castle and do some snooping on my own. Have to admit that cats are great for sneaking around and getting inside info."

He padded toward the door. "I'll find the castle's restaurant first and then find Brynn. After I steal a snack, I'll do some heavy-duty spying to see if he really hates my compulsion as much as you say he does." Mede turned to look back at her. "What's good on the restaurant's menu? Gotta keep up my strength, you know. Hope they have ice cream and cake."

Oh, jeez, no. Sparkle hopped off her stool and raced around the counter to stand in front of the door. "Wait. You can't just wander around the castle. They'll all get upset if they see another cat running loose. And don't even think about going near the restaurant. The Board of Health will be on the place like fire ants on an ankle if someone spots you there."

Mede paused, growing still as only a cat can. "*Another* cat? Something you're not telling me?"

Sparkle sighed. She'd put off telling him about Asima, but it looked like she didn't have any choice now. "Asima's in the castle. She's a messenger of the goddess Bast, and she always takes the form of a Siamese cat. I don't know why she's hanging there, but she's a royal pain in the butt."

Mede looked intrigued. "Is she a babe?" The wicked expression in his amber eyes said he knew exactly the response he'd get to that.

Never let it be said that Sparkle Stardust disappointed. "Remember the whole 'hell hath no fury' thing? Well, a cosmic troublemaker scorned is so much worse." She smiled sweetly. "Can we say instant chop chop? No more manly package."

"Ouch."

"Oooh, yes." She really hated playing to Mede's expectations, but he got such a kick out of her acting the jealous bitch that she couldn't deny him. Sparkle was way too secure with her own sexual appeal to worry about a snooty goddess gofer like Asima.

"You know, I think you're right about too many cats running loose. I need to keep a low profile, so I'll kick back and snooze in this Kim's room when I'm not stalking Brynn. I don't know who she is, but I know how you work. I free Brynn. You hook him up with Kim. They go through hell together. You're happy."

"Exactly." He'd given in a little too easily, but she didn't have time to worry about his motive. Every minute wasted was a minute more for her nail color to remain chipped. Sparkle moved away from the door. "Wait while I get the carrier, litter box—"

"Uh-uh. Isn't going to happen. I walk to the castle on my own cat paws without you tagging along. You'll only cramp my style."

That was it. Sparkle was officially ticked off. "Fine. You want to do it your way? You can ask me for help after you fall flat on your fuzzy face."

Mede chuckled. He loved irritating her. "You can tie a note around my neck with a few basic instructions—doesn't need a litter box, doesn't eat cat food, doesn't respond to baby talk, and won't chase mice. Just the important stuff."

Sparkle's smile was all about payback. "Wait while I get something to tie around your neck.

Maybe Kim had used up all her weird-is-wonderful moments for the day, because she'd gotten through the whole afternoon with no demon sightings, no talking cats, no virgin action heroes, and no klutzy fishermen. Of course, she'd practically barricaded herself in her room and only opened the door to room service.

Eric had called to officially invite her to share her ideas for the castle with them tonight. Kim wasn't sure who comprised "them," but she'd be ready. She'd gone over her presentation during the afternoon. That was good.

Then she'd called Lynsay again. She'd laid out every reason she could think of to convince her sister she shouldn't come to the castle. Lynsay said her gut told her the castle was overrun with demons. Hey, who was Kim to argue with her sister's gut? Lynsay was still coming. That was bad.

And when her sister said she and Uncle Dirk would be there later tonight . . . Well, that had been downright ugly. Other than hiring Wade to stomp on their demon detectors, she wasn't sure what she could do.

The unexpected knock on her door made Kim jump. Fine, so she was a little nervous about this presentation. Taking a deep breath, she smoothed the jacket and skirt of her black suit. She'd tried to balance deadly dull professional with good-time girl by wearing a sexy lavender top.

She picked up Fo. Call her paranoid, but she wasn't going to be caught unarmed in an iffy situation again. Hoping desperately for a normal human on the other side of the door, she pulled it open.

Brynn smiled at her. "Thought I'd go down to the meeting with you. It isn't much fun walking into a roomful of strangers by your-self." He glanced at Fo. "How you doing, Fo?"

"I'm fine, Brynn." Fo's eyes shone with the joy of having another sentient being accept her small self as an individual.

For a moment, Kim felt like all the air she'd just breathed in had been sucked right out of her. Who was she to wish for a normal human when she could have the most beautiful demon in the uni-verse at her door?

And that was wrong, wrong, wrong. How would she ever reach her goal of being the Queen of Normal with an attitude like that? Besides, the first thing Dad had taught her was that a demon's gorgeous wrapping hid unspeakable evil. But no matter how hard she tried, she couldn't sense a demonic nature in Brynn. Surely she should at least get a whiff of Fire-and-Brimstone cologne when he was near. She sniffed. Nope, just hot and tempting male animal.

She tried to ignore his "gorgeous wrapping," but it was so to-tally . . . there. He must be dressed in costume for the night's fan-tasies she'd read about in the brochure Holgarth had sent her. He'd pulled his spectacular hair away from his face and secured it at the nape of his neck with a strip of leather. He wore a long white robe edged in gold, and logically she knew that beneath his robe he wore the rest of his costume.

But in her personal fantasy, he'd slowly slide the silky robe from his shoulders and let it slip to the floor, revealing his magnificent body in its entire naked splendor. As he strode toward her, his muscles would ripple smoothly beneath golden skin, and she'd drop her gaze the length of his ripped torso to—

"Yo, Kimmie."

Not now, Fo. Where was she? Oh, she'd drop her gaze the length of his ripped torso to stare at his oh-so-yummy sexual organs nestled—

"Kimmie, there's a—"

"Uh-huh." . . . nestled between strong thighs.

"There's a cat with a pink bow watching you, Kimmie. And I don't think he's really a cat either."

Kim blinked, but instead of looking down she glanced up to meet Brynn's amused gaze. Only the memory of what Deimos looked like in mid-blush kept her from turning red. "Umm, I'll get my stuff."

She let her hungry stare drop away from him. In the dropping away process, her gaze skimmed the floor and met the annoyed glare of a huge black cat with a pink bow tied around his neck. He sat just behind Brynn, and he didn't look friendly.

"Is that your cat?" She knew the answer even as she asked the question. The cat's narrowed amber gaze said he'd just like to see the human who'd dare claim ownership of him. But a pink bow? Kim fought back a smile. This wasn't a cat you laughed at and survived to tell the tale.

"What?" Brynn glanced behind him. "Where'd you come from, fellow?" He returned his attention to Kim. "Looks like another of Conall's strays. He feeds them every day outside the restaurant's service entrance. Brynn frowned. "A few have sneaked into the castle, but they never got this far before."

Kim couldn't help it, she grinned. "Does Conall always tie pink bows around their necks?"

The cat rose, padded around Brynn, and stopped in front of Kim. He stared up at her. "Hardee-har-har. Okay, let's cut the crap. The pink bow is Sparkle's idea of payback. I'm your rent-a-pet, so read the note and then get this frickin' bow off my neck."

Wide-eyed, Kim lifted her gaze to Brynn. The weird stuff just kept on coming. "*Who* is this?" Whoever he was, he had a husky male voice made rougher by bad temper.

"I'm down here. Ask *me*." The cat peered around her to look into the room. "I'm Ganymede, a being of immense power, so don't mess with me." He looked up at Brynn. "Hey, Brynn, mind if I hang with you sometimes? There's just so much shoe talk a cat can stand. We can watch a few TV shows filled with violence and gratuitous sex. You know, guy stuff."

Brynn studied Ganymede. There was something about the cat's eyes that seemed familiar. He shook his head. Forget the eyes, he needed to do some damage control before Kim ran screaming from the castle. He couldn't throw the cat out of the castle because Sparkle sent him, and he liked Sparkle. Besides, the castle was home to a whole range of unique beings, so he couldn't reject Ganymede just because he was out there.

"You can hang with me, but I don't think Kim needs a pet. We'll find someplace else for you to stay." *And I'll find out exactly what you are*, Brynn thought for a moment while he tried to gauge Kim's panic level. "Got it? I'll introduce you to Asima. Bet you guys will have a lot in common."

"Sorry, can't do. Sparkle wants me to provide some caring companionship while Kim's here, sort of to offset all the other freakiness in the castle." Ganymede glanced up at Kim again. "Got any snacks in your room? Maybe you can pick up a cake next time you go out. I like chocolate icing. Oh, and I sleep on the bed. On a pillow. Hope you don't snore."

"Uh, Kimmie. Is he a demon? If so, you might want to press my button." Fo sounded tentative.

Brynn figured the detector was dealing with a confidence issue after finding out she couldn't tell a demon from any other nonhuman entity. Kim seemed to be handling things okay, considering. He didn't know how calm she'd be, though, when she found out exactly what Holgarth, Eric, and Conall were.

But he'd worry about the others later. Right now he needed to take care of Ganymede. "You know, for a 'being of immense power' you're not too smart. You would've had more chance of staying with Kim if you'd kept your mouth shut."

For just a moment, the cat's eyes changed, allowing Brynn to see something dangerous beneath the smart mouth and pink bow. No way was this cat staying with Kim.

"That's what *Sparkle* wants. Maybe that's not what *I* want." Ganymede glanced at Fo. "What's that?"

Fo answered for herself. "I'm not a what. I'm a who. I'm Kim's demon detector. I sense demons and then turn them into roadkill."

"Cool. Great eyes, kid. Love purple. But you need to adjust your sensors, because I'm not a demon." Ganymede looked expectantly up at Brynn. "So take the note off. And toss the bow while you're at it. I could've done it myself, but that would've ruined Sparkle's little revenge. Gotta humor the women once in a while."

"Sure." Brynn bent down to take off the bow with its attached note. He glanced at it before handing it to Kim without comment.

Kim frowned as she read the note. "Well, what we have here is a manifesto of kitty don'ts and won'ts." She skewered Ganymede with her glare. "May as well add mine to the list. I *don't* share my room with furry loudmouths. Good-bye."

"See. Demon hunters have no sense of humor." The cat looked at Brynn. "Hey, if Sparkle asks, you can tell her that I really tried to be a lovable feline for Kim, but she turned me down flat."

Brynn exhaled impatiently. "Which is what you wanted to begin with."

Ganymede's amber eyes turned sly. "A guy's gotta do what a guy's gotta do. I'm off now. Got people to see and things to do. Oh, and make sure you put your remote where I can reach it, Brynn."

Brynn watched him pad to the nearby elevator instead of the stairs. Ganymede stared at the button, and in a few minutes the door opened. He stepped inside, the door closed, and he was gone. Brynn shook his head. Lazy cat. Lazy cat who intended to move in with him. Uh-uh. Wasn't going to happen.

"Okay, today hasn't been all bad. I pawned off two plants that get their jollies from sexual energy, and I kept a cat with attitude from bunking down in my room." Kim glanced at her watch. "Only six more hours before this freaky day is over." She held up her hand as Brynn opened his mouth to speak. "Don't say anything. I can accept everything I've seen since I got here. Sort of. But don't even try to explain it. There're some things in life that are beyond explanations."

He nodded. "I'll help carry your stuff downstairs."

Brynn stood in the elevator holding Kim's easel while she clutched a large pad and notebook. She was cute when she was nervous. Cute? A word he'd never applied to women. They'd been many things to him, including ruthless and predatory, but not cute.

She was trying to look professional in her black suit, but she'd be horrified to know her sexy top that dipped a little too low for his self-control canceled out the suit. Her red hair tumbled around her face, and her eyes were wide and anxious. He watched her swallow hard, and he wanted to put his mouth on her neck at that exact spot. Then he'd slip her suit jacket off her shoulders and kiss a path to where the edge of her top lay just above the swell of her breast. He'd push the material aside and nibble . . .

The hell with nibbling. He'd rip off her damned jacket, top, and bra. Then he'd put his mouth on her ripe breast and tease her nipple to a hard nub with his tongue.

He took a deep, calming breath. What was that about? When he was under the compulsion, lust was a cold affair—plastic and artificially enhanced. It was as though he stood outside his body and watched it perform. Not this. This was hot, immediate, and personal. It was the first time he'd ever felt real sexual hunger, and he wanted to howl at the moon with his need.

Brynn forced himself to stare past Kim, but the elevator was mirrored, so her reflection stared back at him no matter where he looked. He'd have to talk to Holgarth about getting rid of the damned mirrors.

Her eyes grew even wider if that were possible. "Umm, it hasn't been an hour yet."

"I know." Uh-oh. His expression must be sending her I'm-going-to-gobble-you-up signals.

She offered him a nervous laugh. "I bet you keep these elevators in tiptop shape. Wouldn't want to be trapped in here"— her gaze skittered around the small enclosure—"for very long."

"Depends on the company." Come to think of it, this wouldn't be a bad place to lay her down and drive himself deep into her welcoming heat. A small, intimate space surrounded by visuals of her smooth, tempting body. If he were going to make love with a woman *he'd* chosen, he wouldn't want to do it in a bed. Over the centuries, he'd grown to hate bedrooms. Most of the women who'd accepted his offer of sex had taken him to their beds. There weren't many good memories attached to mattresses and pillows.

Kim had relief written all over her face as the elevator doors opened. "Who's going to be at this meeting? Eric didn't elaborate."

"There won't be a mob, if that's what you're afraid of." Brynn guided her to the small meeting room attached to the restaurant. "Probably just Conall, Holgarth, Eric, and his wife, Donna."

She visibly relaxed. "Won't the owner want to be here?"

"The owner pretty much stays out of sight." He shrugged. "Why all the mystery? No one knows. I do my job and don't worry about it." Which was a lie. He'd gone so far as to look up tax records in a vain attempt to discover the owner's name. No luck. The owner hid behind a corporation that didn't have so much as a Web site.

They entered the conference room to find Eric, Donna, Conall, and Holgarth already there. Brynn introduced Donna and Conall before helping Kim set up her easel. Then he took a seat beside Eric. Kim was about ready to begin when the door opened and Liz entered.

Brynn's muttered curse carried to those with enhanced hearing in the room. All the vampires glanced his way. Liz smiled. She deliberately walked around the table to sit beside him.

Liz put her hand over his. "Hi, gorgeous."

Brynn didn't look at Liz. Instead he watched Kim. Her frown told him she understood what was happening, and somehow her knowledge shamed him.

He could get up and move away from Liz, but doing that while everyone watched would make him feel less than a man. Sure, it was just his stupid pride talking, but his pride was all he had right now. And he knew Eric and Conall would reluctantly honor his wish for them not to interfere.

He glanced at his watch. Not that time mattered. Liz was a vampire. He couldn't run from her, any more than he could run from what he was. And so he leaned back to listen to Kim.

"I'm sure you want to know why I'm here, Kim." Liz's voice was a low, sensual purr, filled with all her sexual expectations for the night. "You already know one of my reasons, but I do have another. I'm a friend of Taurin. He usually works in the castle, but he's away now searching for his brother. The castle is home to him, so I told him I'd let him know what's happening. I hope you don't mind if I sit in on your presentation."

"Would it make a difference if I did?" Kim looked like she wondered where a stake was when she needed it.

"No." Liz leaned close to Brynn, and he purposely pulled his protective cloak of nothingness around him—blocking out all emotions, all sensory stimuli, all caring.

"I don't think Kim likes me, Brynn." She offered him a phony expression of sorrow. "I bet she's jealous because she's trapped up there giving her talk and won't be able to interfere this time. Poor her." Liz's light trill of laughter flowed around the nothingness Brynn had created, touching no part of him.

"I can tell Taurin what he wants to know." Conall's expression was thunderous. He wore his warrior face.

Brynn knew all he'd have to do is nod at Conall, and his friend would heave Liz out of the room.

He didn't nod. Instead, he listened as Kim began to discuss her ideas.

"I don't want to take away any parts of the existing castle, only add some elements that will make it more authentic and interesting to the customers who tour it during the day. You could incorporate these into your nightly fantasies as well."

Brynn watched as Kim forgot about her audience and became involved in her ideas. Great ideas. Unfortunately, some of her listeners spoke before they thought.

Conall got carried away when she suggested an authentic medieval kitchen and bakery. He regaled everyone with how it felt to ride in from a day of battle to a hardy venison stew and willing wenches.

Kim looked thoughtful.

Holgarth couldn't control himself when Kim suggested the small theater area Asima had wanted. He had to share his story of the time he'd gotten revenge on Shakespeare by making all the actors suddenly appear naked right in the middle of *Macbeth*.

Kim looked more thoughtful.

And when Kim suggested an authentic medieval chapel where real weddings could be performed, all the vampires grew very still. The negative energy in the room would've reduced Sweetie Pie and Jessica to bare branches.

Kim looked resigned.

She took Fo from her pocket, placed her on the meeting table, and narrowed her gaze on her audience.

"Okay, let's have it. I want to know what each one of you is. And human is *not* an option."

7

Kim nodded at Holgarth. "Why don't you start? Who exactly are you under that cheesy wizard outfit?" She hoped she sounded calmer than she felt.

Maybe she shouldn't have challenged the whole room at once. She was already upset about Liz and didn't need more craziness piled on top of that. Why did she give a damn what Liz was doing, anyway? Brynn was a big boy. He wouldn't appreciate her outrage on his behalf. But she did give a damn. Right now her feelings were all out of whack.

Probably her emotional balance would've stayed on a more even keel if these wild and weird revelations had come over a longer period of time. But she needed to know if there were any other demons in this group and then move on. Otherwise Fo would drive her crazy. She hoped Fo was paying attention.

Fine, so this wasn't just for Fo's sake. Her mind had to be straight about things before Lynsay and Uncle Dirk hit the drawbridge. Kim already knew she couldn't let them run rampant through the castle zapping everyone they suspected might be a demon. She wanted to keep this job. That wasn't all, but Kim refused to do any deep internal searches right now.

Holgarth somehow managed to look down his nose at her even though he was seated and she was standing. "I am a very old, very powerful, and very offended wizard. And this 'cheesy wizard outfit' is quite authentic, I assure you."

A *real* wizard? Uh-oh. Could he turn her into something small and slimy? Ugh. Yuk. Time for major damage control. "Yes, well, I knew that. Blue is you. Don't ever change the color." She shifted her gaze to Donna before Holgarth had a chance to skewer her with a few well-chosen insults. "How about you, Donna? I noticed you weren't too enthusiastic about the chapel." She smiled at Donna so she'd know Kim respected her opinion . . . no matter what she was.

Donna smiled back. Kim's tension eased in the warmth of that smile. What a nice woman. "I'm a vampire, Kim. Eric turned me using Taurin's blood because Eric's clan can't make other vampires. Since Taurin is a night feeder, that makes me one, too. Night feeders aren't compatible with things you find in chapels. So Taurin and I won't be paying any visits. But if you really think visitors would enjoy a chapel, go for it."

Kim gripped the back of the nearest chair to steady herself and to keep her hands from shaking. Okay, she could deal with this. *Breathe in, breathe out. Repeat as needed.* "Eric, I guess you're next."

Eric's smile was friendly and relaxed. "You're wound too tight, Kim. We never bite architects until they've fulfilled their contracts." He put his arm across Donna's shoulders. "I'm a vampire, but I belong to the Mackenzie clan. Mackenzies don't have any problems with holy water and crosses."

Kim pulled out the nearest chair and sat down. Okay, she collapsed. *Information overload.* This was her own fault. She'd asked a simple question, and well, everyone had answered it. That would teach her to only ask questions about the weather. She looked at Conall. One more to go. She could do this. "How about you, Conall?"

He shrugged his massive shoulders. "My real name is Conall O'Rourke, and I'm an immortal warrior. Morrigan, the Irish goddess of war and death, cursed me because I killed one of her favorites in battle. My punishment was to protect the descendants of the useless piece of crap I killed. The last one lives somewhere in Galveston. When I find him and make sure he never breeds any future pieces of crap, Morrigan will release me."

Uh-huh. Didn't need to know any more about that. "That's . . . amazing, Conall. Just wondering why you guys told me all this neat stuff. Does this mean you have to kill me now?"

Conall's laughter was as big as he was. "We don't need to kill you. What do you think would happen if you went to the police and told them a vampire, a demon, and an immortal warrior were running the Castle of Dark Dreams? Bet they'd hook you up with a kind and caring member of the mental health community."

Kim nodded her agreement.

"And what're you when you're not being an architect, Kim?" Liz wasn't even pretending to be friendly now. "And what's that phony cell phone with the purple eyes?"

Kim took a deep breath. Time to stop pretending. She'd symbolically pushed aside her duster and reached for her holster when she put Fo on the table. Now she had to shoot from the hip. She paused to organize her thoughts.

"Ms. Vaughn belongs to a notorious demon-hunting family." Holgarth reached up to adjust his tall, conical hat. "Since the only demon in the room is Brynn, and he looks reasonably intact, I would assume she doesn't use her demon destroyer impulsively." He offered Kim a supercilious smile. "Unlike other members of her family."

Kim stared at Holgarth. "How did you know that?"

Holgarth's gray eyes glittered with triumph. "Even a wizard with a cheesy outfit knows many, many things." He frowned. "Actually, I Googled the Vaughn name. One of your family members was stupid enough to have a Web site." Scanning his audience, he continued, "I advised the owner against hiring Ms. Vaughn because of her unfortunate family ties and my worry about putting Brynn in harm's way."

Brynn's surprised expression said Holgarth wasn't in the habit of worrying about anyone but himself. The pompous old fart.

"I heard that thought, Ms. Vaughn." Something that could've passed for humor touched his gaze and was gone. "The owner chose to ignore my concerns in favor of hiring, and I quote here, 'a person who'll bring some kick-ass excitement into the old pile of rock.' And since I live to serve, I acquiesced."

"Relax, Holgarth. I'm wearing my architect's hat while I'm here." Good grief, who used the word *acquiesced* in real life? Kim closed her eyes and rubbed her forehead where a headache was trying to form. "I'll take questions and suggestions now." She opened her eyes to see everyone's hand up and Brynn and Liz gone. What the . . . ? She glanced at her watch. Almost an hour. It hadn't seemed that long.

For the next twenty minutes, she was inundated with questions. And if Eric, Conall, and Donna looked worried, that worry didn't translate into action.

Not your business, not your business. Fine, so she was making it her business. She held up her hands to stop further questions. "Look, if anyone wants to talk to me, catch me tomorrow. Gotta go." Kim scooped Fo from the table. "Can someone tell me Brynn's and Liz's room numbers?"

There was a moment of dead silence, and then Eric spoke up. "Brynn is in the Wicked Desires room, number 205, and Liz's room is number 310, Wicked Intentions." He glanced around at everyone staring at him. "What? Someone needs to do something. Brynn won't let *us* help."

Donna looked confused. "I don't understand. What's going on?"

Kim left it to Eric to explain things. She was outta there.

"Where're we going, Kimmie? Did you notice how quiet I was?" Fo blinked her eyes. "Of course, I didn't have to tell you they weren't human because they told you themselves. Don't you think

Eric is a beautiful vampire? And Conall is so big and sexy. Do you think Conall would be interested in dating a very small being?"

"Haven't a clue, Fo." She'd try Brynn's room first. "And we're going to stop Liz from doing something . . ." *Cruel? Obscene?* Brynn would tell her to butt out, that he'd been used this way for centuries. Well, too bad. The using wasn't going to happen on her watch, not if she could help it. "Stay alert, Fo. I might need you."

Fo's eyes grew wide with excitement. "Really? Please let me zap the blond vampire slut? Pleeease?"

When things calmed down, she'd have to find out where Fo had come up with the word *slut*. She wanted to expand Fo's vocabulary, but not in the wrong direction.

"Hey, Kim, where you going?"

Kim glanced down to find Ganymede staring up at her. His belly was so stuffed it almost dragged on the floor. "I see you found the restaurant." She stopped at the elevator and pressed the Up button. "I'm going to find Brynn." As the door opened, and she stepped inside, she glanced around to make sure no one had seen her talking to a cat.

"Don't worry, I look before I talk." Ganymede padded into the elevator with her.

No, no, no. She didn't want company. But things just got worse. Asima sat in the corner watching Ganymede from huge blue eyes. Great, just great. Kim punched the button for the second floor with a little more ferocity than necessary.

"Whoa, would you look at the sexy lady. You must be Asima. Lookin' good, kitten." If a cat could leer, Ganymede was leering. He padded up to Asima and reached out to touch noses with her.

Asima calmly lifted one elegant paw and swatted Ganymede across his nose. Then she began washing her face.

Ganymede jumped away from her and went to look at his nose in the mirrored wall. "Hell, woman. What was that about? Can't a guy get a little friendly? You scratched my nose."

Asima looked up at Kim. *"Who is this . . . animal?"*

"I'm Ganymede, sis, and you don't have to do the mind-talk when we're the only ones in the elevator. Why'd you hit me?" His cat face expressed his complete shock that any female would meet his advance with a swat.

"You have a typical tomcat mentality. You're fortunate we weren't in our human forms, or else I would've aimed somewhat lower on your anatomy." She stopped washing her face. *"By the way, what are you?"*

Human forms.. Did that mean Ganymede was a shape-shifter? She added that tidbit of info to her growing weird-stuff pile. The elevator doors slid open. Kim paused to get her bearings and then strode toward Brynn's room. The cats padded after her. "Ganymede, you can get things straightened out with Asima while I'm taking care of business."

Fo laughed. "We're going to kick some vampire butt."

Both cats looked interested as they stopped outside of Brynn's door.

"Wait outside. I hope we won't be long." Kim could hear Liz's muffled voice through the door, so she'd picked the right room. Now to get inside. No use knocking and announcing her presence. The element of surprise was important. She quietly tried the door. Damn. Locked.

"Do you want me to go inside and tell you what's happening, Kim?" Asima looked eager to spy out the situation.

"No. You guys have to stay outside. Brynn will be embarrassed enough when I go in without me sending you in, too." How was she going to get inside? She narrowed her gaze on the cats. Hmm.

"Embarrassed? Why would he be embarrassed?" Asima looked truly puzzled.

Ganymede made a rude noise. "Because he might be doing something of a sexual nature. Duh?"

"Asima, you have more power than I do, so why don't you open the door for me?" Kim had witnessed firsthand Asima's ability to unlock doors.

Asima seemed torn. *"I have a curious nature, but as much as I'd like to see what's happening, it might not be right to barge in if Brynn's—"*

"I'll open the door for you." Ganymede didn't sound puzzled. He sounded like he understood what was going on.

Kim decided she'd wonder about that later. Right now she needed into that room. And if she thought too long about what she intended to do, she might be tempted to walk away. "Do it now."

With an almost inaudible click, the door swung open.

"I still don't understand why Kim has to go into that room in the first place. And I think there's one too many cats in this hallway." This aimed at Ganymede. Asima had shifted from puzzled to irritated.

Kim stepped quietly into the room. As the door swung closed behind her, she heard Ganymede's whispered reply. "I'll explain, and then after this is over maybe we can raid the kitchen together. I'm a good guy once you get to know me."

Kim didn't have to sneak, because there was some sort of Celtic New Age music playing. Besides, Liz had her back to the door and was so focused on Brynn that she wouldn't have heard an army of vampire slayers charging into her room. But then Kim had no room to criticize, because she was so riveted by what she saw that the same army of slayers could've trampled her into the carpet on their way to Liz, and she wouldn't have cared.

Kim covered her mouth to muffle her gasp.

Brynn lay on his stomach, naked and spread-eagled across the bed. Liz had evidently been in too much of a hurry to do anything more than yank the pillows from the bed. She'd left the deep red bedspread in place, a crimson pool around his golden body.

Eyes widened in horror, Kim stared at his wrists and ankles tied to the bedposts and then skimmed the angry welts marring the smooth, muscular expanse of his back and buttocks.

"No man has excited me this much in two hundred years. It was almost worth losing you to that bitch last night." Dressed as the dominatrix from hell with stiletto-heeled boots, black fishnet stockings, and leather everything, Liz looked in her element. She trailed the tip of a wicked-looking whip over his abused body until it slid between his open thighs. She let the tip rest against his exposed balls. "I mean, if you hadn't gone off with her, I wouldn't have an excuse to punish you. Now that you've learned your lesson, you can give me pleasure for the rest of the night. How does that sound to you, hmm?"

"If that's what you want, then I want it, too." Brynn had turned his face away from Liz, so Kim couldn't see his expression, but the absence of any emotion in his voice said it all.

Kim took her hand away from her mouth and exhaled on a hiss of fury. The noise was too loud for even Liz to ignore. She spun to face Kim, her mouth twisted into an angry snarl.

Kim had learned a long time ago that perception was everything when dealing with demons and hopefully vampires. She slid into her kick-ass demon-hunter persona. "Hi, Liz. Oh, and the bitch is back."

"Where the hell did you come from?" Liz took a threatening step toward Kim. "Didn't anyone ever tell you what happens to people who interfere with a vampire's recreational time?" Her smile was slow and confident. "They end up a dry husk."

That should've been Kim's signal to run like the devil, but she was too ticked off to pay attention to signals. "Let him go."

Liz laughed, but beneath the light trill of amusement moved a malevolence Kim could feel as a cold slide of danger across her skin.

"He's mine until tomorrow. Aren't you, gorgeous?" Liz didn't turn her head to look at Brynn. Her unblinking stare stayed fixed on Kim.

The silence dragged on for so long that Kim thought he might not answer. But finally it came. "Yes." Once again, there was no inflection in the one word to give Kim a hint of his feelings.

Liz's smile widened in triumph. "See. He wants me. Now, if you leave like a good girl, I might not rip your throat out."

Okay, that did it. Kim didn't like to hurt things, but she felt a really unholy need to hurt this woman. She couldn't remember ever being this mad. She lifted Fo and turned her to face Liz. "Let him go."

Liz yawned. "You've officially bored me. And as much as I'd like to drink a toast to Brynn with your blood, I can't risk everyone getting bent out of shape. So I'll settle for beating the crap out of you." She sneered at Fo. "And your toy won't stop me. I'm not a demon."

With that contemptuous dismissal of Fo's power, Liz became vampire. Jeez, instant ugly. Liz in her vampire form was almost as disgusting as the demons that had mooned Kim. Huge black eyes and long, sharp fangs. Ugh, ugh, ugh. She didn't look cute and perky anymore. Hey, things weren't all bad.

Behind Liz, Kim could hear Brynn struggling to free himself. He'd evidently come out of whatever trancelike state he'd been in. "Get out, Kim."

"Not until I take care of Fang Girl here." For the first time, Kim smiled. "Fo might not be able to destroy you, but she can sure give you something to think about." She pressed Fo's red button and watched the powerful beam score a direct hit on Liz's face.

Kim winced at Liz's shriek. Liz threw her hands over her eyes. "You blinded me! I can't see. I don't care what the others say, I'm going to kill you." She growled her fury as she flung herself in the direction of Kim's voice.

"Um, I'd watch out for that chair . . . Oops. Bet that hurt." She watched Liz untangle herself from the fallen chair. But before Kim could say anything else, the door crashed open, and Ganymede padded to her side. Asima stood in the doorway, watching with wide blue eyes.

"Relax, your favorite cosmic troublemaker is here to save your butt. Just step aside." He glared at Liz, but then his gaze slid past her to where Brynn still lay tied to the bed. "Wow, that doesn't look like fun, pal." Forgetting about Liz, who was staggering around bumping into furniture, Ganymede padded over to Brynn. The bindings immediately fell away from Brynn's wrists and ankles.

Brynn winced as he rolled over and sat up. He didn't look toward Kim. But he didn't have to, because his emotions hit her with enough force to back her up. Anger, embarrassment, and self-loathing washed over Kim. He must've been holding them in check until now. She took a deep breath and forced the emotions aside.

Fine, so he was royally steamed at her for turning this into a circus. Could she help it that Ganymede and Asima had tagged along? Absolutely not. And as it turned out, she'd needed them. She understood his anger and embarrassment, but they needed to have a long talk about his self-loathing.

Right now though, Kim had other things to worry about. Like how to get Liz under control. She didn't fool herself. Blind or not, with Liz's strength, she could rip Kim apart if she caught her.

"I'll get her out of here for you, Kim." Asima had finally decided to enter the room.

Liz was still screaming obscenities. Luckily, it was early in the evening, so most people with rooms on the second floor were somewhere else. But the noise would eventually draw attention. And more attention was exactly what Brynn didn't need.

"For crying out loud, Liz, you'll be able to see again in a half hour. Cut the screeching." Kim frowned. Her assurance hadn't lowered Liz's volume one decibel.

"Don't worry, I'll take care of her. You take care of Brynn." Asima stared at Liz, and the vampire grew silent. *"Come with me into the hallway."* Strangely passive, Liz left the room with Asima, only knocking over a lamp and walking into the wall once.

Kim couldn't begin to wrap her mind around the kind of power she was seeing from both Ganymede and Asima. All she cared about now was getting Brynn some privacy. "Thanks for your help, Ganymede, but Brynn can handle it now. And Asima could probably use your help." She didn't try to make eye contact with Brynn.

Ganymede ignored her and spoke to Brynn. "Hell, talk about crazy broads. Okay, so some people like their sex kinky, but it looked like she was the only one having a good time. Why'd you let her tie you up like that?" Something furtive shone in Ganymede's amber eyes.

Brynn didn't try to cover himself. He didn't care about his nudity.

Kim had seen him tied, whipped, and helpless. She'd rescued him. He should feel gratitude. He only felt anger. She'd stripped him of whatever little pride he had left after Liz got through with him. So now she could look at his body or not, because he didn't give a damn.

But Ganymede wanted an explanation. Brynn would tell him the bare-bones truth, because he found that he did have a little pride left. He didn't want the cat to think he'd given in to Liz without a fight.

"I'm a demon of sensual desire. If I spend more than an hour with a woman, she owns my body for the night." He shrugged. "I have to give her pleasure in whatever way she wants." That's all Ganymede needed to know.

"So you're a sex demon? Cool. Bet it's good most of the time, right? Sex with lots of different women? You gotta love it, right?" Ganymede looked a little too hopeful.

Was he crazy? "I hate it. I don't know who or what made me, but turn me loose in a room with the bastard for five minutes, and there won't be enough left to chuck back into hell."

Ganymede's gaze skittered away from Brynn. "Yeah, I guess I see your point." The doubt in his voice said he didn't see it at all.

Brynn had purposely avoided looking at Kim. He looked now. She must've gone into the hall while he was talking to Ganymede because she was just returning.

"Donna took Liz away. After Eric explained what Liz was up to, Donna yelled at all of them for not telling her sooner, and then she rushed up here to help." Kim didn't look ready to meet his gaze either. She was studying a spot about a foot above his head. "Donna is really ticked off. At Liz for being such a bitch and at all of you guys for keeping her out of the loop about what Liz was doing. She said you needed to lose the ego thing and let your friends help. She promised that Liz would never bother you again."

Bother you. Such a weak phrase to describe what Liz had in mind. "Yeah, that's great." Now he'd have to listen to Donna's lecture. Didn't any of them understand that he'd rather spend a thousand nights with Liz rather than be viewed as a powerless sexual pawn?

"Well, since everyone's okay, guess I'll get moving." Ganymede seemed a little too anxious to leave. "Maybe I can catch up with Asima. Hot babe." He paused in the doorway. "Oh, how about not telling Sparkle what I just said." And then he was gone. The door closed behind him.

"Thanks for your help." Brynn knew his voice didn't say thanks. It said, *Butt out of my life.* "I need to get my head together for tonight's fantasies." He swung his feet to the floor, stood, and walked to where he'd carefully folded his clothes over the back of the chair. He dreaded feeling the scrape of cloth against his welts, but at least Liz hadn't broken the skin, so he wouldn't bleed on his white costume.

"You're kidding."

He met her gaze. She didn't look particularly apologetic about anything. "I have a job to do." Brynn forced himself not to grimace as he pulled on his costume. Damn, that hurt. The castle's Handsome Prince wouldn't be carrying any fair maidens to safety tonight. Liz had really put a hurting on him.

"Don't you dare leave this room. I'll buy some cream from one of the stores in the lobby to put on your back and . . . Um, on your back." She edged toward the door. "And you're crazy if you try to work tonight."

"Don't bother. I'm fine." Lies. All lies. He wasn't fine. He hurt inside and out. Brynn waited until she'd hurried from the room before making his way slowly and painfully to his kitchenette for a glass of water.

As much as he hated to admit it, Kim was right. His costume rubbing against his skin was torture. Exhaling in disgust, he called Holgarth to let him know he needed a sub for the night. Holgarth didn't complain or make one sarcastic comment. Brynn wished he'd done both. Right now, he viewed all kindness as translating into pity. He didn't want people's damned pity. Raking his fingers through his tangled hair, he consigned all vampire bitches to the deepest depths of hell. Oh, wait, couldn't do that. He was already there.

Ripping off his costume, he flung it to the floor. Then he paced naked. Would she come back with the cream? He didn't care. But if she did, let her walk in and find him like this. He didn't care. Would she apologize for calling humiliation down on him? He didn't care. Would she offer to smooth the cream over his body? He . . . did care.

As much as he hurt, the thought of her fingers sliding over his flesh had one part of his body on the road to a quick recovery. How could she do that when he was so ticked off at her?

While he was busy trying to convince his cock it needed to get with the program and buy into his I-don't-care philosophy, she opened his door and walked in.

Kim froze with the cream in one hand and Fo in the other. For a moment her eyes grew wide with shock. With her hair a tousled halo around her face, and her prim suit warring with her sexy top, he briefly sympathized with his cock's point of view. But the sympathy died a quick death.

She jammed Fo into her pocket even as Fo complained loudly.

"That's not fair, Kimmie. You never let me see the good stuff. I bet this place has an adult channel on their TVs, but do I ever get a chance to observe human sexual behavior? Ha! Not a chance. How can I learn if you don't even want me to see a naked man? I'm not a baby, but you treat me—"

Kim sighed. "Give me a break, Fo. This has been a rough day, and it still isn't over. I can't help Brynn if I have to fight with you. So will you be quiet until we get back to our room?"

Fo continued to mumble from Kim's pocket. "I'll be quiet for Brynn because he saved my life."

Carefully averting her gaze, Kim took off her jacket with Fo in it and laid it over a chair. The sexy top clung to her, accentuating the curve of her breasts. He focused his attention on the lotion in her hand while he silently repeated his litany of grievances against her.

She'd enraged Liz, thereby causing his punishment. Yeah, yeah, so he'd had a little to do with it, too. She'd interfered where she wasn't wanted. Fine, so she'd had no way of knowing he didn't want her help. She'd involved Ganymede and Asima—two more who now knew his secret. Maybe she didn't purposely involve them, but it was still her fault. His logic wouldn't bear close scrutiny, but it worked just fine for him now.

He finally lifted his gaze to her face. She watched him out of those big green eyes that reflected confusion, outrage for him, and the beginning of awareness.

"You're naked."

He allowed himself a bitter smile. "That should bother me? I've spent five centuries giving women what they want, and I guarantee they don't want anything but my body. Getting naked stopped embarrassing me a long time ago. Does my body bother you?"

She'd get red now and tell him he was a jerk. Then she'd storm out of here never to return. Good. He wanted to be able to pigeonhole her response as he had the responses of all the other women he'd known. Yeah, she'd run. She'd expected gratitude from him, and she had to be pissed at his whole attitude now.

"Yes, it bothers me." She purposely dropped her gaze to his cock. "Looking at your body makes me hot for you, but if I did what I wanted, I wouldn't be any better than Liz." She lifted her gaze back to his face. "Now let's get this cream on you."

Brynn stared at her. For the first time in five hundred years, a woman had surprised him.

8

"And since I'm into honesty mode, I'm not sorry I saved your bare butt from the vampire bitch. No one should be used like that." Kim swallowed hard at his thunderous expression. Had she been a little too honest?

"You can leave now." His voice was a dangerous murmur.

How could he scare her witless and still ooze sex from every pore? It would be so easy to run back to her room. But then who'd put the cream on his back? He certainly couldn't do it himself. And he'd probably spend the night in agony rather than bend his pride to ask anyone else for help. She sighed. "No."

"No?" His expression said he'd misunderstood her reply.

"No. I'm going to put this on you, and *then* I'll leave." She stopped short of telling him to lie down. He'd probably had enough of women telling him to lie down tonight. "If you'll turn around, I can get it over with. The cream will take some of the sting from the welts." Too bad she didn't have a magic cream that could heal emotional wounds. Uh-oh. She hoped he wasn't in her mind. He'd hate that kind of thought. "You're not in my mind, are you?"

He'd turned his back to her. "No. Why would I want to wade through all that overblown sympathy?"

"Not as sympathetic as you'd think. You're a hard man to feel sorry for." She uncapped the tube of cream and squeezed some onto her fingers.

"Demon, sweetheart. You seem to have forgotten that. What would your family say?" If he was trying to goad her into an angry response, he was halfway home.

"I don't know. I'll ask them when they get here tonight." She probably shouldn't have blurted that out just yet.

"Like to explain that?" He sounded casual, but the muscles in his back tightened.

She stepped close and smoothed the cream over the first welt with the tips of her fingers while trying to ignore his scent of warm healthy male. Up close he overwhelmed her. It wasn't just that he was over six feet tall with a beautiful body. She could find plenty of men on the Galveston beach who fit that description. It was the sense that like an extraordinary piece of architecture, he'd remain breathtakingly magnificent while refusing to lose his roof in high winds. And even though he might sway in the face of a hurricane's blast, he wouldn't collapse. An awesome blending of form and function.

She hadn't known him long enough to really get a handle on his character, but demon or not, he'd survived centuries of being forced to service women. That any kindness remained in him at all was a miracle. By now he should be nothing more than a savage beast.

She had the feeling, though, that like her imaginary building, he'd be tested by category-five Hurricane Lynsay blowing into town. She wondered who'd be left standing when it was over.

"Remember the call I got from my sister Lynsay? She and Uncle Dirk—whoever Uncle Dirk is—are paying the castle a visit because Uncle Dirk heard rumors of demon activity here. Know anything about that?"

"Lots of people come through here. I don't check all of them out. So how would I know?" He'd neatly sidestepped a straight yes or no answer. "Just so we're clear on this, I'm going to warn the others about your sister and uncle. From what I've heard, your family isn't choosy about who they label as a demon. If they do to guests what you did to Liz, we're going to take a financial hit."

"Financial hit? Lynsay and Uncle Dirk will destroy you if they can, and you're worried about money?" Kim humphed her disbelief.

"Contrary to what you saw tonight, when I'm not under the compulsion I can take care of myself." She heard the amusement in his voice.

"Why not have Holgarth tell them they can't stay here?" She'd survived smoothing the cream on his first welt with only some minor tingling and a little shortness of breath. She put more cream on her fingers and started on the next welt.

"Uh-uh. Wouldn't work. They'd want a reason. We wouldn't have one unless we ratted on you. Whatever we told them, they'd be convinced we were protecting a whole castle full of demons. They'd just bring in people we wouldn't recognize. People even you might not recognize." Experimentally, he moved the muscles in his shoulders.

"Makes sense." What didn't make sense was the heat pooling low in her stomach. "Okay, since you're probably the only demon in the castle, why don't you take an extended vacation somewhere? After Lynsay and Uncle Dirk zap the first guest, Holgarth can throw them out without arousing any suspicion." Arousing. Not the best word to use under the circumstances.

Kim was now down to the welts low on his back. It was getting tougher to maintain her Nurse Jane mentality—*I'm here to heal your body not drool over it*. As she moved lower, she found herself using more than the tips of her fingers to smooth on the cream. The cop-a-feel officer in her brain was shouting at her through its tiny mega-phone, *Move away from the body and drop the cream*. Ha, like she was going to do that.

"This is my home now. I didn't run from Liz, and I'm not running from your family. Holgarth, Eric, Conall, and I stand together."

Did he realize he was starting to lean into her strokes? She lingered on the welt at the base of his spine, allowing the heat and texture of his skin to drive her senses crazy.

"Then things could get ugly fast." She eyed the welts on his taut, beautiful cheeks. Did she want to go there? You bet. Did she dare? Uh, yes?

She drew her fingers slowly and lovingly across the rounded perfection of his buttocks, admiring the way each one clenched at her touch, wondering at how her stomach clenched in time to his clenching. They were obviously on the same clench . . . er, wavelength.

"Don't you think you should put some cream on your fingers first?" He sounded like he was talking through clenched teeth. Probably trying not to laugh.

"Oops." Between the two of them, they had the market cornered on clenching. She put the cream on her fingers, and then followed the same breathtaking path of a few seconds ago.

She'd like to blame her pounding heart, her obsessive fascination with his body, and her really wow fantasies about what she wanted to do with said body, on demonic pheromones or something. The sad truth? It was pure—okay, not so pure—lust. She, the descendant of legions of dedicated demon destroyers, was in lust with one of the evil ones.

"Getting a little melodramatic, aren't you?" Without warning, he turned to face her.

She remained frozen in place, poised to administer one more soothing sweep of her fingers across his luscious bottom. Kim now found her fingers poised over his erection. His very impressive erection. If the old wives' tale was true about big feet being an indicator of the size of a man's sexual equipment, then Brynn must wear size twenty-five shoes.

"You can put the cream away, Kim. I don't have any welts on my cock." He was laughing openly at her now.

"Melodramatic?" Right now, Kim could only manage one five-syllable word at a time.

"Yeah. I'm not an 'evil one.' I'd know if I were. I'm more of a cursed one. There's a difference." He walked into the bathroom and emerged a few seconds later with a towel knotted loosely around his waist. It rode low on his hips, teasing and taunting with what it hid.

She avoided meeting his gaze by slowly and carefully screwing the top onto the tube. "I'd appreciate it if you'd stop rooting around in my mind." There was just so much screwing she could do to the top—oops, another Freudian slip—so she finally looked at him. "You know, I can't believe you got hard after what almost happened to you a little while ago."

He watched her from those incredible eyes that made her breaths come quickly but told her nothing about the man inside. "Over the centuries, I've learned to compartmentalize. Once a compulsion is finished, and the woman leaves, I forget her." He reached out to slide his fingers lightly along her jaw. "You, my demon destroyer, might be a memory I choose to keep."

Oh boy. He was good. Time to change the topic. "So how are you going to handle my family? You can't avoid them for the whole time they're here."

His eyes darkened, and for the first time she got a hint of exactly how dangerous he could be. "I won't go out of my way to confront them, but I'm not going to hide in my own home. I have a few powers tucked away for times like this, and Holgarth, Eric, or Conall will always be close by." His oh-so-sensual lips lifted in a cold smile. "Your family will get more than they expected if they mess with anyone in the Castle of Dark Dreams."

Kim swallowed hard. Chilled to her heart, she backed toward the door. "Guess I'll head to my room." Potential disaster loomed on her personal horizon. She was caught smack-dab in the middle of a war zone without a clue how to head off what was to come or how to distance herself emotionally from either side.

When he made no attempt to soften his stand or stop her from leaving, she grabbed her jacket with Fo still in the pocket, and fled. Just outside the door she found Ganymede.

Kim looked around to make sure they were alone before talking. "Didn't you find Asima?"

"Yeah, I found her." Ganymede's narrowed gaze said it hadn't been as erotically fulfilling as he'd hoped. "She got really pissy when I told her I was a friend of Sparkle's." He looked resigned. "Sparkle has that effect on lots of people."

Kim bit her lip to keep from smiling. "Show some enthusiasm for her interests, and she'll come around."

She watched him turn that idea over in his mind. "May as well give it a try. So how's Brynn doing?" Ganymede poked his head around the corner of the still-open door.

"I took care of the welts." She wasn't about to discuss Brynn's coping skills with this shape-shifter friend of Sparkle's.

"He's not too happy with what he is." Ganymede sounded like his interest in Brynn's happiness ran a little deeper than mere curiosity.

Interesting. Which reminded her: "When I came out of the meeting room and told you where I was going, you didn't sound confused like Asima did. Any reason for that?"

The cat's eyes shifted away from her. He twitched his ears. "Sparkle filled me in on Brynn's problem. And since I'm a sensitive, caring kind of guy, I wanted to help."

Yeah, right. Most demons were dirty low-down liars. So part of Kim's training had involved spotting a lie. Ganymede's eyes, body language, and voice all screamed that he'd just told her a big fat one. But why? She watched the cat slip into Brynn's room just before she quietly closed the door.

Shrugging away the question that was Ganymede, Kim pulled Fo from her pocket as she headed for the elevator. First she'd go down to pick up her stuff from the meeting room, and then she'd wait for Lynsay and the mysterious Uncle Dirk.

* * *

"Look at it this way, you have the best of all worlds. You have a new furry buddy—someone smart, funny, and lovable. Someone to share your worries with. Someone who can offer you great advice when—"

"Get out of my fridge, cat." Brynn glanced up from where he was spreading a sheet over the couch. No way was he sleeping on that bed again. He'd buy a new bed tomorrow. Maybe he'd take Kim with him to help him choose. *Bad idea, pal.*

"Got any ice cream in this freezer?" Ganymede stared at the freezer door until it swung open.

Damned cat wasn't going to leave him alone until he fed it. Brynn abandoned the couch to go into his kitchenette. Grabbing a bowl and spoon from the dishwasher, he pulled an ice cream carton from the freezer and then pushed the door closed. "I don't know why I'm doing this. You can probably get your own ice cream without my help."

"Yeah, but it's so much more fun when I can irritate someone into doing it for me. It's all about the power trip." He watched with greedy eyes as Brynn started to spoon ice cream into the bowl. "Whoa, big fella. Just put the carton on the floor. I'm going to eat the whole thing anyway."

"So what are you when you're not being a pain in the butt?" Brynn really didn't care, but caution demanded that he know something about his furry roommate. Then he'd find a way to get rid of him.

"I'm a cosmic troublemaker like Sparkle. We go back a long way. I'm in cat form because I like to, you know, get a feeling for the place and the people." Ganymede frowned at the ice cream carton still in Brynn's hand.

"You like to spy on people." *Why here and why now?*

"Yeah, so?" He was still staring at the ice cream. "Why here? Here is where my hot candy mama is. Why now? She lured me with promises of hot sex." Ganymede glanced up at Brynn from eyes that said, *I'm sneaky and proud of it.* "But see, she got sort of pissed at me—you noticed the pink ribbon—and thought she'd pawn me off on Kim for a while. Hey, I don't pawn. So I decided I'd bunk down with you until she got over her mad. Oh, and when I'm not being a lovable cat, I'm the best lookin' guy in the world."

"You were in my head." Brynn rubbed his hand across his face. Jeez, he was tired. Normally, he would've made it harder for the cat to get into his thoughts.

Ganymede didn't deny it. "Uh, the ice cream carton? I don't see it in front of my face yet." He tracked the carton with lust-filled eyes as Brynn leaned over to set it on the floor.

"This isn't Ben & Jerry's. You've got zero ice cream taste, demon. I'll upgrade your frozen dessert choices tomorrow." Ganymede's disdain for Brynn's ice cream didn't stop him from burying his furry face in the carton once it was on the floor.

As Brynn grabbed his pillow from the bed and threw it onto the couch, he thought about the instant gratification he'd get from tossing the cat out the door. Two things stopped him. He didn't have to take a second look into Ganymede's eyes to recognize the power there. Kicking the cat out when he didn't want to leave might take more effort than he was willing to expend tonight. Besides, he had a gut feeling Ganymede had an agenda. No one could look at that shifty amber gaze and think differently. So he might be wise to keep the cat close until he found out how that agenda would impact him.

He gritted his teeth and tried not to react when Ganymede finished his ice cream, leaped onto the coffee table, and plunked his paw onto the TV remote.

Ganymede burped noisily and then stretched out on the table next to the remote. It looked like Brynn was in for another viewing of *Men in Black*.

Brynn glanced at his watch. Too early for the fantasies to be over, but he needed to warn everyone about the Vaughns. Reaching for the phone, he called Holgarth's cell phone and passed on the bad news. Holgarth would tell everyone.

Then he called the desk and had them ring Wade's room. Luckily, he caught the demon in. "Just wanted to give you a heads-up. Kim's sister and Uncle Dirk will arrive sometime tonight. They're loaded for demons. You might want to move to another hotel."

"Uncle Dirk?" Something about Wade's voice didn't sound right. "You know him?"

"Dirk Vaughn? Sure, I know who he is. We both like to fish. Made sure I never met him face-to-face, for obvious reasons. Guess he's here for the fishing tournament on Saturday. Thanks for the warning."

"Kim has never met him either, but evidently he got a tip that the castle was crawling with demons. I'll be keeping a low profile until they're gone." He was a fool for staying, but something in him didn't want Kim to see him running away from her relatives. And why he gave a damn what Kim thought of him was an unsettling mystery.

It wasn't until he'd hung up that he realized Ganymede had turned off the TV. Trying to ignore the cat's interested stare, he sank onto the couch. "Won't be able to sleep on my back until tomorrow night." He'd drape the towel across his hips, but that's about all that would touch him tonight.

The trigger words *touch* and *night* pulled up the memory of Kim's smooth fingers sliding across his flesh—comforting, undemanding, and incredibly arousing. And when he'd turned around to find her fingers poised above his cock, the impact had been more erotic than all the practiced sensuality of the endless stream of women who'd touched his body in passion.

"So what's it like being a sex demon?"

Brynn waited for the expected leer, but it didn't come. He shrugged. "You like ice cream, but what if you ate it every day for centuries?"

"I have." Ganymede blinked. "Your point is?"

"Okay, wrong example." Brynn raked his fingers through his hair. "What happens to anyone who tries to force you to do something?"

The cat narrowed his amber gaze on Brynn. His tail whipped from side to side. "The world gets one more stupid dead person."

"Do I have to spell it out for you?" Brynn was growing tired of this. He wanted to lie down and lose tonight in sleep.

"Well, can't you just make sure you spend your time with great-looking chicks who aren't pushy like Liz? You know, sweet and submissive babes?" He looked hopeful.

Then Ganymede's hopeful expression faded to wistful. "Sweet and submissive sounds good right now. Guess they're a little hard to find, though. Personally, fiery and kick-ass does it for me. But sometimes those kinds of women are a little harder to manipulate. I didn't get to spend even a half hour with Asima. I mean, Sparkle's my main squeeze, but sometimes it's nice to be around a different face, get another woman's perspective." His cat scowl said that Asima's "perspective" wasn't even on his radar. "You don't know when you have it good, demon. You can spend all your time picking those ripe cherries off the tree."

Brynn wanted to shake Ganymede's chubby black body until he rattled. "You just don't get it, do you? You think my life is all great sex with beautiful women? Most of the time I don't get to choose, cat. Want an example? A few hundred years ago I was ordered to guard the eighty-year-old mother of an important official. I had to stay with her for a whole day, couldn't leave her out of my sight." He winced at the memory. "When the first hour was up I did my thing—ripped off my clothes, offered her my body, the usual."

Ganymede stared at him with avid interest. "Bet she was pissed. Did her old heart give out? Did her feeble old legs fold from the shock?"

Brynn reached over to turn off the lamp. "No, she ripped off her clothes and then used her feeble old legs to jump me. And her feeble old heart was beating just fine after a full day of sex. Lesson learned, mature women have a hell of a sex drive."

"Ouch. Bummer." Ganymede remained silent in the darkened room. "How do you feel about Kim?"

"She's okay." He closed his eyes, remembering his red-haired warrior charging into battle against Liz. Brynn smiled into the darkness. She'd embarrassed the hell out of him, but she was the first person in five hundred years who'd braved his wrath to save him. "Yeah, she's really okay."

"What're you going to do about her?"

Brynn thought about trying to keep track of the time every minute he was with her. About seeing her expression if he miscalculated and had to go off with another woman while she was watching. About her knowing how many women he'd been with and would be with in the future.

"Nothing. I'm not going to do a damned thing about her."

9

So far, today felt like a normal day. Of course, she'd only been up for an hour. And what constituted "normal" had grown a little fuzzy since she'd arrived at the Castle of Dark Dreams.

Kim had showered and then pulled on her jeans and an old Dallas Mavericks T-shirt. Lynsay had called a few minutes ago. She'd gotten in late and wanted Kim to meet her for breakfast. Kim glanced at her watch. She still had a half hour to kill.

"Are we going somewhere today, Kimmie?" Fo didn't sound like she'd suffered any ill effects from her accident. "Maybe Brynn will go with us if he feels okay. I'm glad you used me against the vampire bitch. When I saw what she'd done to Brynn I wished she was a demon so I could turn her into a pile of ash."

Kim frowned. Fo's evolution from machine to sentient being was taking a few turns Kim wasn't sure she liked. "After breakfast I'll probably just come back here and work on the ideas everyone contributed last night."

"I think this castle should have an oubliette, you know, one of those deep holes you can dump a Liz into and forget about her forever." Fo the fiendish.

"Bloodthirsty little thing, aren't you?"

Fo's eyes looked happy. "I'm becoming more human."

"Uh-huh. And where did you learn about oubliettes? More to the point, where are you learning words like *bitch* and *slut*?" Fo's learning curve was upwardly mobile, and Kim wasn't too comfortable with that. What happened when Fo became human enough to resent what she was?

"I have access to many online sources." Fo blinked. "And I learned those words by listening very carefully to what people were saying around me. Is that wrong?"

"Uh, no." Nothing Kim could say to that. She sure couldn't go around warning people to watch their language in front of her cell phone.

For the moment, Kim pushed the problem of Fo from her mind. Instead, she pulled up a visual from last night. Not the one of Brynn stretched out on the bed. Thinking about that made Kim want to sit right down and design an oubliette.

No, the particular mental picture guaranteed to rev her up until she got her first shot of caffeine was the one of Brynn standing facing her, all broad, muscular shoulders, sculpted pecs, six-pack abs, and strong thighs roped with muscle. A weaker woman wouldn't venture further, because the heart could only take so much excitement this early in the morning. But Kim believed in finishing what she'd started, so she remembered . . . everything. The length, the breadth, the exact degree of arousal . . .

"Yo, Kimmie, you're getting all red like Deimos."

Kim exhaled sharply, releasing her visual, just as someone knocked on her door. Before opening it, she picked up Fo. Who knew what might be on the other side of any door in the Castle of Dark Dreams?

A smiling Wade waited for her on the other side this time. He stepped inside as soon as she swung the door open. "How you doing this morning, little lady?" His gaze narrowed on Fo. "I came over to see what I could do to replace your cell phone, but I see it's just fine." His expression said he didn't understand how the hell it could be fine after he'd stomped all over it.

Kim smiled up at him. "Lucky for me, Brynn was able to put it back together again." Since Wade seemed to be an ordinary person in a castle where ordinariness was at a premium, Kim set Fo back on the bureau.

Without warning, the object of her lustful mental pictures strode into the room. Kim could almost hear the air crackling and sizzling from all that awesome sensual energy Brynn brought with him. Her hair had to be standing on end. She resisted the urge to touch it. And could anyone in the universe look that good in worn jeans and a plain white T-shirt? She didn't think so.

Kim gave her lust some downtime while she wondered how much pain he was in with the cloth rubbing against his back and buttocks.

"Hope I didn't interrupt anything." Brynn cast a guarded look at Wade.

Guarded? Nah. "Wade just stopped over to talk about replacing my cell phone. I told him not to worry because you put the old one back together again."

"Thanks for saving me money." Wade didn't look grateful.

Kim could've sworn what he wanted to say was, "What a stupid thing to do." *Alert. Alert. Imagination overload.* The castle was messing with her, suggesting undercurrents where none existed.

The two men stood staring at each other. No one said anything, not even Fo. Kim prepared to leap into the breach and loose a full-blown babble attack, but just as she opened her mouth, Sparkle rushed into the room.

"Oh, goody. You haven't left yet." Dressed in a short black leather skirt, a black silk camisole, and teetering on metallic silver stilettos, Sparkle was enough to warm the heart of any man who yearned for the ultimate mistress of pain.

Kim wondered where she'd left her whip. Then Kim noticed the clothes draped over Sparkle's arm along with the shoes dangling from her fingers. Uh-oh.

"Hi, guys." Sparkle's whole persona changed as she turned to greet the men. Her mouth became poutier, and she slid her tongue across her lower lip to call attention to its lusciousness. Her amber eyes shone with appreciation for all things male. She blinked, just in case the males in question had missed her message. Ha, as though any man could miss Sparkle's invite to all things sexual.

Okay, no need to morph into Super Bitch. It wasn't as though she was jealous of Sparkle. Kim glanced at Brynn, whose attention was riveted on Sparkle. Okay, maybe just a twinge. Not enough to even mention. Definitely *not* mentioning it.

"So what brings you here, Sparkle?" Kim noted that Wade's stare was fixed on Sparkle, too. "Oh, I don't think you know Wade. He's here for some fishing. Wade, meet Sparkle Stardust. She owns Sweet Indulgence, a candy store right outside the park."

"Well, well." Sparkle the Sexy had a new dimension. She was now Sparkle the Sexy Hunter. "I never knew they made fishermen so big and beautiful." She moved closer to him, every motion a sensual shimmy of swaying hips and bouncing boobs.

Kim frowned. *Give me a break*. Wade wouldn't fall for that, would he? She glanced at Wade's rapt expression. He would. Better say something before Sparkle sucked Wade dry and then turned to Brynn. "Can I help you with anything?"

"Uh . . ." Sparkle visibly forced her attention from Wade, sort of like hearing the pop when you yank a suction cup off the wall. "Oh, yeah. I forgot." She offered Kim her brightest smile. "I had to run right up here to tell you that you won!"

"Won?" Kim pictured Sparkle running up the steps in those four-inch slut-queen heels. Ouch. But if anyone could run in them, Sparkle could.

Sparkle raised one brow. "My contest. The prize is the loan of some ultracool clothes guaranteed to turn any man—or a reasonable facsimile of such—into a hungry male animal. You get one outfit a day for a week."

"When did I enter your contest?" Confused here.

"When you bought that pitiful bag of lemon drops. Anyone who buys my candy gets his or her name entered in the weekly contest. The prizes change from week to week, but lucky you, this week the winner gets to wear some awesome clothes. I have to say that no one more worthy entered. Anyone who'd pass on chocolate for lemon drops is in deep need of my help, sister." Sparkle's expression said everything should be perfectly clear now.

Brynn was staring at the clothes draped over Sparkle's arm.

Don't ask. Kim wanted to reach out and clap her hand over Brynn's mouth.

He asked. "So what do you have there?"

Rats. So much for Kim's ordinary day.

"Glad you asked." Sparkle's expression said it was really unusual to find an incredibly hot stud smart enough to ask a meaningful question.

"I think that's Monday's outfit." Kim eyed the shoes still dangling from Sparkle's fingers. The heels weren't as extreme as Sparkle's, but they were still major owies.

Sparkle beamed at Kim. "This is your first day's prize. Each day for a week I'll bring you an outfit that'll burn Galveston to the ground."

"And I need these why?"

"Because what you're wearing is pitiful." Sparkle was all business now. "The Dallas Mavericks? Using one of your most sensual assets, your chest, to promote a sports team? Do the Dallas Mavericks say sexy? I don't think so. Really sad, girlfriend." She handed Kim the first piece of clothing. "A sexy Versace beaded halter top. The beads are a Sparkle Stardust modification. One hundred twenty-eight dollars."

Wade's eyes brightened. "Funny thing, I just bought a G. Loomis tackle box for one hundred thirty dollars. Needed a new one for this week's fishing tournament." He shifted his gaze to Brynn. "Great tackle box."

Sparkle didn't look impressed. She handed Kim the next item. "Ultrahot Gucci studded black low-rise pants. The studs are also a modification by *moi*. Three hundred ten dollars." She stared at Wade, daring him to match that.

Wade accepted the challenge. "Picked up a pair of top-of-the-line Van Staal pliers for taking hooks out. Three hundred fourteen dollars." He didn't bother even trying to include Brynn in the conversation anymore. His gaze stayed fixed on Sparkle.

Sparkle raised one expressive brow. "Christian Louboutin black leather slingbacks. Four hundred ninety-five dollars." She shoved the shoes into Kim's hands.

Wade's eyes lit with triumph. "Got a Shimano CTE200DC reel for four hundred ninety-nine dollars and ninety-five cents the other day. Can't wait to use it in the tournament."

Sparkle patted Kim's hand, but her gaze never left Wade. "Put these on and have Brynn take a picture of you in them so I can see how you look."

Wade's gaze warmed. "I can tell you're a woman who appreciates the best in life. How about coming with me so I can show you my boat?"

"I admire a man who can outspend me. Only a special few have that kind of talent." Sparkle's smile was whipped cream with a plump red cherry in the middle. "Deimos can watch my store for another hour. I'd love to see those really expensive pliers."

Yeah, right. Kim watched as Sparkle walked to the door with Wade. She turned for one last word with Kim. "Remember, it's not just what you wear, but how you wear it. Get yourself some attitude." Her gaze slipped past Kim and then froze. "Where's Sweetie Pie and Jessica?"

"Who? Oh, the plants." Kim was still focused on the clothes. Not what she usually wore, but hot, definitely hot. "I told Deimos to keep them."

"Deimos?" Sparkle's tone said Kim might as well have dumped a jar of aphids on them. "Deimos is a virgin. They'll be nothing but bare sticks by the end of the week. Sweetie Pie and Jessica are the owner's favorites." She speared Kim with a hard glare. "Why'd you make Deimos take them?"

Kim toyed with asking her why she was so bent out of shape over the plants but decided it would only prolong Sparkle's stay. "Deimos said the plants needed lots of . . . stuff happening to keep them happy and healthy. They weren't going to get it in my room."

Sparkle's gaze turned sly. "Oh, I wouldn't be too sure of that, sister." With that parting shot, she followed Wade out.

It was a testament to the weirdness of the castle that neither Brynn nor Wade had tried to question Sparkle about the leafy sexual-energy guzzlers.

Okay, two down and one to go. Although Kim was a little conflicted about the go part. "I didn't get a chance to find out why you dropped by."

Brynn smiled, sucking all the air from Kim's lungs. Jeez, she wished he wouldn't do that.

"I'm going mattress hunting today." He didn't spell out why he needed a new mattress. He didn't have to. "I have a few things to do here first, but I thought you might want to get away from the castle for a while."

Common sense said the worst thing she could do was to go mattress hunting with the enemy. Well, maybe not the enemy, but certainly Lynsay would count him as one of the unfriendly spirits.

Kim thought about what Lynsay would say, and then she thought about what she wanted to do. No contest. This was a day to wear sexy clothes and go shopping with a demon.

She glanced at her watch. "I'm meeting my sister for breakfast in about ten minutes. How about if I meet you in the hotel lobby at eleven?" Kim frowned. "How will you know if Lynsay or Uncle Dirk are close by?"

His smile was slow and supremely sensual. "Once I leave here,

I'll make some calls. I wouldn't be surprised if you had a few people join you for breakfast. By the time I meet you, everyone will know what your sister and uncle look like." He leaned close. "Don't worry about my safety." His breath fanned her cheek, setting off a remote explosion that released all kinds of erotic possibilities. "Worry about your own. Shopping for a mattress with me can be lethal."

Kim smiled up at him. Sexy teasing? She wondered if he realized what he was doing.

He did. She watched the playfulness fade from his eyes to be replaced by a guarded expression. He moved away from her. After his centuries of thinking of women as the enemy, he probably didn't get playful very often. In fact, she'd bet he was regretting asking her to shop with him.

Time to change the subject before he took back his invite. "Does your back still hurt?" No, she wasn't going to ask about his bottom. He'd just have to assume she meant that, too.

"It's okay." Translation: it hurts like hell, but men don't admit they're in pain. "I heal faster than a human."

Kim kept her smile firmly in place. "Well, if the okay doesn't feel better by the time we get back, I can always put more cream on it."

The gold flared in his eyes, but his expression didn't change. "I'm sure I'll be a lot better than okay after I get my mattress." And right before he turned away, a smile touched that wonderful mouth. "But if not, I'll be sure to let you know."

As a parting shot, it was pretty good. But she couldn't let him get away without asking something important. "Look, would you tell these people you say will be joining me for breakfast not to mention that I'm working here as an architect? My family thinks I'm demon hunting."

He paused, and she thought he would say something, but he must've thought better of it. "Sure."

Kim watched him leave and close the door behind him. Finally, she allowed herself to relax.

Why exactly were the two of them going shopping together?

Talk about your fatal attraction. And it would definitely be fatal to Brynn if her family had any input. Kim firmed her lips as she walked over to pick Fo up from the bureau. She'd just have to make sure her family didn't find out about him. *When did you get into the demon-protecting business?* She hadn't a clue.

Fo. Kim had sensed there was a missing mouth during the conversation. Fo hadn't said one thing. Not normal behavior. Kim picked up the demon detector—couldn't really call Fo that anymore—and paused to look into the wide purple eyes. "Why didn't you say anything?"

"I was afraid of Wade. He looked at me with mean eyes. I thought if I talked, he might throw me on the floor and step on me again." Fo somehow managed to convey fear with just her eyes.

Fear, another very human emotion. Kim carried Fo to her purse. "Oh, he's an okay guy. He didn't step on you on purpose." She slipped Fo into the outside pocket of her purse where Fo continued to peer up at her.

"I think he did do it on purpose, Kimmie." Fo sounded plaintive. "He's not human, you know."

Kim slumped onto her bed. Damn. She would've sworn that Wade was a normal guy. She didn't know which way was up anymore. Fo and she were useless, wandering aimlessly among hordes of supernatural beings. She'd probably meet a werewolf on her way down to the restaurant, maybe strike up a conversation with a fairy while she was browsing in the hotel bookstore, or excuse herself to an ancient goddess that she bumped into on her way out the door. And then she'd stroll away with a dumb smile on her face because she . . . didn't . . . have . . . a . . . clue.

After staring into space for a few minutes, she heaved a sigh and stood up. "Okay, pity party over, Fo." She picked up her purse and slung it over her shoulder. "We do know one thing for sure. Brynn is a demon, but we like him because he was kind to you." That wasn't the only reason Kim liked him, but she wasn't about to admit anything else to Fo. Fo didn't keep secrets well.

"And we have to protect him from your family." Fo had perked up. "Right."

Kim chose to use the stairs instead of the elevator. No way did she want a surprise meeting with Asima again. She sensed storm clouds on the horizon if Sparkle found out that Ganymede was chasing Asima or if Ganymede discovered Wade was giving boat tours. The explosion would probably send Galveston to the bottom of the Gulf.

As she made her way down the narrow stone stairway lit only by authentic-looking wall sconces, Kim's imagination drifted to a picture of what Brynn would look like walking down the stairs ahead of her. Naked. His broad shoulders would gleam in the fake candlelight. The muscles in his back would flex beneath smooth, golden skin. The taut, perfect cheeks of his . . .

Okay, why was she obsessing? Reluctantly, she banished Brynn's hot bod from the step in front of her and tried to think logically. She could chalk it up to being twenty-seven with hormones popping like overheated kernels of corn. Hey, her hormones wanted to have Brynn's baby.

Or could her fixation have a more sinister origin? Dub in scary music here. If Brynn could read her thoughts and change women's memories after they had sex with him, then maybe he could make her lust for his body. She frowned as she reached the lobby and headed for the restaurant. Hmm. Flaw in reasoning. Brynn didn't *want* women to desire him.

That left only the hormone theory. Personally, she preferred the other one. Because if Brynn wasn't doing this to her, then that meant she was doing it to herself. Which made her really uneasy, because she couldn't remember feeling this level of lust for any man in her past, no matter how yummy.

Kim paused in the doorway to the restaurant. As she scanned the room she saw Lynsay waving madly. A man sat at the same table. The mysterious Uncle Dirk? Weaving her way to the table, she sat down.

"This place is amazing, Sis." Lynsay grinned at her. "I can almost feel the demonic vibes all around me." She motioned to the man sitting beside her. "Meet Uncle Dirk. I think we'll need his help here." She widened her smile for Uncle Dirk—the same smile she used whether she was opening birthday presents or offing a demon. Lynsay had an equal opportunity smile. "And this is my sister Kim, Uncle Dirk."

"Glad to meet you, Dirk." Kim was damned if she'd call a man she'd never met before Uncle Dirk. As she smiled and shook hands with him, she took inventory.

Overall impression? Ordinary. Ordinary height, ordinary face, ordinary everything. Middle aged, maybe fifty. Gray suit, blue shirt, tie—business type and not adventurous so far as his wardrobe went. Washed-out brown eyes to match short brown hair fading to gray. In a guess-my-profession contest, no one would ever peg him as a demon hunter. And that's exactly the bland impression he'd want to project. So all in all, a perfect cover.

He offered her a polite smile, not showing a lot of teeth. "I'm sure the Castle of Dark Dreams will be a satisfying experience for all of us." He shifted his gaze to someone standing behind Kim.

Kim turned her head in time to see Holgarth in full wizard costume. He offered her his usual supercilious smile. "I thought I might join you for a few minutes." Without waiting for anyone's objection, he sat in the empty chair to Kim's right.

Kim frowned. Brynn had said a few people might join her for breakfast, but before she even ordered? Sheesh. "Lynsay, Dirk, this is Holgarth. He . . . does things at the castle." What *was* Holgarth's title here? "Holgarth, this is my sister and uncle. Both Vaughns. We're a big family."

Holgarth nodded and offered them a thin-lipped smile. Holgarth the Jolly. "Please go ahead and order. I won't be here long."

By this time a waitress decked out in medieval dress was hovering. Kim ordered orange juice, pancakes swimming in syrup, and coffee. Not healthy, but she deserved some comfort food this morning. Then she leaned back to hear what Holgarth had to say.

Holgarth reached up to center his tall conical hat—did he sleep in that hat?—and then speared Dirk with a piercing stare. No one did piercing as well as Holgarth. "I'm assuming you're on vacation from your business. What exactly would that be?" He could be so subtle when he chose.

For just a moment, something flared in Dirk's eyes and then was gone. Kim blinked, not sure she'd seen what she thought she'd seen. Whatever it was, it didn't leave her with a warm fuzzy feeling.

Holgarth must've seen the same thing because he narrowed his eyes and tightened his lips to a thin, disapproving line.

Dirk's expression remained bland and slightly amused. "Good to meet you, Holgarth." He politely refrained from asking, "Holgarth what?" He took a sip of the coffee he'd evidently ordered before Kim arrived. "I have business interests in various parts of the world. I'd decided to do some fishing near Galveston, so I called Texas members of the Vaughn family to see if any of them would like to join me here. It's always nice to touch base with relatives you've never met." His gaze rested on Kim and Lynsay with fake benevolence.

Fake? Where'd that thought come from? "Yeah, family get-togethers are always fun." Not.

Holgarth remained tight-lipped as he nodded and then stood. "I'm gratified that you chose the Castle of Dark Dreams." He didn't look gratified. "I hope your stay is enjoyable." Holgarth stared at Lynsay. Evidently, he didn't give a damn whether Dirk had a good time. "Feel free to come to me with any concerns you might have." This was aimed directly at Kim, and he didn't smile when he said it.

Uh-oh. Holgarth's first impression of Dirk hadn't made him a happy wizard. Dirk, on the other hand, seemed perfectly satisfied with Holgarth. He turned away for a few last words with the wizard.

"Kimmie, aren't you going to introduce me?" Fo's whisper sounded as though her feelings were hurt.

"No." Kim hoped Lynsay and Dirk were too busy saying good-bye to Holgarth to hear her hissed reply.

What was she going to do with Fo? More and more Fo was interjecting herself into conversations, demanding that she be treated like a human. Kim couldn't hide her away. That wouldn't be fair to Fo. But she had to make her aware that talking to strangers could be dangerous.

Once Holgarth was gone, Lynsay and Dirk turned back to her. Thank heavens, Fo had subsided into a silent pout.

"An unusual man." Dirk looked thoughtful.

"Uh-huh." Kim figured uh-huh was ambiguous enough to be safe. "So how was the drive from Dallas? Whose car did you take?" Maybe a change of subject would get Dirk's mind off of Holgarth.

"We didn't come together." Lynsay watched the waitress approaching with their breakfasts. "I drove down by myself. More of the family would've come, but the Texas Paranormal Phenomena Convention is this weekend in Austin. I decided I'd rather meet Uncle Dirk and do some serious demon hunting."

"I trailered my boat here from Florida. It's at a local marina." He frowned. "My timing was unfortunate. I didn't know about the convention."

"Don't worry about it, Uncle Dirk. The rest of the family will ride to our rescue if we get overrun by demons." Lynsay looked gleeful at the possibility. "Do you still have that useless piece of crap you laughingly call a demon detector, Sis?"

Kim tried to ignore the angry hiss coming from said useless piece of crap. "Yes." She refused to apologize or make excuses. Fo was more amazing than Lynsay would ever know.

Lynsay shook her head at the futility of trying to snare demons without a state-of-the-art detector. "Take a look at this baby."

She fished in her purse and came up with a detector that had a case much like Fo's, but there the similarity ended. At the base of the screen were enough small buttons to land a 747. And the screen itself showed row after row of words and numbers that meant squat to Kim. Scary.

"Top-of-the-line. It scans everyone who comes within twenty

feet, analyzes them in ten seconds, and recommends destruction when necessary." Lynsay's face glowed with the pride of a mother.

Kim tried to control her laughter as she got a mental picture of her sister in labor and the doctor's face when Lynsay popped out her precious demon detector.

"That looks interesting. What is it?" The deep voice belonged to Conall, who'd sneaked up on them while Lynsay was bragging.

Kim smiled up at him. "A demon detector. Doesn't have much personality, but I guess it does its job." She motioned to the seat Holgarth had occupied.

Lynsay gasped and then glared at her. Dirk still wore his blandly amused expression.

Conall gave the response Lynsay and Dirk would expect. "Yeah, right. Well, if I see any demons hanging around, I'll give a shout." He laughed.

But Conall's amusement never reached his eyes as he studied Lynsay and Dirk. "How's the castle treating you?"

"Conall, this is my sister Lynsay and my uncle Dirk."

He nodded his greeting. "I'm Conall McNair. My brothers and I see that the castle runs smoothly. We also act in the fantasies that run from eight p.m. to four a.m." He winked at Lynsay. "Drop by some night, and we'll do a fantasy especially for you."

Lynsay flushed with pleasure. Who wouldn't? Conall had shaggy dark brown hair that framed a face so masculine it made Kim's teeth hurt. His face was a series of contradictions. It was hard with the memory of too many battles and too many deaths. But his full, sensual mouth promised that in between the battles he'd made lots of women happy. The dark slash of his brows and the hard line of his jaw would make most men pause before challenging him. But his gray eyes fringed with long, dark lashes softened the impact enough to make him simply gorgeous to women.

"What, no fantasy for me?" Dirk smiled his semi-smile. The one that looked like he was conserving lip energy.

Conall cast a sharp glance his way. "We have a fantasy to fit every taste." His smile was polite, nothing more.

Hmm. Looked like Holgarth and Conall found Lynsay likable and Dirk not so. Of course, that might be because Lynsay had long blond hair, big blue eyes, a pouty mouth, and a curvy body. Dirk didn't. That was just Kim's guess, though.

The thing everyone would have to understand was that behind Lynsay's big blue eyes lurked the heart of a serial killer. Lynsay loved to destroy demons, and if a few luckless humans got in her way, so be it. The family spent lots of time and money getting Lynsay out of trouble.

"Have to get back to work now." Conall rose to his full six feet whatever, towering over them. A little intimidation? Probably. "Enjoy your stay."

Dirk watched Conall leave from eyes that gave none of his feelings away. "Lynsay told me you've only been here since Saturday night, but everyone seems to know you." He turned his inscrutable gaze on Kim.

Think fast. "I barged into the great hall while the Vampire Ball was in full swing. I hadn't a clue what was happening, so Holgarth sort of took me under his wing and introduced me to the three Mc-Nair brothers who run the place." Weak, really weak. Kim got this mental picture of a giant vulture with its wing draped over her shoulders.

Dirk simply nodded. "Live the Fantasy is a fascinating concept for a theme park. Open twenty-four hours a day and allowing adults to indulge in dozens of role-playing situations. I'd say the Castle of Dark Dreams is the most intriguing of all the attractions in the park. An authentic-looking castle, hotel, and fantasy world all rolled into one." Suddenly, his gaze sharpened. "Have you found any demons?"

"No." A direct lie. Kim felt ashamed and defiant at the same time. She might have avoided her demon hunting duties at times, but she'd never out-and-out lied about them.

Brynn didn't deserve to die, though. *How do you know? You only know what he's told you, and demons lie. If he was really gross-looking would you still be as sympathetic?* She didn't know, but she hoped she'd still care enough about any being's life to make sure they really deserved to die before pushing that red button.

Kim took a deep, cleansing breath and shifted her gaze to Lynsay. Her sister was frowning at her demon detector.

"It just went dead." Lynsay poked at the small buttons, but the detector's screen remained dark. "It was fine a few minutes ago, but now I'm getting nothing. What the hell happened to it?" She looked at Dirk. "What do I do now? I can't just call Dad to overnight another one. We don't have any extras at home right now. He'll have to order another one and then send it on to me. That'll take almost a week."

Dirk shrugged. "No matter. You have good instincts. If you sense a demon near, tell me, and I'll destroy it." For the first time, he really smiled. It wasn't a pretty sight. "Let me show you my detector. It's quite something else." He reached into his jacket pocket and pulled out a detector that looked like the prerequisite cell phone. He flipped it open and turned the screen toward them.

Kim gasped. Looking back at her were two large red eyes with black slits for pupils. *Demon eyes.*

"The eyes give it a distinctive touch, even though I can't take credit for them. Its creator built this beauty and then died. Too bad. What *was* his name? Sergei something or other." Dirk didn't sound very sorry. "Mine is the only one in existence. The eyes just appeared on the screen one day. At first I tried to delete them, but then decided it wasn't worth the effort."

Kim was about to pull Fo out and announce that yes, the creator *had* built another one, when she changed her mind. For whatever reason, her instinct was telling her to keep her mouth shut. Lynsay had seen Fo, but that was before Kim had claimed her, before Fo had created her own designer eyes, and before Fo had said her first word, which had since led to an endless stream of words.

Lynsay stared at Dirk's detector. "How does it clue you in to a demon if those eyes take up the whole screen?"

Dirk smiled some more. "It speaks. Just a few basic sentences, enough to pinpoint the demon."

Lynsay nodded. "Cool."

"Umm, mind if I sit down for a minute, Kim?" That deep, hesitant voice could belong to only one person.

With a sigh of resignation, Kim pointed to the same empty chair Holgarth and Conall had occupied. Deimos sat down, dwarfing the chair, the table, and the people sitting around it.

Lynsay's eyes widened. "Wow, did anyone ever tell you that you look just like Vin Diesel?"

Deimos found that observation blush-worthy, and everyone watched, mesmerized, as the red marched up his neck, across his face, and then over the top of his shaved head.

"Cute." Lynsay had spoken.

Once again, Kim made introductions all around. "Deimos works part-time in the castle and in Sweet Indulgence, the candy store you passed on the way into the park."

Deimos didn't even pretend to pay equal attention to Dirk. He stared at Lynsay with open admiration, his amber eyes glowing with adoration. Kim did a few mental eye rolls.

"If you have some free time, Lynsay, I'd really like to show you around the castle and the rest of the park." His blush deepened in response to his daring invitation. "They have a neat mock-up of New York City, and you can pretend to be any superhero you want. Then you get to kill all the villains."

Lynsay leaned forward, her eyes bright with interest. "Really? Hey, I'd love to do some role-playing as Cat Woman."

Kim figured Deimos had gotten lucky—or not, as the case may be. "Kill all the villains" had been the magic words. But Kim didn't know how Lynsay would react when she found out that her big bad superhero was a virgin. Lynsay loved men, and not for their minds. Kim hoped Lynsay would be gentle with Deimos. She couldn't control the smile that tugged at her lips. Maybe Sweetie Pie and Jessica wouldn't lose all their leaves after all.

"When will you be free?" Deimos looked as though he wanted to grab Lynsay's hand right now and make off with her.

Lynsay looked at her watch. "I'll be sitting in the lobby at one. We can eat lunch and then do the tour." She glanced at Dirk. "Did you have anything planned then?"

Dirk shook his head. "Go and have fun. If things develop the way I think they will, you'll be kept busy destroying demons the rest of the week."

That pronouncement sent a shiver of dread down Kim's spine. She ate the rest of her breakfast in silence while Lynsay and Deimos discussed the strengths and weaknesses of the superhero population. Dirk didn't have much to say either as he watched every person who entered the restaurant with unwavering interest. Did he expect demons by the dozen to be rolling in for a late breakfast? Obviously.

Finally, Deimos left, and the others finished their meals. Kim urged them to leave when they offered to sit with her until she finished eating. After they left the restaurant, Kim relaxed. But not for long.

"Yo, Kim, up here." Ganymede's mental shout bounced around in her brain.

She winced and then looked up. Ganymede and Asima crouched together on the exposed beam above her. Quickly, she scanned the restaurant to make sure no one had spotted the two cats. Luck was with all of them. Most of the diners had left, and the few who remained were busy with their food.

"Your uncle looks like a sneaky, manipulating kinda guy. I like that in a man. But I think you need to be careful around him. Don't let him use you to get to Brynn." Ganymede shifted his gaze to a woman sitting at a nearby table. *"Whatta you think my chances are of snitching that last piece of bacon?"*

Kim scowled at him.

"Yeah, you're right. The Board of Health and all that crap." He turned to Asima. "Any words of wisdom, babe?"

Asima aimed a death glare at him. "*Call me babe again, and you'll have another scratch on your nose to match the one already there.*" She looked down at Kim. "*I think your sister is dressed like a tart. If I didn't know better I'd say she shopped at the Sparkle Stardust Boutique of Bad Taste. No wonder Deimos was drooling all over her. Immature boys like clothes that are blatantly sexual. I'll have to take a look at her wardrobe and suggest a few elegant upgrades.*"

Oops. Better keep her contest win to herself. And Kim could tell Asima that Lynsay would eat dirt before she'd wear something that could be described as "elegant." Finishing her coffee, she pushed away from the table. As she reached down for her purse with the still-silent Fo glaring up at her, Ganymede made a final comment.

"*I couldn't get into your uncle's mind. That's a big neon warning sign. There aren't many humans who can keep me out when I want in.*" Ganymede cast a speculative glance at the lonely piece of bacon the woman had abandoned. "*You know, I think I can get it. I'll sneak from table to table, jump onto the chair, reach up with a faster-than-light paw, and whip that baby off the plate.*"

Asima looked at him askance. "*Give me a running start out of here before you humiliate me in front of everyone.*"

Kim left the two to fight over the bacon and headed for the elevator. She'd just have time to freshen up and put on her tart outfit.

10

Brynn stepped off the elevator and looked around the lobby. He spotted Conall standing by the registration desk. Conall nodded at him, a signal that Lynsay and Dirk weren't nearby.

At least he knew what they looked like now. Holgarth had snapped a picture with his camera phone before stopping at their table this morning. Dirk looked pretty ordinary. That made him all the more dangerous. It was easy to dismiss the ordinary as non-threatening. And Lynsay looked young, cute, and enthusiastic. It was the enthusiastic part that worried Brynn.

He walked across the lobby searching for Kim. When he spotted her, his surge of pleasure surprised him. After he'd left her room, he'd tried to convince himself that it made good sense to keep her with him today. Sure it would be a hassle. He'd have to make an excuse to leave her for about five minutes at the end of each hour so he wouldn't have to embarrass them both by offering his body. But didn't it make sense to keep her close by so her sister and uncle couldn't draw her to the dark side? Yeah, that was stretching it a little. Kim wasn't the second coming of Darth Vader.

But wanting to spend time with Kim *was* dangerous. The more she knew about him, the more info she'd have to accidentally spill to her bloodthirsty relatives. Then why was he still walking toward her?

She'd been sitting in one of the lounge areas scattered around the lobby, but when she saw him she smiled and then stood. Now he knew why he was still walking toward her.

Wow. Give Sparkle a hand. A sexy little purple top that dipped low and clung to parts that deserved the attention, sexy black pants that emphasized every dangerous curve, and sexy little shoes with heels that made her legs go on forever. *Sexy.* That outfit touched his soul. Well, maybe not his soul. A soul wasn't standard equipment with a demon. But it sure touched something. And that something was growling its approval. He sure hoped she didn't decide to put on the jacket she was holding.

As he reached Kim, he glanced at his watch. He'd have to walk away from her in exactly fifty-five minutes. "You look good enough to eat." He frowned. That was Eric's line. Or maybe the werewolf in room 220. Brynn never said things like that. He never encouraged women to think he liked them except when the compulsion was in control.

"Really? Thanks." Her eyes shone with the happiness his comment had given her. "Let's get out of here before Asima spots us. She thought Lynsay looked like a tart, and I got the feeling she'd turn vicious if she saw me wearing a Sparkle creation. I don't want to chance a wardrobe malfunction if she tries to rip the clothes from my back."

Brynn grinned. Good thing she couldn't look into his mind. It wasn't the visual of Asima ripping the clothes from her *back* that had him looking around hopefully for the cat. "Let's get out of here then."

She stuffed a brochure she'd been holding into her purse. "A Miss Abby gave this to me right after I met you on Saturday night. I was taking a closer look. She owns Ye Olde Victorian Wedding

Chapel. From the photo, I'd say she ruined a beautiful Victorian home. It's amazing what a few cans of pink, blue, and yellow paint can do to a perfectly wonderful house."

"Never heard of the place." But then why would he? He wasn't planning a trip to a wedding chapel.

Kim smiled. "Maybe you should keep closer track of the brochures people leave lying around."

"Hi, Brynn." Fo's big purple eyes peered at him from the outside pocket of Kim's purse. "Kimmie says I can't talk with strangers because they might take me away from her and do terrible things to me. I'm not sure I believe her." For all her bravado, Fo slid her eyes to the left and right, checking to see if anyone was listening to her.

Brynn tried not to smile. "Kim's right, Fo. Scientists would like to take you apart to see what makes you so special, and the government would want to own you."

Fo seemed to think about that. "No one can own me, because I belong to me. But I'll try to keep quiet."

Kim smiled down at the detector. "When we go into a store, I'll turn your pocket toward me so no one will ask about you. You can still analyze everyone we meet, but I'd like you to wait until we leave the store before telling me what you think."

Kim might be smiling at Fo, but Brynn couldn't miss the worry in her eyes. She had to be torn between how to keep the developing intelligence that was Fo safe and yet not stifle her.

As they exited the castle, Brynn lifted his face to the sunny and surprisingly warm Galveston day. He felt good. Really great. Even with the threat of the demon-destroying Vaughns hanging over him. Go figure.

"I guess I don't need this jacket." Kim sounded almost disappointed.

He watched her fling the jacket onto the backseat of his car and put on her sunglasses before she slid into the passenger seat. She wasn't as secure in her new look as she'd like him to think. The jacket would've covered up at least half of it.

Once in the driver's seat, he turned to look at her. "You look great—sexy and beautiful." If he knew anything, he knew what sexy and beautiful women looked like. Not that he'd ever cared much about their looks. They'd been nothing more than a never-ending line of bodies he'd had to pleasure and a bunch of inter-changeable faces flushed with the ecstasy he'd brought them. He did ecstasy well. "But Sparkle was right. You need some attitude to go with those clothes."

"I can give her some of mine." Fo might be new to the conscious world, but she'd stored up an overflow of attitude.

"Thanks, Fo." Kim laughed as he turned off Seawall Boulevard and drove toward the island's only mattress store. "But attitude's easy. Every woman will know I have some serious stuff going on when they see me with you." Her smile lit up her face. "Just look at you." She leaned over to slide her fingers the length of his arm. "They'll wonder what I did to deserve running with a man who has such a fine . . . mind."

Surprised, he smiled at her. Kim wasn't the first woman to tease him, but she was the first one to do it and not earn a scowl. A scowl was protection. It said, *Leave me alone because I'm not a fun guy to be with.* Maybe he didn't feel he needed protection from Kim. Wrong assumption. The kind that could get him killed.

She studied him, but her glasses hid anything her eyes might re-veal. He could slip into her mind, but somehow he didn't want to do that. Not today. Today he wanted to be an ordinary guy out with his woman. Okay, so he could only be ordinary for fifty-five minutes out of each hour, and she'd never be his woman. But other than that, he wanted to pretend he was like every other man on the street.

"What do you want out of life, Kim?" Stupid question. He didn't need to know anything more than he already knew. Knowing things about people brought them closer. He didn't want to be closer to any woman. *Right. That's why you invited her to help you choose a new mattress. You didn't want to get closer to her.*

"I want to be ordinary." She seemed definite about that.

Uh-oh. They had something in common. Not good. He didn't need to do any bonding here.

"I want to be an architect who's normal in every possible way. Normal husband, normal children, normal house, normal everything." Her expression turned wistful.

That left him out. He was glad, right? He didn't want to be on her list of "normal" men. But if he felt like it, he could tell her that no matter what she did, she'd never be ordinary to him. He sensed she'd *always* be an extraordinary memory. He frowned. Where'd that thought come from? Thankfully, they reached the mattress store before he could explore its source.

As Kim climbed from the car, she put her finger to her lips to signal quiet for Fo. The detector mumbled her dissatisfaction but then lapsed into reluctant silence.

Brynn walked into the store behind Kim and immediately stopped to look at the first mattress he came to. "How about this one?" He sat on it. Felt okay. "I'll take this."

"Whoa there." Kim bit her bottom lip in concentration as she looked at the mattress. "You shop like a man. A mattress is an important investment. You don't buy the first one you see."

For a moment, Brynn lost all interest in mattresses as he watched her release her lip, and he thought about sliding his tongue across its soft fullness.

"Let's keep looking." She turned to study some of the others. "What are you looking for in a mattress?"

One that's only big enough for me, so that I never have to share it with a woman while I'm under the compulsion. Usually the woman took him to her place, and that was fine with him. He didn't want the memory of what he was haunting his bed.

He shrugged. "I like a firm mattress."

She nodded, happy. "There you go. That's a start."

"Can I help you?" The woman's voice was like melted butterscotch—sweet, thick, and sticky.

Brynn turned toward the voice. Two people stood watching

them. The woman was tall with breasts that were . . . He'd try again. The woman had long black hair that tumbled around her face, and she had breasts that were . . . Umm, she had long bare legs and breasts that were . . . He gave up and turned to Kim to see if she'd noticed the woman's breasts.

No, Kim was looking at the man standing beside the woman. And her gaze was fixed a lot lower than chest level. Brynn scowled. He'd never seen so much muscle on any guy, and he was wearing jeans that were so tight you could see . . . Jeez, he had to be kidding. No equipment was that big.

Brynn raised his gaze to meet the woman's expectant stare. And froze. Something glittered in her eyes that said nonhuman loud and clear. Without hesitation, he slipped into her mind. No real surprise when he heard the frenetic thought patterns of a demon. He'd known that no human could have breasts that big, that firm, and that pointed. He'd bet the guy's package was made in hell, too.

"I'm looking for a mattress." He'd buy the damn mattress, get Kim out of here, and then try to figure out what two demons were doing selling mattresses in Galveston.

The woman moved in close, brushing her breasts against his arm. "Mmm, I'm going to enjoy fitting you to the perfect mattress. Here, lie down on this one." She patted the mattress. "Then I'll lie down beside you to make sure the fit is right for two people"—she slid her tongue across her lower lip and took a deep breath—"snuggled really close together."

Brynn couldn't help it. His gaze slid down to where her bionic breasts swelled to gigantic proportions, struggling to escape the flimsy prison of her minimally-there pink top.

He lifted his gaze to her face. "What kind of demon are you, and why are you here?" Brynn doubted the demons had been here long, or Galveston would've felt the effects.

Kim had moved on to assess another mattress with Mr. Big. Brynn would have to make sure the male demon didn't draw her too far away.

The woman's eyes widened in shock and then narrowed. He felt the slight pressure that told him she was trying to probe his mind, but he'd already raised his shields.

She looked thoughtful. "Hmm, not human, but what?" She shrugged. "It doesn't matter. No one would believe you if you tried to tell them." Her gaze dropped the length of his body. "You're gorgeous enough to be one of us."

"And *us* would be?" He took another quick glance at Kim. The demon was standing closer to her now while he pointed out something about the mattress. He'd better not be suggesting that he test it with Kim.

"I'm Kiki and he's Reese. Succubus and incubus to you." She made a wide, sweeping gesture that encompassed the store. "Isn't this perfect? A mattress store. I mean, who better to sell them?" Her expression turned sly. "The real owners are on an extended vacation in here—she tapped her head. They've asked us to fill in for them. Like, how could we refuse to lend a helping hand? Of course, while we're in charge of the Lamberts' bodies, we decided to upgrade the original models." She slid her hand across the endless expanse of her breasts.

"Uh-huh. I thought night was your time. Not many dreams to go around during the day." Possession. From what he'd read, the easiest way for a demon to exist outside its demonic realm. And in this case, the smartest. Anyone who knew the Lamberts might think they'd gone berserk with cosmetic surgery, but they wouldn't doubt their identities. Brynn moved closer to Kim. The incubus now had his hand on her back. He felt his inner beast—the one he was forced to beat down during the compulsion—roar to life.

"He told us to do it this way. Play the good citizen during the day and then have our fun at night."

"He? Who's *he*?" Brynn felt he was standing on the edge of something important.

Kiki shrugged. She looked as though she regretted the *he* word. "The One Whose Name Cannot Be Uttered."

He slipped back into her mind just long enough to realize that was the only name she knew this "he" by. And she must've sensed his presence in her head, because she raised her mental shields. He wouldn't get anything more from her now.

Kiki guided him over to another mattress. "This is perfect for a great-looking guy like you. King-size for all those three-on-one situations." She slid her gaze over to Reese and then smiled. "Your woman is a churning caldron of sexual frustration. She needs a man to turn up the heat and watch her burn." She looked back at Brynn with sly amusement. "I guess Reese will be paying her a visit."

Brynn's inner beast snarled. "Tell Reese to stay away from her, or else he'll be ordering a new set of oversized organs from hellinc.com."

Kiki widened her eyes in mock wonder. "Mmm. Lots of passion. I'll have to add you to my nightly rounds."

Brynn turned away from the succubus and strode over to Kim. He arrived just in time to watch Reese slide his hand down to Kim's behind as he described how said part of her anatomy would sink into the mattress. Ha. Old Reese was about to get a demonstration of Brynn's fist sinking into his face.

He didn't bother with politeness. Grabbing Kim's hand, he pulled her away from the incubus's side. "Hey, thanks for your help, but we'd like to look at the mattresses on our own."

With a shrug, Reese transferred his attention to a new customer who'd entered the store.

Kim frowned. "I don't know what you think, but I think these people are a little strange." She glanced around the store. "Great mattresses though." Smiling up at him, she sat down on a mattress and patted the spot beside her. "Okay, now we start trying them out."

It seemed like Brynn had bounced and lain on every mattress in the damn store. Luckily, a trickle of customers had kept the terrible twosome busy. Kim now stood with him in front of an open door that Brynn assumed was a storeroom. She glanced over the entire store. "From what you've said, I guess it's between the mattress by the door and the one over in the corner."

Brynn really didn't give a damn. "Which one do you think is the best buy?"

She glowed with the joy of being asked to make the choice for him. And that made him inexplicably happy. His happiness was short-lived.

As Kim looked away to see where Kiki was, Brynn felt the compulsion rolling over him. Damn, he hadn't kept track of the time. Yanking his T-shirt over his head, he glanced at his watch. What the . . . ? That wasn't right. He had no more time to think.

Kim had just spotted Kiki when she felt Brynn's arms wrap around her. His breath moved over her neck, a warm slide of pleasure.

"Take my body, Kim." The heat of his words coated her in sweet temptation, and the hard-muscled pressure of his chest against her back did amazing things to her breathing. "Lie with me on this bed and let me strip the clothes from your body slowly, touching every bared inch of flesh with my mouth."

Ohmigod! She turned in his arms to stare up at the face of his alter ego, and once again was blown away by the change. His eyes actually blazed with the golden shine of sexual desire. His mouth was fuller, needier. It begged her to explore its texture, its power to excite, to arouse.

His sheer sensual impact left her speechless for a moment, but she could still act. She couldn't let anyone in the store see this. Kim laid both palms flat against his bare chest and shoved as hard as she could. Her shove caught him by surprise, and he stumbled back through the doorway.

The room was dark, but she could still see enough to recognize that it was a storeroom. Right inside the doorway lay a new mattress. Kiki and Reese must've been in the act of carrying it out of the storeroom when Brynn and she came into the store.

Brynn's momentum didn't allow him to catch his balance before the mattress tripped him. As he fell, he grabbed her hand, carrying her down on top of him.

Minor interruptions didn't interfere with the compulsion's

single-mindedness, because Brynn cupped her buttocks in his big hands and pulled her tightly against his erection.

In a moment of weakness, she responded. As he thrust his hips upward, pressing between her splayed thighs, she closed her eyes and slid back and forth over his arousal. Her body clenched around the imagined sensation of his freed cock rubbing back and forth, back and forth right *there*. And when he removed his hands from her buttocks to put them on both sides of her head so he could guide her mouth to his, she let him.

His lips were heated and hungry, slanting across her mouth and demanding that she respond. He traced the shape of her mouth with his tongue, asking that she open to him. He didn't have to ask twice. She parted her lips and tasted the promise of all he wanted to do to her. In a distant part of her mind, she was aware he was reaching between them to unbutton his jeans, but all she could think about was the magic he was creating with his mouth.

"Oh goody, you've chosen your mattress." Kiki smelled a sale. "Great choice. Notice how the pressure of two butts doesn't make it sag. I mean, a good bed just screams fantastic-for-sex. We can arrange payments if you like. Are you sure you don't want Reese or me, or maybe even both of us, to test it with you for those special times when two aren't enough?"

Kim froze, her heart pounding and the heat that had been building low in her belly now churning with embarrassment. Still caught in the throes of his compulsion, Brynn kissed a path over her jaw and down the side of her neck.

She leaned close to his ear and whispered, "I don't want your body, Brynn."

He went still beneath her. She rolled off the mattress and climbed to her feet. He followed. Even though she didn't look his way, she was aware of him pulling on his shirt.

He said nothing to her as he walked to where Kiki and Reese stood. "I'll take this mattress."

Reese grinned. "Have to say I've never seen anyone give a mattress that kind of test ride. You guys rock."

Kim expected Reese to pat Brynn on the butt in recognition of a great play. She trailed after everyone as they went to the front register where Brynn paid for the mattress, a box spring, and a frame with his credit card and then arranged for delivery. Afterward she followed Brynn out to the car.

"Kimmie?" Fo's eyes filled her whole screen. "They aren't human." Fo's eyes slid all the way to the left as she tried to look at Brynn. "Are they demons like you, Brynn?"

"We'll talk about it later." His tone quelled even Fo.

Silence stretched between them as Brynn drove away from the store. Finally, Kim couldn't stand it anymore. "Maybe you should stop at that big discount store we passed on the way here. You've moved up to a king-size mattress, so you'll need new sheets."

He nodded and kept driving.

"I never asked why you live in the castle. You'd have a lot more privacy if you had your own place." There, let him try to answer that with just a nod.

"When Eric, Conall, and I signed on for the job, we agreed to live in the castle." He shrugged. "It doesn't bother me."

"Oh." She was all out of safe topics.

He exhaled deeply and glanced across at her. "We have to talk about what just happened."

"No we don't." When in doubt, deny.

"If Kiki hadn't interrupted, we'd still be on that mattress." Surprisingly, he sounded like he was simply making a statement of fact. No accusation in his voice.

Because she felt so guilty, Kim immediately leaped to the attack. "I never lose control like that, so there had to be something else going on." She thought for a moment. "You must have some demon power that makes women lose control around you. I'm surprised you never realized it." And yes, she totally believed that. Sort of. Okay, maybe.

"Sure, but I wasn't using it on you." He didn't even glance at her as he dropped his bombshell.

"No kidding? Really?" Talk about a lucky shot in the dark.

"I've always had the power to call women to me sexually." He narrowed his lips to a hard line. "I've never used it. I never *will* use it."

"Any woman? Young, old, nonhuman? *Any woman?*" The possibilities boggled her mind.

"Small sentient machines?" Fo.

"Any woman." His expression said he was sorry he'd mentioned this particular power. "But we've gotten off topic here." He slid Kim a quick glance. "You wanted me."

"That might be a yes. Or not. I haven't decided yet. I have to think about all the variables connected to what happened and arrive at a logical conclusion." Prevarication was a gift.

He didn't say anything else for a moment, and that gave her a chance to think about their exchange. Strange, he didn't seem upset with her like he'd been with Liz. Of course, she hadn't tied him to the bed, just laid on top of him.

"Something important happened back there." He glanced at her, and his eyes gleamed with excitement.

Kim frowned. Sure, it had been a wonderful few minutes, and his kiss had speed-dialed her desire, but she got the feeling that wasn't what he was talking about.

Brynn pulled into the store's parking lot and found a spot close to the door. Then he turned to look at her. "Kim, I'd been with you for exactly one hour and five minutes when the compulsion hit."

Where did the extra five minutes come from? "Are you sure?"

"I checked my watch as soon as I felt the change start." He reached over to clasp her hand. "The change is *never* late."

He didn't say anything else as they went into the store. She could understand that. After five hundred years, he wouldn't want to give himself false hope.

They were looking at the sheets when Brynn finally spoke. "Does something about the store feel strange to you?"

She looked around. "A lot of people seem to be changing tags on stuff."

Even as she spoke, a woman stopped in front of her and whisked the set of sheets from her hand. As Kim gaped, the woman put a sticker over the original price. Oh, good. Maybe they'd walked in on a storewide sale. Then Kim looked at the new price. "A hundred dollars? You've got to be kidding. This is a discount store, like in *cheap* prices."

The women giggled. "New owners, new prices. Take it or leave it. Oh, if you want to sell your soul, we'll give you a really competitive deal. Just go to the service desk."

Kim had opened her mouth to voice more outrage when she got a look at the woman's eyes. If the eyes were windows to the soul, then as far as Kim could tell, nobody was home. An involuntary shiver skidded down her spine.

Brynn leaned close. "Leave the sheets, Kim. Let's get out of here." He took her hand and hurried her from the store.

Kim watched openmouthed as other angry customers streamed from the store. "What's going on?"

Once inside his car, Brynn leaned his forearms over the steering wheel and stared straight-ahead. "Kiki and Reese are demons—a succubus and incubus. The people working in this discount store? All demons. Galveston has a problem, Kim."

"My time, my time!" Fo's joy in landing in a hotbed of demons was the only positive emotion in sight. "Take me back inside, Kimmie, and I'll destroy all of them for you."

Kim looked uncertain. "Are you sure, Brynn? Where'd they all come from? Maybe I should call Lynsay and Dirk to help. I've never seen so many in one spot. It's kind of freaky."

"No destroying just yet." He started the car and pulled out of the parking lot. "First off, if demons have taken over the only two stores we stopped at, we can assume they've taken over other stores in Galveston. The question is, why?"

Uh, because they're evil soul-sucking dirtbags? But she couldn't make a blanket statement, because Brynn didn't seem to fit that description. Her life would be a lot less stressful if she could see the world of demons like the other Vaughns did. Demons bad. Destroy. "So why can't I start getting rid of them now?" She hated her demon-destroying job, but in this case she didn't have a choice. She couldn't just let them take over a whole city.

"Think, Kim. The mattress store owners and all the people working in that discount store were possessed. If the same thing is happening all over the island, we're talking more demons than you, Lynsay, and Dirk can handle alone. The demons are trying, in their own demented ways, to keep low profiles, to fit in with the rest of the population. Kiki let it slip that someone she called the One Whose Name Cannot Be Uttered was calling the shots." He paused as he turned onto Seawall Boulevard. "What we have here is a huge influx of demons under the control of a leader. I'd say they're getting ready to . . . Ready to what? That's what we need to know."

Kim frowned. "So the demons are here for some kind of big event?" She couldn't wrap her mind around a demon invasion this large.

He nodded, his gaze intense as he glanced her way. "If you start destroying the demons right now, they'll know you've made them. There're too many of them. They'll wipe you out in one night. The trick will be to find out what they have planned and then cut off the head at the same time you attack the army." A line of concentration formed between his eyes. "We've got to close the portal."

"Portal to hell?" This just got scarier and scarier.

"This many demons in one place means that a portal has opened somewhere in Galveston. Worse than that, only an archdemon could've opened it. Archdemons don't usually make personal appearances. When they do, chaos follows."

"So your suggestion is?" She'd heard about archdemons and portals to hell, but she'd never experienced any of them. She didn't think any of the Vaughns had. It hadn't happened in living memory. No matter what he said, she'd have to tell Lynsay and Dirk. They'd have to call in the whole Vaughn family to save the city from whatever was about to happen. But she agreed they'd have to control the urge to rush out and start zapping demons until they had more people and a plan.

He pulled the car into his personal parking space. Then he sat for a moment staring at the castle. "I know you'll have to tell your family about this." He raked his fingers through his hair. "And to think I was hoping for something to happen that would draw attention away from me." His laughter was short and bitter. "Be careful what you wish for and all that stuff. Eric, Conall, Holgarth, and I have to find the archdemon and his portal, then we have to shut both down."

"I'll help." Every Vaughn in the world would have to answer the call for this one.

He turned to stare at her. "I guess it wouldn't do any good to demand that you stay in the castle until all this is over."

"Nope. Wouldn't even make me blink. But I probably should stick close to you, because you can spot demons without a detector. Fo can destroy them, but she's not too great about identifying them. How do you do that anyway? Is it a case of like recognizing like?" Maybe she should try, just once in a while, to remember that he was a demon. She wasn't afraid of him, but she shouldn't get too comfortable when he was around. Too late. She was already comfortable with him, except when sexual awareness slithered into view. Which was pretty much all the time. So maybe she wasn't as comfortable as she thought.

"Demons have different thought patterns—hyper and scattered. They don't hold a thought for more than a few seconds. But then they don't have to, because the archdemon is pulling their strings." He watched as she opened the door.

Kim paused as a question formed. "Do you answer to an archdemon?" She hoped not. If he had to be a demon, she wanted him to be his own demon.

He shook his head. "I've always been alone."

And somehow, that was the saddest thing she'd ever heard.

II

Brynn pushed open the door to his room, his mind on more things than he could comfortably handle right now. Before coming up here, he'd told Holgarth they had to have a meeting tonight. All nonhumans in the castle needed to be there. And Kim. He couldn't leave Kim out.

Thinking about Kim led to lots of related thoughts, like how much his body wanted her. *Way to go, blame it on your body.* As he pulled up memories of what had almost happened on that mattress—what he'd *wanted* to happen, but not during a compulsion—his thoughts rewound to the moment he glanced at his watch. The compulsion had been five minutes late. It was *never* late. What did that mean? He'd have to run a test. Soon. With Kim. If she was willing. Because she must be getting tired of him ripping off his clothes without warning.

His thoughts scattered as he got his first look at his room. Ganymede sprawled on the couch, one paw resting on the remote as he watched a soap. Chip and cookie bags along with candy wrappers littered the cushions and floor around him. An open carton of ice cream sat on the coffee table, the melted remains pooling on the table's glass top.

"Where the hell did all this come from?" Brynn waved his hand at the monument to pigginess.

Ganymede burped and then turned to stare at him. "Hey, a guy's gotta eat. I spent a tough morning trying to get close to Asima. She's into all this culture crap, and after listening to her rattle on about operas, ballets, and plays, I felt the need to feed my inner slob."

Ganymede pressed the remote with his paw, turning off the TV. "I phoned the snack order in, told them you'd pay for it later and to just dump everything on the coffee table, and then I unlocked the door. They left the stuff for you, and I ate it. Most of it. I left a little for you." He stood, did his cat stretching thing, and then planted his butt on the couch. "So what's happening with you?"

Brynn fought through his urge to toss the feline freeloader out on his overstuffed ass. But he had the feeling he'd need all the help he could get with the demons. "Galveston has a problem. Kim and I went shopping today. Demons have possessed everyone in both stores." He dropped onto the couch and then reached for a cookie. "Kim's going to call in her whole family to help destroy them. They'll turn the island into a war zone." Hordes of Vaughns descending on the castle would be bad news for him.

"Not really."

Brynn almost didn't hear Ganymede's mutter. "What?"

"You're safe from the Vaughns."

Wait, he hadn't said anything about being safe from the Vaughns out loud. "Get out of my mind, cat. How would you feel if I rooted around in your head whenever I felt like it?" Then he realized what Ganymede had said. "Why will I be safe?"

"Give it your best shot, demon. No one gets into my mind unless I let them in." The cat looked away from him. "They'll know you're not human, but they won't know you're a demon. The only way a detector can ID you as a demon is by scanning your organs.

Demons have crazy brain activity, their hearts have a weird rhythm, stuff like that." He took time out to yawn, exposing small, sharp teeth. "Your brain activity is normal. Don't know about your heart rhythm since you met Kim, though."

Brynn didn't react to Ganymede's comment about Kim. The cat would enjoy it too much. "How do you know all this?"

And if he was a demon, why didn't he have demon characteristics? Why didn't he answer to an archdemon? Brynn mentally pounded his fists against the futility of asking questions that had no answers. At least for him.

Ganymede met his gaze and for the first time let Brynn see exactly what he was—a being ancient beyond belief and wielding unspeakable power. And then the cat's eyes were once again the ones he showed to the world. "I know a lot of things, demon."

Brynn tried to put everything together. "So you're a cosmic troublemaker like Sparkle, but a lot older and a lot more powerful. Powerful is good."

Would Ganymede be able to handle an archdemon? "From research I've done over the centuries, I'd guess that portals to hell don't usually stay open long. Maybe a few seconds. Only one or two demons can slip through before it closes. But this? An archdemon must be keeping the portal open while it calls its minions through. The nonhumans in the castle along with the Vaughns can probably cast out the regular demons, but I'd bet no one's had experience with an archdemon."

Ganymede tried to look wise, but it was tough to look wise with ice cream on your whiskers. "Any idea which archdemon?"

"Not a clue." Brynn rolled the empty cookie bag into a ball and tossed it into a nearby trash can.

"If I help take down this archdemon, what do I get out of it?" Ganymede stayed focused on number one. "You have to understand my situation here. See, in the good old days, I pretty much did what I damned well pleased—knocked planets out of orbit, created ice ages, anything for a giggle. But after thousands of years, that got old. So I decided to go small and mess with human emotions. That ticked off the Big Boss—who has zero sense of humor—and he grounded me. He took away all my fun, said I couldn't do anything to hurt any living creature. I thought maybe I could play with some of the nonliving ones instead, but he stopped that, too. Can't even off a vamp."

"Who's this Big Boss?" Brynn thought he owed the Big Boss a huge thank-you for reining in Ganymede.

Ganymede flattened his ears and whipped his tail back and forth to demonstrate his contempt for the top dog, or maybe the top cat. "He's the supreme party pooper, the almighty can't-do-this and can't-do-that." He hissed his frustration with all higher authorities. "A regular no-fun guy."

"Yeah, I can see how that would cramp your style." *Don't laugh.*

Ganymede's expression turned sly. "He said I couldn't curse either, but he got tired of keeping count. Sometimes I let loose with a whole string of f-bombs just because I can."

He hit Brynn with a calculating stare. "I don't know if the Big Boss would get pissed off if I whacked this archdemon. Maybe I can just shove him through the portal and close the damn thing. Have to be careful not to twist the Big Boss's tail, because there's no upside when you cease to exist. So if I'm taking this big chance by helping you guys, I want you to help me impress Asima."

"How?" From what Brynn had seen of Asima, this might be beyond any being's skill.

Ganymede began washing his face with one black paw. "She likes this Shakespeare guy, so I used your laptop to Google famous lines from Shakespeare, and then I memorized some of them. You can tell me if they work. Guess I should've read all his plays and stuff, but that kind of crap makes my eyes cross."

He paused for effect. " 'But, soft! What light through yonder window breaks? It is the east, and Juliet is the sun.' What's that all about? So he's saying this Juliet babe is big, round, and orange? If I said that to Sparkle she'd haul off and flatten me."

Luckily, Brynn didn't have to comment, because someone knocked on his door. As he went to open it, he glanced back at the debris field surrounding Ganymede. Nope, nothing he could do to hide all that.

With Kim's sister and uncle in the castle, and a lot more Vaughns about to join them, he decided to start being more cautious when someone showed up at his door. He looked through the peephole. Kim and Sparkle waited on the other side.

Brynn opened the door and glanced at Sparkle. She looked past him at Ganymede. "Well, hello, cuddly bunny. I see you've been keeping yourself happy."

Not as happy as he'd like to be. For Ganymede's sake, Brynn hoped Sparkle never found out about Asima. But then he forgot about Sparkle as Kim stepped into the room. Automatically, he glanced at the time.

She put her hand over his watch, but she may as well have put it over his cock, because the reaction was the same. Women had touched him in every possible way, and some not so possible, but none had gotten his body's instant attention by simply touching his wrist.

"I saw Lynsay in the lobby. She was with Deimos, so I couldn't say much. I agreed to meet her for dinner. I'd like you to go with me." She moved far enough into the room so that he could close the door.

"And here I thought you liked me." Holgarth got really pissy when guests ran out of the restaurant without paying. That was a given if Lynsay got up halfway through dessert and tried to zap him with her detector or separate his head from his body with her steak knife.

Kim walked over to a chair facing the couch and sat down. She put her purse on the floor, and he could see Fo peering at him from the side pocket.

Sparkle bent over to clear the empty bags and wrappers from the couch before she joined Ganymede there. Ganymede was enjoying the bending-over experience. Not hard to do with Sparkle. The scooped front of her top scooped a little too low for safety, and her tight black skirt showed off her tight behind. Personally, Brynn thought the cat should stick with Sparkle. Who knew what Asima looked like in human form.

Kim smiled up at him. "Don't worry, you'll be safe. Lynsay's detector stopped working this morning, and Dirk won't be around for dinner. I'll need you to back me up when I tell her about the demons. She doesn't believe Fo is worth squat as a demon detector, and she knows I can't sense them." She frowned. "Maybe we should check out a few more places before I call in the whole family."

Brynn tried to throttle back his happiness that Kim had invited him to have dinner with her, no matter what her reason. He didn't get many dinner invites where he wasn't the main course. And he refused to get all psyched at the thought of going with her to check out the demon population in other places on the island. He had to keep one truth front and center. Kim and he didn't have a future together. A few great nights maybe, but definitely not a future.

Insight. He'd gotten good over the centuries at raining on his own parade. Maybe it was time he stopped. Just maybe he'd let himself enjoy being with Kim for the time she was here. Enjoy a woman? A revolutionary thought. "I think she'd believe you if you told her Kiki admitted to being a succubus, and that a clerk in the discount store told you where you could sell your soul. But I think you want me there for another reason."

"Could be." She twirled a strand of her hair around one finger as she watched him. "Fine, so I want Lynsay to see you as a regular guy, someone I'd like to spend time with. Besides, Lynsay and Dirk would start to get suspicious if they never got a look at you. If you have dinner with us, Lynsay can tell Dirk she met you."

"So you're trying to protect me." A day ago, he would've felt offended. Now, it was sort of nice to have someone value him enough to want to keep him safe. The truth? It was nice to have *Kim* wanting to protect him.

Before he ended up drowning in a sea of warm fuzzies, Brynn looked away, only to meet Sparkle's interested gaze. She'd finally planted herself in the middle of the couch. Ganymede had crawled into her lap. Chalk a point up for Sparkle. Brynn might not know what Asima looked like in human form, but he'd bet no one sat in her lap.

Sparkle studied him with a small secret smile that said she knew something he didn't. "I met Kim in the lobby, and since she was headed up here, I decided to tag along to say hi to Mede." She tried on a regretful expression. "I was so disappointed when Kim told me he hadn't worked out for her. And imagine my surprise when she said he talked to you guys." The glance she sent Ganymede said to expect reprisals. Soon. "I told him specifically not to do that."

"Don't get your panties in a bunch." Ganymede looked thoughtful. "That's if you're wearing any today."

Sparkle abandoned her happy smile and narrowed her eyes to angry amber slits. "I don't give rewards to bad kitties."

"No rewards?" Ganymede looked as though someone had taken away his ice cream.

Brynn wondered what Sparkle had promised Ganymede. It had to be food or sex. More to the point, why had Sparkle wanted Ganymede to masquerade as Kim's pet? Kim might buy Sparkle's story about wanting Kim to have a pet, but Brynn had known Sparkle longer than Kim had. Sparkle was working an angle. Too bad he didn't have the time to find out what it was.

"Hate to interrupt, but all nonhumans have to meet in the conference room at seven." He'd distracted Sparkle. Ganymede looked relieved. "We have a demon problem in Galveston, so we need to make plans." Brynn glanced at Kim. "Can you be there?"

Kim nodded. "Try to keep me away."

He grinned at Ganymede. "Why don't you fill in the details for Sparkle? Maybe you can try out some Shakespeare on her." He ignored the cat's glare. "I think Kim is right. We need to hit a few more places to see how widespread the problem is. See you guys at the meeting."

Kim stood, and Brynn followed her toward the door.

Sparkle frowned at Ganymede. "Shakespeare?"

Ganymede puffed himself up and delivered his line in a James Earl Jones voice. "In thy face I see honor, truth, and loyalty."

Sparkle's smile wasn't comforting. "No, sweet cheeks. In my face you see mad, bad, and a need for payback."

Brynn stepped from the room and then quietly closed the door as Ganymede's eyes widened in panic.

Can we say overwhelmed? Kim had ridden with Brynn from one end of the island to the other, and she was still trying to come to grips with what she'd seen. "Demons are everywhere." She slipped on the jacket she'd discarded earlier in the day. With the night came a chill breeze off the Gulf.

Brynn leaned against his car, arms folded across his spectacular chest, and eyes narrowed in thought as he gazed around Live the Fantasy. "We have enough time to check out at least one of the attractions to see if the demons were stupid enough to possess anyone in the park. They have to know what Eric, Conall, Holgarth, and I are."

Darkness was falling, blurring the harsh lines of worry etched in Brynn's face, but doing nothing to diminish the wonder of his hair as it blew around his shoulders. "Or maybe not. Ganymede claims I don't give off demonic vibes. I wonder why?"

There was something important imbedded in Brynn's question, but Kim was too shaken to think about it now. She pushed her blowing hair away from her face. "The Grand 1894 Opera House was a real shocker. I guess I always thought of it as a symbol of Galveston, indestructible. It survived the 1900 hurricane, for heaven's sake. And now *this*?" She opened her arms wide to indicate the vast horror of what she'd seen. "Our peek inside blew me away. Can you believe they were performing Dante's Inferno onstage? And then everyone in the audience jumped up and screamed 'Hell rocks.' It doesn't get any weirder than that."

"They weren't human, Kimmie. None of them were." Fo seemed energized by the knowledge. "You should've stepped forward and pushed my red button right then."

Brynn's smile was a mere baring of his teeth. "You might've gotten a few, Fo, but then the others would've rushed Kim. They would've ground you right into the carpet."

Fo's purple eyes widened. "Oh." She peered nervously from the pocket of Kim's purse.

Kim walked beside Brynn as he strode toward the Wild West area of the park. It was almost dark, and the lights came on, bathing the scene in a pale glow. "Shouldn't the lights be brighter?" Somehow everything seemed more muted than she remembered from Saturday night. *More menacing.*

He nodded. "A drop in power, maybe?"

Kim didn't want to think about who or what might be messing with Galveston's electricity. "Let's stop at the Dead Eye Saloon." Music and voices drifted out of the bar. *Ordinary* sounds. She needed some ordinary stuff right about now.

Inside the saloon, everything looked normal, or as normal as an old Western saloon where people were acting out their fantasies could look. Everyone except them was in period costume. The dancing "girls" were middle-aged women kicking their legs in time to the piano, giggling, and having lots of fun. Kim wondered how much giggling they'd be doing if they knew what was gathering all over Galveston.

In darkened corners, men and women were acting out more sensual pretend games. And by the door two men were taking their make-believe argument into the street where it could be settled with a make-believe gunfight. Cool.

"How do the park's fantasies work?" Kim figured that Brynn was perfect for this park, a fantasy man living in a fantasy world. Make that a *dark* fantasy.

Brynn leaned against the bar and looked around. Every woman's cowboy. Maybe his jeans, biker boots, and black T-shirt didn't shout *cowboy*, but he wore an aura of oneness with his body, a lithe grace that said he could handle a wild horse or a wild woman with equal ease. A dangerous man. Clothes didn't make the cowboy, and from the stares he was getting from all the women in the saloon, Kim wasn't the only one who thought so.

"We keep the costumes in a small building next to the saloon. Before coming inside, people choose the costumes they want. If you weren't with me, someone would've stopped you for not wearing one." He moved closer to be heard above the crowd noise, and she braced herself to resist his sensual pull. "Look around, and you'll see people wearing park badges. If you have a specific fantasy, you tell them, and they'll supply a costume and help you act it out. For example, one of those gunfighters who just left is a park employee." As he spoke to her, he continued to scan the crowd. "Or you can just come in and enjoy the atmosphere."

Kim took Fo from her purse. She shielded the detector's screen with one hand. "What do we have here?"

"All humans, Kimmie." Fo sounded disappointed.

Brynn glanced at his watch. "It's time again. I'll go out and watch the gunfight, and then we can keep looking."

Kim watched the crowd part for him as he left. Brynn had that effect on people. Surprised, she realized she felt a little lonely without him. That hadn't happened before. Especially with a man she'd only known for a few days. Putting Fo back into her purse, she ordered a drink from the bar and stood sipping it. This is how it would always be for him if he wanted to stay with one woman. Someone would have to love him a lot to go through a lifetime with a man who couldn't say no. To *any* woman.

"Looks like you've been deserted." The male voice held a note of laughter in it.

Kim turned to the man standing next to her at the bar. First impressions—average height, short dark brown hair, bright blue eyes, and a nice smile. But he looked too civilized to ever feel at home in the cowboy outfit he was wearing. "He just stepped out to watch the gunfight. He'll be back."

The man nodded. "I'm Vic Burton. I teach in Houston, and I'm staying at the castle over spring break. I saw you in the restaurant this morning. Have you tried any of the castle fantasies yet?"

Kim returned his smile. "Kim Vaughn. I'm staying in the castle, too, but it's strictly business. I'm an architect, and the owner hired me to plan a few changes to the castle." A teacher? Couldn't get more ordinary than that. Then why wasn't her heart singing with joy?

"So is that guy your husband?" Vic smiled his wonderful, ordinary smile at her and watched her hopefully from his ordinary blue eyes.

"No, just a friend." Who happened to be an anything but ordinary demon of sensual desire.

"How about doing a castle fantasy with me? I'm not here with anyone. Bet it would be fun together."

Wow, she was having a conversation with a real human male, an *ordinary* human male. She couldn't pass up a shot at a normal guy, even if there wasn't instant chemistry on her part. "How about Wednesday night?" Brynn had said he was off tonight and tomorrow night, so she'd have to keep that time free to do demon stuff.

He nodded, and his smile widened. "Terrific. I'll meet you in the great hall at eight."

Without warning, Brynn's emotions flowed over her—anger, confusion, and a feeling he tried to hide. What feeling? Inquiring minds wanted to know. This was only the third time he'd lost control of his emotions enough for her to pick up on them. The very fact that she could read them reminded her she wasn't as normal as she'd like to be.

While she tried to make sense of his emotions, she felt Brynn behind her—his heat melting into her back to warm her all the way through, and his scent, a mixture of raw need and male possessiveness. Wait, possessiveness didn't have a scent. So how did she recognize it? Interesting.

"If you're ready, we can leave now." Brynn's voice had all the warmth of an Arctic ice floe.

Kim turned and smiled up at him. He'd wiped his face clean of all expression, but his eyes were hot with something very male and very primal. Jealousy? Satisfaction filled her before she could plug the source. She didn't want a demon to feel either possessive or jealous about her. *But do I still think of him as a demon?* She wouldn't go there right now.

"Brynn, this is Vic Burton. He's staying at the castle for spring break." She glanced at Vic. His expression was open and friendly. Couldn't he feel the danger swirling around him? Guess not. "Vic, meet Brynn McNair. He and his brothers run the Castle of Dark Dreams."

Back to Brynn, whose expression was still, well, expressionless. But his eyes blazed with a desire to stake his claim. "Vic asked me to do a castle fantasy with him on Wednesday. Should be fun." And it would be, but not because of Vic. Okay, so she wanted to see Brynn in action during one of his fantasies.

Brynn nodded at Vic, but he didn't offer his hand. "Nice to meet you." His eyes said *not* loud and clear. "I'll have to make sure your fantasy is memorable."

Uh-oh. That sounded like a warning to her. Vic's smile faded. He couldn't help but feel the waves of aggression hitting him in the face.

"Sure. Can't wait." He cast an uncertain glance toward Kim.

She shrugged. "Guess we'd better get going, Brynn. We have to be back at the castle by six or else Lynsay will come hunting for us."

Kim let Brynn guide her out the door before saying anything. Once outside, she moved away and then met his gaze. "What was that all about?"

He didn't try to hide his confusion. "Damned if I know. I wanted to rip him apart for planning a fantasy with you." He shifted his gaze somewhere past her shoulder. "Jealousy? I've never felt possessive about any woman." His expression hardened. "I don't want to feel that way now."

"Because?" She knew why, but she wanted to hear him say it.

He started walking toward the next building on the Wild West street. "Because wanting to be with you, feeling possessive, is an invitation to disaster." Abruptly, he stopped and sat down on a bench. She sat next to him.

"Look at me." He sounded way too serious.

Kim looked. She understood why Vic had acted uncertain. It didn't matter what term you used, dominant or alpha male, Brynn would always be the leader of the pack. So that would make it twice as hard for him to submit to women like Liz. She pushed aside the sympathy he'd hate.

"I have to keep leaving you every fifty-five minutes, and if I forget, then I start ripping my clothes off no matter where I am. Suppose you were in a meeting with an important client and that happened? You'd be ashamed of me." His expression said his own shame would trump hers every time.

Kim shrugged. "No problem. First off, I don't think you'd want to be sitting in on any of my meetings. If you were, I'd just make sure you were sitting next to me. When I sensed the change starting, all I'd have to do is lean over and whisper that I didn't want your body." A lie, but she wouldn't tell him that.

He raked his fingers through his hair and stared into the darkness. "How about if I timed things wrong and ended up being with another woman for more than an hour? How would you feel then?"

Okay, he had her there. If Brynn were hers, she'd probably be the ultimate jealous bitch. She wouldn't be able to handle that, even if she knew it wasn't his fault. It surprised her to realize how fierce she could feel about this imaginary relationship that definitely *wasn't* going to happen.

Kim had to tell the truth. "I'd want to rip out her heart and kick her very dead body down the stairs." Whoa, mega-violent images here. Her family would stand and applaud if she brought the same savagery to her demon hunting.

"That's what I thought." No self-pity, no accusations, just acceptance.

It was the acceptance that got to her. "There's something not right about this whole thing. Ganymede said you didn't have any demon characteristics. Why not? And if you're a demon, why hasn't an archdemon or some other demonic authority figure ever contacted you? Oh, and another thing, demons are evil in all things. For example, Kiki cheated you on that mattress. After we'd left the store, I glanced at your receipt. She charged you more than the price on the tag. I didn't say anything, because I didn't think either of us wanted to go back."

"And your point is?" Sarcastic but interested.

She drew in a deep breath of courage and voiced the thought that must've been forming ever since he told her about Ganymede's comment. "How do you know you're really a demon? Sure, you woke up believing you were one. So what? I mean, now that I realize there's a whole underground of supernatural beings out there, I think some of them might be powerful enough to wipe your memory clean and give you a whole new purpose in life."

"Why?"

She shrugged. "Just because they can? To demonstrate their power? I don't know." Her theory sounded farfetched, but not any stranger than a demon that didn't remember hell.

She thought about her theory and her aching feet during the next fifty-five minutes as they covered every inch of the Wild West. For a chance to slip her feet from Sparkle's tootsie-torturing shoes, Kim even talked Brynn into taking a short stagecoach ride. Surprise, surprise, she forgot about demons for a short time and had fun.

Now they stood outside a building with a Coming Soon banner stretched across the front. Kim looked up at the sign above the door. "The Cock Crows at Dawn?"

Brynn grinned as he led her around to the back. "The best little bordello in all of Texas. Donna named it. We'll go in the back so no one will think it's open and follow us inside."

"You think there might be demons inside?" The streetlights didn't reach back here, and night closed around them as Brynn searched through his keys before opening the door. Spooky.

"No." He strode through the darkened building until he reached what must be the front parlor. Then he drew the heavy drapes closed across the window and threw a switch next to an impressive-looking fireplace. Fake flames created a credible impersonation of a blazing hearth. The light from the flickering flames cast a constantly changing pattern of shadows across the room. "But it's almost time for the compulsion to hit."

"And?"

"And I'd like to test it this time." He glanced at his watch. "It should begin in about two minutes." He sat down on a plush crimson sofa.

Kim sat beside him. And waited. And then waited some more. After a few minutes she had to look away from the silent man beside her. It was sort of like waiting for a hiccup when you thought they were over, but you sat almost afraid to breathe for fear they'd come back one more time. But then this was a lot worse. Brynn's hiccups had lasted five hundred years.

The room was everything a bordello parlor should be. Red that bled down walls and gathered in the crimson puddles of area rugs. Velvet that coated everything like red mold—drapes, chairs, their sofa, and a huge round couch in the center of the room. Silver candelabras that rested on the intricately carved tables scattered around the room as well as on the piano.

Ladies of the night who'd never ever need breast enhancement smiled down from paintings hanging on the scarlet walls. Fine, so she was jealous. All in all, it was an awesome whorehouse.

Kim wanted to look at her watch but controlled the urge. Brynn didn't need any reminder of the time creeping by. The compulsion must be a lot more than five minutes late this time. Whatever the reason, she was fiercely happy for him.

Finally, when she didn't think she could stand the silence for one more minute, she felt him shift beside her. She could feel the sexual flow of his change wash over her, so when she turned her head to look at him, she knew what she'd see.

He'd already stripped off his shirt, and she knew she should speak up right now. But a tiny unrepentant part of her waited a moment to enjoy the sculpted perfection of his muscular chest. The otherworldly beauty of his face caught at her and shook her in its sensual teeth.

He leaned close, his heat and scent of aroused male making mush of her common sense. Kim understood why down through the centuries women had taken what he offered. He was raw sex and all the fabled delights of the flesh.

"Take my body, Kim. Use me in any way you want." His husky murmur said he'd never needed anyone as much as he needed her.

Low in her belly, heat coiled and spread. Representatives from the parts of her responsible for primitive erotic stimulation whispered, *We took a vote. We all agreed. Go for it.*

She wanted to. She *really* wanted to. She couldn't. He was a strong man—yes, *man*—who was helpless now and needed *her* strength. She sighed. "I don't want your body, Brynn." Sometimes moral victories sucked lemons.

He leaned even closer, his whiskey-colored eyes reflecting the fire's glow. "But I want yours, Kim."

12

Brynn watched her eyes widen, her lips part, and for one scary moment he thought the compulsion still held him. He wanted her that badly.

He wanted to cover her mouth with his, slide his fingers along her sleek inner thigh, and take joy in the first real sexual excitement he'd felt in five centuries.

"Are you okay, Brynn?"

She moistened her lips with the tip of her tongue, a nervous gesture he found sexier than all the erotic acts countless women had practiced on him. He growled his appreciation.

She stood and then walked away from the sofa. "Is that a player piano?" She didn't turn to him.

Brynn sensed her uneasiness. He'd better keep his growls to a minimum. No matter what doubts she might have about his demonic nature, he was still a demon until proven otherwise. And she was still a demon hunter.

"The compulsion is gone, Kim." He rose and then hesitated before walking to stand behind her. "But I still want you. I haven't said that of my own free will in five centuries."

She turned slowly to look at him. He'd expected to see fear in her eyes, but it was something very different he saw there.

"I want you, too." Her lips curved in a warm smile that touched all the important parts of his body and fed his growing arousal. "And I guarantee I've never said that to any demon before." She slid her fingers the length of his bare arm. "It scares me."

He moved closer, invading her space. She swallowed hard, and his gaze slipped to the base of her throat where he knew her pulse beat hard and fast. He'd never shared Eric's fascination with the female throat, but right now he thought Kim's neck was a definite sexual hot spot.

Kim couldn't back up because the round velvet couch was behind her. She sat. "You do looming well."

Brynn smiled at her, allowing her to see all the sexual knowledge in his eyes, all the pleasure he could give her.

Her smile faded, to be replaced by something darker, more elemental. "Talk to me, Brynn."

He wanted to keep this light, playful, but he couldn't. "This is all new to me, but I don't want to waste one minute of my time with you. We don't know what will happen in the next few days." *You might decide to embrace your demon-destroying side. I might be claimed by the archdemon.*

Did he believe that would happen? No, but through the centuries he'd learned he couldn't count on anything remaining the same except the compulsion. And now even that was changing.

He reached down and slipped off her shoes.

She sighed her relief and wiggled her toes. "I'm crippled for life, but I'll have to tell Sparkle they worked." She offered him a teasing grin, but there was a question behind it.

Brynn smiled back, the remembered smile of the sexual creature he became during the compulsion, the smile that filled women's eyes with lust. He didn't know any other smile that said what he wanted. "Let me show you what I've learned of pleasure." He slipped easily into the language of the compulsion.

Her expression said she wasn't too sure about his wording. She studied her toes rather than meet his gaze. "Something about that doesn't sound right, like you're bringing all those women from your past into the room with us."

"Believe me, you're the only woman in this room." What could he say to her? When it came to sex, he didn't know how to be anything but what he'd always been. And this *was* about sex. He wouldn't let it be about anything else.

Kim studied him, and she must've seen something in his eyes, because she nodded. Slipping out of her jacket, she dropped it to the floor. Then she handed her purse to him. "Please put this in the kitchen we passed on our way in. I don't think Fo needs to enlarge her life experiences any more than she has today."

The pocket of her purse did some serious vibrating. "You're no fun, Kimmie." Fo was in full whine. "I want to see. Why can't I see? Besides, I sense a demon nearby." She paused to consider her demon statement. "Of course, it might not be a demon, because all entities feel the same to me." Fo qualified her statement a little more. "Okay, so I don't see any demons. But one might be around. Somewhere." She sounded hopeful.

Brynn didn't wait for Kim to answer. He took the purse into the kitchen and set it on a chair. Then he put Fo on the table so she could see her surroundings. "A lesson in human interaction, Fo. Sometimes, people need privacy."

"Humph." Fo didn't sound convinced.

"And if you see a demon, just yell, and we'll come get you." Leaving Fo a little less disgruntled and on the lookout for rogue demons, he went to the back door and locked it before returning to the parlor. Kim was still sitting on the couch, but he sensed her sexual excitement had given way to doubts in the few minutes she'd had to think. Damn.

He'd deal with them. "Second thoughts?" He knelt in front of her, making himself shorter, less threatening.

"Try third and forth." She reached out to run her fingers through his hair.

And even though he knew his hair couldn't "feel," he'd swear each strand she'd touched turned to liquid fire.

"I was into the moment. Translation: my lust burned with the white-hot intensity of a thousand suns. Diane Chambers, *Cheers*. And I think she was talking about hate, but it fits lust, too. Now I've had time to think."

Brynn smiled. "Ah, the brain. The body's ultimate party pooper." He cupped one of her feet and massaged gently.

She frowned. "Here and now might not be the best place and time."

"I'm a big fan of spontaneity." Brynn switched to her other foot. "But you're right. This isn't the best place for all the things I want to do to you. Besides, we have to be back at the castle by six."

Kim nodded as she reached for her shoes. She was disappointed that he'd given in so easily. Which made no sense at all. It was dumb to even think about rolling around on the floor of a bordello with a man who might or might not be a demon. And she'd known him how long? Uh, one night and two whole days. Amazing what kind of stupidity hormonal surges caused.

She still wanted him. "Right. Let's get going. By the way, how many minutes past the hour did—"

He abandoned her feet to press his body against her knees. Surprised, she forgot about her shoes in favor of leaning back on the couch to keep distance between them.

His eyes gleamed with the feral glow of a hunting cat. "But pleasure takes many forms. I think we have time to explore one of them. Hmm?"

Kim was lying almost flat on the couch, supporting herself on her elbows. "I think we can squeeze in a mini-pleasure session." She fixed her gaze on his sensual mouth. Yep, tons of pleasure potential. "But I'll be looking forward to the extended version with lots of time to savor you." She watched his sexy lips tip up in a smile that made her clench her thighs.

Scary. Kim hadn't made love with many men, and she'd never made a decision this fast and felt this definite about what she wanted. She'd take what she could get, when she could get it. Her yearning for Mr. Ordinary was fading fast in her rearview mirror.

Brynn held her with his gaze as he leaned over, pressing his body against her thighs, her stomach. She spread her legs on either side of him to make it easier. Her breathing quickened, and her heart pounded. Her body hadn't taken long to get into pleasure mode.

Her feet were still on the floor and he was still kneeling, but he was a lot taller than she was. His yummilicious chest brushed her breasts through her top, and her nipples hardened into sensitive nubs. She didn't know if she'd survive the pleasure-pain when her bare breasts actually touched his skin.

His face was close to hers, his mouth so near she felt his breath warm on her cheek. His heat touched her in an elemental way, singing through her in waves of anticipation.

He supported himself on his forearms as he whispered in her ear, "I'm going to lift you onto the couch, and then we'll play."

She felt the word *play* as a soft expulsion of breath that tickled her ear and sounded an erotic rhythm along her nerve endings.

He stood, lifted her easily into his arms, and deposited her gently in the middle of the large couch. Her feet were no longer planted firmly on the ground, physically or symbolically. She lay back and looked up at him.

Kim knew she should be contributing some meaningful conversation, but for the life of her she couldn't force words past lips that had a whole other agenda in mind. Who knew she couldn't have a full-blown lust attack and talk at the same time?

He straightened, turned his back to her, and then stripped off the rest of his clothes. It wasn't a slow peeling to excite her. He ripped the clothes from his body with barely contained violence. And something dark and primal in her responded to his ferocity.

Kim slid her gaze the length of his body. Even though he'd healed overnight, she could still see the faint marks left by Liz. She wanted to trace those marks with her tongue, erasing the memory that went with them. "Does your back still hurt?"

He turned to face her. "I've hurt worse." His easy smile belied the tension that stretched taut between them. "I heal more quickly than a human would." Once more he was reminding her that he wasn't human and giving her a chance to back out. The wary look in his eyes said he half expected her to break and run.

Sheesh, if the tension stretched any tighter, she'd be able to pluck it like a guitar string and watch it vibrate. Luckily, it didn't come to that because he moved.

Brynn lowered himself to the couch in one lithe motion and knelt facing her. But not close. For some reason, he'd left lots of space between them. Maybe he thought by giving her room, by not looming, he'd relax her.

No chance. He was within easy stalking distance. And the hungry glitter in his eyes assured her that *stalking* was the right word, as in large, sexy creature of the night.

She stuffed a red velvet throw pillow under her head to prop it up so she could see him better. After all, there was so very much to see.

Instead of pouncing on her, he raised his arms above his head and stretched. His body was a supple flow of hard muscles moving beneath smooth, golden skin.

He was fully exposed, every yummy inch of his body shouting, *Look at me*. Hey, sounded like a good idea to her. She inventoried his torso, taking notes for future pleasure excursions. Hard male nipples, ripe for nibbling. Sexy little navel, perfect fit for tip of tongue. Six-pack abs, delicious hills and valleys her mouth could travel until it got to his best part.

His best part. His sacs hung large and heavy between his strong thighs, his cock jutted thick and long, and sexual energy flowed from him like a flood-swollen river. It wouldn't do any good to swim upstream, so she went with the dominant sensual current. All six feet plus of him.

Touch. It became the most vital sense to her. She wanted to roll around and coat herself in it. Touch touch touch.

"What are you thinking, Kim?" His voice was a raspy purr, a reminder that he really was a sexual animal.

"I'm thinking that if I don't get to touch you soon, you'll have a really ticked-off demon hunter on your hands." She glanced around the room. "Do you think they'd mind if I sharpened my claws on the furniture?"

His laughter rolled over her, warm and real. She wondered how many times he'd laughed with a woman during the compulsion. She'd guess none.

His amusement ended as if he'd thrown an off switch. Still kneeling, he leaned forward to support his upper body with his hands. He watched her. His hair hung tangled and beautiful around his face, the shadow of his beard and those gleaming eyes increasing the aura of danger.

And then he crept toward her. He should've looked awkward crawling on his hands and knees. He didn't. He moved with the loose-limbed, fluid motion of a large predator, muscles rippling beneath all that bare skin.

When he stopped beside her, she exhaled sharply. Kim hadn't even realized she'd been holding her breath.

"Sit up." He still didn't smile.

She didn't smile either. This wasn't party time with Mr. Ordinary. Brynn had lived for five hundred years. Five hundred years of pleasing women. You had to respect that. She sat up.

Brynn drew her top over her head with the same controlled violence he'd used while undressing himself. He was good at the push-pull thing. The tiny germ of fear he'd planted with his ferocity pushed her away, but at the same time he pulled her to him with a sexuality so potent she could taste it on the back of her tongue. It was thick, hot, and rich.

He paused to breathe deeply, and she saw a glimmer of amusement in his eyes. "You make my beast roar without even trying. Do you have any idea how sexy you look lying on this damned couch? No, I guess not. It seems strange feeling this aroused without the compulsion driving me." He fumbled at her waist in the first clumsy movement she'd seen him make.

As she shifted her hips so he could skim everything off from her waist down, she removed her bra. Kim was too excited, too impatient, to wait for him to do it. She lay back on the red pillow, and he followed her down, his lips only a breath away from hers.

"Mmm. I sort of like your beast." She reached up to cup his cheek, and he turned his mouth into her palm.

Kim felt his tongue slide across her skin and shivered at the warm, wet glide of sensual pleasure. And when he covered her mouth with his, she was more than ready.

He traced her mouth with his tongue, and she parted her lips, welcoming him in. He tasted of sex. No exotic flavor, just the heated essence of desire. Tempting. Irresistible.

When he finally broke the kiss to nibble a path down her neck to the swell of her breast, she mourned the loss. But as long as he still had his mouth on her body, life was good.

She arched her back and murmured his name as he closed his lips over her nipple. Her murmur turned to a moan when he flicked the nipple with his tongue.

Kim grasped a fistful of his hair, holding him close to her breast, trying to make the sensations he was creating with his tongue and teeth go on, and on, and on. Every part of her being was so focused on her nipple and its joyous message of erotic satisfaction that for a moment she didn't realize Brynn was in her mind.

"Enjoy the whole, Kim."

"What?" Even in her mind, his voice was a soft brush of seduction.

"Feel the total sexual experience." He moved down her body, his tongue trailing a warm, wet path over her stomach. *"Think about sinking into the red velvet, feel it surrounding you—red heating every inch of skin, velvet strands stroking your body."* He ran his hand over her inner thigh to demonstrate the stroking concept.

"You weren't through with my breasts. I know you weren't. *They* know you weren't." Even as she whined for her abandoned breasts, she had hopes for other body parts. "And I can't do the total experience thing. Whatever part of me you're touching at the moment takes precedence. Sorry, but I always compartmentalize. It's a weakness."

He moved in one smooth motion to kneel between her legs. Slipping his hands beneath her buttocks, he lifted her.

"Whoa, wait. I haven't had a chance to touch you yet." If he put his mouth on her *there*, it would be all over. Lots of pleasure for her complete with cheerleaders and marching band but nothing for him. That's not how it was supposed to be.

His soft laughter was like a warm slide of silk between her legs. He said nothing aloud as he put his mouth on her.

"This isn't about equal time. This is about pleasure for you. Feel the air touching your breasts still wet from my mouth. Remember my mouth on yours, and the velvet beneath you, soft and smooth as your body moves against each strand."

She was trying to remember all those things, but all she could feel was his tongue rubbing back and forth across the very tiny but ultrasensitive center of her personal sexual universe.

Her breathing quickened, her heart pounded, and if he was giving her any other instructions on how to enjoy the total experience, she didn't hear them.

A heavy come-and-get-me feeling was building low in her stomach, the open, wanting sensation of her body needing to be filled. She clenched around the image of his cock, thick and hard, sliding into her and then plunging in and out, in and out.

He slipped his tongue into her, mimicking the rhythm of sex while she arched her back in an attempt to get closer, so much closer, when closer wasn't possible. Her needy whimpers quickly became guttural cries, even as she tipped over the cliff and fell straight down, screaming all the way to the bottom.

And within that moment of climax, she felt his emotions—

intense arousal, joy in her satisfaction, and something not com-pletely formed, something warm and intimate.

When sight and sound finally made sense again, when her trem-bling stopped, and when her orgasm loosened its hold on her and faded to sporadic aftershocks, she looked at Brynn. What had that been about? Her orgasms usually built slowly and predictably. This one had come at her with the speed and intensity of a runaway train and blown her right off the tracks.

He'd lowered her to the couch and was watching her with cau-tious eyes. He was still hard. She'd fallen off the cliff alone. But Kim could fix that. And she didn't give a damn if she kept Lynsay waiting at the restaurant.

"You've always given, haven't you?" She sat up but didn't take her gaze from him.

His smile held the shadows of all those centuries. "It's what I do best, and I wanted you to have my best."

Kim lay back down and studied the sweat-sheened glory of his body. "Pleasure isn't a one-way street for me. You haven't seen *my* best. But you will. Now." She smiled. "Of course, I'll want you to enjoy the whole experience."

He started to glance at his watch.

"Uh-uh. Don't worry about the time. It hasn't been an hour yet. And Lynsay will wait a little while before she calls me." She reached for him.

Suddenly, Fo shouted an alarm from the kitchen. "Demon! I saw it! Told you, told you, told you. Come and get me *now*."

That's when the piano began to play.

They turned to see a woman sitting at the piano. She wore a red dress that came straight out of an Old West saloon scene. Her hair was blond and piled high on top of her head, and her face said thirty-something, married, with two-point-five kids. Nothing ex-traordinary except for her eyes. Her hazel eyes gleamed with a de-monic light she didn't attempt to hide. A gun rested atop the piano. The piano was playing "Let Me Call You Sweetheart."

Most important item in that little collection of facts? The gun, definitely the gun.

Brynn stilled, a complete cessation of movement that radiated danger. "Where did you come from?"

"I was in the bathroom putting on fresh lipstick when you came in. Gotta look great before hitting the streets. But sex just revs me all up, so I stayed in there and listened." She smiled as she picked up the gun. "Oh, did you mean where did I originally come from? You're in my head, so I think you know the answer to that, Brynn."

"Demon." The word was a quiet hiss.

He rolled off the couch and came to his feet with the same fluid grace that promised explosive speed and power. The woman's gaze never left him. She'd probably pegged him as the biggest threat in the room. Then again, you never knew with a demon. A naked Brynn was well worth possessing, in every sense of the word.

The woman's smile widened. "You betcha. Gotta tell you, you're the finest piece of naked tail I've seen since I crawled out of hell. Shame I have to blow you away." She glanced at Kim. "Won't bother me at all to blow you away, bitch."

"Why?" Brynn edged closer, and the woman's eyes narrowed.

"Wouldn't come any closer if I were you." She seemed to relax a little as Brynn stopped. "You, your brothers, and the wizard have to go. You guys are the only ones who could stop us from taking over the city." She looked smug. "You just sort of fell into my lap here. Didn't think I'd get a chance at any of you without going into the castle. Lucky me."

While the demon's attention was fixed on Brynn, Kim crawled off the couch before sidling toward the doorway leading to the kitchen. She prayed Brynn would keep talking. *Please, please, don't rush her and get shot.*

Logically, Kim knew if Brynn was a demon, he'd only die if the woman took his head. But a gun could do the same amount of damage to a head as a sword. Come to think of it, why didn't the woman recognize that Brynn was a demon like her? *Never* like her. Kim knew that instinctively.

Brynn's eyes were cold and empty. No fear, no anger, nothing. "Not too powerful if you need a gun, are you? Bet you're fresh from the lowest rung in hell. Which archdemon called you through the portal?"

The demon's eyes narrowed at his insult. "The One Whose Name Cannot Be Uttered called all of us through."

That tells us a lot. Kim took another step toward the kitchen. Brynn never looked her way, but she knew he was aware of every step she took.

"What park employee's body did you possess?" Brynn didn't move, but Kim sensed his need to fling himself at the demon.

For only a second, the demon glanced down at the name tag pinned to her dress. In that moment, Kim made a break for the kitchen, and Brynn flung himself toward the piano.

Kim heard the gunshot behind her. No! She half turned to go back to the parlor but then forced herself to keep running. If the demon had taken Brynn out, she'd be after Kim next. The only way Kim could help Brynn was by destroying the demon, and for that she needed Fo.

This was all her fault. Kim knew she was supposed to keep Fo within reach all the time. She'd gotten careless, and Brynn might've paid the ultimate price.

The piano was still going strong, so no one probably heard the gunshot. That meant she was on her own. Kim wasn't sure at what point tears started sliding down her cheeks, but she couldn't let images of Brynn lying in a pool of blood stop her. If he was dead, she had to make his sacrifice worth something. That meant she had to nail the demon bitch. Her family would've been proud of her savagery.

Kim barreled into the dark kitchen with the click-clack of the woman's heels echoing in the hall behind her. *The demon.* Despair touched her. If Brynn was okay, the demon wouldn't be chasing her.

And then she forced everything out of her mind except surviving the next few minutes. She scooped Fo off the table and spun to face the kitchen door.

"You forgot your clothes, Kimmie." Fo blinked. "He must've been really good to make you forget—"

"Demon, Fo. Get ready." That's all the warning she had time to give Fo.

The demon paused in the doorway, its eyes glowing red in the darkness. Gone was the human voice, and in its place was the deep growl of a hell-spawned monster. "You can't hide from me. Your puny attempt gave me a giggle, though. So thanks. See you in hell." It raised the gun.

"Don't hold your breath." Kim hit Fo's Destroy button, and the beam caught the demon between those glowing eyes. It shrieked and flung its hands over its face. Too late, much too late.

Then it was over. A small pile of ash marked the demon's passing, and the screaming host stood with her hands over her eyes. "I can't see. I'm blind. What happened? Where am I?"

The woman was careening toward hysteria, but Kim didn't have time for this. She had to get back to Brynn.

She pushed the woman into a chair as she glanced at her name tag. "I'm Kim, and everything's going to be fine, Clarice. Stay here. I'll get help. Don't worry, your sight will come back in about thirty minutes." She had to hope the woman understood her and followed directions. Kim grabbed her purse and then raced back to Brynn.

Kim had Fo clutched tightly to her as she reached the parlor. Even Fo seemed shaken by the violence, because she remained silent. *Please let him be okay, please let him be okay.* She played and replayed her mantra as she got her first look at him.

He lay sprawled across one of the scarlet throw rugs while blood spilled down the side of his head. So much blood. Positive thought. At least he still had a head, so he'd survive. Red coated his hair where it had fallen across his face. As she dropped to her knees beside him, Kim put Fo on the floor and then pulled her cell phone from her purse. She started to punch in 911.

"Don't." His command was a hoarse whisper.

That one word was the most wonderful sound she'd ever heard. "You need help."

He looked up at her through the fall of hair. "It's a head wound. Bleeds a lot. Hurts like hell, but don't think it's serious. No ambulance. No police." He reached up to touch his head and winced. "No way to explain that a demon shot me, but it's okay because I'm immortal."

Put that way, it made sense. "Fo destroyed the demon, but you have a hysterical employee in the kitchen who'll be blind for about another twenty-five minutes. She'll want some answers."

Brynn slowly pushed himself to a sitting position. Kim supported him.

"Call the castle. Tell Holgarth we need help. And then we get dressed before the guys get here. If they walk in and we're still naked, they won't ever get off our cases." He watched her from eyes that gave away nothing as she pulled on her clothes.

Then she helped him into his clothes before calling Holgarth.

"I'll call Lynsay and tell her we can't make dinner." Now that the scary part was over, she couldn't keep her hands from shaking.

"Just tell her we'll be about a half hour late. I can make it." He smiled at her. "The demon was a lousy shot. She just grazed me. If you help me up to my room, I can take a shower, change, and the wound will be almost healed by the time I'm dressed again."

Kim nodded. Reaction was setting in. She'd destroyed demons before, but not when the life of someone she cared for was on the line. Someone she cared for. How much did she care? It'd seemed like a lot when she was racing back to the parlor and didn't know if he was alive or dead. She lifted his hair away from his face and tried to ignore the blood staining her fingers. He was alive, so all the might-haves in the world didn't matter now.

"What about the woman in the kitchen?" What would Clarice remember when she calmed down? How would they explain the temporary blindness?

"Eric will take care of her."

Kim didn't have time to ask how, because at that moment the front door blew open, and Eric, Conall, and Holgarth rushed into the room.

They gathered around Brynn while he told them the short version of what had happened. Minus the part where he'd gotten naked on the velvet couch with her.

Fo finally found her voice. "I kicked some serious demon butt." She narrowed her eyes. "I could've saved Brynn if he hadn't put me in the kitchen so I wouldn't see what he and Kimmie were doing."

Kim seemed really interested in the crystal chandelier. "Can we say duct tape, Fo?"

Eric raised a sardonic brow. Holgarth donned his all-wise and all-disapproving expression.

Only Conall seemed oblivious. He frowned. "So demons are in the park." He turned to Kim. "Better make that call to your family tonight. We don't have much time." He returned his attention to Brynn. "Holgarth and Eric don't need conventional weapons. I'm going to make sure my sword is with me wherever I go. What about you, Brynn?" Conall slid his gaze to Kim. He smiled. "Never mind. You already have your own personal demon destroyer. Lucky bastard."

Brynn ignored Conall in favor of Eric. "Better go back and take care of the woman." He looked at Kim. "She might appreciate having you nearby."

Kim nodded and then trailed behind Eric as he walked to the kitchen. Exciting stuff. Her first vampire action.

He paused in the kitchen doorway to stare at the small mound of ash. "And this is?"

"What's left of the demon after I cast it out of Clarice. Demons always set up housekeeping in the brain, so I had to aim at Clarice's head. Ergo her blindness. The ash is my proof the demon was really destroyed and didn't just move into another home." She shrugged. "Don't ask me how Fo works and where the ash comes from because I don't know. I'm just the executioner."

Eric nodded. He pulled a chair up next to the sobbing woman and sat down. "Hi Clarice. I'm Eric McNair, and everything's going to be fine."

Clarice the hysterical stopped crying. Wow, how'd he do that?

His voice. It was deep, warm, comforting. Kim felt herself go all soft and squishy inside. Anything Eric told her was the truth. She could trust him to take care of her. He'd wrapped her in a fluffy blanket of security.

Wait. Kim did a mental headshake. What was this about? She didn't know Eric, so why the warm fuzzies? But then she glanced at him, looked into his eyes, and knew.

This was heavy vampire stuff. He was changing forms right in front of her. His eyes grew larger and elongated. His pupils swallowed his irises until his eyes looked black, the kind of black you figured you could stare into and see a person's soul. Under different circumstances she would've taken some time to consider the viability of vampire souls, but this wasn't a night for deep vampire thoughts.

Everything sensual about him seemed to intensify. His lips looked fuller, sexier. Probably because of the fangs beneath them. His hair lay in a black tangled glory around his face. Even his body seemed bigger, more muscular.

And yes, she did recognize how really weird her response was. Even as he changed, she should've been rummaging through the kitchen for a clove of garlic, making a cross from two pieces of celery, or whittling a stake from a chair leg. At the very least, she should've screamed loud enough to wake the dead, no, the undead. But after a day filled with demons, a vampire seemed sort of anticlimactic.

He must've felt her stare, because he turned to study her. Something that looked a lot like laughter moved in those black eyes.

She swallowed hard.

He hissed at her.

She squeaked her alarm.

He lifted his lips away from deadly-looking fangs.

She backed into a chair and sat down hard.

He laughed.

"Okay, you've had your chuckles. So what're you going to do about Clarice?" Kim's heart was still trying to hide in her throat.

Eric put a finger to his lips and then stared at Clarice for several minutes. Then he turned to Kim. "How long before Clarice will be able to see again?"

Kim glanced at her watch. "About ten minutes."

He nodded and stared at Clarice for another minute. "I'm finished. We can talk. She won't hear us."

"What did you do?" This was fascinating. A small voice reminded her she wouldn't meet people like Eric if she married Mr. Ordinary. For the first time in her life, she entertained the thought that Mr. Ordinary could be a wee bit boring.

"I have the power to create fantasies for people." He reached out and tapped the side of Kim's head. "Here. Right now, Clarice is leaving her job at the Dead Eye Saloon. She doesn't feel well and wants to go home early. Her boss isn't around, so when she saw me come in here, she figured I could tell him what happened and arrange for a sub to fill in for her tonight. At the end of ten minutes, she'll open her eyes to see me bending over her. I'll tell her she fainted, have someone take her over to the park's doctor so he can look her over, and then arrange for someone to drive her home. Clarice is pregnant, so she'll believe she needs to rest more."

"And this fantasy will seem . . ."

"Completely real." He returned to human form. "Ask Donna someday about the time we played naked on a cloud. She was just getting the feel for cloud sex when Air Force One flew by. The president waved at her. Pretty embarrassing."

"You have to be in vampire form to create the fantasy?" This was so cool. What fantasy would Brynn like? Probably one that took place on a planet where women were extinct. Kim allowed herself a small, secret smile. Maybe not all women. He'd looked really interested on that couch.

"Right." Humor touched his gorgeous blue eyes. "When you want to share a special fantasy with Brynn, come see me."

Okay, getting all defensive here. "What makes you think I'd want that?"

His smile was slow and wicked. "Because I was in your head just now." He held up his hand to stop her rant. "I won't do it again. But Brynn's birthday is coming up on Sunday. He didn't have a birthday until we gave him one. Everyone deserves a good time on their birthday, and Brynn deserves it more than most. Just think about it."

Kim nodded. She stood and took a last look at Clarice. "I have to help Brynn back to his room." She needed to think about what Eric had said.

And as she walked toward the parlor, Kim could feel the sucking sound of desire dragging her down to disaster.

13

Brynn was standing when Kim walked into the parlor. Barely. He was healing, as he always did, but he still felt shaky. Holgarth had done what he did best—manipulate reality—so Brynn could walk back to the castle without people noticing he was a bloody mess. No one had warned Kim, though.

She stared at him, her eyes wide with shock. "You look like nothing happened to you. No wound, no blood."

Brynn shrugged. "I'm still bloody, but Holgarth did his wizard act and hid the gore so I wouldn't scare customers when I left here."

"Are you strong enough to walk?" Kim shook her head. "Of course you are. You're immortal. Superfast healing and all that stuff." She stared at Holgarth. "So what other wizardy things can you do?"

"Wizardy things?" Holgarth raised one brow. "What a delightful turn of phrase. I can do oh so many 'wizardy' things, Ms. Vaughn. For example, I could wait until you leave Galveston and then correct with a twitch of my nose any unfortunate design faux pas you might have inflicted on the castle."

Kim looked like she wanted to snarl at him. "Are you always such a snot?"

Holgarth widened his eyes. "But of course. I live to annoy."

Even in the face of a demon invasion, Holgarth made Brynn smile. "Don't believe him, Kim. Underneath that hard crust is a marshmallow."

"Marshmallow?" Holgarth looked horrified.

Brynn figured now would be a good time to get out of there. "I'm still feeling a little weak. Would you walk back to my room with me?" He offered Kim his wounded-hero expression while ignoring Conall's eye rolling.

"Sure. Do you need to lean on me?" Her eyes were warm with sympathy.

"No. I should be okay. But I'd appreciate the company." Amazing the depths he'd sink to just to keep her with him.

Conall smothered a grin. "Eric will take care of the woman, and we'll see you guys at the meeting."

Brynn nodded and then followed Kim from the bordello. For a few minutes they walked in silence, and Brynn allowed himself to enjoy small pleasures—the soothing darkness, the clean, crisp gulf breeze, a woman who walked quietly beside him demanding nothing. No orders to touch her body or put his cock inside her on cue. Startled, he realized his greatest pleasure was just being alive. He'd survived and was glad of it. When was the last time he'd felt that? Probably never.

He frowned. Brynn knew damned well all this glad-to-be-alive crap was because of Kim. Not good. He wanted Kim to only be about sex. But his great feeling about life in general, even though the demons and Vaughns wanted a piece of him, felt like more than just a sexual high. He'd have to make sure it *didn't* become more. For both their sakes. And so he resisted the urge to take her hand.

It wasn't until they entered the lobby that Kim spoke. "With everything that happened back there, I forgot to ask how long it took for the compulsion to hit this time."

"An hour and twenty minutes. Longer than the last time. I don't know what's happening, but whatever it is, I hope it keeps up." Brynn glanced at his watch. He kept forgetting to check the time when he was with Kim.

"We'll have to test it again." Kim's smile said she'd enjoyed at least part of what the last test had led to. "This time without the pianist from hell."

Fo paused in her scanning of nearby people to gaze up at Brynn from Kim's purse. "I have to stay next time. What if another demon sneaks up on you, huh? Who you gonna call?"

"We'll see." Translation: never going to happen. Brynn looked down at Fo. "Who you gonna call? Been watching some online movies?"

Fo blinked at him. "Of course. How else would I learn what normal human behavior is like?" Calmly, she went back to scanning for demons.

"Normal. Right." Eric figured Fo's view of the world was going to be really scary.

They'd almost reached the elevator when Donna stopped them. "Are you guys okay?" Dressed in jeans and an oversized T-shirt, Eric's wife didn't look anything like what she was, a vampire and the host of a popular late-night talk show. "Eric called and told me what happened."

Brynn smiled. He teased Eric about being chained for all eternity to the queen of late-night radio, but he liked Donna. "We're fine. But the demon was armed. We have to protect the humans in the park. We'll talk about it at the meeting."

Donna nodded and turned to Kim. "How about coming on my show tonight for about an hour? We don't need to give your real name if you don't want to, but I've never interviewed someone who destroyed demons. My listeners would love it. Most of them are pretty knowledgeable, and I guarantee you'd get interesting questions."

Kim paused before answering. "Sounds like fun, but that might not be a good idea right now. I don't want the demons to know a hunter is in town. Get back to me after this is all over, and I'd love to do it."

"You're right about the demons. I didn't think of that. I do a lot of phone interviews, so my listeners wouldn't know you were in Galveston unless you told them. But the people who come to watch me each night in person would spread the news. And you're welcome to come on the show whenever you like. If you're still up around midnight, stop by the lobby and watch a little of the broadcast."

"Will do." Kim smiled, but Brynn saw the strain behind the smile. It was tough to concentrate on much of anything when demons were taking over the city.

Donna seemed to pick up on Kim's mood. "*Donna Till Dawn* could score a radio first. I bet no one else in the media ever got to cover a war with demons. Eat your hearts out, CNN and Fox." She touched Kim's hand and smiled at Brynn. "Gotta go. I told Eric I'd help him get Clarice home."

They watched Donna walk away before continuing on to the elevator. Brynn hit the button and waited for the doors to open. Once again, Kim grew silent. By the time they reached his door and she still hadn't said anything, he began to wonder if she regretted coming with him.

"Look, I feel okay. You probably need to freshen up before dinner." He pushed the door open.

"Lynsay's my sister. I don't need to clean up for her." She stepped into the room with him.

They both paused in the doorway.

All the lights were off, and flickering candlelight gave the room a soft glow. A vase of fresh flowers sat in the middle of the coffee table. Everything was suspiciously neat, not a candy wrapper in sight. The TV was off, and the swelling notes of an aria filled the room.

Opera? Brynn had pretty eclectic taste in music, but he didn't have any opera CDs.

Ganymede and Asima sat on the couch, each with a wineglass in front of them on the coffee table. As Brynn watched, an almost-empty wine bottle hovered in the air above Asima's glass.

"Here, have some more wine, babe." Ganymede's amber eyes gleamed in the semidarkness.

Asima didn't answer because she'd locked her blue gaze on Kim. *"Tell me you aren't letting Sparkle dress you."* She was broadcasting her thoughts to everyone, and she sounded steamed.

Leaping from the couch, she padded over to take a closer look. *"This outfit is a total disaster. You may as well wave a red light over your head. I see Sparkle's tawdry claws all over these clothes."*

Brynn studied Kim—sexy top, sexy pants, and sexy shoes. "This is a great outfit. I like it."

Asima's stare was a power drill through his heart. *"You would. You're a man. A man's taste in clothing is attached directly to his sexual organs."*

"Come back to the couch, beautiful kitty, and drink your wine." Ganymede glared at Brynn behind Asima's back.

Asima ignored him. *"Don't you dare wear one more piece of trashy clothing supplied by Sluts-R-Us. You're a professional. You need something simple but elegant. I'll do some shopping tomorrow and put together a wonderful outfit. Expect me on Wednesday morning."*

Kim looked worried. She should be. Brynn wouldn't want to get in the middle of a fashion war between Sparkle and Asima.

Fo spoke up from Kim's purse. "Um, I'd love to get some fashion tips from an expert, Asima." Her small voice sounded hopeful.

Asima looked down her aristocratic nose at Fo. *"See, even your small sentient being understands that I have superior taste."* She nodded her head regally. *"My first rule, little one, is to keep an uncluttered wardrobe. Classic styles are always excellent choices."*

Brynn didn't need to hear this. He walked around Asima to get to the couch.

"What the hell happened to you, demon?" Ganymede wasn't fooled by Holgarth's trickery.

"Kim and I had a run-in with a demon. Fo took care of it. Don't forget the meeting tonight." Brynn headed toward the bathroom. He'd only have a short time to get cleaned up before they'd have to head down to dinner.

"Yeah, yeah. We'll be there." Ganymede reached out to paw the remote, and the music soared. "Gee, I love opera. Come back to the couch, babe, and listen to it with me."

Brynn winced. "I don't know if you've thought too far ahead, but Sparkle will be at the meeting, too."

Ganymede's eyes grew wide. "Shit. I didn't think of that." He glanced over at Asima to make sure she wasn't listening, but she was still involved in telling Kim what was wrong with Sparkle's outfit. "Look, make sure I'm between you and Kim at this meeting. I won't look like I'm with either one of them. Man, can you believe that music? Asima better be one hot mama to make this all worthwhile."

"You're a lech." Brynn watched Kim walking toward him.

"And your point is?" Ganymede's gaze slipped past Brynn as Asima leaped onto the couch.

"Nothing." Brynn pulled some clothes from his closet and then strode to the bathroom door. Kim hurried to catch up with him.

Asima watched Kim walk across the room before turning back to Ganymede. *"Isn't that outfit really crass?"*

Ganymede stared deeply into Asima's eyes. "There is nothing either good or bad, but thinking makes it so."

Asima seemed doubtful. *"I suppose so. But don't you think my elegant and sophisticated style will look better on Kim?"*

Ganymede looked a little desperate. "This above all: to thine own self be true."

Asima blinked. *"You're right. I have to stay true to my fashion convictions."* She rubbed her head against Ganymede's shoulder. *"You're so in tune with the inner me, and I do appreciate a cat who knows Hamlet."*

"Hey, babe, I'm a regular font of cultural info. How about listening to more of whatever it is we're listening to?"

Brynn shook his head before grinning at Kim. "If he had eyebrows to waggle, he'd be waggling them."

Kim started to answer him but paused at Asima's next words.

"It's Aida, *and this is one of my favorite arias. The music moves me. Doesn't it move you?*" Asima's eyes were slitted in kitty ecstasy.

"Oh, yeah. Moves me." Ganymede's expression said, *Like a bowl of prunes.*

"*I can't help it. I have to sing along.*" And she did.

It took every bit of self-control Kim had not to stick her fingers in her ears. Instant flashback. Jacob Risner in second grade. Whenever the teacher was out in the hall talking to someone, Jacob got his jollies by dragging his fingernails across the chalkboard. Asima's voice had that exact quality. Kitty vocal cords weren't created to sing arias from *Aida.*

"The breaking glass should start any second now. Let's get somewhere safe." Brynn reached into the pocket of Kim's purse, pulled Fo out, and set her on the table next to the door.

Fo caught on fast. "You'd better not leave me out here, because if you do I'll . . . Well, I'll do something really bad." Since she couldn't think of a threat horrible enough to strike fear into his heart, Fo resorted to a full-blown tantrum, complete with angry shrieks that blended right in with Asima's singing.

Brynn grabbed Kim's hand, dragged her into the bathroom, and closed the door behind them. "Ganymede's doomed. I bet his eardrums are bleeding by now."

"Ha, he's getting what he deserves. He's cheating on Sparkle. The only thing worse than listening to Asima sing would be if Sparkle found out what's going on." She thought about that. "I won't be the one to tell her, though. Sparkle would kill the messenger."

"You're right." Brynn glanced at his watch before pulling off his shirt. "It'll be close to one hour by the time I finish my shower. I want to stay in the bathroom until the compulsion hits. Ganymede and Asima don't need to see the show. Besides, Asima might still be singing."

"Uh-huh." Kim stared unblinkingly at his chest. She should've thought of the implications before charging into the bathroom with him. "So, you're just going to strip naked right here, huh?"

His smile was slow and sensual, more of a temptation than Eve's apple ever was. "That's what I usually do before I get in the shower." To demonstrate his stripping-naked technique, he got rid of his shoes and then made a big deal of sliding his pants and briefs off.

"You do that well." The trick was to stay calm, cool, and in control.

"I've had lots of practice." He watched her, something in his eyes saying that her response was important.

A test? If so, she didn't know what he expected her to say. "That's yesterday's news, Brynn. Maybe we should concentrate on figuring out why the time between compulsions is lengthening. And when we find the cause, we keep it going."

He nodded. She thought about asking him if she'd passed, but decided against it.

"As much as I'd like to ask you to share the shower with me or at least wash my back, I'd better do this alone. Otherwise Lynsay will be waiting a long time." He took off his watch and set it on the sink. Then turning his back to her, he stepped into the shower and slid the frosted door closed.

Kim gulped in a huge, fortifying breath. Not many men had a butt beautiful enough to suck all the air from a woman's lungs. Brynn was one of the fantastic few.

She sat on the closed toilet seat and watched the indistinct shadow of his bare body through the door. And yes, she'd love to be in there with him, helping to wash all those hard-to-reach and just plain fun-to-reach spots on his body. But beyond her transparent lust for him, other things about him were intruding that had nothing to do with what part of his body he was sliding the washcloth across at that exact moment.

Was he really a demon? More and more she was thinking no. Okay, so she really wanted it to be no. Why? She didn't have a personal stake in him. Did she? And what about his compulsion? Why did the ugliness of it feel so personal to her?

All questions she wasn't yet ready to answer. Thank heavens he'd shut off the water. As he emerged from the shower, she could return to good old uncomplicated lust.

She had his towel ready when he stepped out. Silently, she handed it to him. The slight lift of those sensual lips said he'd love to feel her rubbing that big fluffy towel all over him.

Kim smiled. "Mmm. Who needs a towel? How about if I spend the next hour licking every drop of water from your body, slowly and with lots of attention to detail?" What could she compare the experience to? "It would be sort of like when you lick those Wicked Red Blow Pops. Each swipe of your tongue isn't just about flavor. It's about the tactile sensation and the anticipation of all those yummy licks to come."

His eyes widened, and then he laughed. Really laughed. It was one of the few times the shadows completely disappeared from his eyes. "See, now I'll be fantasizing about that for the rest of the night." As his laughter died, his eyes darkened to a delicious promise. "After the demon stuff is finished, we'll have to explore all the things tongues can do."

Kim sighed. "Demons. You made me forget about them for a while."

"A little ironic, considering what I am."

His laughter was gone, and Kim mourned its loss. "Have we been together an hour yet?

Brynn glanced at the watch he'd set on the sink. "Right on the dot. Now we wait." He dried himself slowly, purposefully, with evil intent evident in every slide of the towel across his body. He rubbed a wicked path up his inner thigh, and then cupped his balls. He patted them dry. Carefully. Then he slid the towel the length of his cock. He had to keep going back and drying it again because it kept getting longer.

All the condensation on the mirror wasn't coming from the shower. Kim could almost feel steam rising from her body. Hot, hot, hot.

When he'd finished getting his kicks at her expense, he quickly dressed. Except for his shirt. "May as well wait until after the compulsion. I'd just have to put it back on again after ripping it off."

Well, if she had to sit around for a while, at least she had something to look at. Brynn had pulled on a pair of black leather pants and soft leather boots. Leather, a nice contrast to that bare, hunky chest. Mesmerized, she watched him blow-dry his hair until it lay gleaming and tempting across his broad shoulders.

Then they waited, staring at each other across the sterile whiteness of the bathroom, until Kim couldn't stand it anymore. So she asked the question she'd been saving for just the right moment. "You know, I've never had a serious compulsion. What's it feel like?" Maybe it wasn't a compulsion, but she had a very strong need to slide her fingers across his spectacular chest and then explore the tactile sensation of leather-covered muscle and delish body parts.

He seemed to look inward, and what he saw didn't make him happy. "It's a dark beast clawing at your insides, ripping you apart as it fights to get free. And it leaves you in bloody shreds if you don't give it what it wants. It makes you do things you don't want to do, makes you hate what you are, and drives you to despair. You can't run from it, and you can't hide. Ever."

Okay, she was officially depressed. How strong did a man have to be to stay sane after five centuries of that? Not daring to meet his gaze because he'd hate the pity and ignore the admiration he saw in her eyes, Kim called Lynsay to tell her they'd be there soon. Her sister seemed pretty mellow, considering how late Kim was. Strange. Lynsay wasn't a patient person. Mellow wasn't where she was.

Finally, at exactly forty-five minutes past the hour, Kim saw the telltale signs in Brynn's eyes at the same moment he reached for his nonexistent shirt.

He leaned close to her, his scent of warm and clean male animal making her want to wrap her arms around his neck and pull him close.

"I offer my body—"

She put her finger across his lips. "Not now. I don't want your body." Maybe later. Later sounded good.

He nodded and then straightened away from her. "Forty-five minutes late. What the hell is going on?" He shrugged into his shirt. It was black silk and oh so touchable.

"You know, if you tried to look a little grungy, women might turn you down more." She slid her fingers across the silk. Some temptations weren't meant to be resisted.

He simply stared at her.

"Or not." She shrugged. "Let's get going."

Brynn pulled open the bathroom door, and they both listened for sounds of kitty screeching. Nothing. In fact, Asima was gone. Ganymede sprawled on the couch looking blankly at the darkened TV screen.

Kim picked up a silent Fo. No purple eyes. She was sulking. Good. Kim didn't need to listen to a whiny detector right now.

"So how'd it go?" Brynn paused next to the couch.

"Talk a little louder. I can't hear you. I think Asima nuked my eardrums." Ganymede roused himself enough to jump across to the coffee table and stick his face in a wineglass.

"Where's Asima?" Kim tried to keep the smile off her face, but it was tough.

Ganymede turned to give her a long, deadly stare. "She went to *bathe*. I told her cats didn't bathe, but if she felt a little dusty I wouldn't mind giving her a once over with my tongue. She got pissed and said if I put my tongue anywhere near her she'd bite it off." He whipped his tail back and forth. "This scene is getting old. Sparkle's a lot more fun. She understands my complex needs. Besides, I don't have to memorize Shakespeare or listen to opera for Sparkle."

Complex needs? Uh, like sex and food? Kim had to ask. "Why were you so hot for Asima in the first place? I mean, you have no idea what she looks like in human form."

Ganymede's glance said if she had to ask, then she'd never get it.

"It's the challenge, the chase. You see a new babe, and you seduce her because you can. It's a man thing."

Brynn looked thoughtful. "You know, the demonic asshole who made me would've had better luck if he'd given *you* the compulsion. You have the right attitude for it."

Ganymede glanced away. "Guess I'll take a quiet nap before I show up for your big meeting." Without another word, he curled up on the couch and closed his eyes.

Once out of the room, they walked to the elevator in silence. All the way to the lobby, Kim thought about what was bothering her. "Is it just me, or did Ganymede act strangely when you mentioned the compulsion? He just stopped talking, and he *never* stops talking." She shook her head. "I'm letting all the weirdness get to me."

Brynn thought Ganymede's strangeness was pretty much who he was. "Give the guy a break. He'd just survived Asima's singing. That would make anyone act a little off."

"I guess you're right." Kim walked into the restaurant ahead of him. She made her way toward a table where a blond woman he recognized from Holgarth's photo as Lynsay was waving madly.

Brynn stared. Someone was with Lynsay. Someone he knew. Uhoh. A complication.

They reached the table, and Kim turned to introduce him to her sister. "Lynsay, this is Brynn. Brynn this is my sister, Lynsay." She looked at the man seated with Lynsay. "I hope you and Lynsay had a good time today, Deimos."

Deimos blushed, and Lynsay giggled. "Isn't he the cutest thing?"

Brynn stared at Deimos. Cute? Deimos might be many things, but cute wasn't one of them. Big, bald, and bashful didn't translate into cute. But then what did he know about how a woman's mind worked? "Hey, Deimos."

Deimos nodded at him and then looked at Kim. His blush deepened. "Uh, we spent the day doing a bunch of superhero fantasies together. Lynsay's a great Cat Woman." He turned his attention back to Kim's sister, his puppy dog adoration written all over his face.

Brynn was worried. Deimos wouldn't out him to Lynsay on purpose, but Deimos in love might be a loose cannon.

Lynsay patted Deimos's arm as Kim and Brynn sat down at the table. "After we got back to the castle this afternoon, Deimos took me to his room. We were just getting comfy on the couch when he asked me to do this really big favor for him." She looked up at Deimos from under her lashes.

From Cat Woman to the queen of coy in one afternoon. Impressive. Brynn didn't know if Deimos was at a Lynsay level in his sexual development. He hoped she'd be gentle with him. Something of his thoughts must've shown in his face because Kim frowned at him. She probably thought Deimos was "cute," too.

"Here I am with this big hunky guy, and he goes all wild-eyed on me." She smiled at Deimos. "He says I have to help him save his plants." Lynsay shrugged. "I'm thinking this is some weird come-on line. But you just have to reward that kind of creativity. So I let him show me these two plants. Sure enough, they look all droopy, and some of their buds are falling off."

Deimos's gaze skittered from Kim to Brynn and then back again. His blush was gaining speed and power. It should wash over the top of his head within the next thirty seconds.

"Anyway, he gives me this story about the plants needing sexual energy to stay healthy, and they're not getting any of that from him." Lynsay squeezed Deimos's hand, fast-forwarding his blush. "And then he asks if he can kiss me to help his plants. Like if they don't get something soon, they'll lose all their babies. Isn't that cute? He called the buds babies." She shrugged. "I thought a couple of shots of plant food would perk them right up, but Deimos said only a kiss would do the trick."

The smile she turned on Deimos was brilliant, and Brynn realized for the first time that Lynsay was a beautiful woman—long blond hair, big blue eyes, and a smile that was turning Deimos to mush. Funny how he didn't notice what other women looked like when Kim was near. Later on he'd think about what that meant.

Lynsay walked her fingers up Deimos's arm. "So I kissed him. It was just so . . . sweet. He made me feel like I was the first woman he'd ever kissed."

You were. Maybe Deimos being here wasn't so bad. With Lynsay all wrapped up in him, she wouldn't pay much attention to anyone else. Now, if Deimos would just keep his mouth shut about things Lynsay didn't need to know, dinner could roll along without any life-or-death decisions.

Deimos wasn't saying much, but his head was saying a whole lot. He could use his head to guide Santa's sleigh and give Rudolph the night off.

Lynsay finished up with a flourish. "Since Brynn was coming to dinner with you, Sis, I decided to bring Deimos." For the first time she gave Brynn her undivided attention. "I saw your name in the ad for the fantasies. Who do you play?"

He relaxed a little. This was going to be okay. She wasn't suspicious. "I'm the good prince who rescues all the fair maidens." Brynn smiled at her.

She smiled back. "Good prince? I don't think so. I'd guess you're very bad in all the ways a woman wants a man to be bad. That makes you an interesting man." Lynsay glanced at Kim. "Go for it, Sis. A bad man is hard to find."

Conversation stopped while everyone ordered. As she waited for the waiter to leave, Kim pulled Fo from her pocket and set her on the table. Fo gazed at everyone but didn't say anything. Not a Fo-like behavior so Brynn assumed Kim had told her to keep a low profile when Lynsay was around unless she picked up on a definite demonic presence.

Lynsay speared Fo with her disapproval. "Still using that piece of junk, Sis? You need to upgrade to a . . . cell phone that can do the job."

Fo glowered, and Kim sighed. "Fo works just fine for me, Lynsay. And Brynn knows what we are. Deimos doesn't. You and I have business to talk about. Tonight. We can talk now or later tonight. Your call."

Lynsay glanced at a puzzled Deimos. She shrugged. "It doesn't matter. He'll either believe us or not."

Brynn decided to be proactive for a change. He slipped into Deimos's mind. *"No matter what Lynsay says, keep quiet. We don't want her to know what we are, and definitely not what Eric, Conall, or Holgarth are. Oh, and Sparkle would be royally pissed if you gave her away."*

Deimos turned to glance at him but didn't say anything. Good.

Lynsay met Deimos's stare. "Here it is straight, Deimos. Kim and I are demon hunters."

His eyes widened, but he didn't say anything. Deimos was probably trying to figure out why Kim and Brynn weren't trying to kill each other.

Lynsay forged on. "Hey, I'll understand if you want to leave now. Not everyone can handle the news that demons exist and that we hunt them. No hard feelings."

Her words sounded tough, but Brynn didn't miss the vulnerability in her eyes. Well, what do you know, Ms. Big Bad Demon Hunter really did have a soft spot for Deimos. Brynn found himself hoping that Deimos wouldn't blow this.

Deimos grinned at Lynsay. "No way would I leave. I'm training to be an action hero. I have lots of cool action hero stuff in my room that you didn't see. I sort of forgot about it after the kiss. I'll show you later. I could help you guys." His gaze slid to Brynn. "I'd only kill the evil demons, though."

"First rule of the Vaughn family, Deimos: *All* demons are evil." The light of the true zealot shone in Lynsay's eyes. "We kill every one of those suckers."

Okay, Brynn didn't want to listen to her go off on demons. "Galveston has a problem, Lynsay. Kim will fill you in."

He sat back while Kim told her sister everything, except that the man sitting at the table with them was a demon. Deimos's gaze kept shifting back and forth between Kim and him. Brynn could almost hear the wheels turning as he tried to figure out what a demon and a demon destroyer were doing together. Kim only paused in her story while dinner was being served, and then she talked while she ate.

Kim finished off with a slice of apple pie and a call to arms. "We need the whole family here. It'll take everyone to destroy the demons already on the ground. I don't know how we'll find the archdemon or what we'll do when we find him, but we'll take one thing at a time."

Lynsay nodded while she tried to contain her excitement. "I've never had to save a whole city before. If my damned detector wasn't down, I could hit the streets tonight."

"Not a good idea." Brynn couldn't keep quiet about this. "Your family will have to be organized. You've never dealt with this many demons at once. I'd suggest always traveling in twos. I guarantee the demons will be hunting for you in mobs once they realize what's happening. You need to plan how to sweep the city without alerting the authorities. In fact, I'd bet the demons have already possessed a lot of Galveston's police force. If we need people in the community, we'll approach the religious leaders."

Lynsay cast him a long, considering look. "How do you know so much about hunting demons?"

Oops. Okay, he was a demon, and demons lied like hell. "I worked in law enforcement for a while. Whether you're hunting demons or criminals, you'd better have a plan of action or else you'll end up dead. The bad guys aren't going to sit still and let you shoot at them."

Lynsay nodded. "Makes sense."

Brynn glanced at Kim. She reached under the table and patted his knee. Since her hand was already under the table, he wished she'd make better use of it. The gleam in her eyes said she knew exactly what he was thinking.

"This is so great." Lynsay sounded happy about something.

Brynn doubted she was commenting on Kim's hand under the table. He turned to look in the direction she was staring.

Oh, crap.

Uncle Dirk had just entered the restaurant.

14

Kim turned to follow Brynn's gaze. Her eyes widened. "I thought you said Dirk wouldn't be here."

"That's what he told me. But now that he's here, he can meet Brynn, and we can tell him about the demons." Lynsay waved to Dirk just in case he hadn't spotted them.

Panicked, Kim glanced at Brynn. He looked tense but calm. Good. She'd be hysterical enough for both of them. Scanning the restaurant, she spotted Conall and Holgarth at a nearby table. They nodded at her, and she relaxed a little. If a wizard and an immortal warrior couldn't stop Dirk from turning Brynn into a pile of ash, then no one could. But just in case, Kim put her hand on Fo. One move toward his detector and she'd nail Dirk in the eyes.

The enormity of how far she was prepared to go in defense of an admitted demon boggled her mind. Not only would Dirk be royally ticked, but also the rest of the Vaughns would drum her out of the family business. Sure she wanted out, but she wanted to go with dignity. She'd be lucky if any Vaughn outside of her immediate family even talked to her anymore.

Was this how important Brynn had become to her? Pause for deep soul searching. Yep.

Dirk offered them a perfunctory smile as he pulled out a chair and sat down. Kim held her breath, waiting for his detector to sound an alarm. Brynn edged his chair away from the table. Deimos looked worried. Two tables over, Conall and Holgarth stopped eating to watch.

"I'm glad I caught you still here. I hate eating alone." Dirk motioned the waiter over and got a menu. "I had some business to take care of, and then I spent time getting my boat ready for the tournament." He seemed oblivious to the tension thrumming around the table.

Kim expected his detector to go off at any minute. Maybe he'd left it in his room. Could they get that lucky? When in doubt, talk. "You're here for the fishing tournament? Wade, the man in the room across from mine, is competing in it, too."

Dirk leaned forward, his gaze intent. "Wade Thomas? Tall guy? Brown hair and eyes? Looks to be in his early thirties?"

Kim nodded. So far so good. Maybe Brynn would actually get out of this in one piece. "You know him?"

"I know *of* him." Dirk looked thoughtful. "I've never met him personally. I went to his Web site to see what he looked like, and I have to admit his list of tournament wins is impressive." His smile didn't bode well for Wade. "But he won't win this one. Definitely not this one."

Lynsay shifted impatiently. She'd evidently heard all she wanted to hear about fishing. "Uncle Dirk, this is Brynn McNair. He's with Kim. And you already know Deimos."

Kim felt Dirk's reluctance to drag his thoughts away from Wade and the fishing tournament. He nodded at Deimos and reached across the table to shake hands with Brynn. "A pleasure, McNair. Are you one of the McNairs who run the castle? I met Conall at breakfast."

Brynn's smile looked relaxed, as if he weren't shaking hands with a man capable of destroying him. "Guilty. I hope you enjoy your stay here, and good luck in the tournament."

There were secrets in Dirk's smile. "I intend to have a wonderful time here. I'll be doing the two things I love most, fishing and hunting demons." Almost too casually, he reached into his jacket pocket and pulled out his detector.

Time seemed suspended for Kim as he flipped it open. Tensing, she wrapped her fingers around Fo. And then he set it on the table. She breathed out a relieved sigh. Glancing around, she noted that everyone except Lynsay—who hadn't a clue—was doing the same thing.

Still smiling, Dirk looked at Brynn and Deimos. "I hope I didn't just give away any secrets. You do know that Kim and Lynsay are demon hunters?" He switched his attention to the sisters. "Honesty is always the best policy. You should be proud of your heritage. If the men in your lives can't accept that demons do exist and that you hunt them, then it's best if you find out now." He leaned back to witness the result of his disclosure.

Brynn shrugged. "Deimos and I already know that."

Dirk looked disappointed. The jerk. He'd been hoping for a mass exodus by "the men in their lives." It didn't look like he was going to see any action, so Dirk disappeared behind his menu. Finally Kim felt secure enough to release her death grip on Fo, but she still kept her hand resting lightly on the detector.

She frowned as she stared at Dirk's detector. It stared back at her with big red eyes. Why hadn't it identified Brynn as a demon? Kim glanced at Brynn. He shrugged. Since the same man had made both detectors, maybe they shared the same problem. Or not. Fo thought anything that moved was a demon. Dirk's little buddy didn't have anything to say at all. Strange.

Fo vibrated gently, and Kim panicked. No. She'd told Fo that under no circumstances was she to talk in front of Lynsay. Kim lifted her hand to glare at Fo, hopefully forestalling anything the detector was about to say.

But Fo wasn't looking at her. She'd rolled her eyes to the side and was gazing at Dirk's detector. Dirk's detector stared back at her. Fo's vibration grew more frantic. Uh-oh. She turned Fo to face her before putting a finger over her lips. Fo's eyes looked mutinous, but she kept quiet. Which was more than Lynsay did.

"Wow, I just noticed. Fo and Uncle Dirk's detector both have eyes. That Sergei guy must've made both of them." Lynsay grinned at Dirk, who'd emerged from behind his menu. "I hope yours works better than Fo. She's useless."

Dirk stared at Fo with the same attention he'd give a spider crawling across the table. "Your detector is still working, Kim?"

Not what Kim had expected him to ask. "Sure. Why shouldn't it?"

He shrugged. "Lynsay's went down, so I just wanted to make sure yours was still working. We need every detector up and running to fight the good fight against demons."

Fight the good fight? She thought about Brynn—his kindness to Fo, his humor, his desire to protect his home and friends, and his hatred of what he was forced to do. Dirk would destroy Brynn without a twinge of conscience in the name of righteousness. Everything in Dirk's world would always be black or white. Kim was running into lots of gray lately.

And there were still the lingering doubts about Brynn's demonic nature. Too many things in Brynn's life didn't line up with what Kim knew of demons.

Brynn leaned back and studied Dirk. "You call demon hunting your business, so I assume you don't do it for the good of mankind. Can you make a living from it?"

"You'd better believe it." Dirk seemed happy to spread the good word about demon hunting. "People all over the world believe in demons and want the Vaughns to get rid of them. The people who come to us are the ones who don't trust exorcisms or whose clergy don't believe they have a demon problem. They're willing to pay the price for a demon-free life."

"Lucky for you."

Only Kim seemed to hear the sarcasm in Brynn's voice. She jumped in before he had a chance to say something more that might antagonize Dirk. "You seem to think you'll find demons here. If you do, who will pay you to destroy them?"

Dirk shrugged. "Probably no one. I'll just count this as recreational hunting."

Kim shivered. Thank heavens she didn't have to think up anything else to say because the waiter returned for Dirk's order.

Lynsay waited until Dirk finished ordering before hitting him with the demons-are-taking-over-Galveston news.

Words to describe Dirk after finding out he'd have a whole city full of demons to zap? How about overstimulated and foaming-at-the-mouth enthusiastic? Jeez, he was one scary man when he was in demon-destroying mode.

He couldn't even sit still long enough to finish his meal. After only a few bites, he told the waiter to box the rest up. Then he left with his detector and his uneaten meal. He figured it would take the rest of the night to contact as many Vaughns as possible.

Everyone was quiet for a few seconds after he left.

"Hard to believe, but he's more obsessed than I am about offing demons." Lynsay cast Deimos a smile that had sexy intentions written all over it. "Why don't we go up to your room and take a look at your action hero stuff. See if there's anything we can use in the coming battle."

Deimos lit up. "Yeah, I didn't think of that. This'll be my first real chance to be an action hero."

Kim watched them leave the restaurant. They were holding hands. She frowned. As much as she knew her sister could take care of herself, she didn't know how she'd feel if things got serious. Deimos had Sparkle's eyes. Were they related? The thought of Sparkle as part of her family froze her blood.

Kim closed her eyes for a moment of intense meditation. *Please, please, don't let them get serious.* When she opened them again, she felt better. She was foolish to worry. Once Lynsay found out that Deimos wasn't human, she'd be gone. Or maybe not. Damn, a new worry. Lynsay was consistent in her belief that all nonhuman entities were demonic and therefore kill-worthy. Deimos had to make sure Lynsay didn't find out what he was.

Brynn glanced at his watch. "Look, I'll meet you outside the conference room in a few minutes. I can't take a chance of the compulsion hitting while I'm in the meeting."

She watched him stride away and wished fiercely that she could find a way to rid him of the damned compulsion.

"Kimmie?" Fo was using her small voice, an indication of extreme uncertainty.

"Hmm?" Kim walked slowly toward the conference room.

"That detector is like me." Excitement bubbled beneath the surface of Fo's voice.

"Sure looks like it." Where was this leading?

"I want to talk to him." Fo looked up at Kim, longing clear in her big, purple eyes. "I've never met anyone like me before. It gets lonely being the only me."

What could Kim say to that? "Are you sure the detector is a him?"

"Uh-huh. Very sexy, too. I wanted to . . ." Fo blinked. "It doesn't matter how sexy he is because I can't do what humans do, can I, Kimmie?"

A moment of truth. Fo smacking right into one of her limitations. But Kim would always be honest with her. "No, you can't, Fo." That sounded so cold, but she didn't know what else to say.

Fo seemed to think about that for a moment. "I can still talk to him. Will you ask Dirk if I can visit with his detector?"

Kim should nip this now before Fo got hurt, but she was helpless in the face of all that hope. "I'll ask, Fo, but I wouldn't count on spending much time with him. We don't even know if he's as . . . aware as you are."

Brynn rejoined Kim in time to catch the end of her conversation with Fo.

"Who does Fo want to spend time with?" He was finding more and more that he hated having to leave Kim to avoid triggering the compulsion, because those minutes away from her were a constant reminder of what he was. And of what he could never be.

Kim linked her arm with his and looked up at him. "Dirk's detector. She's hoping he'll be like her. I don't know, Brynn. I'm probably being overprotective, but I don't want Dirk to know what Fo is. Any ideas about how to allow Fo to visit when Dirk isn't around?"

Brynn shook his head. "I get the feeling Dirk isn't the kind of guy to let his detector out of his sight."

"I love the concept of star-crossed lovers. It's a classic theme in the world's greatest dramas. Romeo and Juliet *for example."*

Brynn turned at the sound of Asima in his head. He looked down to discover she wasn't alone. A worried-looking Ganymede stood beside her. Asima was dressed for the occasion with a blue velvet collar that matched her eyes exactly.

Asima stared at Fo. *"Although comparing two overachieving cell phones to Shakespeare's most tragic lovers is a bit of a stretch."* She glanced at Ganymede expectantly.

"What's in a name? That which we call a rose by any other name would smell as sweet." Ganymede didn't look like his heart was in all this Shakespeare stuff anymore.

"You're absolutely right. It doesn't matter what they look like or what their names are—although the name Fo does lack a certain rhythm and grace—they're still lovers in need of my help." Asima nuzzled Ganymede's ear. *"Only you would know Shakespeare's plays so well that you could come up with the perfect quote from* Romeo and Juliet *to put everything in perspective. You're brilliant."*

"Yeah. I'm so smart I've outsmarted myself." Ganymede cast Brynn a panicked glance only another male would understand.

Asima leaned into Ganymede. *"He was on his way down to the meeting all by himself when I ran into him. Now we can sit together."*

Brynn met Kim's amused stare. Looked like the main event would have a sideshow tonight.

"Does that mean Asima will help me meet Dirk's detector?" Fo stayed focused on what was important.

Brynn held the door while Kim walked into the room. "Sounds that way." He didn't want to think about what form that help would take.

Almost everyone else was already there—Eric, Donna, Conall, Holgarth, and a werewolf that had checked in four days ago.

Kim and Brynn sat down. Ganymede and Asima leaped onto chairs beside them.

Brynn glanced at them. "Why didn't you guys change to human form for the meeting?"

Ganymede gave his imitation of a cat shrug. "It's tough to change. Why spend all that time and energy just for a meeting?"

Holgarth scanned the room. "It is precisely seven o'clock. Where is Sparkle Stardust? I have a schedule to maintain." He picked up a gavel lying in front of him and brought it down on the table once. "And before anyone complains about me being dictatorial, let me remind you that he who wields the gavel is the boss."

As if on cue, Sparkle flung the door wide and swept into the room with Wade in her wake. "I bet you were just bitching about me being late, Holgarth. Too bad. I had to wait for my nails to dry. Wade has a great boat, but it's hell on nails."

She looked around the room, sensual smile firmly in place. Until her gaze reached Ganymede and Asima.

Brynn felt everyone in the room suck in their collective breaths as Sparkle's eyes narrowed to dangerous slits.

Holgarth was no dummy. He rushed into speech. "Yes, well, sit down, Sparkle. We have a lot to talk about."

Sparkle grabbed Wade's hand to pull him around the table. They sat directly across from Ganymede and Asima.

Holgarth didn't give any of them a chance to do more than exchange dirty looks. "We've called all the nonhumans in the castle together because Galveston has a crisis. Ms. Vaughn and Brynn have discovered that demons are taking over the city. This isn't something the city authorities could handle even if they did believe in demons."

"Whoa." The unnamed werewolf stood. "Count me out. I just came down for a few days of R & R. No way am I getting in the middle of a war with demons. I'm checking out right now." He hurried from the room, leaving a moment of silence behind him.

Sparkle took advantage of the quiet. "So, Mede, has Asima introduced you to the finer things in life?" Her lips smiled, but her eyes promised he'd better enjoy those finer things quickly because life could be damned short.

Ganymede flattened his ears and whipped his tail back and forth. "Who's your friend? And here I always thought you hated boats. Last time I took you out on one you puked your guts up."

Sparkle's smile turned wicked. "This is Wade. He's a demon. And I didn't get sick on Wade's boat."

"Probably because we didn't leave the dock." Wade shifted uneasily. The winds of war blowing gale force back and forth across the table must be buffeting him.

"You don't deserve someone as cultured and refined as Ganymede, Sparkle." Asima must've decided Ganymede needed some backup. "Find someone who rips beer caps off with his teeth and farts in time with the marching band at halftime." She leaned into Ganymede. "Ganymede enjoys fine wine, opera, and Shakespeare."

Sparkle looked set to throw herself across the table onto Asima.

"I don't mean to interrupt this really fine fight, but did anyone else catch that Wade is a demon?" Conall glared at Wade. "Not that I'd accuse you of sleeping with the enemy, Sparkle, but we need to find out which side of the fence old Wade is on."

Brynn decided this was as good a time as any to get the discussion back on track. "Feel free to take personal disagreements somewhere else, because right now we have important decisions to make." He glanced at Wade. "You want to tell everyone a little about yourself?"

Wade shrugged. "What's to tell? I'm a eudemon. One of the good guys. Eudemons are pretty laid back. I don't answer to any archdemon. I do my own thing, and that's fishing. Okay, maybe I cheat a little when I fish, but that's the extent of my demonic activities." He glanced around the room. "Looks like you have a big problem, though, if a bunch of cacodemons are trying to take over. They're typical A-type personalities, really motivated to do as many bad things as they can in the shortest amount of time. And if an archdemon is doing the organizing, you're in a world of shit."

Kim leaned toward Brynn. "Wade is a *demon*? Did you know he was a demon?" Her whispered question was a quiet hiss of anger.

He was tempted to lie. That's what demons did.

He told the truth. "Yeah, but he's not your stereotypical evil entity. He's not a danger to anyone."

"Well, he was sure a danger to Fo. Did he purposely try to destroy her so she couldn't identify him?" Kim's voice was a little louder.

"He was just trying to protect himself. Wade was afraid if Fo identified him as a demon, you'd try to destroy him." He raised his own voice.

"Yo, folks, I can talk for myself." Wade rested his elbows on the table and speared Kim with his gaze. "I'm sorry for trying to stomp on Fo, but you have to admit the Vaughns have a reputation for kicking demon ass."

Kim frowned. "Yes, but—"

"I sort of like my existence, so I did what I needed to do. And Brynn didn't know you well enough to predict how you'd react to having a demon for a neighbor. He couldn't tell you the truth." The demon shifted his gaze to Fo. "I'm sorry for causing you trouble, little lady. Am I forgiven?" He offered Fo his best good old boy grin.

Fo looked uncertain. She still wasn't used to being treated as a sentient being. "I guess so. Just don't do it again. Brynn had to work really hard to put me back together."

Wade looked around the room. "By the way, who's the idiot responsible for putting a demon right across the hall from a demon hunter? Don't tell me it was a coincidence, because I don't believe in coincidences."

Eric rubbed the back of his neck. He looked weary, and the meeting had hardly begun. "The owner always checks out the reservations a few days in advance. Don't ask me why, because I don't know. I seem to remember that the owner told Holgarth to change your room to the one across from Kim's."

"Pretty hands-on owner, wouldn't you say?" Wade's eyes began to glow, hinting at the power hidden behind his easygoing facade. "Maybe I need to have a little chat with this owner."

Eric shrugged. "If you find out the owner's name, let us all know. We haven't a clue who owns the park. Holgarth—"

The pounding of the gavel captured everyone's attention. Holgarth held his wooden attention-getter ready to bring it down again. "As fascinating as all these glimpses into your personal lives are, we have a city to save."

Wade nodded. "I won't do any hand-to-hand stuff with the cacodemons, but I can act as your demon consultant. Sort of give you some insight into how they think." He paused. "Of course, except for the archdemon, they don't do too much in the way of thinking at all."

Holgarth nodded. "We wouldn't ask a guest to put himself in harm's way."

"Dirk is calling as many of the Vaughns as he can reach. They should start arriving tomorrow. They'll need places to stay." Kim looked expectantly at Holgarth.

Kim seemed focused on the demons, but Brynn had no doubt she'd have a few words to say about Wade once they were alone.

"If we don't have enough rooms here, we'll find places nearby. With so many spring breakers in Galveston, it won't be easy, though." Holgarth straightened his pointed hat and smoothed his blue robe, signaling he was up to the challenge.

"We have to find the archdemon, get rid of him, and then close the portal. Otherwise demons will keep coming through to replace the ones the Vaughns destroy." Sounded pretty simple, but Brynn knew lots of things could go wrong. The demons they'd seen today hadn't seemed particularly dangerous, but once night fell, true evil came out to play.

Kim nodded her agreement. "Finding the archdemon will be tough. I remember reading that an archdemon has the ability to completely cloak his presence. Our detectors won't be able to spot him. And I assume if he's that powerful, he'll also be able to shield his thoughts from you guys." She lifted her hands in a gesture of helplessness. "Where do we start looking?"

Conall offered her a wolfish grin. "Catch one of those suckers outside a human body, and I'll make it talk."

Brynn shook his head. "That's the problem. We can't harm the humans they're possessing, and I don't think any of them will manifest in their true forms just to help us. We also have to take care of the humans after we destroy the demons. Eric will have to run around changing memories like crazy. We don't need a panic in the city."

After throwing ideas back and forth for almost an hour, Holgarth finally rapped his gavel for silence. "I think we've agreed that finding the archdemon and the portal are of paramount importance. We'll conduct an ongoing search while we wait for the Vaughns to arrive. They can destroy the demon hordes while we deal with the archdemon. I'd suggest we travel together, since none of us has ever dealt with a demon as powerful as we assume the archdemon is."

There was a murmur of agreement.

Holgarth took a deep breath. "It's time to wake the gargoyles."

Kim looked at Brynn. "Wake the gargoyles? What's that about?"

Brynn frowned. "Gargoyles guard the four corners of the fence surrounding the park as well as all the doors. They're more than just decorations."

"This is one of the 'wizardy things' I do, Ms. Vaughn." Holgarth gestured imperiously, and everyone rose obediently to follow him. "Conall, please have someone reroute people away from the entrance to the great hall until I'm finished."

Conall nodded and left. Holgarth led them into the courtyard, and then he turned to face the two massive gargoyles guarding each side of the great hall doors. Grotesque faces with huge bulging eyes and fanged mouths open in silent screams were enough to make Brynn think twice about waking them. They were scary enough asleep.

Holgarth smiled at Kim, a slight lifting of his lips that was his official token smile. "You once asked what my job description was. In my own tacky way, I protect the park."

Kim sighed as she looked at Brynn. "He never forgets an insult, does he?"

"Never. He can tell you the exact date Napoleon called him a useless old pretender who couldn't conjure horse shit. That's the day Holgarth left his employ and the day before Napoleon got his butt kicked at Waterloo. Wizard vengeance isn't pretty."

Brynn was trying to concentrate on what Holgarth was doing, but Kim's closeness was raising hell with his attention. His close encounter of the scary kind with the piano demon hadn't done a thing to dampen his anticipation of spending more quality time with Kim. Maybe after Holgarth finished with his gargoyles.

"I will now call forth the power of all the gargoyles in the park through these dominant two." Holgarth raised his arms and chanted in a language Brynn didn't recognize.

Kim moved closer to Brynn. "What will happen now?"

"I don't know. He's never had to call on them before." He *did* know what was happening to his body with her so near.

Suddenly, Holgarth flung his arms wide and shouted one final word. Like well-rehearsed special effects, lightning flashed across the clear night sky followed immediately by booming thunder that shook the ground.

He cast his audience a sly glance. "I don't actually need the lightning and thunder, but I so enjoy the drama of the whole thing." Holgarth turned back to the gargoyles and spoke to them in English. "We call on you and yours to protect those within this park from all—"

Brynn held up his hand. "Whoa. Don't forget to stick in an exception there, or else they'll kick me out, too." The hope-springs-eternal part of him wanted to see whether the gargoyles would keep him out if Holgarth made a blanket demon statement. The ignorance-is-bliss part of him thought that was a stupid idea. Since meeting Kim, he'd wrested a sliver of hope from his centuries of hopelessness. He'd guard that sliver fiercely.

Wade tapped Holgarth on the shoulder and whispered. "Cacodemons. If you say all demons, your watch-gargoyles will toss me out. And I'm here for the whole week." He slid a considering glance Brynn's way. "You're a demon, too? Could've fooled me. Never got a hint." His gaze shifted to Kim. He smiled. "A demon and a demon hunter. Whatta you know."

Holgarth glared at Wade. "Cacodemons." His gaze moved to Brynn. "Brynn will be allowed to dwell within the park."

Deep rumbling growls echoed from all sides of the park. The eyes of the two gargoyles guarding the great hall glowed yellow, and their huge mouths stretched wide in terrifying roars. They then grew silent, but their eyes still glowed in the darkness.

"Well, hell." Eric's soft expletive said it for everyone.

Holgarth turned once more to his audience. Lines of weariness creased his face. "These kinds of rituals take more out of me as the centuries pass."

He took off his tall conical hat and ran his fingers through his gray hair. It was the first time Brynn had ever seen him without the hat.

"Any demons within the park when the gargoyles took over protection duties will be expelled along with their human hosts. Any new demons trying to enter will be unable to do so." He put his hat back on. "I think I'll retire early tonight to renew my energies for the coming battle."

Brynn watched Holgarth leave, and then he looked down at Kim. "Looks like we have a few hours to kill." *Spend them with me.*

She reached up to touch his head where the demon's bullet had skimmed him. "Almost healed. Amazing." She smiled. "Eric promised me one of his designer fantasies. After the day we've had, we deserve a good fantasy."

15

Sparkle paced behind her counter, the sharp click-click of her heels punctuating her rising fury. "You slime-sucking, cheating worm. I gave you sex like you've never had it before, and what do you do? You slither around behind my back with that tight-ass bitch."

Mede watched warily from his perch on top of her chocolate covered cherry display. "Hey, the cheating street runs both ways. I've taken you on some of the best adventures of your life, and you run off with a demon *fisherman*. What's that all about? Big deal, he drops a hook in the water and then waits all day to catch a fish he could've bought in the nearest supermarket. Woohoo, Mr. Excitement. Besides, you hate boats."

Sparkle narrowed her eyes to vengeance-filled slits. It was a good thing she'd put a Closed sign on her door. She didn't want any customers walking in on the carnage. And there would be carnage. "Don't you dare try to justify what you did. I only toured his stupid boat, while you . . ." Her lips wouldn't form the words to express what she thought he'd done, so she let her hands do the talking.

Reaching into her glass display case, she grabbed two fistfuls of jelly beans and flung them at him.

With a startled hiss, Mede crouched as jelly beans rained down on him and bounced off the walls and floor. "Whoa, getting a little emotional, sugar tart."

"I'll sugar tart you." Sparkle shrieked her rage as she scooped up handfuls of liquid-center chocolates. She heaved them at him. One made a direct hit on his forehead, while the rest went splat against the wall and sort of oozed down to the floor. "I gave you the best centuries of my existence, you toad."

"Okay, okay, maybe I made a mistake going off with Asima." He pawed at his face and only managed to spread the sticky goo to his feet.

"You had sex with the one woman in the universe who drives me ab—"

Incoming fudge bombs. Mede covered his head with his paws.

"so—"

Hailing peanut clusters. "Ouch, that hurt."

"lute—"

Chocolate buttercream missile attack. "Losing my patience here, babe."

"ly—"

Lethal truffle twister at twelve o'clock. Mede jumped aside just in time.

"crazy!"

Mede had evidently had enough. He leaped to the floor and hid under the display. "Don't make me use my power, Sparkle. Put the nougats down."

Sparkle had exhausted her anger. The only thing left was sadness. She dropped the nougats onto the counter.

"Now step away from the nougats." Mede peeked out from under the display.

She walked around to the front of the counter and sat on the floor amid the destruction. "We had lots of good times, Mede. Why wasn't that enough?" Stupid question. They were cosmic trouble-makers, and cosmic troublemakers didn't form emotional ties. He had a right to be with any woman he chose. But why the hell did he choose Asima?

Mede emerged cautiously and then padded over to sit beside her. "I didn't have sex with Asima."

"Ha. I bet you busted your butt trying, though." But she brightened marginally. "Why bother with her at all when we were planning a good time of our own?"

Mede made another attempt to clean some of the sweet goop from his paws, face, and whiskers. "I don't know. Maybe I wanted to see what kind of woman could piss you off like that. And maybe I got tired of you only calling me when you needed something. It would be kinda nice if you just wanted *me* for a change, with no strings attached. It's like I always have to earn my good times. That does a job on a guy's pride."

Sparkle frowned. Okay, now she was starting to feel a little guilty. Not much, just a little. She glanced at her nails. She'd broken one of them while she was flinging candy. And for probably the first time in her existence, she didn't care.

"Wade's a lot of fun, but he's not you." That was as close to an apology as he was going to get.

Mede gave up on his face. "Yeah, I know what you mean. Asima was driving me crazy with her operas and plays. Funny thing, when she was telling you to get a guy who ripped the caps off beer bottles with his teeth, I was saying, 'Hey, that's me.' "

Sparkle smiled. "Really?"

He chuckled. "It's true. I kept missing your fire, your passion, your temper." Mede frowned. "Maybe not the temper so much."

She looked around her. "When I lose it, I lose it big-time. Jeez, Deimos and I will have to clean this mess up before I open tomorrow."

Mede moved a little closer. "Forget about the mess. How about if I change to human form and spend the night creating some serious heat?"

She thought about that. Was she ready to forgive him completely? Probably not. She'd make him pay in little ways for a long time, but tonight she wanted the great sex only he could deliver. A full-blown screaming rage always made her horny.

Sparkle nodded. "Sounds like a good idea. Oh, have you decided what you want to do with Brynn?"

Mede glanced away. "You were right. He hates what he is. But I've got a problem. I tried to reverse everything, and it didn't work. I always get this tingle when I make something happen. No tingle this time." He frowned. "For thousands of years I've been a do-it kind of guy. I don't know how to undo it."

"What about the demons? Should we care?" The only truly important word in her vocabulary was *me*. And demons couldn't harm a cosmic troublemaker.

"I sort of like Brynn." Mede looked a little uncertain.

Interesting. Mede was never uncertain. "Yeah, Kim has possibilities. She looked great in my outfit. And I wouldn't like to see demon scum wipe out Eric, Donna, Conall, or Holgarth." Asima? She'd stand on the sidelines and cheer for the demons.

"Don't get me wrong, I don't give a damn about anyone but us, but I guess it wouldn't hurt to help." His narrowed eyes suggested that helping others wasn't at the top of his to-do list. "If we weren't doing anything else, I mean."

"Sure. Like if I was trying on a new pair of Jimmy Choos, the demons would have to wait." She didn't want Mede to think she was getting soft.

"Right. I'm glad we got that straight." He still didn't look comfortable with the concept of joining the goodness-and-light team. "Have to be careful, though, and not be too helpful. Wouldn't want to tarnish my reputation for being a badass."

Sparkle sighed. She'd used up all her emotion for tonight. She'd have to worry about Brynn tomorrow. "Maybe we'll think of a way to get rid of Brynn's compulsion after a good night's sleep."

Mede stretched and padded toward the door. "Wouldn't count on that good night's sleep. I have some creative moves to lay on you." He mumbled under his breath as his feet stuck to the floor. "First thing I'm gonna do as soon as I change forms is to jump in the shower." He leered at her from those amber eyes that were so Mede, no matter what form he took. "Wanta wash my back?"

She turned off the lights and joined him at the door. "Mmm. Sounds like an invite to steamy fun." She glanced at her broken nail. Fine, so a girl couldn't ignore her nails forever.

Eric followed Kim and Brynn into her room. "So what kind of fantasy do you want?"

She looked at Brynn. "You choose. I don't feel too creative right now." *Just make it hot and totally sexy.*

Brynn nodded before turning to Eric. The two men stared at each other for about a minute, and then Eric grinned. "You're weird, man."

She'd missed something. "What?"

Eric laughed. "Brynn chose a two-part fantasy. He gave me the details mentally. Wants it to be a surprise."

Kim sat on the side of her bed and kicked her shoes off. Oooh, yes. She'd never known how good absence from pain could feel. "How do your fantasies work? Do we have to do anything special?"

Eric shook his head. "Just get comfortable, and I'll do my part. I set up the parameters of the fantasy in your minds, and then you guys do the rest. While you're in the fantasy, it'll seem completely real and make perfect sense no matter how outrageous it is. Once the fantasy is done, you'll remember it but realize it wasn't real."

She was curious about this vampire with the freaky power. "Do you have other options when you create fantasies?"

"Definitely." His smile caught at her, and Kim understood why Donna had chosen to become vampire. Forever with this man wouldn't be a hardship. "I could make you believe in the realness of the fantasy long after it ended. For the rest of your life, if that's what I wanted. Clarice, for example, will never remember what happened during the time she was possessed." He shrugged. "But I'm a good guy, so I wouldn't do that to you." His smile widened. "Especially with this fantasy. You've got an evil mind, Brynn old buddy."

"Sounds awesome." Kim was still skeptical. She had a firm grasp on reality—or at least she had before visiting the Castle of Dark Dreams—and if the fantasy got too wild she'd recognize it for the make-believe it was.

She watched Eric go completely still, that total absence of movement no human could attain. And then he became vampire—his eyes changing from blue to black as they grew larger and more elongated, his mouth becoming fuller to accommodate his fangs, and his aura of power and danger filling the room.

He focused on them for a few minutes while he planted the fantasy in their minds, and then he returned to human form. "You could travel the universe and never leave this room." Eric winked at Kim. "See, hanging with a creature of the night has an upside." He walked to the door. "I don't have to be here during the fantasy. Just relax, and it'll come." He closed the door softly as he left.

It made her uneasy to know Eric had messed with her mind, and she hadn't felt a thing. Silence wrapped around them. "I guess I'll relax right here." She propped herself against the headboard.

Brynn nodded. "Sounds good to me." He took off his shoes and joined her.

"So . . . Here we are." *Just relax.* Easy for Eric to say. Her body wasn't listening to her brain, though, because tension still made her insides quiver.

His soft laughter caused the quiver to expand exponentially. "This will be fun. Nothing to worry about." Brynn reached across to clasp her hand.

"That's what my dad said the first time he took me on a roller coaster. When we got off, I threw up on his shoes." The warmth of his big hand seeped into her, and she felt the tightness inside her ease.

"Then I guess it's lucky I took off my shoes." He squeezed her hand gently. "Close your eyes and concentrate on something that makes you feel good."

She glanced at him and smiled. "I'd have to keep my eyes open for that." Was that too obvious? Uh, yeah. But if she really grinned a lot, he might think she was only being playful. The sad truth? She was totally serious. No matter what kinds of weird things happened around them, he made her happy when he was near. If he made her any happier, they'd have to treat her for an overdose of bliss before she left the Castle of Dark Dreams.

He didn't return her smile, but an emotion she couldn't identify touched his gaze.

She closed her eyes so she wouldn't have to see him struggling to say something meaningless and noncommittal.

It felt good to rest her eyes and allow the sleepy lethargy to flow over her. After being up most of the night with the baby, even a few minutes of oblivion was great. Too soon she had to open them.

Her son, Billy, raced past her and out the door. "Hi Mom, hi Dad. I'm gonna ride my bike around our ordinary neighborhood for a while." And then he was gone.

Her husband, Vic, sat across the kitchen table from her. He sipped his coffee as he checked his stocks in the *Wall Street Journal*.

He glanced up and smiled as he sensed her watching him. His smile was still really nice, even though his hairline was receding at the same time his waist was expanding. Lose some gain some.

He glanced at his watch. "Looks like it's almost time for Ordinary Guy to hit the streets."

She sighed. "It would be nice if you could stay home for just one day. We could do things together—change diapers, take out the trash, bake a tuna casserole."

He reached across the table to pat her hand. "I'm sorry, dear. I'm a superhero, and people depend on me. Ordinary Guy already has lots of people to save today." He opened the day planner that always rested beside his orange juice glass. "Let's see, I have to stop Carl Lisle from making a disastrous low-yield investment. And Sonia Gerlich is about to choose Henson's Electric to rewire her old house. Bad choice. But Ordinary Guy will be there to save the day. Hmm, Lily Madison bought a size twelve dress yesterday. She's a size sixteen. I'll have to be there for her when she comes out of denial."

Kim felt her eyes crossing.

"There are dozens more like them walking the streets of New York City, all crying out for Ordinary Guy to make their pitiful lives better." He brushed toast crumbs from his suit jacket and tie. Closing his day planner, he stood.

Kim knew she was begging, but she couldn't help herself. "Tonight is New Year's Eve. Can you get home early?"

He frowned. "I suppose I can reschedule a few of the poor suckers who need my help." He smiled at her. "Sure, why not? We can sit on the couch and at midnight watch the ball drop in Times Square. Maybe make a little popcorn. If you're lucky, the baby won't need her diaper changed while the ball is dropping."

She was pathetically grateful. "Afterwards we could make love on the couch." Kim held her breath. He always made love on Sundays and Wednesdays. Today was Friday.

Vic looked thoughtful. "You're right. Tonight's special." He opened his day planner again and penciled in 'make love' for twelve fifteen. "But not on the couch. We'll make love in our bed because that's where ordinary people do it." He waggled his eyebrows at her. "We might even get a start on our point-five child."

He walked to the door, and as he did every morning, donned the pocket protector he'd found after an alien from a far distant galaxy had dropped it. Immediately, he was transformed into the superhero, Ordinary Guy, able to perform amazing feats of . . . ordinariness.

She watched him drive away in his white SUV that was exactly like the white SUVs their neighbors drove. Then she closed her eyes again.

In the blackness behind her closed lids, a woman with long blond hair and a slinky silver dress held up a sign that read: And Behind Door Number Two . . .

Kim opened her eyes and blinked. And blinked again. The sound of tens of thousands of screaming people beat against her ears. Terrified, she glanced around, trying to figure out where the hell she was. Nighttime. Outside. Someplace high. She glanced down. Ack! She was on the roof of a building overlooking . . . No. It couldn't be.

With her heart pounding so hard she didn't know why all those people didn't look up, she peered over the side of the building. Far below her, Times Square teemed like a giant anthill. Uh-oh. She looked at the other buildings. Sure enough, there was number one Times Square, the pole, and the crystal ball all lit up. New Year's Eve.

She ran suddenly clammy hands over her dress. Dress? Well, almost a dress. It was a glittery gold piece of cloth that hit strategic spots. Most of the time. As she stumbled back from the edge of the roof, she almost fell. Jeez, no wonder. Her matching gold sandals had heels that added another story to the building.

Frantically, she looked around for stairs she could use to get off the roof. No stairs. That couldn't be right. There had to be stairs. How was she going to get down? In a reflex action, she rubbed her arms to keep warm. If it was New Year's Eve in Times Square, then it must be cold. Strange, she didn't feel cold, even though her hair was blowing in the breeze.

She didn't know why she was here, and she didn't have a clue how to get off the roof. Only one thing left to do. She screamed bloody murder. But even as she shrieked into the wind, she realized no one below would hear her.

Won't panic won't panic. She panicked. "Help! Save me. I'm stuck on the roof, and I can't get down. Send a helicopter. Send Spiderman, Batman, any man at all. I'm not picky."

"Would Naked Man do?"

Huh? The man's deep, sensual voice with a touch of the South in it spun her around.

"A beautiful woman shouldn't be alone on New Year's Eve." His soft murmur promised that her New Year's Eve was about to get a lot better.

She gaped. Yes, actually dropped-her-jaw gaped at him. She'd remember to blink again in a minute or so. "Um, love your costume." Well, what else could you say to a naked superhero? And he *was* a superhero. She knew that because he had a giant *N* on his chest. It began at one nipple and ended at the other one.

His chuckle skittered up her spine. "I love yours, too, sweetheart." Before she could react, he stepped close. "I like the way the back only covers your cute behind and the front plunges almost to your navel."

"Can you get me off this roof?" She knew her eyes were wide as she stared up at him. Way up.

He was tall, with broad, muscular shoulders and a gleaming chest that a woman could rest her head against while her fingers explored his intriguing male nipples, sculpted pecs, and washboard abs.

"I can do many things, Night Woman." He lowered his head toward her, the tangled glory of his blond hair falling around the most sensual face she'd ever seen.

"Night Woman?" A girl could die happy after getting a glimpse of that face.

He nodded. "I've chosen you to be my mate. After we've made love with enough sizzle to blow out all the neon signs in Times Square, I'll share my power with you." The heat in his gaze said he had a lot of other things to share with her. "We can wear matching *N*s."

He watched her from eyes that glowed golden in the reflected light from the square below, and his smile was an erotic invitation to lose herself in the texture and taste of his mouth.

She dropped her gaze, only marginally aware of his strong thighs roped with muscle. His whole sexual package was a fitting tribute to a superhero. His sacs hung heavy between his slightly spread thighs, and while his cock had not yet officially reached the excited stage, Kim was confident that when he chose to become excited it would be a . . . huge event.

Reluctantly, she returned her gaze to his face. "I know you. Somewhere in a past I can't remember, I know you." She frowned. "You're Brynn."

His smile broadened. "Not now. When night shadows cover the big city I become Naked Man." He flung his arms wide to encompass the world around them. "I can bring you all that's pulse-pounding, outrageous, and *erotic*."

"But can you get me off this roof?" This was becoming less of a priority as his sensual energy swirled around her.

"Of course." With no warning, he scooped her into his arms and leaped from the edge of the building.

She screamed like a banshee until she realized they were sailing high above Times Square. Unlike the movies, no one looked up and shouted, "It's a bird! It's a plane! No, it's Naked Man!" Bummer.

After she got over the fear that he'd say, "Oops!" and drop her on her head in the middle of all those very drunken revelers, she had to admit it was an exhilarating experience. He held her against his hard chest while they flew effortlessly through the air. She felt . . . safe. Go figure.

Then she noticed where they were headed. "Uh, aren't we supposed to be going down? I mean, the crystal ball is gorgeous, but I don't think I need a close-up of—" Urp. Too late. He landed on the roof of number one Times Square and set her down. She stared up at the glittering ball with its Waterford crystal panels and gulped. Then she glanced around the roof. "There's no one here. Shouldn't there be lots of people running around making sure everything is okay?"

He pressed her against his side, his heat branding her from shoulder to hip. "In our reality, we're alone up here. And I promise you'll never forget this New Year's Eve."

"No kidding." She glanced down at the sea of people twenty-five stories below as they all stared up at the huge ball.

He brushed her hair away from her face and traced the line of her jaw with his fingers. "Forget the ordinary tonight. Allow yourself to experience the extraordinary."

Sliding his finger across her lips, he lingered on her bottom lip. "New Year's Eve is for resolutions. Let's resolve to live large with no limits to what we can enjoy or how we can enjoy it." He lowered his head to touch the side of her neck with his lips and then whispered in her ear, "Make love with me here. Now. With the whole world present but not seeing."

All of her normal arguments paraded across her mind. They'd just met. No pockets, ergo no condoms. Someone might see them. They'd just met. He wasn't someone she'd take home to Mother. He was really really different. *They'd just met.* She opened her mouth to voice a few of her concerns, but he spoke first.

"When the moment comes, I'll have protection." His grin was wicked temptation. "Let tonight happen. Indulge your secret fantasies—the rush of making love with a stranger, the thrill of possible discovery, and the danger of playing with someone who isn't part of your ordinary world. Expand your horizons, Night Woman."

She wanted to. Even though she couldn't quite remember her past, she knew this was something she wouldn't have done. But as he'd said, this was their reality, and she was going to let it happen.

Reaching up, she wrapped her arms around his neck and smiled up at him. "Mmm. I've never made love with a superhero." She frowned. "At least I don't think I have. I would've remembered, wouldn't I?" Impatient, she pushed aside a vague recollection of someone named Ordinary Guy.

He put his hands on her waist, lifted her into the air, and then swung her around. They laughed together as he pulled her down with him onto what should have been the cold surface of the roof. Instead it felt warm and soft. She didn't question the discrepancy. Tonight wasn't a night for questioning.

"I want to slide my fingers the length of your bared body, touch every part of you with my mouth, and then fill you completely." His breath was hot against the side of her face.

"This will be an equal deal. There are lots of places I'd like to slide my fingers, and you don't even want to get me started on what I want to do with my mouth." She nibbled a path along the side of his neck and felt him shudder.

She lay on her back while he propped himself up on his elbow beside her. "Time to get rid of that sensational dress."

He simply passed his free hand over the dress, and it peeled from her body like the shimmery gold skin of a designer banana. She'd already discarded her shoes.

"Whoa, that was so cool." She stared into his eyes gleaming with laughter. "Can we say impressed?" Distracted, she stared down the length of her body. "I'm not wearing a bra or panties. Where'd they go? I would've remembered if I left home without them."

Brynn touched her nipple with the tip of his finger, and she sucked in her breath at the instant prickle of sensation.

"You're Night Woman. You're a sensual creature who finds undergarments a restriction on your sexy moves, and you have a whole arsenal of sexy moves." He tipped up the corners of his oh-so-hot mouth.

"I do?" She returned his smile. "Yeah, I do." She smoothed her fingers over his broad, muscular chest, glorying in the tactile joys of his warm, smooth skin and the hard nubs of his male nipples.

His gaze darkened as he leaned over her. "I'll show you my sexy moves if you'll show me yours."

The roar of the crowd grew louder in seeming agreement with their sharing of sexy moves.

Lowering his head, he slid his tongue across her nipple, and she gasped her pleasure. Then he covered her nipple with his mouth and sucked.

She anchored her fingers in his thick hair while she hissed her pleasure. *Oh, yeees!* And it got even better as he teased the nipple with his tongue and then nipped gently. She had to be glowing as brightly as the ball above her.

When he moved to her other nipple, she raked her nails down his back, letting every delicious sensation pool low in her belly.

Touching his back wasn't nearly enough. If this was a night for excesses, let the excess begin. When he released her nipple, she laid her palm flat over the spot on his chest where his heart pounded hard and fast. She pushed, and he rolled onto his back. A hum of erotic anticipation rose on a wave of need.

He locked his hands behind his head and watched her. "You have something in mind?"

"Definitely." She knelt beside him and placed her hand flat on his stomach. His muscles tightened beneath her touch. "I have many somethings in mind."

His lips curved in a sensual smile. "Tell me what will make you scream, and I'll do it." He took one hand from beneath his head and reached between his legs to cup himself. "Would you like to watch my body react to the thought of sliding deep inside you, to the thought of your heat and friction driving me crazy, and to the thought of you tightening around me?"

She drew in a deep breath as his words took form and stroked her imagination. "I love watching your body. It's supremely watchable. But I'm thinking of taking a more active role in this seduction." She'd been right. He was excited. And it *was* a huge event.

Desire flooded his eyes while shadows cast his body in patterns of light and dark that gave the whole scene a surrealistic look. It fueled her sexual hunger. She could do anything tonight. And would.

"What do I want? Hmm. Got it. Tonight I want to make *you*

scream." She thought about that. "Okay, maybe you don't think screaming is manly. So let's say I'd like you to moan, groan, and maybe even shout. No loss of masculinity in that."

"Really?" His smile said he didn't believe her, and that he thought once the seducing began he'd take over.

Ha. Did she have a surprise for him. "Really. In fact, I want you to promise me you'll keep your hands behind your head no matter what I do."

"Is this about power?" His smile faded a little. He seemed to know a little about the desire for power, and what he knew didn't make him happy.

She leaned over and dipped her tongue into his navel, making sure her long hair slid across his stomach in the process. He sucked in his breath. Too bad she didn't have her trusty chocolate syrup with her. It would make the licking a double treat.

"No, this is about giving pleasure. My Night Woman super-intuition tells me you're a man who's always been on the giving end of the pleasure cycle." Even though she was joking, she sensed a strange truth in what she said. "Let me do the giving tonight." She smiled at him. "It'll make me very happy. And after all, isn't your goal as Naked Man to make women happy?"

"I suppose there's a twisted kind of logic there."

"Promise?" She drew an imaginary line with her fingernail around his nipple, and he shuddered. Fine, so maybe there *was* a little power thing going on. She got a rush every time her touch drew a response from him.

He watched her from eyes that gave none of his feelings away. "Promise."

She couldn't help herself. Her gaze returned to his impressive erection. Maybe he wouldn't tell her what he was thinking, but his cock kept no secrets. It thought her idea was a blast.

Kim once more leaned over him until her breasts skimmed his chest and stomach. Her nipples were twin points of sensitized pleasure, and she bit back a moan. It wouldn't look too good if she gave this big speech about making him moan, and then she did it at first contact.

"I want to touch all of you. Turn over." She waited impatiently as he silently rolled onto his stomach.

Was there any view of this man that wasn't perfect? She didn't think so. His broad, muscular back flowed into firm, round buttocks that begged to be kneaded and . . . Well, she could write a whole book on *How to Touch the Perfect Butt*. With illustrations. Many illustrations. From every angle.

"I can't do anything, huh?" He lifted his hips a little to relieve the pressure on his now overexcited cock.

"Nada." Kim shifted to between his thighs and then ran the tip of her tongue the length of his spine.

He gasped. That was a start. Not a moan yet, but a start.

The heavy, achy feeling in her lower stomach drove her now. She brushed his hair aside, put her mouth on his neck, and sucked hard. He'd have a mark there. At least for as long as it took his superhero genes to erase it. Probably all of five minutes.

Abandoning his neck, she scooted forward until she was straddling his hips. The sensation of him between her thighs almost dragged a groan from her, but she bit it back just in time. She pressed down hard, wanting to feel him touching her right *there*.

He lifted his hips, bringing himself more tightly in contact with her. She rubbed back and forth, back and forth. And she moaned. Not very loudly. It was more like a tiny whimper. She hoped he didn't hear it.

"Do you have a plan here?" His voice was low and raspy.

"Uh-uh. I'm going with free association." She sounded a little breathless.

Kim wanted to do so many things before making him turn over. Some kneading of buns, some nipping here and there, maybe some discreet sucking. She had to abandon all those wonderful plans as her personal Orgasm Express thundered down the track, threatening to dump her at the station whether she was ready or not.

But there was one thing she had to do. She slipped off him, bent down, and nipped one perfect male cheek.

"What the . . . ?" His exclamation was part surprise and part laughter.

"Turn over." Her breaths were coming in small gulps. This was moving too fast, but she couldn't slow it down.

If she'd thought he was staying pretty unaffected, she was wrong. When he turned over, he stared at her from eyes that seared her with their heat. "If you're hoping to make this a leisurely tour of my body, forget it."

"How long do I have?" A glance at his cock suggested she might want to keep things moving.

"Not long." He spoke through gritted teeth.

"Okay, only the important stuff." She played with his nipples—rolling them between her thumbs and forefingers, flicking them with her tongue, sliding the edge of her teeth over them.

He moaned.

She kissed her way south, and when she reached her destination, she unpacked and settled in for a long stay. Well, maybe not so long. She ran her tongue over his tight balls, savoring the texture of his skin and the taste of aroused male before taking each one gently in her mouth.

He groaned.

She nibbled along the length of his erection and then swirled her tongue around the head. And when she finally slid her lips over him, he moaned some more. She would've moaned along with him, but she was too busy trying to hold back the flood of emotion that had piggybacked on her sexual frenzy.

Along with her sexual need came another very different need. One that made her want to crawl inside him and stay there. It was a tangle of emotions she'd have to think about later.

He raked his fingers through her hair, and she gently nipped the head of his cock before giving in to her own personal compulsion.

Kim couldn't crawl inside him, so she did the next best thing. She literally crawled up his body, growling low in her throat with the pleasure of his bare skin, damp with sweat, sliding against every inch of her flesh.

His breaths came fast and harsh as he bent one knee, pressing it between her spread legs. She gasped as his knee found the perfect spot and his erection thrust hard and insistent against her stomach.

"All bets are off, Night Woman, if you don't ride me hard and fast soon." His words were hot against her neck.

Sounded like a good idea to her. Still straddling his hips, she knelt up. A roar from the thousands below made her glance up at the ball. It was starting to descend. Perfect. They could descend together.

"Countdown has begun." This was one of life's moments that seemed so *right* she knew it would live in her memory until she took her last breath. Not something she would tell her grandchildren about, but she'd keep it as her own personal magic moment.

She slowly and with delicious forethought lowered herself onto his erection. Kim savored every sensation. The exact second when she felt the head of his cock nudge her open. The feeling of being stretched and filled as he slid into her. The incredible moment when all of him was inside her.

The crowd's roar rose and washed over her as the huge, glittering ball dropped lower.

She rose from him, letting him slide almost out of her, and then she slammed back down, taking him back into her.

He shouted his pleasure, his voice blending with all the other voices rising from below them.

She increased her rhythm, up and down up and down, driving her uncontrollable need before her.

The masses in Times Square started their thunderous countdown to the New Year—ten, nine, eight, seven . . .

His own control gone, he took his hands from behind his head and clasped her waist. "Happy New Year, Night Woman." And arching his hips, he drove into her. Over and over again.

With each powerful thrust of his hips, she screamed her pleasure. His thrusts picked up the chanted count from below even as the massive glittering ball moved lower and lower.

Almost there, almost there! Lights and sounds blurred, a backdrop to the unbearable pressure about to rip through her.

Four, three, two, one.

Ohmigod, ohmigod! The waves of release rocked her. Every sensation merged until she shook with the unspeakable pleasure. She. Would. Never. Feel. This. Incredible. Again. NEVER!

Her scream joined his shout of climax. And in front of them the ball reached its journey's end. The New Year lit up in a flash of blinding light.

She didn't know what year it was. Didn't care. Past and future meant nothing. Only this moment. She closed her eyes and let her orgasm roll on, and on, and—

Behind Kim's closed lids, the blond woman waved at her. "Have you made your choice? Will you choose Ordinary Guy and door one or Naked Man and door two?"

She was kidding, right? It didn't matter what was behind the damned doors, she was taking Naked Man.

"Give me Naked Man and you can keep . . ." Wait. She opened her eyes.

Brynn sat beside her on the bed. He still held her hand. And he watched her with eyes that gave nothing away. But she could feel his emotions—confusion, sexual satiation, and another feeling he was determinedly blocking from his consciousness. What was it? She sensed it was something important to her.

He smiled at her. "Ordinary Guy was a dud. Rethinking that normal life you wanted?" There was smugness in his voice.

Kim couldn't answer for a minute as she made the transition from fantasy to real world, from awesome orgasm to normal heartbeat and breathing. She allowed herself to enjoy the "coming down," that sense of limp satiation when all you're aware of is the slow, relaxed ka-thump of your heartbeat.

"Normal as in that fantasy? Got a little carried away with the exaggeration, didn't you?" If he weren't so damned smug, she'd tell him she'd already had a few doubts about her quest for the normal life. "Ordinary Guy? Please. Give me a break."

His smile broadened. "You're right. He was way over the top. I had a good time with him."

Kim had to smile back. "And what kind of mind spawned Naked Man?" It was scary how real the whole thing had seemed to her.

"A sick one?"

Her smile faded. "I got the message. Ordinary equals boring, and you equal excitement. The only thing I didn't get was why you felt the need to point it out."

He looked away from her, and she couldn't read his expression. "Damned if I know. Maybe I just didn't want to see you get involved with someone like this Vic person."

"Why not?" Something important was hovering just out of sight.

He shrugged and then grinned. "Maybe I think you deserve a superhero like Naked Man. By the way, thought you might like to know how it all ended. In that reality, you became Night Woman and made Naked Man take you along each night to help bring excitement into people's lives."

She'd started to reply when he glanced at his watch.

He met her questioning gaze. "Two hours, and the compulsion hasn't hit." Hope shone in his eyes.

"Would it equate the fantasy as sex?" She didn't want to believe that, but she had to throw it out as a possibility.

He shook his head. "No, nothing fools the compulsion."

It was sort of weird how they both talked about the compulsion like it was a living thing.

Swinging his feet to the floor, he slipped his shoes back on.

"Mind if I stay here until it shows up? I want to keep track of the time between each one."

"No problem. I have to work on my plans for the castle." Climbing from the bed, she walked over to the desk and sat down.

She pretended to be working for the next fifteen minutes until the compulsion hit. Kim said the expected words, "I don't want your body," with complete honesty.

Because she was beginning to realize she might want a lot more.

16

Brynn waited for Kim in the lobby. He'd left her room hours ago so she could get work done on her plans for the castle.

Yeah, yeah, so that wasn't the only reason he'd left her alone. He needed space to think about what the feelings generated by their fantasy meant in real time. And what the hell was happening to his compulsion?

"I can tell you're thinking hard about which strategy will defeat the demons." Kim's Uncle Dirk sat down in the chair across from Brynn. He was still wearing a suit and still looked like he belonged in a boardroom.

Brynn tensed, but no demon detector alarm sounded. Someone would have to tell Dirk his detector wasn't working before he ran into any unfriendly demons. He'd leave that chore to Kim.

"A lot will depend on how many Vaughns show up and if we're able to identify the archdemon." Brynn was keeping an eye out for Kim, so he saw Wade when the demon stepped off the elevator.

Wade spotted him and started to walk over. When he saw Dirk, he paused.

Brynn slipped into Wade's mind. *"His detector is broken. You're safe. But just in case, I'll have your back."* If the detector came alive for Wade, Brynn could move faster than any human to knock it out of Dirk's hand.

Wade nodded and continued walking. He grinned as he took the third chair in the group. "Hey, Brynn. How's it going?" But his attention shifted almost immediately to Dirk. "You're Dirk Vaughn. Recognized you from pictures I've seen in fishing magazines. I'm Wade Thomas. Looks like we'll finally be going head-to-head in Saturday's tournament."

Wade wore old jeans, a flannel shirt, scuffed work boots, and his dumb good old boy persona tonight.

Dirk smiled, but it was more a curling of his upper lip. "I can hardly wait." His expression said Wade was dead meat. "I have my Triton ready. And your boat is a . . . ?"

"Got me a Pathfinder." Wade offered Dirk his happy puppy dog smile.

"Nice boats." Dirk's semi-smile said he'd hoped Wade would be fishing from a wooden raft he'd nailed together. "What about your motor? I've had a lot of success with my Yamaha 250."

"Mercury 250 Verado." Wade's smiled widened.

Dirk leaned forward, evidently ready to accept Wade as a worthy opponent. "What about—"

Okay, Brynn had heard enough. Thankfully, he saw Kim get off the elevator. "I'm meeting Kim, so I'll see you guys later." He didn't think either of the men noticed when he walked away.

Brynn reached her, and when she looked up at him, everything in him clenched around needs that had nothing to do with sex. Such as wanting to sit on the beach with her at night and talk about . . . everything. Maybe take in a Rockets game together. Uh-oh. This was not good. Yanking out his mental hammer, nails, and plywood, he tried to slap up a quick privacy fence to keep out any free-ranging hopes involving Kim.

Demons and demon hunters did not find happily-ever-afters together. *But what if I'm not a demon?* Okay, so he'd be lying if he said he hadn't at least thought about the possibility. But even if he wasn't a demon, what the hell was he?

He couldn't age and die. She'd do both. Not a situation either would find comfortable. Brynn smiled at her and then nailed that last freakin' board up. Too bad he could still see through a knot-hole. Hope springs eternal and all that garbage.

"Ready to listen to *Donna Till Dawn* for a while?" He took her hand. If there wasn't anything for them beyond her time here, he was going for as much physical contact as he could cram into these days.

"Sounds like fun." She glanced at her watch.

Brynn was starting to hate watches and all other symbols of passing time. "Then let's do it." He walked across the lobby to the bookstore with her.

Donna was broadcasting from in front of the store. There were several rows of chairs for anyone who wanted to watch her. Brynn and Kim sat in the back row next to Eric. The rest of the chairs were pretty much taken. Donna waved at them.

Eric grinned at Kim. "Enjoy your fantasy?"

"It was right up there with making love on a cloud." She flushed. "Jeez, I must look like Deimos."

Satisfied, Eric settled back to watch his wife. "I don't get a chance to catch her broadcasts often. She usually works on weekends while I'm busy with the castle fantasies."

Donna had finished her opening monologue and was taking calls until it was time for the night's guest. The wide range of callers fascinated Brynn. Everyone from a man interested in remote viewing to a woman obsessed with secret societies.

Kim leaned into him. "I don't usually stay up late enough to hear this program, but I might treat myself once in a while. Donna's great." She paused to listen to the next caller.

"I am the One Whose Name Cannot Be Uttered." The voice was a low rumble of evil.

Donna's eyes widened, and Brynn felt Kim tense beside him. Ken, Donna's show producer, signaled to her. Probably suggesting they cut this sucker off the air. Donna shook her head.

Brynn glanced at Eric, who'd gone completely still. Time to put out a mental call to Holgarth and Conall.

Donna looked strained but calm. "I respect that you want to remain anonymous. So what *can* you tell us about yourself?"

"I wield unspeakable power and rule an army of evil from where I dwell in the black center of chaos." The owner of the deep voice seemed to savor each word.

The bastard was enjoying himself. Ken was growing frantic. Probably didn't have a clue why Donna would keep this crazy on the line. Brynn hoped she'd keep him talking a little longer.

"Interesting. Doesn't sound like a fun place, though. Uh, would this black center of chaos be a fancy name for hell?"

Brynn could feel the audience's unease growing. He didn't blame them. This was a seriously creepy call. Kim continued to lean into him, and even with his growing tension he could still appreciate the warmth of her body close to his.

"If naming it hell makes you more comfortable, please do so." The archdemon's amusement was a cold slide of malevolence.

Kim shivered. "That is one scary voice. I don't think I'd want to go mano a mano with that particular demonic entity."

Donna forged onward, but she was looking a little uncertain. Even a vampire might think twice about taking on something that projected so much power and evil.

"Why did you call?" She was ready to wrap up this conversation.

"I'm issuing a challenge to all Vaughns. Come to Galveston, and I'll teach you the meaning of true power." Again Brynn got a sense of sinister humor. "And since I'm a stand-up kind of guy, I've left two tokens of my affection in a Vaughn's room."

"Affection?" Donna sounded a little breathless.

"Almost a warm and fuzzy feeling. I love to cause suffering, despair, and death." Brief pause. "Forgive me. Thinking about how much I enjoy inflicting all three of those chokes me up. I live in hope that the legendary Vaughns will try to stop me." Huge evil sigh. "So foolish. Because of course I'll grind them beneath my cloven hooves like so many roaches. No, not roaches. I have a fondness for roaches. Perhaps ladybugs? Anyway, I'm depending on the Vaughns to provide my entertainment, so of course I think of them with affection."

"Tokens?" Donna had been reduced to one-word questions.

"Mmm. Something amusing along with a small temptation. Oh, and any Vaughn who joins me in making Galveston a cozy family getaway can expect similar . . . souvenirs. Until the next time, I am the One Whose Name Cannot Be Uttered."

The call ended with a clap of thunder. Donna stared blankly into the silent audience.

"Pompous jerk. His name's probably Cecil. That's why he doesn't want anyone to utter it. I wouldn't either." Eric's muttered comment sounded overloud in the quiet.

There were a few nervous giggles, and then everyone started talking at once.

Donna recovered and smiled at her audience. "Wow, we haven't gotten a call like that since last year when Taurin, the vampire, called in." She was working hard to make the call just another in the many strange calls the show had received over the years. "If any listeners want to comment, we'll have open lines for another half hour right after the break." As soon as she was off the air, Donna cast a desperate glance toward Eric and then turned to meet her producer's questions.

Eric rose to go to her, but before he could leave, Brynn grabbed his arm. "We'll have to take a look at the rooms of the three Vaughns who're here."

Eric nodded and then went to speak with Donna. Brynn and

Kim walked over to where Holgarth and Conall stood. Kim took Fo from her purse.

Fo sounded motivated. "I could tell by his voice that he was the lowest of the low, the baddest of the bad, the scummiest of the scummy, the—"

"We get the idea, Fo." Kim pushed a strand of hair from her face, and Brynn wished he'd seen it first. Eyes narrowed, she frowned. "I can't believe he tried to bribe members of my family to turn traitor. And how could he get past the gargoyles?"

Brynn shrugged. "Beats me. I guess we'll just have to take a look and see. As far as the bribery, demons are manipulators. The divide and conquer technique might work if the 'temptation' is big enough. Every man has his price."

Holgarth was offended. "I guarantee, Ms. Vaughn, that the demon did *not* get past my gargoyles." He sniffed. "The idea is preposterous."

Eric's return forestalled any snarky reply by Kim. "I'm going to stay here with Donna. The call sort of shook her up. If you need me, give a shout."

"Let's hit Lynsay's room first." Kim looked worried.

Just before they reached her sister's room, Asima joined them. *"Eric told me what happened. Don't you think a mob of immortals plus a demon hunter is overkill? Kim can take care of any demons. Conall, you don't need to be here. What can you do with just a sword? I mean, if you destroy a demon by cutting off the host's head, there's going to be a really ticked off headless human. Oh, wait, you're not wearing your sword tonight. I think you should go back to your room now."*

Conall growled his anger at the suggestion he wasn't needed. "You're not my mother, cat. I'll do what I please."

Holgarth twitched his lips, his equivalent of raucous laughter. "You worry about Conall too much, Asima. I've always wondered why."

Asima whipped her tail from side to side and flattened her ears against her aristocratic head. *"He appreciates cats. I feel a responsibility to keep him safe."*

Conall looked embarrassed that a cat thought she could protect him better than he could protect himself. But he didn't get a chance to retort because they'd reached Lynsay's room. Holgarth used his master key, and they crowded into the room.

Nothing. Kim sighed her relief. "I guess she's still with Deimos. At least she won't get back to her room and find a nasty surprise." No matter how relieved she looked, her voice said she wondered what Lynsay was doing with Deimos.

Brynn grinned. "Relax. He's showing her his action hero stuff. Maybe we should be worrying about Deimos instead." Lynsay looked like she could eat Deimos for lunch.

Kim returned his smile. "You're probably right."

They all trooped to Dirk's room. He answered Brynn's knock and assured them everything was okay. That left Kim's room.

Brynn stood beside her as she cautiously opened her door. She had Fo out, and the detector's purple eyes gleamed with anticipation. Holgarth, Conall, and Asima were behind them.

Something primitive and protective in Brynn demanded he go through the door first, so he slipped in front of her and flung the door wide. He'd braced himself to meet the charge of a dozen enraged demons, but nothing happened. The only thing that met him was a blast of loud music.

He could hear everyone crowding into the room behind him, but he was too focused on the bizarre scene in front of him to think about it.

"Howard Stern?" The amazement in Kim's voice said it for him, too.

The shock jock sprawled across her couch surrounded by four women who'd evidently lost most of their clothes, because they must've started out with more than they had on.

Howard looked up from the women long enough to grin and wave at them. Then he held up a glittering necklace for all to see. He swung it back and forth, a sparkling tease for the avaricious.

"Oooh, a pretty sparkly necklace, Kimmie. Can I have it after I zap the Howard Stern demon? Can I?" Fo would be the only fake cell phone with a diamond necklace wrapped around it.

"*Is* he a demon, Fo?" Kim's cold and calm voice signaled she'd morphed into her demon hunter persona.

Holgarth and Conall moved further into the room, one on each side of the couch. Asima stuck close to Conall.

"Um, I'm not sure." Fo was in tiny-voice mode.

"Okay, is he human or nonhuman?" Kim sounded puzzled.

"I don't know." Fo's voice was barely audible.

Kim looked worried. "Why don't you know? Are you malfunctioning?"

Conall moved a little closer to the couch. "Why hasn't he said anything? Howard Stern wouldn't go this long without running his mouth."

Fo rolled her purple eyes up at Kim. "I'm functioning perfectly. But my sensors aren't sending any information for me to analyze."

The strange Howard Stern image turned his gaze toward Conall. Asima moved in front and hissed at the shock jock.

"Time to rock and roll." Kim raised Fo and pushed the red button.

The beam of light blinded Brynn for a moment, but when he could see again, Howard and the women were simply gone with no little piles of ash to mark their passing.

Brynn could almost feel the collective sigh of relief in the room. "Our archdemon has a warped sense of humor."

Holgarth walked to the couch. "I told you the demon wouldn't get past my gargoyles. This was merely a clever projection. None of it was real."

"I wouldn't celebrate too soon, Holgarth." Kim joined him at the couch. "Howard left the archdemon's 'little temptation' behind." She reached between the cushions and pulled out the diamond necklace.

Asima leaped onto the couch and batted at the necklace with one slim paw. *"Diamonds suit me. They make an elegant statement."*

Fo's possessive growl said she had first dibs on the necklace.

Asima ignored Fo. Royalty didn't brawl with commoners. *"I fear your gargoyles failed you, Holgarth. If the archdemon left the necklace, then he breached your walls."* She stared unblinkingly at the necklace, obviously a lot more interested in the diamonds than she was Holgarth's breached walls.

"Forget the necklace, Asima. You, too, Fo. If we keep it, the demon wins. It goes to charity." Kim walked to her bureau and dropped the necklace into a drawer before returning to sink wearily onto the couch. "An archdemon can cloak his presence from the detectors, so I don't see why he couldn't fool the gargoyles."

Conall made the obvious leap of logic. "So this archdemon could be in the castle, and we wouldn't have a clue."

"Right." Brynn was trying to think things through. "But his demon hordes can't get past the gargoyles. That's one good thing. On the downside, he could create havoc among the guests without any help from his minions."

Kim yawned. "I'm too tired to come up with a plan tonight, but I'd say by the weekend we'd better have our act together. That'll give my family four days to gather from around the world. If the archdemon sees this as some kind of challenge, I'm hoping he won't attack until the Vaughns are all here. We'll have to find him and his portal before then if we want to have a prayer of winning the war."

Conall turned to Brynn. He didn't look happy. "I hate to even suggest this, but we might consider closing down the castle if it looks like the guests are in danger. We'd have to use an excuse like electrical problems." He rubbed the back of his neck. "I don't want to even think what the owner would say about that idea, especially during spring break."

"As the owner's attorney, I would advise that it's better to lose money from canceled reservations than to pay it out in lawsuits if anyone is injured in the castle." Holgarth compressed his lips into a thin line—his lawyer's face.

"That's what I love about you, Holgarth, always putting the public welfare before money. What a guy." Kim sounded too tired to generate much enthusiasm for her sarcasm.

Brynn held up his hand. "Whoa, I don't think closing down the castle is the answer. We'll have to let the Vaughns stay here when they arrive, so that'll shoot down any excuse we make. Besides, guests are probably safer here than they'd be anywhere else on the island. The archdemon might do things to annoy us, but I don't think he'll start his war until the Vaughns are all here. He seemed pretty definite about his challenge." He thought some more about what he'd said. "Besides, that old quote about keeping your friends close, but your enemies closer might have merit. If he's really in the castle, then he's in our world, and he's cut off from the other demons."

"Makes sense." Conall nodded. "Then we'll just have to make sure our guests stay safe." His expression said the archdemon didn't want to mess with him.

Holgarth and Conall left. Asima lingered for a moment. *"Don't forget that I'm bringing you a new outfit on Wednesday. Oh, and you might want to know that Ganymede and I are no longer an item. He admitted he hated the opera, thought the ballet was a bore, and wished Shakespeare would've written his 'damned plays in English a regular guy could understand.'"* She sniffed her displeasure. *"He was not worthy."* She left.

Kim giggled. "God, I'm so tired I'm slaphappy."

Brynn didn't want to leave Kim for a whole bunch of reasons. She'd be asleep before he got through listing them. "Guess I'll go back to my room. Just Ganymede and me." He paused to let her digest what *that* would be like. "Still don't have my new bed, so it'll be another night on the couch. No way would I sleep in the bed anyway. Ganymede wants half of it, and he snores loud enough to wake Eric at noon."

She looked amused, but she didn't say, "Hey, no problem. You can stay with me."

He narrowed his gaze on her. Okay, no more gentle hints. "I want to stay with you tonight." No hokey reasons, no begging.

Her smile faded, and something soft and welcoming filled her eyes. "I'd like you to stay." Kim glanced at her watch. "No sign of your compulsion yet. If you leave, we can't keep track of the time between them." She tried to look serious, but her laughter seeped through. "This is all in the name of scientific inquiry, of course."

Of course. He closed the door quietly and turned off the lights.

Purple eyes gleamed in the darkness. "Hey, you guys. I can't see."

17

Where had Tuesday gone? Last she recalled it'd been Monday night. Now it was Wednesday morning. She seemed to remember a blur that could've been Tuesday. There were fuzzy images of her trying to do her architect thing while Fo whined nonstop because Kim hadn't given her the diamond necklace and hadn't allowed her to off any demons.

Other than that, Tuesday had been about placating Holgarth who was so not happy about searching all of Galveston for rooms to house the Vaughns and trying to remain sane while Mr. Hot slept on her couch.

Wait, she did have one positive memory from yesterday. Brynn's last compulsion to date had occurred Tuesday morning.

Wednesday, ack! Just the thought made Kim want to roll over and cover her head with her pillow. Castle of Dark Dreams? Ha! More like the Castle of Unfulfilled Dreams. Because she knew if she stretched out her hand, Brynn's side of the bed would still be empty.

Not only that, but if she opened her eyes, she'd have to face a high-kicking chorus line of things she didn't want to do. Like refereeing the battle between Sparkle and Asima over what she'd wear today. Like doing a fantasy tonight with ordinary Vic Burton, when ordinary was no longer on her radar screen. Like dealing with all the Vaughns pouring onto the island. And like discussing things with Brynn that would be uncomfortable for both of them. Ah, the good old days of Monday, or maybe even Tuesday.

The worst thing of all? She'd have to face another day with the knowledge she was falling in love with . . .

A demon? His compulsions were coming farther and farther apart. He didn't demonstrate the usual demonic behaviors. And the archdemon didn't exert any power over him. Of course, he could be a eudemon like Wade, but he didn't exhibit Wade's indifference to humanity.

A human? Nope. He didn't die. Not a human characteristic.

Any other recognizable nonhuman entity? Not that Kim could tell. No fangs or unusual cravings. No desire to howl at the moon.

So, she was falling in love with none of the above. Just peachy.

A sudden rattling and rustling forced her eyes open. At the same time, Fo's disgustingly cheerful voice swept away any hope she could just go back to sleep.

"Yo, Kimmie. Asima's here. She brought you lots of neat stuff."

Kim propped herself up on her elbow and met the morning with a grumpy scowl. "It's called knocking, Asima, a pesky human ritual in which you announce your presence and your wish to enter a room. The human can then choose to yell through the door that she's not home and wants to be left alone."

Disbelieving, she watched an equally grumpy Conall stomp into her room and dump a bunch of clothes on her bed. Without a word, he turned and left. Kim winced as he slammed the door behind him, then she shifted her attention back to Asima.

"Are we bad-tempered in the morning, hmm? You are so human, Kim. Immortals aren't a slave to the clock. I've been up for hours."

Asima leaped onto the foot of the bed. *"Get up and see what I've brought you."*

A glance around verified that Brynn wasn't in the room. She didn't hear water running so he wasn't in the shower either. Her mood, which was already pretty low, hit bottom and settled there. Kim glanced at her travel clock on the night table. She groaned. "It's only six, Asima."

"All the better to get you dressed before the Queen of Bad Taste rises."

"The Queen of All Things Sexy has risen and is seriously considering kicking your man-stealing butt all over Galveston." Sparkle swept into the room and laid the things she'd brought on the couch.

Asima raised her nose into the air. *"Men appreciate good breeding and naturally seek me out. You can hardly blame me for that."*

Sparkle rolled her eyes. "Oh good grief, now we'll hear about how the Tight-Ass Fairy whacked you over the head and turned you into the Goddess of Boring Bitches."

Ack! Kim was officially wide-awake and heading for the shower. If she came out and there were bodies, she'd dispose of them. But she'd keep the clothes.

Once in the shower, she forgot about Sparkle and Asima. Showers turned her mind to Brynn and how the water flowing over that incredible torso would bead on his nipples, slide over his abdomen, and bathe his glorious sexual package in warm . . .

Pounding on the bathroom door. "Get out here fast before these two rip each other's heads off." Brynn's voice.

Kim's instant relief was pathetic. No matter how frustrating the last few nights had been with Brynn sleeping on her couch, it was preferable to him sleeping on his own couch. After Sparkle and Asima left, they'd have to talk.

A few minutes later she walked from the bathroom still wearing her robe—why dress when she was getting a new outfit—and prepared to be fought over like a new chew toy.

Speaking of chew toys, Brynn was looking disgustingly relaxed as he lounged in one of the armchairs, his long legs stretched out in front of him. He wore jeans, boots, and a white shirt. He was drinking coffee, and she could see he'd brought some back for her along with a doughnut. Caffeine and sugar, what better way to start the day? *How about hot sex in my bed?* No, she refused to go there until the twisted twosome had left.

She couldn't avoid Sparkle and Asima any longer. "Have you agreed on what I'll wear today?" One should always face life with a positive attitude.

"No." A simultaneous negative blast.

Kim threw up her hands. "Look, ladies, I appreciate that both of you have taken an interest in making me the best I can be, but I have lots to do today, so let's get this show on the road." Had she been firm enough? "And just out of curiosity, Asima, how'd you get Conall to drag all these things to my room?"

"I asked him. How else? He was going to refuse until I pointed out that if I didn't have to help you with your outfit I'd be free to follow him around." Asima sat beside the things Conall had dumped on the bed. *"And no offense, Kim, but my driving motivation here is to emerge triumphant over the slut queen."*

"What she means, Kim, is she couldn't screw Mede, so she wants to screw me." Sparkle swayed over to the clothes she'd left on the couch.

Kim couldn't help but admire Sparkle. How did she manage a sexy sashay in stilettos high enough to give anyone altitude sickness? And her tight leather pants and skimpy black top made a definite statement that said, *I'm here, and I'm sexy.*

"Maybe I'll go down and find Holgarth. We have demon business to discuss." Brynn was poised to escape.

Fat chance. "I don't think even Holgarth will be up for a discussion at six in the morning. Don't you dare move from that chair. You're the only one on my side, and if you leave, I'll tell Ganymede you've missed having him around."

"You're a cruel woman." He stayed but looked all sulky and gorgeous. Did Brynn have any mood that made him look less than incredible? Kim didn't think so.

Sparkle made her presentation with sexual innuendoes dripping from every word. "We'll start with this little black silk camisole edged with ivory lace. It'll drive men wild trying to figure out whether you're a sexy lady in black silk or a tempting innocent in ivory lace. To go with it we have a short black leather skirt with an intriguing slit up the side. I brought you black lace panties so guys will have something interesting to see while they're playing peek a boo with the slit. Add in leather slides with tassels by Manolo Blahnik and a slouchy leather bag from Salvatore Ferragamo, and men will follow you home."

"I plugged my ears so I wouldn't hear the dreadful details." Asima was lying on the bed making a big show of holding her paws over her ears. *"But I didn't have enough paws to cover my eyes. Is it my turn?"*

Not even seven yet, and Kim felt weary. "Go for it."

Asima cast flirty eyes toward Brynn. *"Would you hold up my things? I seem to be short of hands."*

Kim did a mental headshake. Flirty? How could a cat be flirty?

Brynn's expression said he'd rather be out fighting the archdemon to the death than holding up Asima's clothes. "Sure. No problem." Liar.

He walked over to the bed and held up a top.

"You need a high-necked lace top to foster the mystique of the untouched virgin. Men are fascinated with virgins." Asima stared up at Brynn. *"Aren't you?"*

"Fascinated." He stared at Kim. The whites of his eyes were showing.

"I've brought a tulle-and-lace skirt to go with the top. It's swirly and girly." Asmia stared at Brynn until he held up the skirt.

"Hey, swirly and girly, that's me." Kim didn't dare look at Sparkle to see how she was taking this.

"Finish the outfit off with Hermes leather lace-up espadrilles and a suede pocket satchel with leather trim from Coach, and you're ready to face the day with flair." She looked smugly satisfied.

Kim would have to move fast to head off a catfight of monumental proportions. "Okay, here's the deal. I love everything you guys have chosen for me, but obviously I can't wear everyone's stuff at once. So I'll pick and choose." She didn't give Sparkle or Asima a chance to argue. "I'll wear the top Sparkle chose and Asima's skirt. I like the lace-up espadrilles, Asima, and the slouchy leather bag is nice, Sparkle."

Sparkle and Asima glared at each other.

"By the way, where did you get all these great clothes?" Maybe Kim didn't want to know.

"We have connections." Asima's cat eyes turned shifty.

"Many connections." Sparkle busied herself by gathering up the things Kim wasn't wearing.

Kim sighed. Connections. Well, at least they'd found something they could agree on. "Thanks for the outfit."

With much hissing and mumbled complaints, Asima and Sparkle left.

"Why do you let them bother you like that?" Brynn sounded amused now that they'd left.

"For the clothes, of course." She smiled up at him. "Hey, I'm as shallow as the next person, and great clothes make me feel good." Fine, so she wanted to look sexy enough to entice him off that stupid couch he bedded down on each night.

"I'd love to wear pretty clothes, too, Kimmie." Fo sounded wistful.

But before Kim's sympathy could kick in, Asima padded back into the room. She had Dirk's detector gripped in her jaws. She leaped onto the night table and dropped the detector next to Fo. "I forgot this."

"Uh-oh." Brynn's comment sounded ominous. "Where'd you get that, Asima? And does Dirk know?" He shook his head and then answered his own question. "Of course he doesn't."

Asima blinked her big blue eyes. *"He didn't see me borrow it. When you're finished, I'll take it back, and he won't see that either."* Without a backward glance, she leaped from the night table and was gone. The door eased closed behind her.

Fo vibrated with barely contained excitement. "Flip him open, Kimmie. Now."

Brynn walked over and put his arm across Kim's shoulders, lending her his silent support. In that moment, she realized she'd be perfectly happy if he were there to lend his support for the rest of her life.

She swallowed hard. Did she mean that? Absolutely. Funny how the turning points in your life didn't always come when you expected them, like while you were hanging from a cliff by your fingertips or trying to outrun an angry rhino. Turning points crept up while you were doing something ordinary, like enjoying the warmth of a man's arm across your shoulders. And those moments changed you forever.

Okay, so standing beside a demon of sensual desire while you discussed fashion with a demon detector didn't qualify as ordinary. In fact, nothing involving Brynn would ever be normal, mainstream America. But compared to everything else she'd experienced this week, it was a pretty ho-hum moment.

Not that her little life-altering moment meant squat in the grand scheme of things. Because even if Brynn's compulsion eventually disappeared, as long as he believed he was a demon—and she hadn't come down on either side of that argument yet—he'd never commit to forever with her.

"Kimmie?"

Fo's anxious voice pulled her back to what was important right now. Kim didn't want Fo to be crushed if Dirk's detector wasn't sentient, and there was a good chance it wasn't.

"He might not be like you, Fo." She picked up Dirk's detector and flipped it open. "Please don't be too disappointed if he doesn't live up to your hopes. We still love you." *We.* She automatically included Brynn.

Kim glanced up at him. Brynn smiled his heart-stopping smile that made breathing a real chore for her. Forcing her attention away from his smile, she looked down at Dirk's detector. It stared back with those scary red eyes.

"I'll talk to him, Kimmie." Fo was taking charge.

Kim allowed Brynn to lead her to the couch. They both sat down. He leaned close. "This is groundbreaking stuff. Think of the possibilities for online dating services."

Kim smiled, and her mood lightened a little.

"Hi, I'm Fo. Do you have a name?" For all her seeming confidence, Fo sounded tentative.

The silence stretched on and on, and Kim bit her lip to keep silent. She couldn't say anything to save Fo from hurt.

"No. Should I have one?"

The deep male voice was a total surprise. Kim didn't know what she'd expected, but it wasn't this darkly sensual rumble. She stopped herself just short of thinking it was wasted on a machine. It wasn't wasted on Fo. But wow, old Sergei had outdone himself on this one.

"Of course. Everyone should have a great name." Fo was immediately outraged on her new friend's behalf.

"Why should I have a name when no one ever talks to me?" The deep voice sounded truly puzzled.

"No one?" Fo seemed shocked by the admission. "Well, we'll talk to you, and we'll give you a great name, won't we, Kimmie?"

"Sure will," Kim frowned. "Wait, Dirk said you spoke to him when you identified the demons, so that means there was some verbal communication going on."

"I've never spoken to him."

Okay, Kim saw a basic flaw in his statement. "If you've never talked to Dirk, how do you warn him when a demon is near?"

"I don't detect demons." He delivered his bombshell calmly, but his eyes looked uncertain. "Should I?"

"So what *do* you do?" Brynn didn't wait to be invited into the conversation.

"I destroy." He seemed on firmer ground here.

"Demons?" Kim was still hopeful.

"Anything." There was something chilling in the machine's calm declaration. "My creator programmed me to destroy a target with a beam that leaves no evidence behind of how the human or nonhuman died."

Human or nonhuman? "Why would Sergei do that?" Kim was horrified. No evidence left behind? This was a scary machine.

"I don't know." The detector eyed Fo.

"Interesting." Brynn sounded thoughtful. "Has Dirk ever used you to kill anyone?"

"No." The detector's gaze never left Fo.

Brynn cast Kim a meaningful glance. "Why don't we give Fo and her new friend some time alone? We can wait out in the hall." He hoped she didn't fight him on this.

"I guess so." She stared at Dirk's detector like it was the reincarnation of Jack the Ripper.

"Thank you." Fo looked ecstatic. Her new friend's destructive capabilities hadn't dimmed her fascination with him. Love must be blind even with sentient machines.

"Give me a moment." Kim grabbed jeans and a top from her closet and hurried into the bathroom. Once dressed, she picked up her doughnut and coffee and then followed Brynn into the hall.

Once outside the room, Brynn raked his fingers through his hair as he tried to make sense of what the detector had revealed.

Kim paced. "What was Sergei thinking? If Dirk hits the Destroy button to get rid of a demon that's taken a human host, he'll kill the human. He doesn't even know he's dealing with a sentient being."

"We're assuming Dirk doesn't know. After all, he lied to you about the detector speaking to him." That assumption might be wrong. Not a comfortable thought, but one that had to be considered.

"Of course he doesn't know. What good is the detector to him the way it is now?" But Brynn could tell she was turning it over in her mind even as she defended her relative.

"The detector said it had never killed anyone, had never even talked to Dirk. What are the chances, considering how rabid Dirk sounded about destroying demons?" The chances were nonexistent so far as Brynn was concerned, but he'd keep his opinion to himself.

"You're right." She looked troubled. "Either Dirk wasn't telling the truth about loving to hunt demons and tried to make himself look good by saying the detector spoke to him, in which case he doesn't know about his detector because he's never tried to use it, or . . ."

"Or he's used it to kill, and the detector lied to us." Neither scenario brightened Brynn's day.

"Why would a detector lie?" Her eyes widened at the possibility.

Brynn shrugged. "You said this Sergei died. How did he die?"

"I have no idea." Her expression said she knew where he was going with this, and it didn't make her happy. "I'll ask Fo to find out. She can access Web info."

"No matter what we might suspect, someone has to warn your uncle." This would be a problem.

Kim nodded. "Yeah, and then he'll know who borrowed his detector. And I don't think he'll be sympathetic to Fo's plight."

"We can't involve Asima. Even if we were willing to, your uncle wouldn't believe a cat got into his locked room and made off with his detector while he was sleeping."

Kim sighed. "We'll have to let Asima take it back to Dirk's room. He won't catch her. It'd be nice if Dirk was still asleep, but we couldn't get that lucky. He'll just have to be left with an unsolved mystery." Leaning over, she set her coffee and doughnut on the floor and then sat down with her back propped against the wall. "I guess we'll have to figure out how to let him know about his detector without implicating ourselves."

"And if he already knows?" Brynn sat down beside her.

"Then we have a problem." Her expression said she didn't want to consider that possibility because it would mean good old Uncle Dirk had a secret dark side.

Since neither one of them could come up with a way to inform Dirk that his detector was a little less and a little more than he'd bargained for, they sat in silence for a few minutes.

"We have some time to kill, so let's talk about your compulsion, or the lack thereof." She didn't look at him. "We've been together night and day since Monday night. And as of five this morning, it's been twenty-four hours since the last one."

He didn't want to talk about his compulsion. Brynn wanted to sit quietly next to her thinking about her smooth, bare body under her jeans and top, because he knew she hadn't taken panties or a bra into the bathroom with her.

Kim wasn't one to sit quietly when she could worry a problem to death. "We have to at least consider the possibility that—"

He put his finger over her lips. "Don't say it. Don't even think it."

"Why not?" She stared at him from wide green eyes.

Brynn exhaled sharply and rubbed the back of his neck to relieve the tension. "It's like the compulsion is hiding, and if I think or talk about it being gone, it'll jump out and yell boo." That sounded really mature.

She smoothed her fingers over his thigh. "We have to face what's happening."

We. Warmth curled inside him as she aligned herself on his side. "Yeah, I know."

"You'll have to test it." He must've looked horrified because she rushed into her explanation. "You'll have to stay with another woman for twenty-four hours to make sure I'm not the catalyst."

"Another woman?" Surprised, Brynn realized he was unhappy with her idea because it meant he'd be away from her all those hours, not because he feared the compulsion might return.

"It has to be someone who knows about the compulsion. That narrows it down to two women. There's Sparkle . . ."

"And what do you think Sparkle, the self-proclaimed queen of all things sexual, will do the first time I offer her my body?" A no-brainer.

"Right. She'll pounce. It has to be Donna." She didn't look too enthusiastic about her test either, and he immediately felt better.

"When?" The sooner the better. He wanted to know one way or another about the compulsion. But no matter what happened, he'd come back to Kim.

"We can talk to Donna tonight after she rises. I know you have to take part in the fantasies, but when you're finished you can hang around with her for what's left of the night. When dawn comes, you can sleep on her couch. Heaven knows you've had a lot of practice sleeping on couches lately." She didn't try to hide her unhappiness with that fact. "Do you think Eric will be okay with you spending the night in the same room as them? And I never asked if the compulsion cares if the woman is married or single."

She was starting to think of the compulsion as a separate entity. A mistake. The compulsion was a part of who he was. "When the compulsion hits, I don't ask the marital status of the woman, I just start getting naked."

"Okay, then." She didn't sound like it was okay. "You'll be done by early Friday morning." She offered him a warm smile. "Why does that suddenly seem such a long time?"

Warm wasn't good enough. He wanted her to give him a sexy smile that said she'd make love with him wherever he wanted—on the floor, under the bed, in the shower, or on top of a building in Times Square. Anywhere but in her bed. He glanced at his watch. Yeah, they had time to discuss the bed thing.

"I want to make love with you." May as well get it out in the open. "But not in your bed. Maybe on the beach. Making love on the beach at midnight with the moon shining would be incredible." Or not. It was still a little cold on the beach at night in March. But he'd try to generate enough heat to keep both of them hot.

At first she looked startled by his change of subject, but then something in her gaze said he wasn't going to escape that easily. "Maybe I need you to make love with me in my bed." She looked away from him.

Memories of centuries spent as an unwilling visitor to women's beds lay cold around his heart. "Coming to your bed would remind me of the compulsion."

She glanced back at him, and something sad shimmered in her eyes. "I guess I'd like to think I could create a different memory."

She didn't say it, but Brynn didn't have to slide into her mind to understand what she meant. Kim wanted to be special enough to make him forget about all those other women.

He tried to think logically. "For five centuries I've had to climb into women's beds and give them what they wanted sexually. That's a lot of negative reinforcement. I can't reason away what I'm feeling, because it's all about hate, self-loathing, and fear. Logic doesn't get you anywhere with emotions that strong. It would take a more powerful emotion to get past all that baggage."

"Like love?" She showed him only sympathetic interest.

He nodded. "Like love." *Kim could be that woman.* The thought didn't startle him as much as he'd expected. Probably because his subconscious had been playing with the idea for a while.

Of course, love between them wouldn't work. Even if the compulsion *was* gone forever, he still wasn't human. He couldn't ask her to commit to a lifetime with him. Not that she'd want to anyway once she thought about the ramifications.

The irony of the whole thing almost made him laugh. Too bad it wasn't funny. Because if he came to her bed knowing he loved her, he'd have a whole new bed memory to torture himself with once she left him.

All bed discussions ended as the elevator doors opened and Asima emerged. She padded over to them. *"I hate to break up the happy couple, but I have to get our mystery man back to your uncle's room. Dirk just charged down to the registration desk and demanded they find the filthy thief who stole his detector."*

Brynn nodded as he waited for Kim to grab her coffee and un-eaten doughnut. Then he helped her up. They walked to the door and knocked before entering.

Kim hurried over to Fo. "I'm sorry, but Asima has to take . . ." She glanced at Fo's unnerving new friend.

"Gabriel. Fo has named me Gabriel. It's a good name." The gleam in his red eyes said she could've named him Bozo, and it would've been fine with him.

Fo had named him after an archangel. Brynn thought that was kind of symbolic, considering they were hunting an archdemon.

"Asima has to take Gabriel back to Dirk's room right now. Dirk's down in the lobby raising holy hell." Kim looked at Gabriel. "You can't say anything about being here because . . . because it'll get Fo in lots of trouble."

Gabriel widened his eyes in alarm. "I would never do anything to cause Fo grief. I won't answer, even if Dirk speaks to me."

"Thank you." Fo's eyes may as well have had the words *my hero* blinking in their purple depths. "We'll find a way to be together."

"Yes." Gabriel's voice held a dangerous quality that promised un-pleasant consequences for anyone who got in his way.

He might look like a glorified cell phone, but Brynn wouldn't make the mistake of underestimating Gabriel. He was programmed to destroy, and he didn't discriminate between human and nonhu-man. He was an equal opportunity killing machine.

Kim flipped Gabriel closed, Asima picked him up in her mouth, and then she was gone. As it always did, the door closed quietly behind her.

Silence filled the room for a few moments.

"Kimmie, I prayed for a friend like me, but I didn't know if God listened to . . . small beings." Her purple eyes glowed with happi-ness. "He does listen."

Kim smiled. "I'm happy for you, Fo." But the helpless glance she sent Brynn told him she wasn't sure if this love story would have a happy ending.

Brynn drew Kim down onto the couch. He pulled her close against him. "Don't forget, tonight you have a fantasy with Ordinary Guy."

Kim laughed as she gazed up at him. "That's mean. Vic is a nice person, and even an ordinary person can have extraordinary depths. I expect you to give him a super fantasy tonight."

Brynn hoped he wasn't broadcasting his evil intentions far and wide. "He'll have all the fantasy he can handle."

Then he lowered his head and took her mouth in a long, drugging kiss that had him thinking about putting his bed phobia aside for the moment. When he finally raised his head, his heart was pounding, and his breaths came in shallow gasps.

"And you'll have a fantasy that will be the stuff of legends, sweetheart."

18

"So how's your week been going?" Vic Burton guided Kim into the elevator and then hit the lobby button.

"Fine. Nothing spectacular." If you didn't count the demons, vampires, wizards, gargoyles, and immortal warriors.

He nodded. "I've had a great time with the fantasies, and the weather's been warm enough for me to relax on the beach. Makes it hard to go back to work next week."

"You needed a week to unwind." If he was waiting for the tales of *her* week's adventures, he'd have a mighty long wait.

The elevator doors opened, and everyone spilled out into the lobby. They walked the short distance to the great hall.

Vic looked at his watch. "We're just in time. I signed us up for the first fantasy." He offered her a quick grin. "Maybe we could catch a bite at the restaurant later."

"Sure." Why not? Brynn would be working, and besides, she wasn't attached at the hip to Mr. Tall Demonic and Delicious. Nope. Definitely not. Just because he'd be with Donna for twenty-four hours starting as soon as he quit work didn't mean she wanted to spend every moment until then with him. *Liar.*

"Ah, Mr. Burton, you're right on time." Holgarth sounded almost . . . jovial. "Promptness. An admirable trait."

Holgarth looked down his long nose at her, which was pretty hard to do because he wasn't really that tall. His conical hat added at least a foot to his height. The thought gave her lots of satisfaction.

"Ms. Vaughn." He didn't sound jovial anymore. "I assume you've been busy thinking up totally inappropriate changes for the castle."

Kim was trying to think of a scathing reply when Vic spoke up. "Okay, where're our costumes, and what do we do?"

Holgarth was all business now. "Caitlin here will supply your costumes. Once you've changed, you'll simply follow the staff's cues. Enjoy your fantasy." His expression said he was hoping part of Kim's fantasy involved the villain heaving her into the moat.

As she followed Caitlin, Kim resisted the urge to turn around and stick her tongue out at Holgarth. Barely.

A few minutes later, she emerged from the small dressing room wearing an authentic-looking medieval gown. Well, she assumed it was authentic. What did she know? The important thing was it made her feel like a woman from another age.

She patted her pocket to assure herself Fo was still there. After everything that had happened this week, she was afraid to go anywhere without the detector. But she'd warned Fo to keep quiet while Vic was around.

Vic waited for her. Even dressed in hose and tunic, he looked like a twenty-something guy from today's Houston.

A woman approached. "The queen wishes to see you."

Kim looked at Vic. He shrugged, and they followed the woman to the long banquet table where a large woman with many chins and a piercing stare waited. The queen was busy looking queenly. She beckoned imperiously.

When Kim and Vic stood in front of her, the queen looked down her royal nose at them. She did it much better than Holgarth.

"You." She pointed at Vic. "You will take the virgin to Eric the Evil so he will leave this castle in peace."

Vic blinked. "Eric the Evil?"

"Silence, knave." The queen looked grumpy. "Eric the Evil is the wicked vampire who plagues my kingdom. He demands a virgin whenever he visits the castle. I realize you have feelings for this virgin." Her dismissive glance in Kim's direction said she didn't mind losing one virgin, because after all, there were so many others cluttering up her kingdom. "But you must sacrifice her for the good of your queen." She didn't give Vic a chance to mount an argument. "Go." She pointed toward one of the darkened doorways.

"Yes, Your Majesty." Vic bowed and turned away.

Ha. Naked Man wouldn't have meekly led her to her doom. Oops, wrong fantasy. Since Kim didn't have anything to add to the discussion, she followed Vic.

The winding stone stairway was a lot scarier than Kim had expected. Only one or two wall sconces cast a dim glow, and the upper reaches of the stairs were lost in darkness.

"This is creepy." Vic's voice echoed in the darkness.

"No kidding." Kim wasn't particularly sensitive to atmosphere, but even she couldn't miss the miasma of evil and danger drifting down the stairs and twining around them like invisible fingers.

Kim suspected Eric waited at the top of the stairs, smiling as he created their sense of impending doom. She'd already experienced his awesome ability to mess with her mind. But even knowing this, she still wanted to turn around and race back down to the hustle and bustle of the great hall.

Vic clasped her hand as they climbed higher. His palm was sweaty. "I can't figure out why I'm afraid to meet this Eric the Evil guy. He's just a hired actor playing a role. Shows the power of suggestion on the human mind." His laugh seemed overloud in the darkened stairwell.

No, it shows the power of the nonhuman *mind.*

They reached the top of the stairs and stood peering into the gloom. A low, evil chuckle slid around them. Chills slithered along Kim's spine. Vic dropped her hand.

"Who's there?" Vic sounded like he wasn't too sure he wanted to know.

"Eric the Evil. 'Tis a bonny virgin you've brought me." The deep voice was rife with dangerous undertones.

A Scottish burr? Nice touch. "Um, I don't think you'll be too happy with me, Mr. Evil. I, er, giggle a lot even thinking about a naked man with all his dangly parts. And the one time someone told me how a man and a woman do it, I had hiccups for three days. You wouldn't want my mouth near your most precious body part while I had the hiccups. I mean, think about what could happen if I hiccuped right when my teeth were near . . . Uh, that would be a definite owie."

"Silence, woman." Eric sounded fierce enough, but Kim could hear the laughter in his voice.

"You can't have her. She's mine." Vic seemed definite about that.

"Take that, O Evil One." Maybe she should get more into her role. Were virgins meek ninnies back then? She didn't do a meek ninny well. Perhaps she should try a few terrified sobs. Nah.

"You wish to defy me, puny human male?" Eric injected just the right amount of amazement and contempt into his voice.

"You bet." Vic sounded fierce now. "Give me a weapon, and I'll take you on."

"Foolish man." Eric's voice was a whisper of menace.

Slowly he emerged from the darkness, and as if on cue, several wall sconces flickered to life. The play of light and shadow against the stone walls added to the implied threat.

Eric paused when he finally reached them. And even though Kim knew him, she had to swallow her frightened gasp. He was dressed as an ancient Highlander, and he was in his vampire form. Wild black hair framed a face filled with savage bloodlust. He moved into their personal space, using his size and bulk to intimidate. Kim didn't know about Vic, but she for one was damned intimidated.

He hissed at Vic and bared his fangs. "You dare try to keep this virgin from me?"

For a moment, Kim thought Vic was going to say the virgin was on her own and race down the stairs, but then he took a deep breath and met Eric's gaze, not an easy thing to do. "You can't have her."

Smoothly and with an ease that spoke of centuries of practice, Eric drew his sword from its scabbard. "You'll not only be without the virgin but your head as well. If I hadn't just fed I'd simply rip your throat out and have done with it."

Before Vic could voice his reply, assuming he could think of anything meaningful to say like, "Hand me my gun, virgin," there was shouting and a loud clattering on the stairs.

"Hold fast! We come to rescue you." The sound of footsteps grew nearer.

Eric sneered at them. "The prince and his faithful warrior race to save you, but they'll not have you." He curled his fingers into talons and showed more fang.

Brynn and Conall reached the top of the stairs on cue and rushed toward them.

"I'm Prince Brynn, fair maiden. Sir Conall and I will save you and your brave companion from the dark one."

Someone needed to work on the dialogue for these guys. "I can never repay you, Prince Brynn. My virginity is safe." She fluttered her eyelashes to demonstrate that although she valued her virginity, she might be convinced to lose it if he crooked his little finger, or any other appropriate body part.

Brynn's eyes gleamed with his attempt not to laugh, and Kim was reminded of how absolutely spectacular-looking he was. He'd tied his hair back with a strip of leather and once again wore his long white robe edged in gold.

"I will carry you to safety, beauteous maid Kim, while Sir Conall and your companion, Sir Vic, vanquish the forces of evil." He cast

Sir Vic a glance to see how he was taking the news that he'd be staying behind.

Vic's eyes lit up. He clapped Sir Conall—who was looking pretty impressive in his hose, tunic, and ankle boots—on the back. "I did some fencing in college. Let's get this bastard." He turned to Brynn. "Loan me your sword."

Eric's eyes widened as Brynn grinned. He handed Vic his sword and then scooped Kim up in his arms. Instead of carrying her down the steps, he strode across the landing to another stairway winding upwards.

A short time later, they emerged on the curtain wall's walkway. He put her down, and together they gazed over the battlements. There was a moon out tonight, and she could see the moonlight shining on the dark waters of the Gulf. "This is beautiful, Brynn."

His grin was quick and mischievous. It tugged at her heart. She'd bet there weren't many times in his existence when his smile could've been described as mischievous. Had she done this for him? She fervently hoped so.

"Yeah, this is a great view, but that's not why I brought you up here." Brynn leaned over the battlements to stare toward the ground. He frowned. "What the . . . ? There was supposed to be a rope ladder here."

Kim blinked. "A rope ladder?" She'd expected and definitely looked forward to a sensual interlude up here, but a ladder?

Eyes narrowed, he looked around. "I put a rope ladder here so we could climb down and escape to the future."

"Run that past me again?" Not much surprised her anymore at the Castle of Dark Dreams where the bizarre was normal.

"I wanted us to spend time in our own spaceship. A great fantasy. We'd battle alien ships and then relax while we watched the stars for a while. All alone, just us." His grin returned. "I don't think we'd spend much time battling alien bad guys." He glanced away. "Of course, I'd give you the option of staying here to be with Vic when his fantasy ended."

"I'd love to explore the universe with you." Kim knew her voice was soft with all the feelings she couldn't express aloud. "But Vic would be hurt if I just took off and left him here." She stared out at the Gulf. "Why the rope ladder when all we had to do was go down the stairs and out the castle doors?"

Brynn didn't look repentant about Vic. "Eric and Conall helped me come up with a few additions to his fantasy that'll keep him busy for a while. And I got a sub to take over my part in the fantasies until I returned."

Kim's heart did its usual hop and skip as he smiled. "Climbing down the wall would be an adventure. Using a door is what Ordinary Guy would do. It's logical. What's between us hasn't been ordinary or logical from the beginning."

Kim moved closer to him as a light breeze lifted her hair from her shoulders. "Hmm. Am I right in guessing there're no beds in this spaceship?"

He widened his eyes. "Now that you mention it, I don't think there are."

"And I suppose it never occurred to you that if lust for your body overcame me, I'd have to drag you onto the floor." She reached up to release his hair from the leather tie and then ran her fingers through the freed strands.

Brynn shook his head in disgust. "Busted."

She drew in a deep breath of courage. Time for a few truths. "Maybe it's past time we did away with the fantasies between us."

His gaze sharpened, but he didn't say anything.

Please let her find the right words to make him understand. "I want to make love with you in my bed. No special effects. No imaginary world. Just the two of us together in the real world."

"But I'm not part of your 'real world.' I've never been part of it."

The earlier happiness was gone from his voice, and she mourned its loss. "Maybe I *want* you to be part of it." Okay, treading on dangerous ground here. "I want to wake up with you in our bed. I want to be part of your days, your nights." Plural. She hoped he noticed the plural. Kim knew she couldn't get much more direct than that unless she uttered the *L* word. And she still didn't have the courage for that, because his rejection would hurt too much.

He smoothed her hair away from her face. "How would you handle your conscience long-term, Kim? I'm not sure what I am anymore, but if I'm a demon, you'd have to deny your duty every day for the rest of your life."

For the rest of your life. That sounded promising, didn't it? "What you are is a beautiful man, inside and out, no matter what label the world wants to give you."

"Thank you." Bending down, he covered her mouth in a deep kiss that for the time it existed pushed away all the things they hadn't said to each other, maybe would never be able to say. Like how could she grow old and die while he looked forever as he did at this moment? Would the compulsion ever return? How would they handle never knowing who or what he truly was? And what about children? Did he want any? Could he love an adopted child? *And why the hell am I worrying about children when he hasn't said he loves me?*

Kim didn't know how any of this would end, but she could make one concession. "I'd like to do the spaceship fantasy with you before I leave. After we kick some alien butt, we can make love in a galaxy far, far away." If she had to walk away once her job here was finished, she didn't want to look back on a missed chance to make love with him, in or out of a bed.

She'd never know what his reply would've been, because a shout from the base of the wall took them out of the moment.

"Ahoy, ye scurvy dogs. Captain Blood wants a word wi' ye, he does." The rough, booming voice demanded their attention.

They both looked over the wall.

"Aye, there ye be. Ye weren't planning to escape the castle, now were ye?" The man standing on the ground below them was dressed in full pirate regalia including a hook instead of a hand and an eye patch.

His raspy laugh grated along her nerve endings. "Yer ladder came loose from the wall, it did." He pointed to where the ladder lay curled in the grass. " 'Twould have been a sad thing if ye'd fallen to yer death from the ladder, now wouldn't it?" His evil grin revealed several missing teeth. He didn't seem particularly unhappy at the thought of them falling to their deaths.

"Damn. Hell. Bitch. Awk!" The grouchy-looking parrot clinging to the pirate's shoulder flapped its wings and squawked.

Kim winced. "What do you want?"

"I come from the One Whose Name Cannot Be Uttered." He cleared his throat noisily and spat.

Ick, ick, ick. Kim glanced at Brynn. He had that fixed expression that told her he was communicating with someone. Okay, she'd keep Captain Disgusting busy.

"Why can't his name be uttered? Hey, I bet he's ashamed of it. Must be something like David Ulysses Martin Boswell. See, when you look at his initials, they spell *DUMB*." She smiled her most insincere smile.

"Bastard. Slut. Asshole. Awk!" The parrot agreed with her.

Captain Blood scowled. "Ye be not wise to make sport of one so powerful."

"Yeah, like I'm so scared of someone who has to send Captain Gross and Polly Pottymouth to deliver a message. So what's he want?" This time when she glanced at Brynn he nodded.

"The One Whose Name Cannot Be Uttered wants ye to know he won't destroy ye until Sunday. That will give all the Vaughns a chance to be here for the bloody massacre. Until Sunday, he'll just amuse himself by driving all yer guests from the castle."

"Shit. Fuck. Dickhead. Awk!" The parrot thought a bloody massacre sounded pretty neat.

Kim watched as Eric and Conall eased into view, each coming from a different direction.

"Um, Kimmie, do you want me to zap the pirate and his parrot? I bet the parrot's saying all those ugly words because the demon in him is steamed. I would be, too, if I got stuck possessing a bird."

Brynn shook his head. "It's just a projected image, Fo. Only an archdemon could get past the gargoyles."

At that moment, Eric and Conall dove for the pirate. With a grating laugh and another string of obscenities from his parrot, Captain Blood disappeared.

Kim stepped back. "You were right. The archdemon must be creating the images, probably from inside the castle somewhere."

Brynn nodded and headed back toward the stairs. "We have to find him and the portal before Sunday."

Kim sighed for their lost closeness of a few minutes ago. She followed Brynn down the stairs, trying to think of an excuse to explain away her long absence to Vic. But she needn't have bothered.

She reached the great hall to find Vic lounging on a pile of large, colorful pillows in front of the fireplace and surrounded by five maidens who gave new meaning to the word *fair*. One of them was feeding him chocolates, another held a goblet that Kim suspected contained something a little stronger than water, and the other three were massaging his shoulders, brushing his hair, and stroking his chest.

When she walked up to him, he didn't look overjoyed to see her. "This is unbelievable, Kim. I'm a hero for defeating Eric the Evil. My reward is the services of these maidens for the rest of the night." He did have the grace to look guilty. "We can still go to eat if you want?" His expression said he hoped she didn't "want."

Kim tried not to look too relieved. "No, you enjoy your reward. I have work to do anyway."

He didn't try to change her mind. Kim was glad. But now she had free time on her hands. And since the owner of the castle was paying her to design a few meaningful changes, she'd better earn her money. She'd spend the rest of the night working on her plans. By next week—assuming she survived the epic battle between good and evil—she'd be ready to head back to Dallas. She should be happy about that, right? *Waiting for feelings of joy, joy, joy here.* Nope. No joyous feelings. This was all Brynn's fault.

Nursing her bad temper, she stepped onto the elevator. An elderly couple got on behind her, and just as the doors were about to close, Lynsay and Deimos rushed in.

Her sister and Deimos were holding hands and staring at each other with wide, silly grins. Kim had opened her mouth to ask how things were going, when Deimos spoke.

"You've got to come to my room, Kim. We have to show you something." Deimos's full-head blush hinted at a sexual "something" in his room.

"Yeah, you've gotta see this, Sis. It's awesome." Lynsay actually glowed.

Uh-oh. Lynsay looked way too happy. Kim would have to talk to Deimos. Her sister had a right to know what he was. But Kim hated to be the evil sister who symbolically tore the young lovers apart.

"My, my, isn't it wonderful? Everyone here is in love. Even you, dear." The older lady smiled sweetly at Kim. "People in love have that certain glow. Herb and I are going to be married on Saturday in that chapel Mr. Vaughn told us about. You know, the one in those brochures. Is Mr. Vaughn a friend of yours? We saw you with him in the restaurant. Such a nice man."

Kim had to think for a minute. "Oh, you mean Ye Olde Victorian Wedding Chapel." Glow? If she was glowing, it was from sexual frustration.

"Mary and I were sweethearts back in school, but we both married someone else and raised families." Herb squeezed Mary's hand, and she gazed up at him with adoration in her eyes. "We never forgot each other, though. Both our partners died, and now we're going to spend the rest of our lives together."

That was so sweet Kim felt herself tearing up. Fine, so maybe she was getting all teary because it didn't look like she'd get a shot at a rest-of-my-life with Brynn. And she'd definitely decided she wanted one.

As Kim stepped off the elevator with Lynsay and Deimos, she

waved to Herb and Mary. "Congratulations, and I wish you tons of happiness."

Once outside Deimos's room, she watched him fumble with the key until Lynsay helped him open the door.

Lynsay, her little sister who had no patience with any type of clumsiness in others, smiled lovingly at Deimos. "He's so cute when he gets all nervous and excited."

Kim followed them into the room and over to the small table beneath the arrow slit masquerading as a window. Once there, they parted to let her see what rested on the table.

"Ohmigod!" Kim blinked and stared.

Sweetie Pie and Jessica were in full, magnificent bloom. Not only were they completely covered with small pink flowers, but the two plants had grown to the size of small bushes.

Deimos wrapped his arm around Lynsay's waist and pulled her tightly against him. "You tell her, love."

Love? Kim looked at Lynsay. Her sister seemed down with being called *love*. This was serious.

Lynsay blushed. She never blushed. Kim's sister bought into the belief that blushing was against the kick-butt heroine code.

"Deimos gave his virginity to me. Isn't that incredibly sweet?" Lynsay's gaze stayed fixed on Deimos.

"Incredibly sweet." Kim backed toward the door. "I'm going to leave, because I think you want to be alone to celebrate. Oh, and Sweetie Pie and Jessica look spectacular."

Kim didn't think they noticed when she left.

What was the most depressing fact about the last few minutes? The knowledge that if she'd kept Jessica and Sweetie Pie, every one of their little buds would be nothing but withered scraps of unfulfilled promises lying on the floor waiting for the maid to vacuum them up.

Come to think of it, that might very well describe her by the end of the week.

19

Brynn leaned back in Kim's armchair and watched her put Fo into her jacket pocket. "No purse tonight?"

Her stare was deadly serious. "Demons don't die if you hit them with your purse. I travel light when I hunt."

It was Saturday night, and his universe had narrowed down to two truths—he loved Kim Vaughn, and they were going to kick some demon butt tonight. He wasn't quite sure where either of these truths would lead him.

She slipped her cell phone into her other pocket. "I hear more guests checked out today. What's our archenemy with the diabolical sense of humor been up to?" Kim had ticked off both Asima and Sparkle this morning by refusing their outfits in favor of jeans, a T-shirt, boots, and her leather jacket—demon-hunting clothes.

"The Milligans checked out after the ghost of Abraham Lincoln stood at the foot of their bed last night and recited the whole Gettysburg Address. The Santoris left this morning after the spirit of

Mr. Santori's mother kept turning the lights on and off and shrieking that Mrs. Santori wasn't good enough for her baby. The Santoris have been married for thirty years, but I guess the spirit is still into deep denial. Should I go on?"

"I get the picture. Don't you find it kind of strange that our big bad archdemon hasn't tried to kill any humans, just scare them away from the castle?" She slipped a mini-recorder into her bra.

"He's amusing himself." *And putting a big hurting on our business.* "Ordinary humans aren't his main target. He's itching for a fight with the Vaughns. The people who live or work on the island are simply hosts for his army. And he's keeping Holgarth, Eric, Conall, and me busy doing damage control. I've spent the last few days trying to calm terrified guests."

Kim nodded. "If he distracts you guys, you won't have as much time to hunt for him. On the upside, fleeing guests leave more vacant rooms for the Vaughns to fill." She winced. "Okay, that was insensitive. I'm sorry the Vaughns have brought this kind of trouble to your castle. But it should be over one way or another soon. Lynsay says Dirk has asked everyone to meet in the lobby at midnight. I don't think all the Vaughns have ever gathered in one spot before. It should be quite a sight."

Brynn made a mental note to be far away from the lobby at midnight, even though he was starting to lean toward the I'm-not-a-demon theory. "What's with the recorder?"

"It's an exorcism ritual. I'm not a priest, so the words by themselves won't cast out a demon, but they'll annoy him to death. Anything that sidetracks a demon is a good thing." She stuffed a few tissues into her jeans pocket. "Demon ash makes my nose run."

Brynn nodded. "Funny, but today was pretty quiet. Our archdemon gave everyone a break. I wonder why?" There was some important clue just out of reach.

Kim shrugged. "Maybe he had something else important to do." She walked over, knelt in front of him, and put her hand on his knee.

Damn. Physical contact. Major distraction. He forced his attention away from her touch and back to what she was saying.

"The Vaughns are set to go. I had a hard time convincing them to wait until midnight, but they finally saw the wisdom of striking when most ordinary people—read: those not possessed—are in their homes. The fewer uninvolved witnesses to the battle the better. Besides, they need Eric's help, so they had to wait until dark anyway." She met his gaze, and he saw the fear there.

He didn't blame her. They hadn't tracked down the archdemon or the portal, but they couldn't put off their attack any longer. The Vaughns had to hit the streets and start destroying demons before the archdemon launched his own attack. The archdemon must know that's what they'd do, but it didn't seem to bother him. He was confident, and that was a red warning light.

"Here's hoping one of the demons feels threatened enough by the Vaughns to make a break for the portal. We'll be there to follow it home. And we've canceled the Vampire Ball for tonight." If the archdemon decided to take the battle to the Vaughns here, innocent guests would be in danger. Although without his demon army, he might think twice about engaging the combined supernatural forces in the castle.

Kim rubbed her hand across her forehead. "I've put off telling Dirk about his detector until the last minute. Can we say cluck cluck? I've got to tell him now, and I've got to tell him in person. I'm sure some of the Vaughns brought extra detectors. He can borrow one."

Brynn still felt conflicted about Kim's uncle. How could someone who made such a big deal about loving to destroy demons not know about his detector? Something wasn't right with Uncle Dirk. "Did Fo find out anything about Sergei's death?"

"Nope. She couldn't find any info about him at all. It was like someone went in and wiped away any proof of his existence." Kim stood and then headed toward the door. "It's almost time for Holgarth's meeting."

Reluctantly, Brynn rose to follow her. He didn't want to go to any damn meeting with Holgarth. He wanted to forget about demons for the next hour and instead strip Kim's clothes from her hot body, lose himself in her welcoming heat, and feel her clench around his cock. And while they were still joined, he wanted to tell her he loved her enough to tear apart anyone or anything that got in the way of that love, even his own doubts.

Amazing how a few days had changed his perspective. He'd started out with this whole list of reasons why not, and now all he had was one I-don't-give-a-damn. Of course, the twenty-four compulsion-free hours he'd spent with Donna had removed one of the major elephants in his own personal room.

Brynn breathed deeply. *Focus. Demons first and then declaration of undying love.* And he'd guarantee he was the only man who could honestly promise the undying part. "Holgarth did some research on how to close a portal. He wants to pass on what he's learned and make sure everyone's on the same page."

"Uh, Kimmie?" Fo was using her tiny voice, a sure sign she wasn't happy about what she was going to say.

"Hmm?" Absently, Kim glanced down at Fo.

"Gabriel killed Sergei." Fo's words were barely audible.

"What?" Kim pulled Fo from her pocket and stared into the detector's wide purple eyes.

"Gabriel didn't want me to tell you because he was afraid you'd blame him and not let us be together anymore."

Fo blinked rapidly, and Brynn swore he saw tears in her eyes.

"Dirk pushed the button to kill Sergei, so it wasn't Gabriel's fault." Fo's gaze skittered back and forth between Kim and Brynn. "I didn't think it would hurt to keep Gabriel's secret. But I don't want Dirk to kill you. And he'll be really mad when he finds out Gabriel was with me." Fo's voice was a whisper. "I'm sorry. I just wanted to have a friend like me. I should have told you."

"We're not mad at you, Fo," Brynn reassured the detector. *Not much anyway.* What could've driven Dirk to murder? "Did Gabriel say why Dirk killed Sergei?"

"He said Dirk didn't want Sergei to make any more detectors like Gabriel, and he didn't want any of the other Vaughns to know that Gabriel was different." Fo sounded tired, as if revealing her first human deception had worn her out.

Kim slid her finger over the screen in an attempt to console Fo. "Thank you for telling us, Fo." She slipped the detector back into her pocket and then stared helplessly at Brynn. "What's going on with Dirk?"

Brynn guided her into the hallway and then closed her door. "I don't know, but I do know he's a dangerous man. If Gabriel can be believed, he's capable of destroying both humans and nonhumans. We have to get Gabriel away from Dirk."

Just then, the elevator door opened, and Wade exploded into the hall. "That freakin' son of a bitch." He spotted Kim and Brynn. "That cheat won the fishing tournament with a hundred-pound redfish." He speared Kim with a glare that said she was personally responsible for the redfish. "No one has *ever* caught a freakin' hundred-pound redfish."

Kim stepped back and stared at Wade with wide eyes. "Who?"

"Your freakin' uncle, that's who. The tournament was today, and I caught a thirty-five-pound beauty. I would've won if Dirk hadn't caught his hundred-freakin'-pound monster. He cheated. I just don't know how." Wade's eyes glowed red. "But I'll find out."

All the uneasy feelings Brynn had about Dirk suddenly coalesced into a terrifying suspicion. He glanced at Kim and saw that the same possibility had occurred to her.

"No. It couldn't be." Kim's voice shook.

"Yes, it could. It would be perfect. Hiding in plain sight." He turned to Wade. "Come with us. Holgarth wants all the nonhumans to meet in the conference room. I know you don't want to get involved in our war, but I think Holgarth needs to hear what you have to say."

Before going down to the lobby, Kim tried to call Dirk's room. She looked at Brynn. "No answer."

"Ha! He's probably out celebrating how he screwed me over." Still fuming, Wade followed them onto the elevator.

Wade was too pissed to even ask why Holgarth would want to hear about his fishing tournament. Kim didn't say anything, but her face was pale with shock. Two floors down, the elevator stopped, and the doors slid open. Mary and Herb stepped in.

Mary beamed at Kim. "Herb and I got hitched a couple of hours ago. When you see Dirk, thank him for suggesting Ye Olde Victorian Wedding Chapel." Her smile faded a little. "The chapel was lovely, but that Reverend Abby was a little strange. Don't you think she was strange, Herb?"

Herb nodded. "Strange. But it doesn't matter because we're finally married."

"Reverend Abby?" Kim looked bemused.

Mary nodded. "She gave us this as a souvenir." She held up a miniature plastic wedding cake with a screw-on top. "It's a really cute idea." She unscrewed the top to reveal a bubble blower. "Every time I want to remember this day I can blow some bubbles." She dipped the plastic ring in the solution and then blew on it.

Without warning, the elevator car jerked to a stop, and the lights went out.

Brynn blinked to make sure he was seeing what he thought he was seeing. The gasps from everyone else in the elevator verified he wasn't hallucinating.

Glowing bubbles filled the darkened elevator. Big, bright bubbles with gleaming red eyes peering out of them. Evil eyes that even scared him, and he'd thought he'd seen all there was to see over five centuries.

"Everyone down!" Kim's voice was coldly professional and not to be disobeyed.

Brynn hit the floor with everyone else in the elevator except Kim. She whipped Fo from her pocket, pointed, and pushed the red button. As each bubble popped, Mary squeaked her alarm. Finally all the bubbles were gone, and darkness settled around them.

Just as suddenly as the lights had gone out, they came back on. The elevator lurched into motion again.

"What the hell was that?" Herb sounded breathless.

Brynn wasn't even going to try to concoct a lie. People were in danger. "I'm Brynn McNair. My brothers and I run the castle. I think Mary and you need to check out as soon as possible. The castle will compensate you for any inconvenience."

Herb stared into his eyes, and whatever he saw in Brynn's gaze evidently convinced him to not ask questions, because he simply nodded.

"Did Reverend Abby say she'd given the bubbles to any other couples?" Kim picked up the empty bubble container and studied it.

"I don't know about that, but she gave us a whole bunch to put in the lobby." Mary's voice quavered. "She said the little cakes were great promo items." She glanced at Herb. "In fact she said she would've done it herself, but she'd hurt her leg and couldn't get around right now."

"More likely the gargoyles kept her ass out." Wade's murmur echoed Brynn's thoughts.

Kim clasped Mary's shoulder. "This is important, Mary. Did you put any of those cakes out?"

Mary shook her head. "They're all still in our room. The reverend said to take them down to the lobby and just scatter them around. But we thought we'd better ask for permission before we did that."

Brynn couldn't hide his relief. "You did the right thing. Kim and I will be going into your room to get them. Don't go back there until the cakes are gone." He attempted a smile. "Go have a good meal on the castle. By the time you're finished, it'll be safe to return to your room."

"Is this some kind of plot to ruin your business?" Herb was reaching for understanding.

"Yeah, kind of." Brynn didn't know what else to say.

"Well, I hope you catch whoever's behind it. I had my own business, and a man works damn hard to build up a good reputation. No one has a right to take that from him." He patted Brynn on the shoulder.

The elevator doors slid open, and the couple left quickly. Brynn put his hand up to stop anyone from getting onto the elevator. "Sorry, folks. There's something wrong with this car. It's out of commission for a while. The management apologizes for any inconvenience."

Grumbling, the people wandered toward another elevator. He turned to Kim. "Can you tell anything about the bubble container?"

She nodded. "It's lined with some type of metal. Maybe lead? But whatever it is, it got the demons past the gargoyles." Kim shivered. "If those bubbles had been released in a room full of people, the demons would've had their pick of hosts. Thank heaven Mary and Herb didn't put out all the others."

"What's the point, though, if the gargoyles kick the demons out on their butts as fast as they take human hosts?" The demon bubbles had managed to push the fishing tournament from Wade's mind for the moment.

"You're right." Kim stared at the container. "But we've seen examples of this archdemon's power. If he can cloak his own presence from the gargoyles, why can't he cloak an area in the castle from them, too?"

"Like the lobby." Brynn looked grim.

"Where all the Vaughns will be meeting at midnight." Kim felt grimmer.

Red flickered deep in Wade's eyes. He was into the moment. "Looks like the chapel might be your portal. Don't think this Abby is your archdemon, though. The archdemon could get past the gargoyles any old time he wanted. He wouldn't need someone to bring in stuff for him. I'd say the Abby demon is a minion who's been filling the containers for the archdemon, and when she had enough, she used a convenient human carrier to get them past the gargoyles. Probably the big guy was busy doing something else, so he couldn't do it himself."

"Yeah. Like out catching a hundred-pound redfish." Kim wondered how long the archdemon had been using her uncle.

Wade looked at her blankly for a moment, and then his eyes blazed bright red as Kim's implication sank in. "That son of a bitch."

Kim sighed. "I'll have to clean up these piles of ash. We were lucky Mary and Herb were so rattled they didn't notice them. I think they've had enough weirdness for their wedding day."

"I'll take care of the ash." Brynn touched her arm. "You and Wade go on to the meeting. Tell everyone I'll be there in a minute."

It was pitiful how even a light touch on her arm managed to momentarily erase everything else from her emotional chalkboard. Without comment, she went with Wade to the conference room where everyone waited.

Holgarth harrumphed to call attention to her lateness.

Okay, she'd used up every last damned bit of her patience for the day. She narrowed her gaze on the wizard. "You will not make even one snide comment, or I'll come across that table and screw your pointed hat into your tiny brain."

Holgarth raised one brow. "A bit grumpy, are we?"

She glanced at Brynn as he came in and sat down next to her. "You bet. We have some serious stuff coming down."

Kim had everyone's instant attention. She put the bubble container on the table. "Brynn and I think the archdemon has possessed my uncle Dirk and that Ye Olde Victorian Wedding Chapel is the portal to hell." Just saying it sounded ludicrous, but it was the only thing that made sense. She'd let Brynn explain the whole mess while she figured out what she'd say to Lynsay and what they'd both say to the other Vaughns.

A roomful of humans would've all started talking at once. The nonhumans grew still and intense as they waited for Brynn to explain.

Brynn took a deep breath and told them everything Kim and he knew—Gabriel's unique abilities, Dirk's murder of Sergei, the demonic bubbles, and the fact that Dirk steered Mary and Herb to the chapel.

When Brynn was finished, Wade added his postscript. "And the prick didn't scare the crap out of any of your guests today because he was too busy screwing me out of first prize in the fishing tournament. A freakin' hundred-pound redfish. Only demonic power could've put a redfish that big on the end of his damned line. I'll find a way to have him disqualified." His eyes blazed red at the unfairness of the whole thing.

Ganymede burped loudly, calling attention to himself. "You have to get rid of those demons in a bubble first. Kim needs more detectors than just Fo to take care of them." He looked at Sparkle. "You know, I'm a sensitive kind of guy, and all this talk of demons has upset me. I crave a big dish of ice cream to settle me down." He leaped from the chair. "Coming, sweet stuff?"

Sparkle looked uncertain but stood to follow him.

"*Aren't you going to do battle against the demons?*" Asima sounded scandalized.

"Battle demons? Hmm." Ganymede rolled his eyes to the top of his head in pretend thought. "That sounds a lot like work. Nope. Don't think I will."

Sparkle studied her nails, but her heart didn't seem to be in it. "You know, I wouldn't like to see anything happen to anyone here." Her pointed stare said Asima was exempted from Sparkle's "anyone."

Ganymede yawned. "Look, there're enough of you here to take care of the demons. A little ice cream, a little nap, and you can call me if you need me." He stared at the closed door, and when it swung open, he padded out of the room with tail waving in the air.

Sparkle made her decision. She sat back down.

Holgarth sniffed. "Well, those of us who care about something other than ourselves will go forth to defeat the forces of evil tonight."

"Oh, brother." Sparkle rolled her eyes.

Wade didn't look too enthusiastic about battling the forces of evil. "Umm, I've had a long day on the water."

Brynn stood. "No one leaves until Kim talks to Lynsay." He glanced at Kim.

Kim pulled out her cell phone. Thank heavens Lynsay answered. "I need at least three more detectors. We have some demons to take out. Don't bring any Vaughns with you, just the detectors. Meet me up at room . . ." She glanced at Brynn. He mouthed the room number. "Meet me at room one forty-five."

Holgarth took over. "Kim, Brynn, Eric, Lynsay, and I will destroy the demons. Conall, Donna, Asima, and Sparkle will start looking for Dirk. Oh, and while you're looking, make sure none of those bubble containers are lying around anywhere." He speared the Dirk hunters with a gimlet stare. "Do not, I repeat, do *not* engage the archdemon if you find him. Notify me immediately." Finally, he cast Wade a dismissive glance. "Since keeping the world safe from archdemons ranks somewhere below catching the perfect fish, I didn't include you."

If Holgarth was hoping to shame Wade into a commitment, he failed. Wade shrugged. "I'll tag along with Kim and Brynn just for the heck of it. Then I'll go to my room and catch up on my sleep. Had to get up before dawn this morning." He yawned to demonstrate his exhaustion from reeling in his thirty-five-pound beauty.

Asima leaped onto the table to face off with Holgarth. *"Why does Conall have to hunt for the archdemon? Sure he's strong, but physical strength means nothing to a malevolent entity like that. He'll flick Conall aside like a piece of lint from his belly button. I think—"*

"Shut up, cat! I'm a warrior, and I'll do a warrior's work." Conall's thunderous roar made everyone wince.

Except Asima. She simply hissed at Conall. But she didn't finish telling everyone what she thought.

Kim didn't waste any more time. She and Brynn led the way to Mary and Herb's room.

Lynsay waited for them at the door. "What's up, Sis?"

"Where's Deimos?" Up until now, he'd been attached at the

hip—and other places—to Kim's sister. Where was he now when they might actually need him?

"He's watching the candy store for Sparkle." Lynsay sounded like right now she'd rather be hawking gummi bears.

Amazing, since destroying demons had always been Lynsay's reason for being.

Kim took a deep, fortifying breath. Okay, Lynsay needed to know what she was up against. She also needed to know that nonhuman entities were fighting on her side. No specifics. Just enough info to keep her from freaking if Holgarth or Eric outed themselves during the fight. She firmed her lips and her determination. Her sister didn't have to know anything about Brynn or Wade.

As quickly as possible, Kim filled Lynsay in on Dirk, Gabriel, Ye Olde Victorian Wedding Chapel, and the bubble demons. She also hinted that several of the men who'd be going into the room with her were, uh, more than men.

"Holy crap!" Lynsay cast uneasy glances at Brynn, Eric, Holgarth, and Wade. Then she looked at Kim. "Let's get those bubble bastards. And later on we'll talk about this 'more than men' thing."

Brynn stepped forward and used his master key to open the door. The pile of plastic wedding cakes lay on the coffee table. Lynsay handed Eric, Brynn, and Holgarth demon detectors.

Lynsay frowned at Wade. "Sorry, I only brought three."

Holgarth sniffed. "Wade is a noncombatant. He doesn't need one."

Eric turned and stared at the door and then did the same to the window. "I've put a shield across both exits. If a demon gets past us, it'll be trapped in the room."

Lynsay's eyes widened, but she didn't say anything.

"We'll open one container at a time. From what I saw on the elevator, we'll only have to blow once to empty the container of demons." Brynn glanced at Wade. "Since you don't want to be involved in destroying the demons, you can blow the bubbles."

Wade's face lit up. "Hey, cool."

Kim suspected Wade's inner child wasn't far from the surface. "As soon as Wade blows the bubbles, we destroy them. And make sure the bubbles are far away from Wade before you zap them. We wouldn't want to hit him." Message sent to everyone except Lynsay—they didn't want to be sweeping up Wade's ashes.

Eric, Holgarth, and Brynn got the intense expressions on their faces that told Kim they were instant messaging telepathically. Probably reminding each other to make sure none of the demons got near Kim or Lynsay, the only two beings in the room the demons could possess.

Kim took Fo from her pocket. "Ready, Fo?" At this point, she didn't give a damn if Lynsay heard her.

"I'm pumped." Fo's purple eyes shone with battle lust.

Wade unscrewed the first container, dipped the ring in the liquid, and blew. As in the elevator, the lights went out and the big brilliant bubbles with the evil eyes floated into the room. Other than an amazed squeak from Lynsay, everyone was silent as they aimed their detectors, pushed the red buttons, and . . . nothing.

Fo was the only one that worked. Frantically, Kim ignored everyone around her as she focused on the demons and kept pressing the button.

When she heard Lynsay's startled yelp, she knew the "more than men" were going into action. A bubble disappeared in a puff of smoke, and Kim glanced over to see Holgarth pointing his wand at another one.

Lynsay's reaction escalated to a shriek. Eric. Kim took care of a demonic bubble that was floating near her sister. Out of the corner of her eye she saw that Eric had changed to vampire form. He wasn't touching the demons physically, but Kim knew what kind of power he wielded mentally. Bubbles started exploding in showers of light.

When the last bubble was gone, Wade carefully put down the empty container and looked around the circle. "Y'all have some defective equipment there."

Lynsay's face was pale as she glanced at the men. "A vampire and a real wizard? I don't want to know what the rest of you guys are. My brain isn't processing this too well. Right now, I have to deal with the fact that none of the detectors are working except for Fo."

Kim responded to the terrible suspicion in Lynsay's eyes. "Just like your detector stopped working when you first got here."

Brynn nodded, his expression grim. "I'd bet none of the Vaughn detectors are working. No wonder the archdemon is so confident. He's disabled every weapon that could stop him and his demon army."

"Except for Fo." Lynsay stared into Fo's wide eyes. "Why is that?"

Kim shrugged. "Who knows." *Because Fo is a sentient being with a free will, not a mindless machine.*

Holgarth straightened his pointed hat that had gotten a little off center during the excitement. "We have to destroy the demons in the other containers with whatever we have."

Lynsay stared at Brynn. "I didn't notice you zapping any bubbles."

Brynn smiled at her, that sensual smile honed over centuries, able to melt women from the inside out. "My talents lie in other areas."

And Kim's sister reacted accordingly. Her smile was soft. "I just bet they do."

Wade picked up another container and unscrewed the top. "Between Fo, Eric, and Holgarth, we can finish this job."

Fifteen minutes later, they stood staring at the empty containers and the many small piles of ash scattered around the room.

Brynn reached for the phone. "I'll get housekeeping to bring up a vacuum so I can get rid of this ash."

But suddenly he stilled, along with Holgarth and Eric.

Lynsay cast Kim a puzzled glance.

"Telepathy." She moved to Brynn's side. "Have they found Dirk?"

"Yes. He's sitting down in the lobby." Brynn picked up the phone to finish his call to housekeeping. "Probably waiting for Mary and Herb to show up with the cakes so he can scoop them up."

"And turn his army of demons loose on the Vaughns at midnight. Without their detectors, none of them could stop the demons from taking them as hosts." Kim raked her fingers through her hair. "It would be even more satisfying to the archdemon than killing them outright. The ultimate irony."

"Conall has hotel staff unobtrusively moving people out of the lobby." Eric removed his shields from the door and window.

"Like the archdemon isn't going to notice the lobby emptying?" Wade nudged a pile of ash with his toe. "He'll know you've made him."

For once Holgarth wasn't wearing a supercilious smirk. "Let's hope he's arrogant enough not to care. But we can't move on him until all the humans are safe."

"All the humans?" Lynsay edged closer to the door. "That sort of sounds like there're more nonhumans in the castle."

Kim sighed. "Yeah, Lynsay, there are. Now let's hope there's enough nonhuman firepower to bring down an archdemon." She just wished she felt a little more confident.

20

Every primitive instinct in Brynn had howled for him to rip Fo from her hand, shove Kim behind his back, and have at those cursed demon bubbles. Even though he knew she was a professional and had the cool, calm courage to do the job herself. Even though he knew she'd tear a strip off him if he dared try to take Fo away from her. But damn it, his need to protect his woman had almost turned him into a grunting Neanderthal.

His woman. And that's who she was. Maybe she didn't know it yet, but he suspected she did. So now he had a problem. How could he say words he'd never said in five centuries? How about, "Hey, babe, love ya. Don't know if the compulsion will ever come back, and I might still be a demon, and I can't give you kids or much of a life, but how about runnin' off and marrying me, huh?" Right. That would make her realize what a great prize he was.

He'd whispered sensual words to thousands of women, but he didn't know how he'd say "I love you" to the only woman who'd ever been important to him. Maybe this was a show-don't-tell situation.

Brynn didn't have any more time to make plans because they'd reached the lobby. Now he'd have to watch Kim put herself in danger all over again. Freakin' great. A whole castle full of useless demon hunters with their useless demon detectors.

At least Dirk had a physical body. Brynn couldn't do anything but bat at those blasted bubbles, but he could get his hands on Dirk and do some serious damage. Hopefully, the combined supernatural powers of Eric and Holgarth would be too much for the archdemon. Sparkle and Asima had powers, too, but he wouldn't depend on them.

Holgarth glanced at the small army ready to enter the lobby. Donna was the only one missing because she had to get ready for her show. Couldn't cancel that. But no one doubted that Eric counted for two vampires when it came to pure power and danger.

"I think it would be best if you didn't go in with us, Lynsay. You're human and weaponless, an unfortunate combination if the archdemon is searching for a weak link. And I'm certain he will be." Holgarth tried to look kind, but he couldn't screw his face into a benevolent expression that anyone would believe.

Frantic, Lynsay looked at Kim. "Sis, you know demon hunting is my whole life. You guys have to take me with you."

Kim sighed and turned to Holgarth. "I'll keep her safe."

He didn't look happy, but he nodded at Kim. "I'm sure if I say no you'll design some grotesque new addition to the castle."

Kim grinned. "You bet."

Then Holgarth spoke to the whole group. "We'll go in together and then spread out to divide his attention. If he doesn't attack, we'll slowly close in on him. Kim, when you're within range, use Fo at the same time Eric and I throw our combined powers at him."

Conall frowned. "Don't you think we'd have a better chance if we all just rushed him? Won't your plan give him time to escape?"

Holgarth puffed himself up like an outraged rooster. "I advised Napoleon on his battle strategies. Exactly how many generals have *you* advised?"

"And if it doesn't work?" Lynsay didn't sound too confident now that she knew all the detectors were inoperable.

"Then we run like hell." Wade, always the bottom-line guy.

Asima's tail seemed to have developed a nervous twitch. *"You're exceptionally strong, Conall, but this will be a battle of supernatural forces. So stay behind me."*

Conall didn't say anything, but he looked like he wanted to pick Asima up and shake her until her little pointed teeth rattled.

Lynsay looked uncertain. "Did anyone else hear someone talking in their head?"

Sparkle frowned as she peered down at her stilettos. "I won't get that disgusting ash all over my new Pradas, will I?"

No one answered Lynsay or Sparkle.

Brynn kept one hand on Kim's shoulder as they moved into the lobby. He leaned down to whisper in her ear. "No, I'm not going to walk away from you. I thought I'd get that straight before you asked. So save your breath for the important stuff."

"Yeah, like what?" Her voice was breathless as she spotted Dirk lounging in one of the lobby's chairs. Gabriel was on the table in front of him.

"Like making love after this is over." He tightened his grip as they drew closer to the archdemon.

Heaving an exaggerated sigh, Dirk stood, stretched, and then yawned. "Well, damn. I assume you put the pieces together and came up with good old Uncle Dirk's name." His smile was toothy and insincere. "How clever of you."

The archdemon made a moue of disappointment. "I won't be getting any of my delightful little demonic bubbles, will I? One of my more brilliant ideas."

Turning his attention to Kim, his eyes suddenly blazed red. "Your uncle invited me in, you know. It was a trade-off. I'd make sure he won every fishing tournament he entered, and in return I got a cozy home for as long as I needed it."

"Son of a bitch." Wade's input.

The archdemon turned an amused gaze on Wade. "Eudemons are so clueless, such pathetic losers. It was absolutely worth spending the day with smelly fish and a stupid eudemon just to see your face when I brought in my catch. Which of course was no catch at all. But it doesn't really matter where the fish came from, because it'll go down in the record books under Dirk Vaughn's name. I hope he gets lots of pleasure from knowing he beat you, because there's always an ultimate price to pay."

Wade narrowed his eyes to red slits and growled low in his throat.

The archdemon laughed before turning his attention back to the others. "I suppose now you're going to try your puny powers on me. A waste of time, but who am I to deny you your useless little pleasures. If it gives you a chuckle knowing I'll have to come up with another plan to get rid of you all, please feel free to celebrate. But promise me you won't leave Galveston until I think of something else. It would be such a hassle getting you all back together again." He slid his gaze to Kim. "Oh, and I *will* have your detector, even if I have to pry it from your cold, dead hand."

"Asshole! Go chase your tail for a few thousand years." Fo was steamed.

The archdemon grinned. "Delightful."

Brynn felt Kim tense a second before she pressed Fo's Destroy button. At the same moment, the lobby filled with Eric's and Holgarth's immense powers. Maybe Asima and Sparkle were doing their part, too. He couldn't tell.

Fo's beam blinded Brynn, and everyone's combined powers swirled around him, taking his breath away and pressing on him from every side. He put his arm around Kim's waist and pulled her against him even as he resisted the urge to crouch on the floor in a fetal position. He'd have to remember to never make Holgarth or Eric really mad.

And then it ended. Everyone stared at everyone else before staring at Dirk who *was* curled into a fetal position on the floor.

"I can't see! I'm blind. What happened? Someone help me." His pleas degenerated into terrified whimpers.

Everyone raced to Dirk, but Brynn knew Kim wasn't looking at her uncle. Her gaze swept the floor around the cowering man. Then she stared up at Brynn. "We didn't get him."

Silence, tense and thick, fell as understanding spread. Brynn said what everyone was thinking. "No ash. He escaped to someone else."

Each person slid their gaze to the person beside him or her.

Sparkle studied her nails. It must help her think. "The only ones here he could possess are Kim and Lynsay."

Everyone's attention focused on the two humans. Lynsay blinked. "What? Hey, I'm still me." She glanced at Kim. "Sis, hold Fo up to me. Okay, Fo, am I still me?"

Fo's purple eyes were bright with excitement. "You're still you, although if you were someone else it might be an improvement."

Eyes narrowed, Lynsay took Fo from Kim and pointed the detector at her sister. "How about Kim? Is she in there by herself?"

Kim sighed. "The archdemon didn't possess me. But even if he had, you wouldn't know it. Remember that he can cloak his presence from everyone. Even Fo didn't pick up on Dirk. So technically, Lynsay and I are still suspect."

"I'd know about you, Kimmie. We're friends, and I'd know if that scumbag was inside you." Fo's eyes angled toward where Gabriel still sat on the table. "We'll have to adopt Gabriel now. Can we, can we?" She looked at Kim with wide, pleading eyes.

Kim dropped onto the nearest chair. "We'll see."

Brynn walked over and picked up Gabriel. "We'll have to make sure you don't fall into the wrong hands again, buddy."

Gabriel watched him with those red demon eyes but didn't say anything. Brynn flipped him closed and slipped him into his jacket pocket.

Lynsay was standing next to Wade. "So where'd the demon go? And where'd Fo learn to talk smack?"

Kim shrugged. "He's an archdemon. He can go wherever he

damned well pleases. He probably materialized outside the lobby or took a new host and is long gone." She looked frustrated. "Or not. He could still be in the castle because the gargoyles can't identify him." She ignored her sister's question about Fo.

"Do we head for the chapel now?" Eric was still showing fang.

"No." Something in Wade's voice got everyone's attention. "Give me an hour before you try to close the portal."

"Why?" Sparkle seemed fixated on her feet. "Although that'll give me time to change into cheaper shoes."

Wade's eyes still blazed red. "That bastard disrespected all eudemons. He thinks just because we're laid back we're weak." He stared at Kim. "Without their detectors, the Vaughns won't be able to take out the archdemon's army. Within an hour I can have hundreds of eudemons here. We can drive all the cacodemons from their human hosts and destroy them." He paused to think about details. "Eudemons don't take human hosts. We create forms that are acceptable to humans. But to do this job, we'll have to take our true forms." He glanced around. "Uh, our true forms are pretty creepy to the ordinary Joe on the street."

"The humans won't remember seeing you." Eric oozed the kind of confidence that came from immense power. "I'll take care of it."

Wade finally grinned. "The cacodemons can kiss their asses good-bye."

"Woohoo, way to go, Wade!" Lynsay high-fived Wade and then froze. "Wait. Did you say you're a demon?" She stared at Kim. "That's what he said, wasn't it?"

Brynn was officially out of patience. "Yeah, Lynsay, he's a demon. So am I." He frowned. "Maybe. Eric's a vampire, Holgarth's a wizard, Conall's an immortal warrior, Sparkle's a cosmic troublemaker, and the someone you heard talking in your head is the cat. She's a messenger of Bast. Deal with it. And if you ever tell anyone, we'll make your life a living hell. Got it?"

Lynsay stared at him for what seemed forever, and then she nodded. "Got it. Uh, what about Deimos? Is he . . . something else?"

Brynn hesitated. "Maybe you'd better talk to Deimos about that."

"We'll meet back here in exactly one hour." Holgarth was at his bossy best. "Wade can lead his eudemons into battle against the cacodemons while the rest of us attack the wedding chapel. And someone has to let the Vaughns know what's happening."

Lynsay raised her hand. "I'll take care of that." She cast Holgarth a narrow-eyed stare. "Have to prove to some people I can be useful."

Holgarth raised one brow to show how little he cared about her opinion. "I assume it wouldn't do any good to tell you to stay in the castle for the rest of the night."

Lynsay's eyes were now slits of defiance. "Damn straight."

He cast the still-whimpering Dirk a contemptuous glance. "And someone please take care of him."

Eric lifted Dirk to his feet. "I'll leave this one with his memory. He deserves to live with his betrayal." He glanced at Kim and Lynsay. "The archdemon murdered Sergei, but Dirk gave him the control. I assume the Vaughns have their own punishment system in place."

"The family will take care of him." Lynsay sounded grim. It didn't bode well for Dirk.

Brynn put his arm across Kim's shoulders. "Let's go to your room. We have a whole hour to ourselves."

"Maybe I'll take a short nap." She let him guide her toward the elevator.

I don't think so. The elevator doors slid shut behind them.

Brynn watched Kim strip off her jacket, put Fo on her night table, kick off her boots, and flop onto her bed.

She grinned at him. "How should I spend the hour before I go into battle against an archdemon—meditate, write farewell letters to my family, bargain with God?" Kim sounded like she was only half kidding.

Brynn took Gabriel from his pocket, flipped him open, and set him beside Fo. "We're not going to lose, so we don't need any farewell letters. And I don't think God is into bargaining." He slipped out of his jacket and dropped it on the couch. "So I'd say we should spend the hour making love."

"Hmm." She studied him as she absently unwrapped one of his Wicked Red Blow Pops. "Let's see what kinds of interesting options we have here."

She slid her tongue over the blow pop, and he shuddered as he personalized the erotic suggestion in her innocent action. Then he saw her eyes. They shone with wicked intent. Okay, not so innocent. She knew he was imagining her warm, wet tongue gliding over the most sensitive part of his bare body.

"We could make love in the shower. Sexy but done to death. We're looking for innovative and unique." She licked the blow pop again, slowly and provocatively. "How about under the bed?" Kim leaned over the edge of the bed to peer beneath it. "It's doable as long as you don't get carried away and smack your head on the bottom."

Brynn got rid of his shoes and peeled off his shirt.

Kim was in mid-lick but froze for a moment to size up his chest. "Have I told you lately what a spectacular chest you have? No? Well, consider yourself told." She completed her lick.

He gritted his teeth. Every lick was a slide of pleasure-pain across his imagination, his very *vivid* imagination. He dragged his gaze from her mouth and that damned pop only to meet the avid stares of two pairs of eyes. Without hesitating, he swept up Fo and Gabriel and took them to the closet, where he deposited them on the top shelf.

Sentient machines had big mouths. "Kimmie, I want to watch. I'm a mature woman, and I have a right to see." The "mature woman" turned her purple gaze on Brynn and stuck her virtual tongue out at him. "Meanie, meanie, meanie!"

Gabriel wasn't any better. "Yo, dude, like this is so fifties. Let the babe and me watch the action. An audience makes everything hotter." He winked one red eye at Brynn.

Brynn stared at Gabriel. Mr. Cool had experienced a personality spurt and not necessarily in the right direction. No way were those red eyes watching anything he did with Kim. "Talk to each other." And he slammed the door shut before either one could mount another argument.

Kim still looked deep in thought. "Hey, we could move them out of the closet and we could move in. Have you ever made love in a closet?" She held up her hand. "No, don't answer that. You've probably made love everywhere."

Brynn reached for the button on his jeans. "I've had *sex* everywhere. Not the same thing."

She stopped her licking altogether as she watched him slide his jeans off. "Mmm. Black briefs. My favorites."

He stretched, purposely calling attention to muscle definition and advanced state of arousal. Maybe he didn't have a blow pop to lick, but he had his own seduction strategies.

Drawing out the anticipation, he walked over to the bed and looked down at her.

"So where're we going to make love?" Kim suddenly developed an intense interest in the blow pop. She rolled the stick between her fingers and watched the pop spin. "I love you, you know." The pop spun faster. "I want to be with you. Forever."

"I know." His voice was hoarse with all the emotions clogging his throat—love, gratitude for this woman, and fear that somehow she'd be taken from him. And he, who'd always known exactly the right words to make a woman wet and wanting, couldn't say a thing. It was definitely a show-don't-tell moment.

He lay down on the bed beside her and watched her eyes widen with understanding. "We're going to make love here, in your bed."

She nodded. It seemed they were both lost for words. He lifted his hips so he could pull down the bedspread and blanket. She did the same while still holding on to her pop. He wanted their love-making to take place on cool, white sheets.

"I bet you're wondering why I left my briefs on." He pulled her T-shirt loose from her jeans and slid it over her head. "No? Well, I'll tell you anyway." She lifted her shoulders from the bed so he could reach behind her and unfasten her bra. Then he dropped the bra on the floor beside the bed. "Whenever the compulsion hit, I'd have to start stripping. And I'd keep getting naked until the woman told me to stop. If she didn't say anything . . ." He shrugged.

Kim traced his erection with the tip of her index finger, and the sensation through the clingy material of his briefs almost brought him off the bed.

"The briefs are an affirmation that *I'm* in control this time." Supporting himself on one elbow, he leaned over to touch each puckered nipple with his tongue. She drew in a harsh breath. "And when I take them off, it's a promise that this is the woman *I* choose to make love with."

Her smile was a bit shaky. "You have no idea how much I'm looking forward to that moment." She ran her finger along the edge of the briefs, teasing as every once in a while her finger dipped beneath the cloth.

That moment was fast approaching, because no matter how stretchy the material was, things were getting tight in there. But first, he had to finish something.

Sitting up, he slid her jeans and panties off. Then he just stared. "You are more beautiful than any woman I've known in five centuries."

"Uh-huh, and I know *that's* a big fat lie." But her smile was brilliant.

"Let me finish. There's more." He kissed the end of her nose. "You're beautiful to me because you saw past the label of demon, because you chose me over duty, and because you're one fine-looking babe."

She slapped at him, and he fell back laughing. Now it was her turn to sit up.

"Touching you through your briefs was a great appetizer, but I'm ready for the main course now." Making sure he was watching, she parted her lush, tempting lips and slid the pop between them. Then she sucked, slowly slipping the candy in and out of her mouth.

Jeez, pressure was building, and there wasn't a shut-off valve in sight. He slipped his briefs off and couldn't hold back a low groan of relief.

Kim's sound of appreciation was a completely different animal. "As Asima would say, 'Mmmrrrooww!'" She held the pop above him. "Behold my magic wand of impossible pleasures." She waved it around for emphasis.

He grinned. Amazing. Sex had been many things in his past, but fun wasn't one of them. Driven by his compulsion, he'd stayed focused on his partner's orgasm, pushing aside everything else—like finding pleasure in his senses, like laughter, like sharing in the woman's joy.

Honesty made him admit he'd probably been striking back at the bastard that created him in the only way he could. The Big Bad might be able to force him to have sex, but he sure as hell couldn't make him enjoy it.

Kim put a stop to his trip down memory lane by skimming the pop across his lips. Then she leaned over and covered his mouth with her own.

Brynn opened his mouth to the sweetness, the softness, the heat of her mouth. He savored not only the taste of her but also the textures, subtle differences in smoothness but all erotically exciting.

While his brain still retained some control over his body, he plucked the pop from her limp grasp. Rolling onto his stomach, he held onto the pop while he savored the cool roughness of the sheet against his body. The scent of clean sheets would forever after be a major turn-on. "Let's see what impossible pleasures we can conjure."

Kim flopped onto her back and laughed at him. He could picture himself watching her like this down through the years of their lives together. *And after her life ends, then what?* Grimly he pushed aside any doubts.

Hitching himself up to a kneeling position, he took his own turn licking the pop and watched her eyes heat with passion.

"You'd better have great plans for that pop or else I'll take it away and"—there it was again, the slow, sensual smile that made him so hard he wanted to drop the pop and fast-forward to the climax of this scene—"do things to you with it."

"Oh, I have all kinds of plans, sweetheart." He rolled the pop back and forth across each of her nipples until she thrust her breasts into the caress, begging for something more, something sweeter.

He leaned over and flicked each nipple with the tip of his tongue. But Kim was into her own fast-forwarding. She grabbed his hair in her fist and dragged his mouth to her breasts.

Covering her nipple with his mouth, he sucked the sugary taste from it, twirled his tongue around it to make sure he'd gotten all the sweetness, and then realized the sweetness would never end when he was touching Kim's body with his mouth.

She moaned her excitement, and for the first time in his existence, he really listened, really allowed the sound to give him pleasure.

Brynn didn't give her time to recover as he repeated the process with her other nipple and then rolled the pop over her stomach. He followed the sweet trail he'd created with his tongue, tasting the flavor of candy and woman, an irresistible blend.

"I know where you're headed with that candy, O Great Explorer, but if you touch me there, I'll explode. End of adventure." Her voice was hoarse with need. "So go there at your own risk."

He sat back on his heels to think the problem through for, oh, five seconds. Then he smiled.

She looked suspicious. "I'd never trust a man who smiled like that."

"Good." Once again he licked the pop, using lots of tongue. Then he slid his fingers over his swollen cock, calling her attention to it just in case she hadn't noticed.

She widened her eyes, and her breathing roughened. "You're so ready."

He stroked himself with slow deliberation. "I want you so much that every moment I deny myself makes the pressure increase until I don't think I can take one more second. But the pleasure is in holding on just a little longer and thinking about how unbelievable it'll feel when I slide inside you, feel you clenching around me all hot and wet."

Brynn almost stopped there but found he wanted Kim to understand how special she was. "With all those other women I never tried to make it last. As soon as they were ready, I was ready, too. I didn't care about prolonging the pleasure because I didn't care about them. I care about you." *I love you.* He could say it so easily in his mind. Now if he could just make it come out of his mouth.

Tears shimmered in her eyes as she reached up to slide her fingers across his chest. Uh-oh. He hadn't meant to make her sad.

Brynn smiled his sexiest smile as he rubbed the pop over the head of his cock. He closed his eyes and experienced the feel of the candy touching him, smooth and slick from both their mouths. Then he opened his eyes.

Seeing the intent in his eyes, she bent her knees and spread her legs as he shifted to between her thighs. Clasping his cock, he rubbed the head back and forth over the spot he wanted unbearably sensitive for him. Her harsh breathing told him he was right on target.

He slipped his hands beneath her cute bottom and lifted her. Then he lowered his head and slid his tongue across the nub of flesh that held the taste of Wicked Red and wicked woman.

Her hoarse cry was another sensory memory to add to the meager store he'd collected so far. He intended to add many more over the years. All with Kim.

His orgasm threatened to blast him into an infinite number of tiny throbbing bits of energy if he didn't act right now. He couldn't even remember putting on protection. He didn't need it, but Kim didn't know that. His hands shook as he replaced his mouth with his cock. "Sorry." His heart pounded hard and fast. "Can't wait any longer." His breaths came in huge gulps, and he couldn't put together any more words.

Brynn slid into her, slowly at first, but then the beast took him and shook him in its jaws. With a wild shout, he plunged into her, felt her wrap herself around him, felt her warm welcome for all that he was. And as he thrust deeply and withdrew, thrust and withdrew, emotion tore at him. Something hard and brittle inside him shattered forever.

Their orgasms exploded together. Throughout the centuries, Brynn had remained coldly analytical as he brought women to completion. There was nothing cold or analytical about this.

It was rolling, thrashing, pounding flesh against flesh, and animal sounds of pleasure. It was gasping cries as spasm after spasm rocked them. And it was lying bathed in sweat, waiting for the tremors to die away, for breath to return, and hearts to slow their jackhammer pounding.

Brynn still shook as he rolled onto his back and pulled Kim on top of him.

She smiled tremulously down at him. "My God, that must've registered on the Richter scale around the world."

He didn't say anything for a minute as he soaked up the sensation of her soft, damp body plastered against him. Oh, yeah, he could get used to this for as long as they had together.

Then he smiled, and he hoped she saw everything in his eyes he couldn't yet put into words. "You're one hell of a woman, demon-hunting lady." He delivered a playful smack to her bare behind, and then stuck around to gently knead her perfect cheeks.

She made a face at him. "You're pretty much okay yourself."

Brynn widened his eyes in mock surprise. "Only okay? Maybe we need to do this again so I can up my rating."

Kim glanced over at the clock. She sighed. "No time. We have to get dressed and go downstairs."

Nodding, Brynn swung his feet to the floor and stood. "You can use the shower first. I'll get dressed and spring our two disappointed voyeurs from the closet."

As soon as he'd dressed, he opened the closet door. Two pairs of eyes shone in the darkness. Grabbing both detectors, he put them on the bureau. "Have a good conversation in there, guys?"

Fo's eyes were wide and filled with awe. "It sounded . . . wonderful. I'll never feel that, will I?"

Brynn drew in an embarrassed breath. They'd been pretty noisy. "I don't know, Fo. You're just starting to explore what you can experience. You might not feel it in the same way Kim and I do, but who's to say you can't find a different way." He wasn't sure what he'd said, but it seemed to satisfy Fo.

"You're right. I have to keep experimenting." She slid her gaze to Gabriel. "But not with him. He was so nice the first time we met. This time he was saying stuff I didn't like."

Gabriel's eyes glittered with amusement. "Hey, babe, it's all about evolving and getting tuned into possibilities. You and I could do great things together."

Fo glared at him. "It isn't going to happen."

Gabriel winked at her. "Hot, babe. Really hot."

Fo looked uncertain about how being "hot" made her feel.

When Kim emerged from the bathroom, he took his turn under the shower. As the warm water sluiced over his body, he tried to look past the coming battle. He wouldn't even consider that anything could happen to Kim. He'd be there to make sure she stayed safe. Then when it was over, they'd talk.

And do other things. He smiled.

21

They met at midnight in the darkened lot behind the park. Kim, Brynn, Eric, Conall, Holgarth, Sparkle, Asima, Lynsay, Deimos, and two hundred eudemons.

The eudemons were the stuff of nightmares. They were all glowing red eyes, long, pointed teeth, razor-sharp clawed hands, and cloven hooves. Oh, and tails. Couldn't forget the tails.

The other Vaughns had wisely chosen to stay in their rooms tonight.

As Kim listened to Wade, she repeated her inner mantra, *They're the good guys. They're the good guys.*

"Eric has to come with us. Once we drive the cacodemons from their hosts and blister their demonic asses, you're gonna have a lot of freaked-out humans." Wade waved his clawed hands around to emphasize how much they needed Eric. "And stop going all big-eyed on me. You either want my true form that can waste the cacodemons or my hot human form that can't kill squat. Your choice."

Brynn moved to Kim's side. "She'll live without your hot human form for a few hours. And Eric says he'll follow behind you guys to change the humans' memories. Good thing he has that handy vampiric ability to move at the speed of light and be everywhere at once. Or at least that's the way it seems to me sometimes."

Kim was worried. "Uh, no offense, Wade, but you sort of stand out in a crowd. There're still some ordinary people on the streets. What if they see you? It'll start a panic."

Wade grinned, and it was *not* a pretty sight. "We're like shadows in the night. No one will see us except the cacodemons."

Holgarth raised his voice. "We're ready to go forth and slay the enemy. I wish the eudemons and Eric good fortune in ridding Galveston of the evil forces."

Kim sighed. "I think Holgarth's a Napoleon wannabe."

"Everyone else get into the van." Holgarth adjusted his pointed hat and headed for the parking lot with his small but motivated army trailing behind.

Conall drove while the others sat and stared at each other.

Asima crouched beside Conall. *"Stay close to me, Conall. If anything goes wrong, I'll get both of us out of there."*

Conall glared down at her. "You're a royal pain in the butt, cat."

Asima calmly washed her face. *"Thank you. I try my best."*

Sparkle sat beside Kim and Brynn. She was the Deadly Dominatrix tonight. Black leather pants, thigh-high black leather boots, and black leather vest. She sighed as she looked Kim up and down.

"Kim, Kim, it's our duty as women to dress sexy for every occasion. You should've told me you didn't have anything to wear to a demon battle." Giving Kim a last commiserating look, she turned her critical gaze on Lynsay, who sat across from them with Deimos. "Now there's someone who really needs my help. If she's going to date Deimos, I'll have to give her a few tips on dressing sensually with style."

"Are we almost there, Kimmie?" Fo was riding shotgun in Kim's jacket pocket.

Holgarth sat beside Deimos. "There's the chapel. My God, there must've been a sale on Easter egg dye."

Brynn had his arm wrapped around Kim's waist, and he leaned forward with her for his first glimpse of Ye Olde Victorian Wedding Chapel. "Pink, blue, and yellow. Cheerful but ugly. Strip the paint from that sucker and you'd have a nice house."

Holgarth tapped Conall on the shoulder. "There's a parking space right in front of the chapel. I'm sure they know we're coming, so there's no need to do any sneaking."

Conall followed Holgarth's directions, and everyone piled out of the van to stand staring at the chapel. Kim already had Fo out as Brynn pulled Gabriel from his pocket.

"I don't know how much help Gabriel will be, but he did say he could destroy nonhumans." Brynn spoke low to Kim.

"Now what?" Deimos's eyes gleamed with the excitement of being on his first real action assignment.

Kim hoped her sister would keep an eye on him. Lynsay might be the human half of the duo, but she was a rung up on the maturity ladder.

Holgarth held up an imperious hand to get their attention. "There's a light in the chapel, so someone's waiting for us. We'll simply go in together and confront the archdemon if he's there. If not, I'll do my best to close the portal."

"Um, about confronting the archdemon." Kim refused to back down from Holgarth's glare. "I know you have tons of really impressive power, but if you remember, we didn't do a great job of stopping him at the castle. Have you come up with any new strategies since then?"

Holgarth adjusted his hat and looked wise. "This time Sparkle and Asima will help, won't you, ladies?"

Sparkle avoided his gaze by flicking a speck of dust from her leather pants. "I'll do my best, but sex is my thing. If you want me to seduce the archdemon, I'll give it a shot."

Holgarth looked grumpy. "Well, do what you can."

Asima scratched behind her ear. "I have a great deal of power. If Conall's in danger, I'll use it."

Conall cast all of them a helpless look. "Why me?"

"*Messengers of Bast don't have loose lips.*" Finished scratching behind her ear, Asima blinked her big blue eyes. "*I think we need to
stop talking and get moving.*"

"Speaking of power, Sparkle, what's Ganymede doing?" Brynn
thought as Kim did, that this army didn't have nearly enough
firepower.

"When I left he was eating a bowl of ice cream. By now he'll be
watching a late-night movie." Her frown said she wasn't happy
about that.

Evidently giving up on Ganymede, Brynn glanced at the others.
"Okay, let's do it." He led them onto the porch, stood to the side of
the door, and knocked.

"An action hero would kick the door down." Deimos's take on
the situation.

"Yeah, and an action hero would get his head blown off." Kim's
take on the situation.

Beady red eyes peered at them through the small pane of glass in
the door. "Come right on in, dearies. Miss Abby's been waiting for
you."

Everyone looked at the red eyes and then at each other. Kim had
a really bad feeling about this.

Holgarth took over command. "Lynsay and Kim are the only
ones here who aren't immortal, so they go in last. If the archdemon
is inside, everyone will throw whatever power they have at him. I'm
certain it'll be enough. Remember that last time the archdemon escaped from Dirk before the full effect of our combined powers could
harm him. In common terms, he was running scared. This Miss
Abby isn't in the same league as the archdemon. We'll question
her, and then Fo can destroy her."

Kim still wasn't convinced the forces of goodness and light
would walk away from this encounter without a few demonic dings
from the One Whose Name Cannot Be Uttered. "So what if we
give it our all, and the archdemon laughs in our faces?"

Holgarth offered her an exaggerated sigh. "I'm positive that won't happen. But we can always call for Eric to join forces with us." He placed himself directly in front of the door so that he could enter first.

Hey, if he wanted to be first, it was all good with Kim. She shared a glance with Brynn that told her he had his doubts about this operation, too.

She moved to Sparkle's side. "Hypothetically speaking, how long would it take to get Ganymede here if we really needed him?"

Sparkle looked as though she'd been wondering the same thing. "Ganymede can move through time and space at will, so he could be here right after I put out a call."

Brynn nodded. "Keep the lines open to him. Just in case Napoleon's advisor there gets us in over our collective heads."

All conversation stopped as the chapel door swung wide with an ominous creak. Miss Abby stood in the open doorway, smiling at them. "Welcome, welcome, dearies. Come in and relax at Ye Olde Victorian Wedding Chapel."

Everyone crowded into the parlor. Kim kept Fo hidden under the flap of her jacket. A quick glance around showed no big yellow arrows labeled Portal to Hell Here. There were a few folding chairs for guests to sit on, and the rest of the furniture in the room was old and shabby. There was an open area at the back of the room ringed by artificial flowers and backed by a huge pink fake wedding cake that was a larger version of the bubble containers. The four-foot-tall cake rested on a table draped in white lace.

Sparkle leaned close to Kim. "Miss Abby's a trendsetter. She can call her new style shabby tacky." Then she spoke to Miss Abby directly. "You know, a demon can be sensually stylish at any age. You really need to lose the cardigan, flowered dress, and knee-highs. And those chunky shoes are a disaster. Maybe some Hermes goatskin lace-up sandals, hmm? Have you considered lasic surgery? I'm sure you have I'm-as-hot-as-hell eyes, but those glasses don't do them justice. You need to do something with the hair, too, because those white waves are so not sexy. I'd suggest soft brown with blond highlights. Very youthful. A cosmetic surgeon could—"

"Be quiet!" Holgarth thundered, and everyone flinched.

Miss Abby smiled sweetly at Sparkle. "How interesting. Maybe we can chat later, dearie."

"There will be no later, demon." Holgarth sounded as though he was speaking through clenched teeth. "Where is the archdemon and the portal?"

"You want to see the portal?" Miss Abby looked delighted. She walked briskly over to the cake, her girdle squeaking merrily. "It's right here." She reached for a CD player that sat beside the cake, and hit Play.

Carly Simon immediately affirmed that "Nobody Does It Better." Miss Abby smiled at her gaping audience. "The One Whose Name Cannot Be Uttered chose that song."

"Why am I not surprised?" Kim did some mental eye rolls. "James Bond and the One whose Name Cannot Be Uttered. Perfect."

As the music swelled, the top of the cake opened, and a demon leaped out. Probably by demon standards she was pretty hot with her long fake eyelashes accenting her red eyes, her green nail color carefully applied to her claws, and pink glitter on the end of her tail.

But great accessories didn't impress Kim. She pressed Fo's red button. Demon ash rained down on the cake.

Miss Abby frowned. "Now that wasn't very friendly."

"Where's the archdemon?" Holgarth sounded mad enough to crawl into the cake in search of his prey.

"I'm here." Gabriel narrowed his big red eyes. "And you just offed Bon Bon, one of my favorites."

Brynn dropped Gabriel.

"Ouch?" The red eyes looked affronted. "I was going to search for another human host, but this was so convenient. And I guessed that since he was one of only two detectors still working, you'd bring him with you."

Fo's purple eyes were saucer size. "I knew the real Gabriel

wouldn't say those things to me." She looked up at Kim. "Let me get the demon out of Gabriel."

"Hey, give it your best shot, cutie." The archdemon sounded supremely unconcerned. "In fact, all of you have a go at it." His soft chuckle dripped with evil. "And then it'll be my turn."

Horrified, Kim stared at Brynn. "He was in the closet listening to us make love." She knew her whisper said *ugh*, *yuck*, and *ack*.

The archdemon had excellent hearing. "You guys were so hot I almost popped out of that closet and joined you. Can you imagine the rush? Threesomes are the best."

Kim's answer was to aim Fo once again and press the Destroy button. At the same time, expressions around her grew tense and focused. If the total blast of everyone's power at once didn't blow the archdemon out of the water, they'd better vacate the premises fast.

There was the expected blinding flash of light from Fo, but this time there was almost a sonic boom of power from the others. The room shook, and pieces of plaster fell from the ceiling. Kim felt the power like giant hands pressing her body between them.

Then there was silence. The little black dots stopped dancing in front of Kim's eyes, and she looked for Gabriel. He still sat on the floor, his red eyes glittering with wicked amusement.

"You guys are a real disappointment. I expected to at least get a buzz from the whole thing." A deep humming noise started deep within Gabriel. "My turn now."

Brynn stared into space for a moment and then looked at Kim. "I just told Eric to get his immortal butt here fast."

Kim poked Sparkle. "Tell Ganymede to get his fuzzy face out of the ice cream container because we're in big trouble."

Sparkle nodded, her amber eyes filled with real fear.

Lynsay had backed up against the door and was fumbling with the doorknob. Kim didn't need to see her sister's expression to know the door was locked. Not that a locked door would ordinarily stop the beings in this room, but she had a sinking feeling no one would be leaving if the archdemon didn't want them to go.

"Miss Abby will soften you up. She's my second-in-command. A lot more powerful than the demons on the street." The archdemon sounded absolutely jolly. "She's out of range of your detector, Kim. And I'll keep you from getting any closer. I think I'll let her take out the weakest link, your sister Lynsay."

"No." Kim's harsh whisper of denial came at the same time Miss Abby's fingertips began to glow. "Do something, Brynn." That wasn't fair. What could he do? She tried to move toward the demon but smacked into an invisible wall.

Deimos had wrapped Lynsay in his massive arms and put himself in front of her.

Miss Abby cackled. "I don't have to see her to kill her, dearie. You can't stop me."

"But *I* can." Brynn's quiet statement drew everyone's gaze.

Kim watched his face subtly change, and she knew he was purposely becoming the man he loathed, the demon of sensual desire. His eyes heated, backlit in fluid gold. His lips seemed fuller, more sensual. His sexuality was a living, breathing presence in the room.

"Come to me, Abby. Use my body in any way you want. You'll never know pleasure like I can give you." His voice was the call of temptation to every woman from the beginning of time.

Yes! There was hope. Kim had forgotten about Brynn's power to draw any woman to him. She held her breath and steadied her finger on Fo's button.

Miss Abby's eyes darkened with sexual hunger. The tips of her fingers stopped glowing. "Mmm. I'm on my way, hot bod." Girdle squeaking and chunky shoes clumping, she walked toward Brynn.

"Yo, stupid. Don't go any closer to them." The archdemon sounded annoyed but not really worried.

Miss Abby kept walking.

"Abby, I command you to stop." Now he was worried. The archdemon was invoking his seniority.

Miss Abby's gaze never wavered from Brynn. Kim waited until the demon was in range, and then she pressed the red button.

When the beam was gone, Miss Abby was a small pile of ash on her chapel floor.

"Well, well. I underestimated the varied talents in the group." The archdemon wasn't amused. "I'm bored with this whole scene. I think I'll destroy you now."

Everyone froze as they waited for the attack. And waited, and waited.

The archdemon growled his fury. "This damned machine is fighting me. Why the hell would anyone give a machine free will? If I had that son of a bitch Sergei here, I'd kill him all over again."

"Way to go, Gabriel." Kim glanced out a window. Where was the cavalry?

"Oh, fuck it, I'll have to take my true form." The air swirled, and reality seemed to shift. The smell of sulfur filled the room. And then the One Whose Name Cannot Be Uttered materialized in all his demonic hideousness.

Twice as big as an ordinary demon, with scarier eyes, bigger teeth, longer claws, a really impressive tail, and the prerequisite cloven hooves, he was the Big Bad on a gigantic scale.

"Oh, crap." Conall said it for everyone.

The archdemon snarled as he turned his attention on Conall. "Too bad. You talked first, so you die first. I think that's fair." He glanced around the room. "Don't you think that's fair?"

"No." Brynn leaped forward but slammed against the archdemon's protective shield. Holgarth didn't have any better luck.

A feline scream filled the room and reverberated against the walls. Asima leaped in front of Conall. A brilliant white light enveloped both of them, and then they were simply gone.

"How'd she do that?" The archdemon sounded more baffled than furious. "Oh, well. There're a lot more of you to kill."

Without warning, the door shattered as a great gray owl flew into the room. The owl instantly became Eric. Naked Eric. He smoothly changed into vampire form.

"Oh, goody. Another challenge. See, I knew you hadn't shown me the best you had." The One Whose Name Cannot Be Uttered was back into his enjoyment of the whole happening.

Brynn pulled Kim to him and tucked her face against his chest. "Don't watch."

"I have to watch. I owe it to Eric." She held her breath as Eric fought his way past the archdemon's protective shield with the supportive power of the other immortals in the room. But the ending was the same. Eric sat on the floor looking dazed and bloody, but at least he was still alive.

"How can anything be that powerful?" Eric's frustrated question was their death knell.

"Now that we've finished the preliminary stuff, I get to have my fun." True evil now looked out of the archdemon's eyes. "Since you won't be around to watch my master plan unfold, let me run it past you. I'll set up headquarters in Galveston while more and more demons come through my portal and spread onto the mainland with no pesky Vaughns to bother them. Without their detectors, the Vaughns are no longer players. Today Galveston, tomorrow Houston, and then the world. No one can stop me."

"Wouldn't count on that, sulfur breath." Ganymede leaped through the hole in the door Eric had made and padded to Brynn's side. He looked up at the archdemon. "I was into a good movie and just about to dive into a big bowl of buttered popcorn when Sparkle called. No one gets between me and my popcorn."

"What's with all the cats?" The archdemon's whole body was starting to glow.

Brynn could feel the evil building, expanding, filling the room.

"I'm not in the mood for small talk, sucker. I have a bowl of popcorn calling my name. So let's just get this over with." Ganymede looked up at Brynn. "Pick me up. Now."

Brynn felt as confused as everyone else looked. "Why? I don't have any power."

Something ancient and more frightening than even the archdemon moved in Ganymede's eyes. "Remember that morning at the inn five centuries ago, Brynn? Remember the black-and-white cat?"

Brynn froze, unable to move, as the horrific truth of his beginning crept closer on silent cat paws. He wanted to know. He wanted to run.

"Yeah, me. You are what I made you all those years ago. Now I need the part of my energy that still remains in you to send this thing back to hell and then close the portal forever."

While everyone else made startled noises, Brynn felt the cold misery of all those centuries well up in him. If he looked anything like he felt, he could match the archdemon red eyes for red eyes.

Brynn concentrated on his breathing—in and out, in and out. He couldn't lose it here with the archdemon about to make his move. And then he felt Kim's arms around him, felt her holding him tightly. He looked down into her eyes sheened with tears.

She tried for a watery smile. "I'll cry and curse in your place while you're busy kicking demon butt."

Glaring down at the cat, Brynn reached for Ganymede with his mind. "*Go scriosa Dia thu.*" May God destroy you. Funny how when he wanted to curse Ganymede with every four-letter word in the English language, he instead returned to the Celtic language he'd spoken those many centuries ago.

"Yeah, yeah. Demon destroying first and then curses." For just a second, wry humor slid into those amber eyes. "And you might just get your wish someday, but I wouldn't hold my breath."

If Brynn thought about it too long, he'd squeeze the immortal life from Ganymede once he got his hands on him. So he quickly picked up the cat and faced the One Whose Name Cannot Be Uttered.

The archdemon narrowed his red eyes, for the first time sensing power that might threaten him. But you had to give him points for balls of steel. He smiled, showcasing a mouthful of sharp teeth that would qualify him to swim with the great whites.

While his tail whipped from side to side, he murmured, "Here kitty, kitty." And then the archdemon loosed his power.

Big mistake. Ganymede lay relaxed in Brynn's arms. He even aimed a bored yawn in the archdemon's direction. But suddenly the One Whose Name Cannot Be Uttered was flung into the air as if by a giant hand, whirled around, and thrown headfirst down through the top of the cake. Then the cake collapsed on itself and disappeared.

There was shocked silence for endless seconds. Then Holgarth asked the question they all wanted the answer to. "Good Lord, where did you get that kind of power?"

It was the first time Brynn had ever heard true respect in Holgarth's voice. But he was still too killing mad to savor the moment. He dropped the cat and wrapped both arms around Kim. "I'm not trying to murder him because I love you, damn it, and with his power he'd make you a widow before we ever got to the altar."

Kim lifted wide eyes to him. "You finally said it. Took you long enough."

Most cats would've landed lightly. Ganymede landed with a thud and then glared up at Brynn. "Let's have some respect for the one who just saved the world's ass. Yeah, I know you're all bent out of shape—even though I personally don't get it—but we need to talk about the situation like civilized beings."

"Five hundred years of thinking I was a demon, and you tell me I'm supposed to talk nice with you? Go to hell." Too bad he didn't have the power to make it happen. "Anytime you want to shift to human form and drop your powers, I'll show you exactly what I thought of those years."

While he and Ganymede traded snarls, Kim and Sparkle exchanged meaningful glances.

Kim slid her fingers over Brynn's jaw. "Be mad. You have a right to your anger. But nothing's going to change what you've suffered for five hundred years. Talk, and at least you'll understand what happened to you and why."

Eric and Holgarth hovered behind Brynn. Eric was once again in vampire form with fangs on full display, and Holgarth was making threatening motions with his wand toward Ganymede.

Brynn nodded. He didn't need to be the cause of a second battle. "We'll go back to my room."

Ganymede brightened. "I'll get to finish my popcorn."

Sparkle scooped the cat up in her arms and wisely got him out of the house before Brynn reverted to raw, primitive rage.

Once back in his room, Brynn pulled Kim down beside him on the couch. Ganymede was crouched beside the bowl of popcorn on the coffee table while Sparkle hovered nearby in case hostilities broke out. She should've brought the whip that went with that outfit.

Brynn wasn't wasting words tonight. "Tell me about it."

Ganymede cast a regretful look at the popcorn and then gave Brynn his complete attention. "There's only one cosmic troublemaker older than me in the whole universe, so I'm about as powerful as a being can get. Back in the beginning I got my kicks by putting major hurts on whole civilizations—war, famine, pestilence, drought, even the occasional exploding planet."

"Real nice guy." *Control the sarcasm.* Brynn didn't want Ganymede leaving before he finished the story.

"Yeah, those were the bad old days. Just ignore me if I go all nostalgic on you." Sparkle threw a warning glance his way, and Ganymede continued. "After thousands of years the mass destruction routine got old. I was bored. So I decided to go small, see what kind of trouble I could brew between individual humans. That was sort of fun until the Big Boss brought his hammer down. Said I couldn't kill or do physical harm to any living thing. Bummer. Took most of the fun out of life."

Kim had her mouth open to ask who the Big Boss was until Brynn caught her eye. He needed to keep Ganymede focused. "So where did I fit into all this?"

"I was still raising hell five hundred years ago—hadn't mellowed out yet—when I came across you at the inn. I was in human form, and we both got drunk. You're lucky. I didn't do really mean stuff when I was sloshed."

"Could've fooled me." *Close your mouth.* "Wait. You mean I was *human?*"

Ganymede nodded. "You were young, skinny, and putting up zeros with all the women. You said you'd give anything if you could have sex with every woman you met." He paused for a popcorn break.

Human. He'd been *human.* "I can't believe I said that."

"Believe it. I felt sort of sorry for you. I always got sentimental when I got drunk. So I gave you a great body, a great face, immortality, and—"

"The compulsion." Kim finished for him. "You thought you were doing him a favor."

"Smart lady." Ganymede threw Brynn a look that said he was dumb as a rock next to Kim. "I took away your memories and gave you new ones of being a demon. See, if you thought you were a demon, you wouldn't feel guilty about screwing all those women." He cast a long-suffering look at his audience. "I did everything out of the goodness of my heart, and all I get in return are threats and curses."

"Stuff it, Mede." Sparkle reached down to wipe dust off the toes of her boots.

"So you came here to make things right out of the goodness of your heart?" Kim sounded doubtful.

"Ha!" Sparkle sat on the edge of the coffee table now that the threat of violence had lessened. "He came because I promised him kinky and unforgettable sex if he'd make things right for Brynn. The park's owner knew Brynn's history and told Holgarth. And I weaseled the info out of Holgarth. I decided matching Brynn up with a demon hunter would be a stimulating challenge. But I couldn't do much with the compulsion interrupting things every hour."

Brynn frowned. Was it just coincidence that Sparkle knew Ganymede? And that a demon hunter just happened to fall into her lap? He didn't believe in coincidences, but he had other things to think about right now. "At least you got rid of the compulsion for me."

Ganymede and Sparkle stilled.

"Hey, wasn't me. I tried, but no luck." Ganymede forgot about his popcorn for the moment. "Are you telling me it's gone?"

Brynn nodded.

Ganymede twitched his whiskers. "Well, there ya go. Life's good."

"Except for those five centuries of sexual slavery." He was starting to sound like a whiner. He hated whiners.

Ganymede's amber eyes turned sly. "Maybe I'm wrong, but I get the feeling you guys love each other. If I hadn't messed with your life, Brynn, you'd never have met Kim. So how do you feel about that?"

Brynn gazed at Kim. "I'm glad I'm alive to love her." He took a deep breath. "And marry her. If she'll have me." With that admission, he conceded the battle. "Now maybe you need to take your bowl of popcorn and move in with Sparkle."

"Sure, sure. Get the popcorn, babe." This to Sparkle. "Maybe I do feel just a little bit guilty. Not much, just a little. So since you guys love each other, I'll give you an early wedding present." He glanced at Kim. "There *is* going to be a wedding, isn't there?"

Kim leaned into Brynn and smiled her secret woman's smile. "Oh, yes, definitely."

"You already know I'm not great at undoing things, so I can't take Brynn's immortality away from him. But I *can* give you a life span to match his. Do you want this?"

Sparkle smiled. "See, he's learning. Once in a while he asks people what they want."

"Yes." Kim never took her gaze from Brynn. "I want to share his life, every single century of it."

Ganymede nodded. "It's done." He glanced away. "I can't help you guys have kids. When I gave you the compulsion, Brynn, I figured you didn't need thousands of kiddies calling you Daddy down through the centuries. So I made sure it wouldn't happen. But who knows. I never thought the compulsion would go away by itself, so anything's possible."

Sparkle picked Ganymede up and headed for the door. "I'll see you guys soon. And absolutely do *not* let Asima help you plan the wedding. It'll be a disaster."

When Sparkle opened the door, Deimos was on the other side. He edged past Sparkle to hand Gabriel to Brynn. "You forgot this little guy back in that house. He was pretty brave to fight back against the archdemon. I didn't think he deserved to be left behind." He backed out the door. "Talk to you later."

Brynn met those big red eyes. "Sorry, buddy. I wasn't thinking straight back there. I didn't mean to forget you."

"*I* didn't forget him." Fo peered out from Kim's pocket. "I was going to remind you as soon as you got finished talking about your stuff."

Brynn put Gabriel into his pocket, stood, and then pulled Kim into his embrace. "I'll have to get rid of all my Wicked Red Blow Pops."

"Now why would you do that?" She looked at him with all the wonder of their love in her eyes.

He ran his fingers through the shining strands of her flame hair. "Because I have the only Wicked Red I'll ever need." And then he covered her mouth with his.

Fo sighed wistfully. "I wish we could touch like that, Gabriel."

Red eyes locked with purple eyes. "I'll find a way." Gabriel's voice held a promise.

Epilogue

Married. Kim still got a rush just thinking the word. And best of all, they'd said their vows in the castle's new chapel she'd designed. "Wow, I just realized I have almost forever to hone my nagging-wife skills." Kim lay beside Brynn on their new bed. She wore the sinful silk thingee Sparkle had insisted would drive Brynn to uncontrolled lust. Brynn wore nothing. She liked his outfit better.

Brynn ran his finger along the swell of her breast. "You can nag me through eternity if you wear things like this to bed."

The sound of laughter in the next room caught her attention. "I forgot. I promised Fo and Gabriel we'd stop over before the end of the night to see something Gabriel's been working on." She swung her feet to the floor and slipped into her robe.

Resignedly, Brynn pulled on his robe as well. "This better be worth me letting you out of bed."

Kim patted his supremely fine butt. "I'm glad Fo's so happy. They have their own room, and they're in love. What if Sergei had only made one of them? It would've been so sad." She knocked on the connecting door and then entered.

Fo and Gabriel were propped up in front of a large monitor. Gabriel had a lot more advanced programming than anyone had suspected. And Kim widened her eyes as she realized how he was using his impressive brainpower.

An eye-popping graphic of a naked couple in bed filled the screen. The woman's eyes were purple, and the man's were red. They were, um, doing things. Okay, didn't need to see any more. Kim fixed her unblinking stare on Gabriel.

"Interesting." Brynn sounded fascinated.

"We can experience physical sensations through the computer." Gabriel was eager to explain. "I've been able to duplicate the five senses, so in our own way we can have a sexual relationship. I'll keep upgrading it as I learn more."

"That's amazing." Kim thought Gabriel's intelligence was so far off the chart he'd find a way to get whatever he wanted.

Fo looked at Kim. "We might not have human forms, Kimmie, but I think Gabriel and I are part of humanity. It doesn't matter what name people give you, it's what's in your heart that makes you human." She shifted her gaze to Gabriel, and her purple eyes glowed with her love for him.

"You're right, Fo. We'll leave you guys alone now." Kim felt tears welling as she followed Brynn from the room.

Once back in bed and wrapped in Brynn's arms, Kim voiced her thoughts. "You know, Fo's right. I think our love for each other gave you back *your* humanity. All those centuries, you only felt hatred and bitterness. The compulsion ruled you, and you let it. But once you reached outside yourself to love, the compulsion couldn't hold you. No one knows the real power of the human will, and I think you willed it away because you finally found something worth fighting for." Jeez, she sounded like the happily-ever-after last line of a romance novel.

Gabriel didn't say anything for a long time, and then he laughed softly. "I think you've nailed it." He deftly slipped the silk thingee off her. "Let's celebrate the power of the human will."

For Curt Groff

This will probably embarrass the heck out of Curt, but yes, Virginia, real-life heroes do exist. Curt is married to one of my best friends, and when he realized I'd have to evacuate for Hurricane Rita, he rode to my rescue in his trusty SUV. He fought traffic to get to my condo before taking control of the chaos surrounding me. He waited in line for an hour to buy plywood, carried the wood up three flights of stairs because the sheets were too tall to fit in the elevator, and then boarded up my sliding glass door. He helped tape my windows, took photos of all my rooms, and risked his life to catch my panicked cat who'd made her last stand under my toilet and was threatening to rip apart anyone who tried to cram her into a carrier. Then I followed him all the way to his home—a drive that should've taken less than four hours took twelve instead.

Curt also contributed all the fishing information for this book. Is there no end to the talents of this man?

He wouldn't let me give him any kind of thank-you gift, so I decided to dedicate this book to him instead.

This one's for you, Curt.